"A compelling read which had me both laughing and crying!"
Alice Running

"Black Rainbow is beautifully written, entertaining, informative, and yet at times heartbreakingly sad."
Laura Kerbey

"Filled with warmth and humour, and frequently emotional and eye-opening, Black Rainbow is ultimately an uplifting story of redemption, self-discovery, finding personal freedom and discovering your own truth."
Rebecca Huseyin

"This book is amazing. Danielle has written a fiction book that mirrors real life for many families who have children with Pathological Demand Avoidance."
Steph Curtis

"Black Rainbow made me laugh out loud and weep with relief that I wasn't alone and isolated on this topsy-turvy journey of parenting a child who will not squeeze into societal boxes."
Tina Mac

"A beautiful book which speaks to the worry, heartbreak, and unseen battles faced by countless parents whose children are failed by the system. Compelling, funny and gut-wrenching, this book is here to tell you that you are not alone and it's not your fault."
Rachel Moseley

Black Rainbow

Danielle Jata-Hall

PDA PARENTING

Book Cover by **Mandi Patterson**.

Illustrations by **Samantha Webb**.

A CIP catalogue record for this title is available from the British Library and the Library of Congress.

ISBN 978 1 80517 912 2

Also by Danielle Jata-Hall

I'm Not Upside Down, I'm Downside Up: Not a Boring Book About PDA

Jessica Kingsley Publishers

ISBN 978 183997 117 4

"A brilliant insight into the mind of the PDA child and a unique and engaging guidebook for those who need to understand it. ie everybody!"

Melanie Sykes - Broadcaster and editor in chief of The Frank Magazine

F*ck That Sh*t

Hey everyone and it's lovely to see you here! My name is Danielle and I am a single, autistic parent to three children and when I'm not silently shouting "F*ck That Sh*t" at the world around me, I can be found making content under my pseudonym *PDA Parenting*.

My debut children's book *I'm Not Upside Down, I'm Downside Up* reached number 1 in Children's Nonfiction on Disabilities and number one in Children's Autism on the *Amazon* bestsellers list. I am also a public speaker, PDA advocate and a disability rights campaigner.

As a parent I have repeatedly faced blame due to the misunderstanding around what it means to parent a multiplex, neurodivergent household - in fact I narrowly escaped the trap of child protection as a result. Family profiling has been used on my family multiple times over the years and just, as I write this introduction I am pulling myself out of yet another accusation that has been going on for the last nine months. It's always there, lurking in the background, as a tactic many services use when we don't fit the typical boxes.

These experiences have propelled me to write *Black Rainbow* as I wanted to fictionalise a character who would show the world what it is really like to navigate the system and tell our community's truth. I like to think that this book might be the novel that those facing similar will cheer for and the authorities will dread to be released!

If you or your family, or anyone close to you, has faced discrimination and you feel strongly about that injustice then this book is written for you.

We all need to be heard together.

In the mean time, you can find me with a glass of wine and dancing my mid-life behind off at one of the following places:

www.pdaparenting.com
Facebook: @pdaparentinguk
Instagram: @pdaparenting

Acknowledgements

The first thank you must go to my three spirited daughters who have shown me how to see the world through a new lens, and who have taught me more about my own neurodivergent identity than I could ever wish for and without whom I'd still be masking my authentic self. You each have colourful personalities that inspire us all and with the right support I hope you find your own ways to thrive.

I am also truly grateful to my parents, Sue and Dave, who have not only done a great job the first time around to their own children - but they have generously given up their time to nurture their grandchildren too. They have single-handedly kept our family unit together which is something I cannot repay with words.

Jodie and Karen, my trusted allies, who volunteered their precious time to attend desperate meetings and to fight back the poisonous gaslighting - this book would never have been possible without your support and dear friendships. Jodie, you gave me the confidence and drive to continue with this book, that was laying dormant without your passion. Eleanor, too, for the expert advice and encyclopaedic knowledge. A force of genuine kindness and strength, again I'm grateful for all of your help along the way.

Lor, you have been an amazing editor to work with. I'm so glad that you were on the team, your advice and ideas have managed to shape this project perfectly. Mandi - thank you for supporting us designing the covers for the book. It took a long time but we got there. An added thanks to Sam for all of her illustrations and for making these pages come to life with her vibrant colours.

I am very indebted to the huge PDA and SEND communities that I feel have been behind my blog and my writing so supportively. I have made genuine connections with each and every one of you. This book will represent a piece of each of us - a story about our community. Thank you all for being on this journey with our family.

There have been so many bloggers and professionals who have given up their time to read and review this novel, too many to mention individually, but I am so grateful for your help to get this book into print and for your kind words. Steph, my dear friend, thank you for being a champion to others; a beacon in our glowing PDA community. Becca, you have been awesome too, thanks for going that extra mile to do one last final proof edit.

Lastly, but definitely not least, a special mention to my besties Lois and Lindsey, for being there every step of the way and moulding yourselves into the friends I needed you to be. Thank you for helping me to find my own rainbow again and for teaching me to go wild now and again! Keep giving me the material to write with!

Dedication

This book is dedicated to the memory of **Doris May Loveday**.

Thank you for teaching us the art of raising strong women and for your generous contributions made to the swearing jar.

"There's no better way to dismantle a personality than to isolate it."

Princess Diana

1

Pups on the Double

"**M**UMMY??!" I could hear my name being bellowed from across the room. My body tensed in fear as once again the shriek – that I now recognised meant trouble was brewing ahead – drew my attention away from the very important task at hand.

"Lena! What do you need?!" I called in response through gritted teeth.

Lena's impatience left no room for her to understand the predicament I was in. A half-naked baby and the impending crisis that was about to implode from across the room (by the mini-ruler that was my five-year-old daughter), left me sweating in my new dress.

My boy chose to make his first movements at the same moment as Lena's big voice had rocked the house and I'd opened Charlie's nappy flaps to reveal that this was a bigger job than I'd originally anticipated. Instinctively, with my left hand on his tummy, I grabbed a handful of wipes, whilst out of the corner of my eye I was trying to supervise the smallest boss in the world – whose shriek of the word 'Mum' was now turning into a thunderous crescendo. Unbeknownst to me, Charlie thought it was going to be an ideal time to start wrestling and prove to me Lena wasn't the only boss in this house!

Charlie was wriggling and had turned straight onto his tummy – the sort of trick other mums waited for in anticipation so they could be the first to brag to their antenatal friends that their kid had done it first. The competition between the newbie mummies to see who would win the prize for the fastest baby always made the hairs on my neck prickle. I tended to carry on observing their playground tactics whilst munching on too many biscuits, feeling antisocial, smiling away, trying my best to fit in.

I had been busy preparing his bag for the big event, after giving him a bath, so he looked smart. Then, just at the moment I chose to slip him into the new shirt and shorts combo, he decided to make his physical-developmental debut. I had even ironed his attire which said a lot as I was pretty avoidant with most chores. In fact, it was the only outfit that I'd bothered to get for him that was half-decent. Most of Charlie's wardrobe had come from my daughter Lena's hand-me-downs.

The celebration of this momentous milestone had to be put on hold whilst I scrubbed every crack of his once-cute baby rolls as the squidgy green poo had moulded into every available crevice. I realised I had run out of baby wipes and, just as I searched the side for a replacement pack, Charlie turned once more, baring his smeared butt all over his beautiful, one-off ensemble. As usual, sensing my attention was taken elsewhere, Lena jumped onto my bed to fling a figure from *Paw Patrol*, which I involuntarily caught with my hand (without realising it had also been covered in the remnants of Charlie's nappy).

Lena pressed the button on her accompanying toy pad which bellowed the catch phrase: "*Pups on the double!*"

"Mummy can't play now," I hissed with frustration. "You need to get ready for the christening. Please go and brush your teeth before you put on your new dress!"

Taking my frustration out on Lena is always going to be a recipe for disaster, especially on a day as important as this, I thought, mentally scolding myself for the barrage of demands I just placed upon her.

Lena stuck her tongue out at me and screamed as she stomped out of the room: "You meanie!"

I could feel my pulse racing higher and I was swimming in the stress which was overtaking me like a heatwave. I was so consumed with anxiety that I couldn't even keep the water in my own body happy, nor my children for that matter. I glanced at the clock and noticed the minute hand was moving hastily closer towards the hour. Okay, so I had always been notoriously late, but since having kids, it had admittedly got worse. I used to always blame it on something that was out of my control, such as the time I turned up to my own graduation in my PJs because my fake tan was still wet. The bottle of liquid took the blame for being late and it was never mentioned that I had plenty of days leading up to the event to do it. If I was totally honest with myself, it was more about the fact I had poor time management skills than the reason I ever professed.

I had been dreading this day for weeks. The thought of rocking up at my nephew's christening and facing family judgements had been enough to send me over the edge. My sister, Julie, had already pre-warned me this morning (at seven o'clock, I hasten to add), whilst speaking in her very direct fashion, that my 'tardiness' was not going to spoil their special day. It was always worse when there were outside pressures to conform to, for some reason it frequently led to disaster.

How on earth could I explain to my sister our very unique reasons for being late? My brother-in-law, 'Mike the Psyche' (as I preferred to call him), had already been over-analysing me and what he deemed as my 'poor ability to parent or hold myself together'. Arriving late again would only be the icing on the cake to confirm my ineffectiveness and utter incompetence as a human being. I was sure it would go down well if I began my explanation of the reasons behind my lateness this time. I could just see the look of horror on their faces if I were to tell them the complicated set of scenarios that I'd found myself in this morning, in order to be at their grandiose event on time.

I started to write an imaginary letter in my mind (like I needed any more distractions) as I sat in my brief solitude, daydreaming the time away:

Dear Julie and Mike,

This is only the start, and is certainly not an exhaustive list, of reasons as to why I was apologetically late for your special day:

1. It started with Lena waking up and refusing to get ready until she had played with her marbles.
2. Followed by reasons why it is unfair that Lena is a girl and not a marble!
3. After finishing with the marbles she said her legs couldn't possibly work.
4. Negotiated a deal with Lena that a good time to get ready would be after one episode of Paw Patrol so that her tired legs could recover.
5. Reminded Lena that the episode had finished, to which she screamed "No!" at the top of her lungs (whilst her tonsils danced in shock).
6. Wasted half an hour playing hide-and-seek to find Lena.
7. As if things could get any worse, we were wiped out by Charlie and his poo-like crime scene!

8. I now am looking for a new outfit for Charlie.

From Sarah (aka your useless sister)

I could explain it all, but I knew they wouldn't understand, hardly anyone did – not even Nick, my own husband. My family always said that that's what parenting is and thought I was making silly excuses. So, at this point it was easy to see why I had very little left in my bucket of patience and how much time had been wasted 'trying' to get us all ready rather than the actual 'doing' of it. I started to get cross, where was Nick when I needed him? I wasn't getting anywhere fast and I knew that the obstructions in my path were likely to get far worse.

Without any other options available, I scrambled through Charlie's baby unit and noticed out of my eye one of Lena's toy baby dolls in a smart shirt and trousers. I quickly rushed to undress the doll and put the outfit on Charlie as a replacement for the christening. It was a tight squeeze and those cute baby rolls were once again peeking out of the outfit, but I was creative and used a safety pin to hold the trousers up where the button wouldn't fasten. It would have to do.

I then walked into Lena's room, but she was nowhere to be seen. The only remnants of her presence were her beautiful dress and frilly socks left in a dishevelled heap on her floor. Her room pretty much always looked like an earthquake had just hit it, as the rubble of toys and clothes swarmed the floor. However, there was something about seeing a discarded party dress on its own that emoted a sense of grief in me. The feeling of absence and loss of what I'd expected my life to be was summed up by a lonely, unused party dress on a messy floor.

Suddenly, Lena threw open the shiny wardrobe door and appeared dressed as *Chase* the dog, singing the catchphrase: "*PAW Patrol, ready for action, Ryder Sir!*"

"There you are, darling, for a moment I thought I'd lost you." I squeezed her in close with a pang of guilt from my earlier abrupt response, but she ducked out instantly.

"I need gel for my hair. I can't look like *Chase* otherwise!" Then a new idea suddenly popped into her mind: "Can you be *Ryder*? And what if I take Rex with me? He can be *Rubble!*" She continued rambling on to herself, not even waiting for an answer to her barrage of questions and demands. We ended up negotiating on her plush rabbit going instead of her real-life pet dog, Rex, and despite a lot of exchanges, she finally agreed.

I knew this was the only way that we were getting out of the front door, so I reluctantly agreed that she could go to the christening dressed as a dog – with a canine mask covering her pretty face. I drew the line (despite her insistence) that I would be accompanying her dressed as the character of the pup's handler *Ryder* (I could just imagine the look on my sister's face if I'd complied with Lena's demands). It was difficult to describe it to other people who didn't live it, but it was like Lena's dreamworld had to be her reality instead. Anyone and everything had to comply or else there was warfare to be had.

It was the weekend – it should have been my relaxing time! I already had the dreaded anticipation of it getting nearer to Monday (which meant I had the usual battles to get Lena into school). I just wanted to switch off like I usually did on a Sunday and spend the day in my pyjamas, overdosing on TV and food in equal measures. Having to tart myself up and make an effort was the last thing on my priority list. I also knew that I hadn't properly opened that dreaded letter from Lena's school and had hidden it behind the breadboard – out of sight out of mind. *Try to focus on the here and now*, I told myself, *rather than the problem I can do nothing about.*

Lena finished her breakfast, which consisted of two scrambled eggs and crunchy toast. I knew her routine well and made sure the eggs weren't too 'wet or dirty', or it would be another reason to add to my late list. Just as she had finished eating and was leaving the table, my husband, Nick, walked into the room, fully dressed in his three-piece suit, without a mark or a crease to be seen. I couldn't help but feel peeved as I could feel sweat patches staining under my arms from Charlie's earlier escapades. I knew we couldn't have looked any more incongruous with one another if we tried. It was always the way that Nick only had himself to get ready and I had to pick the pieces up for the rest of the family.

"Lena! Come back and show some manners! Take your plate into the kitchen when you've finished eating!" Nick shouted in his punitive parenting style. He always came in at the wrong time. I could feel my senses rise as it felt like he was about to entice her into yet another one of their battles. I had to find a way to diffuse it. Typically, he was nowhere to be seen whilst all of the emergencies were unfolding earlier, as no doubt he'd had his headphones plugged in and had been watching his precious football highlights.

"It's okay, Nick." I treaded softly. "We can worry about the mess when we get back. Let's just focus on getting to the christening on time."

Nick shot me a look of frustration and then seemed to ignore what I had said as he commanded Lena: "Do it, now!"

Lena articulately retorted: "I'm too busy being a superhero. Besides, paws can't carry plates!" She ran back out of the room.

I smiled at him and shrugged. "If they were giving out awards, she would definitely get one for creativity." My nervous smile turned into giggles. I cherished this imaginative part of her personality, and the pressure of trying to keep the situation under control had tipped me over into laughter.

"That's typical of you," Nick cut through, "always condoning her poor behaviour choices. Maybe if you backed me up more often, then we wouldn't be in this mess!"

Was he for real? Where had he been all morning whilst I had been struggling to get everyone ready? He always saw things so black and white!

I shuffled the chairs around the table and tried to keep my emotions intact, moving them slowly and delicately with effort, attempting to hold back the rage that was spewing from every pore. I had to keep my hands busy in fear that anger could explode unexpectedly. I so desperately needed the day to work that I was forced to bite my tongue, yet again.

Almost as if she had been outside the door eavesdropping, in barged Lena as she grabbed hold of the plate. "*Chase is on the case!*" She swerved out of the room, leftovers of scrambled egg falling onto the carpet. Rex the dog appeared from his basket to devour them all up.

I scooped Lena into my arms and moved her *Chase* mask to the side to give her a big kiss. "That was very kind of you to think about it and come back to tidy up. I'm proud of you."

She beamed her beautiful, gappy smile up at me; relishing that I had acknowledged her attempt to try and make things better: "*These paws uphold the laws!*" Lena declared in her most military of voices.

"What a special pup you are, my darling," I said as I tickled under her tummy. She gave me a big 'woof' as a contented reply.

I had half an hour left until we had to leave and I felt like I was finally turning a corner. Maybe I could get it right. Lena was finally quiet and preoccupied, as well as being dressed – okay so not in her party dress, but dressed as a dog would have to do. I could carry on clearing up the mess in the bedroom crime scene, but I was feeling a bit resentful of Nick. I mean, why couldn't he do it? Why was I the only one doing this stuff? I shut myself in the bathroom and quickly made a call to one of my best friends, Shelley. I convinced myself I could spare ten minutes for some preparation time, and I knew that Shelley would be the voice of reason; she would understand what my morning had been like.

"Sarah!" Shelley's voice greeted me and made my racing heart slow instantly. "I thought you were getting ready for The Christening of the Year!" I could almost picture her dark, curly hair and her assuring light-blue eyes as her words fell down the receiver. Shelley took care of her body and could wear any outfit to make it look outstanding. She oozed confidence and her persona could be felt virtually just as strongly despite being a ten-minute drive away from my house.

"Ha! Yes, I am!" I giggled. She knew exactly what my sister was like. "You know Julie has always been the same. She's still the same teenager who used to only select the friends who would let her borrow their cool *Naf Naf* jacket or take her to a *Take That* concert!"

"Oh my goodness, do you remember that awful boyfriend she had too? The one with the greasy, curtained hair and the *Levi* jeans?" Shelley cajoled.

"Eww! He was gross, wasn't he?" I could feel my face squirming in memory. "The one every girl in our year wrote about on their exercise books that they were going to marry and have kids with!"

We laughed loudly and it was the relief that I'd needed from the pressures at home. Shelley and I had met at school in our first form group and we had remained close ever since. Most of the kids at school were scared of Shelley on account of her direct insults and because she got into scraps (that's what happens when you grow up with a brood of burly brothers). She seemed to have the ability to outsmart anyone with a hidden agenda or a false persona.

"I still can't believe you two are sisters!" Shelley said, bringing me back to the present. "You've always been the opposite of each other!"

"I've always preferred the social misfits – they are far more fun!" I teased, knowing this would please Shelley. "Haha, don't tell Vic I said that!" Vic was the third bestie in our group but I tended to call Shelley over Vic as I knew she had her hands tied looking after her own kids. Shelley, on the other hand, hadn't entered parenthood. I always suspected the pain of not finding the right person was too much to bear as Shelley was always vocal in her desire to be a mum.

"Nothing wrong with being a misfit," Shelley joyfully defended. "It means we're not boring! Anyway, did you manage to get Lena in her party dress?"

"Nope!" I declared. "Not a chance in hell. I currently have her packing a bag of toys whilst being dressed as a cartoon dog."

"Well at least she can be herself," Shelley warmly offered.

"I'm starting to wonder if I gave birth to a baby or a puppy!" I howled. "Well, all I can hope is that she is more comfortable like this and we can wing it. I'm dreading the part when I look around and see all of the perfectly-behaved children and their designer clothes and then..."

"Listen, Sarah," Shelley guided, "Lena is perfect just as she is. Remember, her individuality is destined for greatness one day, just you wait and see!"

I wanted to believe Shelley was right, and that I could hold my head high, confident in the belief that I was doing a good job. There was still a seed of doubt that the pressure of trying to fit into what everyone expected would still take a hold of me. Why couldn't I be more assertive like Shelley? Maybe if I grew a thicker skin then I wouldn't feel the need to worry what other people thought of Lena all the time.

I realised the conversation had gone over schedule and that I had five minutes to leave the house. "I had better dash, Shelley. I'll send an update and some photos to our group *WhatsApp* chat later."

"I can't wait!" Shelley squealed. "Have the best time."

I quickly hung up and scurried the last of our things together, including the children, before we set off on our journey to the christening.

The radio filled the nervous excitement in the car and kept us temporarily entertained enroute to the event (which was routinely broken every few minutes by a yell in the back from a caped-crusader demanding 'are we there yet?').

"Hey!" Nick chirped, manually rolling the volume dial up on the radio. "This is our song, Sarah!"

I smiled and rested my hand on the top of his trouser suit as he pulled his hand away from the wheel and patted my hand. The lyrics, from a *Coldplay* song we had once loved, serenaded across the radio waves to wash over us and we enjoyed the occasion sparked by a memory of us as an earlier couple.

"Look at the stars, look how they shine for you..." Nick sang along tunefully. *"And everything you do. Yeah, they were all yellow."*

I thought about the younger people we were when we first embarked on a relationship together and how free and easy, we both had been. The song held such poignancy – it was playing at the Glastonbury festival when Nick got down on one knee and asked me to marry him. He was lucky I'd said yes and jumped back up so quickly, or he would have been squashed by the swaying crowd! He'd spun me around in circles and I'd nearly knocked everybody around me over with my slipping-off, muddy wellies. The song marked the start of an important journey together.

I thought about the significance of hearing the song on a day like today and it made me wonder: Was this a sign that it would be a magical day for us all? I started to forget some of the stress and worries that I'd had earlier, and felt more in the present – like any other family about to embark on an important occasion.

We pulled up in Nick's car to the approach of a quaint and picturesque church in the village of Nettleden. My sister had selected the Church of St. Lawrence for the christening as it was located in a wealthy village. I suspected that she had befriended the church not long before the preparations, as she wanted the photos on the day to have a quintessentially-olde English heritage look to them. Julie was always aspiring to fit in with the other neighbours and friends that she wanted to be like. For Julie, it was always about money, driven by a hunger for materialism and the superiority of status. I sounded bitter, but I knew that part of the aim for the day was to have a collection of 'social-media-ready' photos to enable those inner-needs, and gain that respect she so desperately required. Having a child dressed as a dog probably wasn't part of the plan!

The church lit up the village, strutting up with its crenelated walls and beautiful bell tower into the clear blue sky. The weather was certainly adding to the picturesque postcard feel of the location. I knew this would make my sister happy. I was soon brought back to reality as I could feel the clunky boots of Lena's Chase costume banging into the front passenger seat.

"Ouch!" She screamed, "The sun hurts my eyes!"

I pulled down the sunblind that I had attached onto her window; it was actually bought for Charlie, but like most things, Lena had claimed ownership of it. Besides, Charlie didn't seem to utter a sound when the light poured through the car window, whereas Lena made the same amount of unwanted noise as an entire school playground could do in one setting.

Nick pulled down the mirror to fix his hair and adjusted the top part of his suit as he muttered, "What a travesty it is driving down these rickety old lanes when I've just had the car washed!"

We'd had an argument about the necessity of attending the christening the day before, to which he had grumpily admitted defeat. Just like the kids, he was another person that I had to walk on eggshells around sometimes. I was using all of my strength to not retaliate and I was using all of my effort to make the day go as planned. I gave a deep sigh. There was no going back and we were committed for the day whether we liked it or not. Maybe it would be alright? I mean, Lena may have had a different outfit on than I would have hoped, but for once we weren't that late and she was seemingly in a good mood too. Heck, Nick hadn't even lost the plot enroute when she'd asked like a bazillion times if we were there yet!

Lena's voice interrupted my internal conversation: "Why does Charlie have my favourite doll's clothes on, Mummy?!" I could feel Nick shoot me a look of disbelief through the front mirror.

"I'll explain it later." I swiftly moved off topic before Nick or Lena exploded any further. "Look, darling…" I paused, knowing I had to get the exact wording right, "let's just enjoy the day."

"*Paw-some*!" Lena replied in full character mode. I wondered if the words had actually sank in as her response was in auto-drive.

"Easy for you to say," Nick groaned. "I still have to drive back through those tiny lanes without damaging any of my car's body-work."

"Oh, Nick." I rolled my eyes and then turned to Lena. "When we get out of the car, I need you to hold Mummy's hand and say hello to everyone. This is an important day for Aunty Julie."

I'd show them… it didn't matter what Lena was wearing, we were here together and we would show everyone that we could have things under control. As I went to open Lena's door to let her out, I tried to think positively and tell myself I could do this, but my self-coaching was suddenly interrupted by Lena who was charging across the open grass.

"Lena!" I tried to covertly cover my yell. "Wait!"

Lena was running, unrestrained, towards the congregation of smartly-dressed guests – all with their perfect hairstyles and im-peccably-behaved offspring – waiting under the arched oak door of the church. My heart was in my throat.

"Hurry!" I screamed to Nick who was preoccupied making sure, under no uncertain terms, that his precious car would get stolen. "Can't you do that later?!"

I made the fastest leap of pursuit onto the grass (which felt like slow motion) as I chased Lena – who was galloping away with her *Paw Patrol* tail swishing from side-to-side. The blur of gaping faces was coming into focus and I narrowed my eyes as I spurted forwards to reign back my wild child. How was I going to get out of this?

2

Christening-gate

As I plucked up the courage to get closer to the congregation, I suddenly spotted Lena. She was chasing a squirrel on the grassy grounds, sprinting out from behind one of the impending conifer trees that lined the stony path to the church.

"Lena, come back!" I called out, desperately, but the pent-up inactivity of the car journey had infused her, propelling her forwards at full speed. The squirrel darted through an opening and scurried past the headstones of the graveyard lying adjacent to the church building. Lena jumped innocently from grave-to-grave in hot pursuit of the grey, furry, real-life toy that she desperately needed to catch. I could hear an amalgamated gasp of disbelief from the aghast crowd.

There was anticipation in the air to see how I would deal with the most disrespectful and feral behaviour no doubt they had ever witnessed. Lena was never aware that she pushed the boundaries of social normality, particularly whilst she was enthralled in a moment of activity. I was caught in the confusion of my mind – feeling like I needed to scold her publicly, whilst my heart was telling me otherwise. Against my nature, I finally opted for the style of parenting that was being expected of me – peer pressure has that effect no matter how old you are.

"Come with me right this instance," I firmly and loudly stated. My voice had raised for the benefit of others to witness, rather than following the natural style that was ingrained in me, as I attempted to take Lena by the hand.

Lena screamed as her canine mask was dislodged and thrown to the floor in disbelief.

"You are mean, just like everybody else!" Lena bellowed, darting away from me and masked herself deep inside one of the conifer trees.

I could hear her sobs just the other side of her makeshift safety den and felt a pang of guilt that I had succumbed to upsetting Lena just to please others. I had to put it right.

"I'm sorry, sweetie," I cajoled as I tentatively took steps forwards into the space she had made safe, offering my hand first, with her much-needed character mask. "I was cross because you had run off. I didn't mean to upset you."

I nestled with her for some time, and once out of earshot, I could return to my usual creative parenting strategies. I was frustrated with myself that I hadn't been brave enough to have followed my instinct in the first place.

"How about we pretend the pups are at a christening where we have to do as we're told so that *Mayor Goodway* will be happy with them? Aunty Julie can be *Mayor Goodway,*" I said excitedly. "What do you say?"

"Aunty Julie doesn't have a chicken as a pet!" Lena answered cleverly, over the nonchalant chatter of the crowd. "But I guess we could just pretend!"

Just as my good work was working its magic (after my earlier faux-pas), my mother arrived to offer her superior support. "Lena, you must NEVER stand on somebody's grave! It's extremely disrespectful!"

"I didn't!" Lena screamed defensively, unaware she had even

done anything wrong and reigniting the anxious emotions from before.

"And where is the pretty dress Mummy bought for you?" My mum continued enticing, "Why do you have a silly costume on? This is a christening not a school dress-up day!"

"It was itchy." Lena's voice became croaky and she looked away.

"Sarah," oh, God it was my turn now, "I hope you have Lena's proper outfit for the photos afterwards?!"

I didn't know how to answer. I was right back to my usual response of trying to please everyone without the ability to stand by my own opinions. Eventually I opted for a diversion: "I think the service is about to start."

"Be good, Lena sweetheart," as my mum leant in to pull her canine mask away to kiss her cheek. Somewhere deep down I knew there was an attachment, but my mum found it hard to express. If she wasn't so stressed about worrying what people thought of her, then she may have been more in the present. It was no wonder where I got it from.

We each left our hiding spot and joined Nick – who was holding Charlie in his carrier by the group of christening goers. We gently eased forwards, attempting to slip back unnoticed, and managed to join the single-file queue through the door and past the vicar (who was welcoming the guests at the door). The service soon got under way and my attention was momentarily diverted by the colourful pattern pouring through the stained-glass window, whilst the vicar began his bibliotic speech at the pulpit.

"For when I am weak, then I am strong. Psalm 16:8," his voice resonated through the echoey hall and his words struck a chord. I was feeling weak, it was like he was speaking directly to me; I wondered if one day I would ever feel strong. My thoughts began to jumble, as they often did, onto my next state of frustration and how undermined I felt about my parenting skills when people like Nick or my mum, or even Julie, were around. Why couldn't they

see how well it actually worked when I had the confidence to do it my own way?

Lena was starting to get uncomfortable. She'd been sitting for long enough, which was a miracle in itself. I sensed she was needing a movement break, but we were trapped in the pews with little room to manoeuvre. As we stood up, I noticed my mum shoot me an angry expression and signalling with her protruding eyes for us to sit back down.

If she sits down now, I thought, *then Lena will have a meltdown!* Couldn't she see I was trying my best to make the day go smoothly? Did she want Lena to explode for every one of those pompous guests to witness? She should have been thanking me for the extra effort I put in, but of course she didn't because she didn't understand. It often felt like nobody in the world understood.

Lena pushed past me with an aching desire for freedom and began hopping over the mosaic-tiled floor to create her own imaginary game. I noticed she was keeping herself entertained by inventing a rule of avoiding any orange diamonds in the pattern. If for any moment she made the mistake of touching one, she dropped her arms down and repeated the same steps until she succeeded. My mum continued to glare at me, and I couldn't cope with the stress of upsetting her any longer, so I quickly retrieved Lena.

"We have to sit down," I began, but realising I was sounding stern, I altered my tactic. "I wonder if I have any special sweets in my bag?"

I couldn't afford for Lena to start screaming or physically lashing out in such an enclosed and busy place, not in front of people who were in the pursuit of perfection – they just wouldn't understand.

Lena pushed past me and dived into Charlie's changing bag. "What's in there?" she demanded loudly. I shushed her back down, planting a lollipop in her hand to pacify her volume dial. It did the trick – although the sound of her sucking was just as vociferous. I wondered if it was humanly possible for Lena to ever remain silent.

I was on eggshells for the rest of the service, but after an eternity, it finally ended and I sighed heartily with relief.

"It's finished," I told Lena. "We can go to the party now!"

"Pups don't like parties," she began, "their ears hurt."

"I'm sure we can find a quiet spot for the pups to play?" I said invitingly.

"Okay."

The group of guests steadily streamed out of the church and performed as if they were a snake-line of zombies in a sci-fi movie. As soon as we were back outside in the fresh air, it was as if the guests were re-spawning out of the apocalypse and could find their voices to speak once again. I gulped down the fresh air, feeling desperately relieved that the hardest part was over. I could feel myself tuning into other people's conversations like I was an imposter scheduling information back to headquarters.

"Wasn't that a wonderful service?" One lady beamed to another as she fixed her fascinator.

"Absolutely," replied the accomplice, her eyes darting speedily around the congregation. "Although, I do think they should have given the service schedules out at the door."

"Oh yes," the first lady retorted. "I accidentally sat on mine as they were sprawled over the seats!"

My ears scanned anxiously to the next conversation, in need to reassure myself we were not being judged. I felt the usual social paranoia as I was used to my parenting (or Lena's 'odd' behaviour) becoming the subject of focus.

"We have a new apartment in Marbella," a deep voice boasted without taking a moment to pause for the listener to join in. "We get to rub shoulders with the rich and famous!" He continued with references to how much the millionaire yachts were worth and how grandiose the paellas were. I was soon bored of the bragging and lost interest.

Just as I was about to walk away, I heard a question directly coming towards me.

"You must be Julie's sister?" one of the ladies said. "You look so alike! Julie said you both were on maternity leave at the same time – now fancy that!"

"Yes, I know," I responded politely. "Strange how the timing has worked out."

"That must be so lovely," she continued, "being off with your sister and having someone to do everything with!"

I took a moment to think about what she'd said. We were both on maternity leave and we both had boys at relatively the same time, and yet we spent very little time together. I smiled on the outside but felt so lost and sad on the inside.

Luckily, I didn't need to provide an answer as the photographer appeared and Julie began huddling the guests together so that he could take a photo of the occasion.

"Why is Lena dressed as a dog?" Julie's eyes narrowed in uncontrollable rage.

"She needed to." I pleaded, "Going to a christening is a big deal for Lena. We wouldn't have made it here otherwise."

"So it's another one of *those days* when you think it is acceptable to bring Lena as a character to an event like this!" Julie blurted out venomously.

"It wasn't like that." I defended as my fingertips started digging into my palms.

"Forget it! I don't have time for this!" Julie placed her hands onto Lena's small shoulders and led her away from me, placing her directly at the back of the group where her vibrant outfit could be covered by those in front of her. A wave of red mist swept over me but I was too scared to be the centre of attention if I confronted Julie about it.

Just as the photographer was ready to take the shot, Lena ran to the side of the group, barked loudly and sprung up into a star jump. She had her iconic tongue sticking out as a final gesture of goodwill. My heart pounded with fear through the silent anticipation from the looks around me. Nick leapt over and tugged Lena roughly by the arm.

"Come with me, NOW!" They disappeared out of view and my thoughts raced about how he would be reprimanding her.

After a few minutes of manic worrying, Nick returned back to the congregation with a tear-stained Lena. He shot me a look, faster than a bullet, but his thoughts could always be read. I knew that he did not want me to comfort her – I had been warned in his own little way. I tried to remind myself he was just cross and things would be alright again soon.

It was only a few minutes' walk to the reception party, but it felt longer as I was carrying Charlie's changing bag. I had learnt that it was imperative I brought a range of activities out with me in my makeshift 'just-in-case' bag in order to deal with any eventuality. I needed to be able to occupy both children with different toys or food bribes in case they were ever needed. I had books, cuddly toys and marbles for easy reach, then deeper into the bag you could find a random set of shiny keys (not to actually open anything but just to buy me a ten-minute window with their sensory enjoyment). Lower in the dark depths – an iPad, a bendy man, an improvised shaker and even a pot of slime. I was sure I'd be arrested under suspicion of plotting an act of terrorism if anyone stopped me and spot-checked my belongings.

Nick held open the door of the rustic local pub. "After you," he politely offered. I traipsed in like a donkey laden down by my belongings and a child in tow. Nick was carrying Charlie. I felt some mercy that we appeared more together as a family unit.

The Cart and Horses had a panoramic view of the crisp farmer's fields that flowed endlessly into an idyllic countryside paradise. For all of my pessimistic thoughts about my sister and her need to show off, for once, I could clearly see the appeal of holding an event in a location such as this. Being around people may not have been to my liking, but the environment was perfectly agreeable. I plastered a smile on my face and tried to refrain from feeling like an outlaw for a change.

Nick pulled me close to speak over the din. "Sarah, why didn't you choose a different outfit? Your dress is too low and it's quite figure-hugging – it's not exactly appropriate for a family christening, is it?"

"You bought me this outfit," I defended, not daring to meet his eyes.

"Yes, for when I take you on holiday." Nick's reply was abrupt. "You should have put something more conservative on."

I remained quiet. I knew better than to challenge his opinions.

Nick switched his mood like the flick of a light switch. He leant in and kissed my cheek in a bravado show of spouse-like affection.

"Look. It doesn't matter now," he swiftly usurped. "You look attractive and I'm sure all of the men's eyes will be on you. I should be proud to walk in with you."

I smiled but felt unsure of what had just happened. There were too many people around and I felt conscious that I wasn't comfortable but was working hard to hide it.

"So, darling – what drink would you like?" Nick beamed.

"A pink gin and lemonade please," I replied eagerly. "And a cola for Lena to keep her quiet." I winked, trying to find solidarity together, but Nick passed Charlie over to me and disappeared into the crowd. I took a deep sigh before I veered around the cesspit of bodies who were busy slurping down their wine and beers and discussing how the pub was registered as one of the 'must-see drinking establishments to visit in the county'. Jeez, did these people ever let up in their competition for who could be the biggest boaster?

Balancing Charlie on my arm, I managed to scrape past the menage of arms and legs, trying desperately not to make eye contact. Lena was holding onto the back of my dress and I was deeply self-conscious that, firstly, my pull-me-in pants were on show and, secondly, my stomach (which had been aptly named as the 'jelly-belly' by Lena) could be seen wobbling with every step. I hated that I felt so frumpy. A pang of inner resentment shot through me that I hadn't spent time on myself lately. Nick's earlier comment had only added to my low self-esteem.

I found an unwanted spot, near the rear of the pub, which basically consisted of a high table with no stools – a fat lot of good that was to me. I had to make do. The sheer relief of dropping the baby carrier down was nothing short of a weightless euphoria. The moment wasn't to last as Lena spotted the door at the far end of the pub and legged it out past a couple of old men who were semi-perched having a smoke.

"Come back, Lena!" I shouted as I bombed it outside with Charlie and the just-in-case bag. For someone so small, she had managed to leap over the pub's garden fence and climb on top of a neatly-stacked bale of hay whilst singing the theme tune of *Paw Patrol* at the top of her lungs. I paused for a moment to let her play and release her pent-up energy – I sensed her relief and how much she needed it. She tried to play leapfrog over the hay bales, but wasn't quite grasping how far each stack was in proximity from one another, and suddenly fell head-first into the hay.

"Mummy! I hurt my face!" she cried, straws of hay tangled into her soft auburn hair.

"Let me kiss it better," I soothed

"You wasn't helping me!" Lena accused as a decoy for her inability to process an accident.

"I was too busy watching you, darling," I reasoned with her. "You are so brave. I couldn't leap that far!" I shouted over-animatedly to distract the onset of a meltdown.

"I could teach you how to do it, if you like?" Lena offered with a sudden mood change. "Just take off your clip-clops, Mummy, because you can't jump in them!"

She didn't wait for a reply as she went into lecturing mode.

"I don't know why you put clip-clops on anyway. *Ryder* wouldn't wear them and I told you which character you could be for the day." Lena often assumed the reversal of parenting role and it felt like she was the mummy and instructing me like I was the child.

I needed a fast plan to change her current train of thought and it needed to be a good one. If it had been any other time, then I probably would have joined her, but it wasn't the time for me to be free. If I said the word 'no' we could be heading into the unknown territory of Lena's non-proportionate ability to rationalise in a situation. She still had what others referred to as 'toddler tantrums'. I wasn't in a moment of creativity, so my first idea for distraction went back to the basic art of bribery.

"Hey, *Chase!*" I shouted over coyly, hoping nobody could hear me. "What do you say if we go back inside now? I think I have some chocolate in my bag! How about we go find it together?"

"Dogs can't eat chocolate, it's poisonous," she retorted

"Why don't we pretend it's doggy chocolate that we picked up at the pet shop as a reward?"

There was no answer for what felt like an eternity. This was always the case when you asked something of Lena or gave her an instruction – it was as if you had pressed pause on a remote control and she was lost via the transmitter or something. When she was younger, I used to just keep repeating my words (which usually ended up with me shouting at her out of frustration), until I finally realised that it was no use. Over time, I'd learnt to reduce my input, whilst also building up a repertoire of strategies to help get her to do the simplest of things. I was sure parenting Lena had equipped me enough if I ever randomly chose to join the army.

Lena finally cut the silence and proposed a deal: "I'll come inside, *Ryder Sir,* if you let me borrow your phone?"

"What for?" I was thrown off-course by another tactical rebound from Lena.

"I need to ask *Alexa* what treats you can give to puppies!" she declared.

"Oh right." The penny dropped that my chosen route had worked.

"Let's pretend *Mayor Goodway* calls you and asks the pups to help rescue a cute sea turtle," Lena reeled off. "Then maybe you could give the treat to me as a reward?" Lena executed her plan in the finest of details. It seemed quite excessive as a response when I'd only asked her to go back inside, but I was used to it.

We returned inside and the air was stifling. The echo of glasses clattered as we tried to find a new space again.

"Where have you been?" Nick suddenly yanked me by the arm. "I've been standing holding these drinks for ages! Who have you been talking to?"

"Lena ran outside so I had to fetch her," I defended, my cheeks flushing. Where did he think I'd disappeared to and who on earth would I have been talking to?

Nick passed me the tall glass of pink gin and handed Lena her cola. Her eyes lit up excitedly to have a fizzy drink as a rare treat.

"Thank you, Daddy!" Lena slurped half the drink magically.

It wasn't long before she began her favourite past-time of blowing bubbles back into the straw and watching the cola erupt – almost like watching lava overflow from an unpredictable volcano. Just at the crucial moment of overspill, she flapped her arms up and down and made an almighty racket of deafening noise. Her enjoyment was curtailed by her father's stoic voice: "Stop that, right now! Just bloody behave, Lena!"

Charlie began murmuring once again and I thanked my blessings that he had slept as long as he had done for the last hour. I shuddered at the thought of how Lena could have reacted if he had been screaming during the service.

"Be quiet, Charlie." Lena was starting to get agitated.

"That's enough, Lena," Nick commanded crossly without realising he was mirroring her exact tone of voice.

Charlie continued whinging and letting us know that he wasn't going to be neglected at the event. I fetched him from the carrier in the hope it would relieve his discomfort, but his cries continued to build.

"I told you to shut up!" Lena's face contorted and a deep, strong frown travelled down her brow. In the blink of an eye she had banged him hard on his head with her flat palm. Charlie's sudden scream cut through the noise of the pub. Everyone turned to see what the commotion was.

Nick yanked Lena from her seat and confiscated the phone into his pocket. I wrapped Charlie into my arms, wishing I could take away the pain he was currently feeling. I was partly angry with Lena and the other half of me understood why she had done it; deep down I knew the noise was painful to her. With Charlie being comforted in my arms, I stood up and swayed side-to-side as if I was being driven by a motor (something I did subconsciously as if the rocking would soothe any worries away).

My parents arrived as if it was a rudimental obligation to confirm how much we'd failed their expectations every single time. Nick continued with scolding Lena as he removed her cola drink. "I think you've had quite enough of that." I watched in horror as he lifted the drink to his lips and slugged the remainder of her cola down.

"Nooooo!" Lena's hands flew to her face as she fell into a sobbing mess.

"Did you *have* to do that?!" I vented, unable to hold back the venom. I could feel the anger burning deep inside like some torrent of rage that couldn't be contained anymore.

"Well, she deserves to be punished," Nick said indignantly. "Can't go around whacking her baby brother over the head just because she's having a tantrum! I mean, what did you think I should do? She has to learn sometime, and mollycoddling her is not the answer."

"Nick's right," defended my dad. "Children have to learn conse-quences sooner or later." My mum stood by his side, silent and nodding. It felt even more isolating when my own parents sided with my husband's views.

At times I often wondered what had brought Nick and I together in the first place. Before we'd had kids it seemed like we got along just fine. There was a part inside me that still remembered the first time we met and how I was bowled over by Nick's good looks and charm. There had always been an edge to him – a side to him that he wouldn't let others see, which was often perplexing but intriguing at the same time. He seemed to arm himself by wearing an invisible mask that smiled, joked, and camouflaged his identity. Sometimes, I often questioned whether I knew the real Nick. I tried to shake my negative feelings, I desperately wanted our relationship to get back on track. If he could just change his outlook on Lena a little, maybe things would be better again.

"Anyway," resolved Nick. "It's my round. How about we get an-other drink?" I could see he wanted to impress my father, who needed no persuasion to head back to the bar. In an instant, they had disappeared into the crowd. Nick didn't actually like drinking, he usually only had one and would drive so that he could stay in control of himself. He also generally left the drinking to me, and despite his athletic and broad stature, I could drink him under the table. Nick often made snide remarks about my drinking habits, which really got to me. It often felt like he didn't understand me… but I didn't understand him either.

I was momentarily distracted by feeding Charlie that I hadn't even noticed Lena had disappeared out of sight. I pushed through the crowd with Charlie on my hip, leaving my belongings behind at the table. I finally located Lena staring up at the four-tiered christening cake which was beautifully embellished like some for-bidden kingdom. Every layer of the cake had been carefully decorated with a variation of the baby blue theme that was dressed over the cake. An ivory, lace bow was pride of place on the bottom tier. There was a photo alongside the cake with a frosted, glittery frame showing baby Andrew in his finest glory. Lena was transfixed by the beauty of the handmade, edible creation.

"Come on, darling," I ushered.

"What's that?" Lena pointed to the three perfectly placed baby blocks at the top of the final blue tier with the letters A, B and C crafted onto them.

"They're just part of the cake," I replied, more concerned that her unwashed fingers might come into contact causing another social taboo.

"No they're not!" Lena's voice went up an octave sensing she was being told a white lie. In slow motion I saw Lena's small, doggy arm reach up to the top tier and pull off a brick. She placed it on the frilly tablecloth alongside the cake and put her hands behind her back as she proceeded to lunge her canine jaws into the block. The blue icing dribbled down her chin like the unwanted remnants of a dog's dinner, which she gracefully used her tongue to lick back up.

"What do you think you're doing, young lady?" Julie shouted with scorn, yanking Lena away from the cake.

"It was a real cake, Mummy, you were right." Lena looked at me sheepishly with her tail between her legs. "I'm sorry I didn't believe you."

"Have you *seen* what your daughter has just done to Andrew's cake?" Julie glared at me intently. The room fell silent. In their collective desire to watch the drama unfold, guests were forming a circle around us. Oh, God, how was I going to explain this?

"Why trash it when you can stash it?" Lena replied in her usual abstract and fantastical fashion with her paws held up.

"I beg your pardon?!" Julie raged, her eyes popping.

"All pups stash prizes when they are superheroes," Lena said, picking the skin next to her fingernail. She wasn't making eye contact and I knew she was confused about why she was in trouble.

"You should have waited until it was cut first and you were given a slice to eat nicely – at a table with cutlery, I hasten to add!" Julie scolded.

"I thought the blocks were just pretend," Lena expressed defensively.

"Don't answer me back!" Julie tried to bring down my child for all to see.

Nick appeared and stood next to Julie as he allied himself in her corner. "That's right, don't answer your Aunty back!"

I tried to lunge forwards to safely bring Lena in closer to me so that I could cushion any response she had next. I didn't need her hitting out at anyone – it would go down like a lead balloon. I accidentally tumbled and managed to catch my step in time before I fell down.

"Don't mind Sarah." Nick grinned. "She's just had too much to drink!"

Julie shot me a look as if to say this was all my fault and I had let her down.

"I've only had one!" I declared defensively.

"That's what she always says." Nick winked. "Don't you, darling?"

I didn't understand why Nick had said that. He knew I'd only had one drink because he'd controlled the purse strings and had been the one to buy it.

"If you had manners, you would have known how to behave at an occasion like this!" Julie shouted at Lena, wild with anger, unable to stop herself from heading into a row on her own special day. "If you hadn't drank so much you would have stopped her in time!"

"What are manners, anyway? And who decides if they are good?" Lena was now fully back in her 'lawyer' role; a strategy that was typical of her if there was a perceived sense of threat to her equilibrium. It usually bought her time to plot her next move. The approach was working and Julie was so shocked that she was momentarily dumbfounded by a question she hadn't been expecting to hear.

"When a dog eats from his bowl he doesn't get told he has bad manners, he gets told he has been a good doggy. What if... I am really a dog living in some strange human world where manners don't make sense to me? The dog world is much easier to understand than the human world – they don't have lots of rules that tell them how to live. A dog isn't forced to say please or thank you just so they can eat. When they see food they are allowed to eat it."

"What are you talking about?" Julie bellowed. "You don't even sound like a five-year-old child!"

"I don't have bad manners because I am a puppy living in a horrible, human world," Lena declared.

"I think we had better go home now," I pleaded as I pulled Lena by the arm. I quickly put Charlie back into his carrier and strapped him in. Fear and adrenaline ran through my fingers as the lock clicked together. I threw the special 'get-me-out-of-jail' bag of stashed distractions and nappy changes onto my shoulder, signalling I was leaving immediately. I turned on my heels as I spat out the words: "Sorry about the cake."

The journey home was quiet and I could see that Lena was pensively lost in her own thoughts. I sat in the back of the car, in between Lena and Charlie, in anticipation that I might have a fallout from the Christening-gate that had just occurred. The tranquility from the peace and quiet was desperately needed and I sat wishing it had gone better. I couldn't help but feel that Nick didn't support me like I needed him to. I was angry with him for telling my family a big lie that wasn't true. Why did he do that? With nobody speaking I was able to let the silent tears fall down my weary cheeks. Our relationship had been so good before we'd had kids, I just couldn't understand how it was falling apart. I wanted Nick to know that it was just a blip and we could get past this. I mean, all couples struggled when children entered the equation. Maybe we would look back at this and realise how tough it was, as we held hands ploughing into the next life transition?

I'm sure my mum must have had my house rigged because, as soon as we opened the front door, only a few seconds passed until the phone pierced the atmosphere. It didn't take a genius to work out what conversation we were about to be having. She was rambling on about the failures of the day and then she went in for the kill.

"When Lena is good she's angelic, but when she chooses to be bad she can be a monster," Mum paused for a brief ceasefire before she continued on, "Father and I were discussing it with Julie... she mentioned that some of the adults she sees on the ward have personality disorders and we were wondering whether you need to ask someone about it? I mean, Lena whacked her baby brother on the head for crying and didn't even feel any remorse. It made us wonder – what if there is something wrong with her? It's not normal to show no empathy like that, I remember seeing something like that on one of those documentaries on psychopaths."

"She... she... is normal!" I blurted out through snotty tears as I tried to retain my voice (which was sounding like a scratchy record). "Of course she feels remorse – she just doesn't understand how to stop herself sometimes."

"She understands well enough, Sarah." Mum continued with her righteous, one-sided parenting conversation. "You have to stop making excuses for her, or else..."

"Or else what?" I demanded.

"Or else nobody will like her and she'll face life being locked away like some kind of social outcast... if not worse! I dread to think! It's your job, as her mum, to enforce those boundaries, because, quite frankly, she is making a mockery of you right now."

There was an uncomfortable silence which Mum soon pierced, uninvited.

"I'm sorry, Sarah, but we don't want you to bring Lena to any more of our family get-togethers until you can change her behaviour. We don't want any more events ruined by a five-year-old child!" Mum was on the rampage and it was all spilling out like an unwanted case of verbal diarrhea. "I was brought up knowing the rule that 'kids should be seen and not heard', your generation has given them too much. You've ruined them. They are the 'we can't-ever-say-no-to kids', in my day we would have had a wallop for even stepping out of line."

I couldn't say a single word. I felt like my whole world was collapsing at that very moment. My mother did not pick up on my silence to deter her from further tirade.

"Father and I always brought you and Julie up to obey the rules and to be polite, well-mannered young ladies. We never had these problems that you and Nick have with Lena. We were the adults and we were the ones in control," she added as the final missile.

With those words stinging my ears, I hung up the phone, the eerie silence piercing my raging thoughts. Mums were supposed to make you feel better, no matter how old you were, mine just added more stress. When it came to Lena, she never could say the soothing words that I needed to hear to reassure me that things were going to be alright, or just be that shoulder I needed to cry on. She never listened, but always proceeded to tell me what I was doing wrong. She never once considered that Julie and I were different from Lena. I couldn't describe it, but there was something about Lena that meant she had a different outlook on the world. My mum always liked to compare my parenting skills to hers, and every time she did, it made me feel like a complete failure. I made a mental note to avoid any communication with her for a few days. When I felt this down, I couldn't afford any setbacks.

Lena charged back into the room with her *Chase* costume hanging down her petite frame and with remainders of blue icing dried down her chin.

"*Pups are on the double*!!" she squealed excitedly as she pulled me gently by the hand out of the kitchen. "Come on, Mummy, let's play."

Her small, innocent hand had no idea of the carnage and disruption it had caused. I pulled it to my face and gently brushed a kiss onto her palm as if to magically erase the day from our memory. She was such a gentle soul and I wished my family could see it.

"Of course, darling," I said softly, "as long as I can be *Ryder* again."

"Yes, *Ryder Sir*." Lena saluted her hand to her brow. "Ready for service again, *Ryder Sir*."

We walked up the staircase, hand-in-hand, as if we were the only two people (or the only pup and dog handler) that mattered in the world. Lena was always calmer and softer when it was just us and she wasn't dealing with the unpredictability of the outside world. She chatted about the emergencies the pups were going to face in the game. I listened intently, at one, joining in with her utopian paradise. It took my mind away from the drama that had unfolded and I could take a break from the worry about how I could make things right with my family again. Or the fear that Monday, which meant the dread of school challenges, was impending closer.

3

The Comedown

The first social comedown day was always the hardest to survive. I felt battered and exhausted from Sunday's christening – almost as if I had been to war. Family life already felt like a constant rollercoaster which I had to ride in order to get through the twisting loops that were unrelentingly thrown at me. Social occasions did seem to take it out of me more than anything with the continual pressure to masquerade around like a family that fitted in, when in truth, it felt like we were anything but. It was the same for Lena too; she needed lots of downtime after any social exposure. It often took a great deal of recovery time for her to regain control of herself again.

When Monday morning came, I had tried to carry her through the usual school routine to no avail. She used as many distraction techniques as possible to avoid the inevitable.

"My legs are too tired," Lena proclaimed. "I can't go to school today."

"We can drive," I offered. "You'll be just fine."

It was no use and she tried to out-manoeuvre once again.

"I can only get dressed..." Lena declared, "if Rex performs a trick for me!"

Of course Rex remained hidden in his basket, sensing the onslaught that was about to unfold. Lena's attempts to dismantle my pursuit towards getting ready for school became more direct.

"Somebody has been playing with my *Paw Patrol* toys without asking!" As she lobbed the figures across the room (distracting my attention from getting ready by compromising the safety of her brother was always a chosen option). There was nobody who could have moved them but Lena.

After a while this lost momentum and she went off to hide her school shoes in the recycling bin. Still, I carried on with trying to rally her through her jobs to get to school, at which point she blew and threw the school shoes – that I had foraged from the recycling bin – across the room. They hit me straight in the mouth.

"Ouch!" I stood in silence and put my hand over my swelling lip, almost robotically. I wondered if my dramatic action would make her realise how upset I felt. The shock took a while to subside but the pain soon came flooding back to pack an almighty punch on my nervous and broken spirit. Lena crumbled and positioned herself under the dining room table at an angle which made it impossible to get to her.

"Go away! I hate you!" She began screaming and crying as she belted out a hurl of insults. "It was all your fault! Mummy is a big, fat meanie!"

"I didn't do anything to you!" My voice had raised and I was now part of the tense exchange.

"You always do! *You* force me to do things that you know I can't do," she vented venomously.

"And what is *that* exactly?" I was embroiled with my emotions and was too busy matching her raise in the stakes to use a level head. I often found myself too lost in the moment and overreacting, which prevented me from talking with my five-year-old child at an appropriate level.

"Stop making me go to school when I don't want to!" Lena

declared full of anger.

"Everybody has to go to school," I said matter-of-factly. "It's how we learn!"

"School is torture! All you have to do all day is boring work, that doesn't make any sense... AND you don't get to play." Lena was spitting out the words, looking fiercer by the moment.

"Well, it's the law!" I shouted, clawing at reasons, and now desperate to explain the gravity of the pressure I felt under.

"Kids should make the laws," Lena declared.

"I've already been issued with a letter because of your bad school attendance! I can't win. Try and get you to school and you hit me, get you to school then they call me because of an incident and tell me to pick you up. And you tell me it's my fault? What did I ever do to you so bad to deserve this?" I instantly regretted the last statement, and I knew that acting the victim wasn't going to help the situation at all, but the rage had got the better of me.

I charged out of the room, full of tears and feeling very embarrassed about my outburst. How could I teach her to stay in control of her emotions when I was such a bad role model? I couldn't bear the flood of emotions that came over me when I knew I'd handled a situation badly. Images of her beautiful, almond-shaped eyes and trailing toy rabbit filled me with guilt and I couldn't cope with the berating of my internal subconscious. I knew that I was adding more pressure onto her and it was making her bolt further. *You are such a shitty mum*, I told myself. My frantic thoughts were accumulating and taking me into a pool of shame. I paced around, eventually going back into the dining room to see if I could somehow undo the damage.

I was worried. I began to think about the other children in Lena's class and how incredible it must be for their parents to just do a normal school drop-off. To walk hand-in-hand with a smiling child who wanted to go to school. Why was my life so different to what I expected it to be? My mother's voice from the day before rang out in my head: "It's not normal! She's not normal!" I looked at my daughter curled up under the table, sobbing... all because she didn't want to go to school.

*Is she normal? What even **is** normal? And what does it matter anyway?* I pushed the worries and doubts out of my head – other people's opinions and society's expectations didn't matter. What did matter was Lena. I knew I needed to make it up to her and show her I was on her side.

My thoughts were propelled into action as Lena saw me re-enter the room. She left the safety of the table. She picked up her favourite *Paw Patrol* toy controller pad and threw it at the wall – it crushed into a distorted heap on the floor as the batteries bounced along making a dramatic end. All at once, the biggest amount of noise came from Lena that I had ever witnessed before in my life.

"Nooooooo!" she screamed, falling to the floor, sobbing uncontrollably, hugging the remnants of her favourite toy as a grieving person would hold their beloved deceased in their arms. The anger had turned into fear. It was unimaginable that the anger was so strong just seconds before. The panic that she had lost something so sentimental to her was too much for her to bear. She was attached to toys and objects as much as she was to her family. They were very real to her and certainly not inanimate. As the panic and fear dissolved, the sadness moved in with full force, battling her infantile nervous system with such ferocity it was hard to not feel the emotion with her.

"I'm so sorry, Mummy, you're not a meanie. I always hurt you. What if one day you don't love me anymore?" The tears were flowing faster than a river thrusting down its course. "I should go to prison for being the meanie, Mummy. AND, I broke my bestest toy. It's... all... my... fault!"

I held her tightly, and rocked her, whispering the words that of course I still loved her and that I always would. I reassured her that she wasn't mean. I apologised for trying to force her earlier and that it was my fault for making her feel upset. We stayed like that for a while. I finally stepped back out of the room to fetch Lena a glass of milk and to retrieve her soft, pink-and-white spotted plush rabbit – which was, unusually, named Chicken Pox.

"Here's Poxy!" I called from outside of the living room (I must have been caught up in the moment because I usually cringed when I followed her preference to nickname her rabbit Poxy).

I stopped in my tracks as I barged open the door because someone else was doing my job for me (and actually a lot better than I cared to admit). Rex, our very clumsy chocolate Labrador, had jumped out of his basket and laid the top part of his body across Lena's lap. She was pinned down and had no other option but to stroke his big, soft ears and feel his silky coat as she ran her tiny hand up and down his back. His eyes were quiet and still, concentrating intently. I picked up my phone, took a picture of the emotive scene and brought it over to Lena so she could see the photo.

"Look! Rex wanted to make you feel better so he came to help you!" I tried to join them and involve myself in their cuddle, but Rex was having none of it. "He wants you all to himself, darling."

Lena beamed her pretty face up at me, the markings of her tears were starting to fade. She stroked under his arms and Rex almost looked like he was smiling.

"This is where he likes to be tickled the most," Lena informed me.

"How about we get the photo printed and you can put it up in your bedroom?" I asked gently. "It can remind us of this special moment and how much Rex cares about you."

"Yay!" she squealed, and with her usual happy persona back in full gear, I softly moved Rex off her and picked Lena up on my hip. I could just about get away with it these days as she was getting bigger every day. She put her small arm around my neck and snuggled into my face, kissing my cheek. You could say anything about Lena, but when she wanted to be, she could be the most affectionate child you could wish for. I squeezed and kissed her. We were back to being partners again. I swung her and spun in circles around the living room.

I started to feel a wave of shame run through my body; I had just witnessed my dog see to my daughter's worries better than I had done. Rex had acted on instinct and knew intuitively what to do. How did I lack the ability to follow my intuition when I needed to? Why wasn't I able to be brave enough to ask school for what she needed? I spent so much of my effort trying to be polite and not let them think anything bad about me, that my priorities were always being compromised. How could I make this situation better? I was scared to make a decision, but as I looked at her innocent bottom lip, I knew I had to create a new option.

"Let's have a rest day today," I said. Lena's eyebrows raised at the sudden retreat in my persuasion to push her into school. She looked on, dumbfounded, as if I was going to say it was just a prank.

"Look, how about we go to the park for a run around to cheer ourselves up?" I suggested tentatively.

"Only if I can go on my blue *Paw Patrol* scooter?" negotiated Lena. She was back in her usual place calling the shots, but in that riding seat, she was a much happier child.

"Of course you can," I agreed. "And maybe we can just speak to school about today being a rest day after all."

Lena ran up the winding staircase excitedly at full speed as if her life depended on it. I knew what she was doing as it was always the same routine. She would be searching the bedroom to locate all of her *Paw Patrol* figures so that she could take them, for comfort, safely in her scooter basket for company. She often told me that her toys were her real-life friends because they understood her and they let her tell them what to do. They were her crutch to leave the house and gave her the type of relationship she craved in the real world.

The pause from needing me at all times gave me the headspace to be able to send an email to school about Lena's absence for the day. I quickly fired up the laptop and the panic soon returned as I began typing:

```
To: receptionclass
From: sarahforte
Subject: Lena's Absence

Dear Miss Orchard,

I have struggled to get Lena into school today. She is
very upset and I have not been able to get her dressed
in school uniform. Lena had such a big meltdown at
home and I just don't know what is causing it. She
has been finding school hard for quite some time. I'm
wondering how we can get to the bottom of what is
causing her school worries?

Kind regards,

Sarah Forte
(Lena's Mum)
```

My anxiety was mixed with an instant feeling of relief that I had taken things under control, that I could concentrate on what Lena needed, but most of all enjoy seeing her smile again. The weight from the pressure of attending had released and I actually felt a sense of excitement for what the day ahead could bring. Maybe if I could forget what society expected of me, I could find a way of us being happier like this more often?

"I'm ready, Mummy!" Lena appeared, fully dressed and uncharacteristically ready, by the door. I shut down my laptop and went to rouse Charlie from his morning nap so we could leave for the park.

"I'm just coming, sweetie!" I called as I hurried down the stairs with Charlie in my arms. "Let me just get Charlie in his buggy and we can go."

We let ourselves out through the back gate – Lena on her scooter leading the way to the park. The air pierced our lungs better than any adrenaline rush I could've wished for. It tasted cold and pure – as if the rain had just fallen and washed any dust or pollution from the air. It was definitely needed to clear the storm of the earlier meltdown.

I looked over, Lena had created her own imaginative game that was keeping her entertained enroute to the playground. I could see that she was following the cracks in the path that adorned the rubble tarmac path that seemed to take a zig-zag pattern all of its own. She was delicately balancing her scooter along the lines so precisely that the wheel did not leave the crack. If at any point her precision failed, then she would pick up her scooter and return to the starting section of the crack so that she could ensure she fulfilled her self-imposed task perfectly.

She suddenly halted mid-game and it took me a few seconds to catch up with her. We were on the corner of the bendy hill as it meandered around towards the recreational area.

"Be careful!" Lena instructed urgently as she made a childlike wall to protect a chunky green caterpillar on the pavement ahead. "Don't kill him!"

"I won't," I reassured. "I wonder how it got there?"

"Look, Mummy, he has spots on his back and spikes at the end of his tail," she began, as if she hadn't heard my question. "We need to save him!"

"We could put it back on the grass?" I suggested.

"I have a great idea!" Lena exclaimed. "He can be my pet and I shall call him Henry."

"That's a lovely idea." I smiled amusedly, not knowing what made Lena decide the caterpillar was masculine.

"Mummy, what do caterpillars sleep in?" she asked pensively.

"They build a cocoon and sleep until they become a butterfly – just like in your bedtime book about the hungry caterpillar." I made a mental note to pick the book out for her bedtime story, hoping she would like to listen to it again.

Suddenly, Lena changed direction on her scooter, expecting me to just be able to keep up. "Let's go home instead, Mummy!" Her words rippled through the air as she went back down the hill.

"I thought we were going to the park, darling?" I called out, confused by the unexpected change of plan.

"Henry is far more fun than a boring old park!" Lena screamed back in excitement.

It took seconds to return home, we really hadn't got that far on the journey. Lena was hyper-focused on something of interest and there was no chance in a month of Sundays that I would be able to get her off topic. She clambered through the back door, catapulted her trainers through the hallway, and sped up the stairs with a caterpillar in one hand and Rex chasing her on the other side.

The brief interlude gave me a moment to compose myself and check my emails before it was time to give Charlie his next feed. There was an email from school waiting in my inbox. Reluctantly I opened it, unsure of what it could say.

```
To: sarahforte
From: headteacher
cc: receptionclass
```

```
Re: Lena's Absence

Dear Mrs Forte,

Your email was received earlier by the class teacher
but it was brought to my attention. I must inform you
that in future, anything relating to school absence,
should be going through our usual communication chan-
nels such as the school office. Lena's non-attendance
has been recorded as an unauthorised absence and I
must emphasise that she must not be kept off in future
or it will be setting a precedent of what is expected
of her. We follow positive behaviour strategies whilst
she is at school and she understands the boundaries
and what is expected of her. We may have to inform
the local authority as Lena's attendance is lower than
school policy's guidelines.

We would like to invite you to a meeting in school
to discuss this issue further. Please could you call
the office at your earliest convenience to secure an
agreed time that is suitable?
Best wishes,
Mrs Ramsbottom
```

The email worried me. What could I do? Maybe Nick and I needed to discuss it? Or maybe someone else could help? Shelley? She was great, but she wouldn't fully understand what to do around the school issue. I made another (yet again) one of my mental notes to remind myself to look into it, maybe there was some information online to help with this kind of thing.

The rest of the day passed relatively peacefully and Lena was so preoccupied with her new pet, Henry, that she hadn't picked up on my mood change. The school couldn't see what I was doing to make Lena feel safe. The fear of having the issue escalated filled me with dread. My brain was riddled with thoughts of the local authority poking its finger at me. Oh goodness, when would this nightmare ever end?

My mum phoned and tried to make smalltalk about the weather and how Julie was settling into life as a new parent. She wasn't getting much back from me, my mind was elsewhere.

"Did you know Julie has started doing Pilates?" My mum informed me. "She's started to get her physique back in only three months!" Mum never seemed to sense-check a conversation before she started one and had no idea what was going on in my life; even after a few minutes, she hadn't bothered to enquire how any of us were. The topic of 'Christening-gate' was certainly never mentioned.

"That's nice for her," I answered, trying to hold back the bitterness. "Some of us don't have time to dedicate to exercise."

"It helps you regain your cervix muscles," Mum carried on beavering away, regardless of the covert undertones in my last statement. "So important to not be leaking wee at your age."

"I don't have that problem," I insisted.

"Well, you can buy incontinence pads," she continued brazenly. "Although you might want to choose the discreet type."

I sighed. I couldn't talk to her any longer. I really needed someone to talk to about what I should do about the school problem, but my mum was not going to be the voice of reason. I made my excuses and hung up the phone. I wasn't in a good place to be drained any further by trying to frequent a call with my own mother.

My mind cartwheeled to the impending thought about school and the fact that I needed to attend a meeting regarding Lena's attendance. I knew I shouldn't put it off any longer, so I made the dreaded call to the school office and spoke to the admin lady in order to book a meeting time. We secured Thursday, which meant I had two more days to prepare myself before I had to attend. The receptionist had been adamant that my husband come along too. Great! Not only did I have to admit that I had made the solo decision to not send Lena to school today, but I would be found out regardless as they wanted us both to be present at the meeting and Nick would no doubt tell them that he'd had nothing to do with it! I tried to park the worry as the more I thought about it, the more paralysed I felt about having the capacity to do anything about it.

Bedtime was lurking so I pulled out the book about the hungry caterpillar and cosied up with Lena under the duvet. She recounted the book, word-for-word, slightly a second or more ahead of me. Just as she was about to drift off to sleep, she sat up and said she had one last question before bed. I succumbed to the request knowing how close we were to achieving the aim of getting to sleep at a respectable time.

"How do butterflies learn to make their cocoons without going to school?" she cleverly asked. "AND... how do they come back as adults and know how to live... all by themselves?"

I was dumbfounded. How do you answer a question like that? Eventually I thought of an answer.

"They figure out how to do it because it's naturally built into them." It was the best I could offer to a child who always outwitted me.

"I could learn to do things all by myself, but I'm never allowed to." She looked over at her newly-acquired pet forlornly. "Just like Henry."

I kissed her palm and ruffled the duvet just underneath her chin like I did every bedtime. I made the conscious decision not to say any more words but to gesture her towards sleep by rubbing her tiny back, rhythmically, in order to induce some form of sleep. I had always thought it was the parent who educated the child, but having Lena had made me feel like it was the other way around.

Once downstairs, I wondered how I could make things better for her. I grabbed my notebook to start preparing for the school meeting. I tried to tell myself I could do this, but there was this niggling feeling that I was in this mess a lot deeper than I cared to admit. What if I was in trouble for keeping her off for the day? How did I know if I had made the right decision? Worse still, I had to face the music and tell Nick about the decision I had made that morning without consulting him. How would he react? I shuddered in fear at the prospect; he would be annoyed that I had kept her off school. How was I going to get out of this mess?

4

Accidents Just Happen

The next morning I heard Lena run down to the back door and fling it open, letting Rex rush past her in full excitement that someone was up and ready to play. He was mistaken. Lena was driven by her own hidden agenda and didn't give him a second thought. The sun was beaming down on the desperately overgrown lawn. The smell of a newly woken dawn filled the air. It tasted of a dew that was about to give rise to a gloriously warm summer's day. The pitter-patter of Rex's paws was in harmony with the early birdsong, only broken by the gushing sound of his first morning wee (which created a gigantic puddle on the dry ground).

"Mummy! Come and say goodbye to Henry. I'm setting him free!" Any hint of an idyllic scene was soon permeated by Lena's boomy voice.

"Bye-bye, Henry." I tucked my head down to the childlike habitat Lena had created. "The whole family will miss you."

I passed him a small leaf as a farewell gift, unconventionally, as if I was a fellow child from reception and not, in fact, a mid-life parent. I had even contemplated giving him a stroke, or worse – petting him a kiss from my finger to show Lena that I had been attached to her chosen insect, but I started to question my own sanity. Lena held the box down, Henry stayed put.

"He needs his freedom." Lena looked at me. I could see a flowery tear falling down her rosy cheek. "I don't want him to feel trapped. He needs to learn to do things by himself."

The profound sense and understanding of the world around her, and the vocalisations of her own innate experiences, were far more mature than her chronological years. It was such a contradiction that she knew and felt so much, but yet she seemed so much younger in her ability to control her emotions. If only school and those around her (including her family) could see the most beautiful soul cocooned inside.

Lena seemed extra quiet during the early morning school routine, almost as if her mind was somewhere else. She ran back out to the empty box one last time before school, to reassure herself that her passing pet had finally made his rightful passage into independence. As she returned, with a sullen face, I knew that the natural course of events had happened. As I dropped her off at school, late, she walked in slowly through the reception to join her class.

Her body drooped, her feet pointed in mirroring one another, soaking up the fear from the body that they traipsed along carrying. I refrained from shouting her name and dragging her back out of the building with me because my gut feeling was that she was going to find the day a struggle. My heart was being pulled in one direction – to retrace our steps and beat the premonition of disaster that was foreboding inside me, but I let my head force me into another strategic direction. I wobbled backwards and forwards in hesitation until I could finally pull myself away and walk back down the lonely school path to leave the gates behind, not knowing how my baby was going to be.

Just as I was leaving, Lena's teacher, Miss Orchard, called out to me: "Mrs Forte! I wonder if I could have a quick word?"

"Yes, of course," I complied. That was the quickest school call back in history, I thought.

Miss Orchard soon joined me on the pavement. I couldn't help but notice how pretty she was; not overly preened, just a natural enhancement of makeup. Her figure-hugging black dress sculpted her shape, she was gracefully decorated by tousled long brunette waves. She was like the 'Early Years Goddess' (or the EYG as I privately nicknamed her). I wondered what the infantile brains thought of her as she demonstrated her knowledge on phonics or times tables and whether they realised how enviously attractive she was to their mums at the door? I couldn't even remember the last time I'd put makeup on or washed my hair, for that matter. I'm sure I had been using my dry shampoo for a week straight. She blatantly couldn't have kids of her own to have that amount of dressing time.

"Thank you, Mrs Forte, I won't keep you long. I appreciate that it's not easy juggling everything at once," the EYG politely acknowledged. It felt like she was showing some compassion towards me – was she on my side?

"That's okay," I replied quickly.

"I just needed a quick word about Lena. You see, last week we noticed we are having a few issues whilst she is outside during child-initiated learning time," she spoke softly. I questioned in my head how she could command a whole class of thirty kids if I struggled to pay attention.

"What kind of issues?" I tried to cover my defensive tone.

"Lena seems to not quite understand how to respond *appropriately* to the other children. She's either very controlling of their games or throwing herself in a heap on the floor." The EYG looked at me as if she was nervous to carry on. What was she about to say? "For instance, when another child makes a mistake or has an accident, she either laughs or shouts at them."

"I've talked to her about this," I explained, feeling like I was on a parenting trial, "but it doesn't make a difference. She just can't seem to change her reaction." I thought about the phrase 'accidents happen' which I had invented at home and used in a sing-song kind of style so as to not make any situation worse.

"I'm sorry, Mrs Forte, but it's making the other children not want to play with her. If she doesn't change her behaviour soon, she won't have any friends."

I could feel myself holding back tears of immense pain as this teacher was joining the group with my parents, my sister and even my own husband in the belief that Lena was just some naughty kid. The image of her all alone with no friends hit a nerve. Was I the only person in the world that could see how kind Lena could be?

"Mrs Ramsbottom suggested that we discuss this issue whilst we talk about Lena's poor attendance," she delivered in her teacher-like fashion. "I've been told we're meeting on Thursday and that you will be attending with Mr Forte?"

I made an excuse that I had to be somewhere and stomped back through the red, spiky gate. I found myself subconsciously muttering the last words I heard back like some woman out of control. My musings were getting louder and more intolerable with every step I took. "Accidents happen," I began. "Accidents *fucking well* happen!" I screamed to myself as the dam to the water works had been dislodged. There was nobody around, or a shoulder to cry on, but I felt embarrassed by my outburst in the street.

Then there was the added pressure that it was expected of me to bring Nick to a meeting. How would he react to that? Would he even be able to get the time off to attend? Nobody asked us what suits our time schedules when they just beckoned us to the school in the daytime.

I picked up my phone and called Nick. I felt like I needed reassurance from a voice I knew well.

"I've just been collared at school by Lena's teacher," I began incoherently. "It was awful."

"Why? What's happened?" Nick asked, confused.

"They say she's having too many issues in school and that she doesn't act right around the other kids," I blurted. "How could they say that?"

"Well, she is bossy," he counteracted. "I think we would both agree on that. Maybe we just need to teach her how to rein it in a bit?"

Was that it? All that he could offer? I just wanted him to understand how I was feeling but he wasn't getting it. Did he not feel the injustice of it like me? Was I the only person on Lena's side? I decided to move on. He wasn't going to be that source of comfort I needed. I should have just called Shelley.

"Listen," I explained, "they have asked us to come to a meeting on Thursday morning to discuss it properly. Please say you can make it as I've already said yes?"

"Well you could have asked me first!" Nick said irritably. "I haven't even checked whether I can sort it out at work. Are you expecting me to take bloody annual leave to attend a silly meeting? I have limited time off as it is!"

"Can you at least try?" I felt vulnerable as if I was begging. He had to come with me. I couldn't face this alone.

"Yes, I'll try," he replied.

"Okay, thanks," I grovelled. I couldn't risk having an argument and him refusing to come. "There is just one more thing..."

"Which is?" Nick questioned.

"They also want to discuss some issues around her attendance," I explained, taking a deep breath knowing I had to continue. "There is something else I need to tell you."

"I have work to do, Sarah!" Nick snapped. "Can you just spit it out?"

"Well, yesterday I didn't send Lena to school because she was too upset to go," I confessed, relieved that the details were finally out in the open.

"You've got to be kidding me!?" Nick bellowed over the receiver. "Why didn't you consult me before you made a decision like that on your own?"

"Look, I'm sorry I never spoke to you." I tried to negotiate. "But she was so distressed there was no way I could send her in."

"I can't believe you did that!" Nick's voice was rising even higher. "She will never learn right from wrong if she knows she just has to cry to get what she wants."

His last statement hurt me deeply. He couldn't understand why I had been forced to do it. He wasn't living this reality day in, day out, like I was. This was going to look great on Thursday! They would probably put down any of Lena's issues as a reflection of marital disputes, instead of investigating the bigger challenges. Why could he not see that it was more than just not wanting to go to school?

After a few closing opinions we hung up and I retreated home with Charlie for a calm cup of coffee to regroup myself. I helped myself to a piece of cake from the kitchen counter (which admittedly was the size of a mountain) and I regretted binging on it instantly – but in the moment it made me feel more distracted from my uncomfortable emotions.

It wasn't long before the phone rang and the contact's name for Sunnybank School appeared on the screen. *Oh goodness*, I thought, *what now?*

My feeling this morning about Lena had been right on target as usual; I was being informed that Lena had been excluded and I was instructed to pick her up straight away. How was this possible? The day before I was being reprimanded about her attendance, and the next day I had a call to pick her up early because she was too much to handle. Either way, both situations resulted in the action being my responsibility.

"How could my five-year-old daughter be excluded?" I felt a concoction of shame, sadness and anger all rolled into one, just like the ingredients of a potent cocktail, which was packing a mighty punch.

It didn't take much time to fetch Lena, she was sitting waiting in the reception, her book bag over one shoulder, her water bottle spilling over the desk, whilst she was doing speedy circles on a spinning chair on one side of the office. I could hear the receptionist shout back past the glass screen to the colleague behind her: "Don't worry, *the mum* is here now!"

Two hands were shoved behind Lena's back as if she was being catapulted like a rubber band as she fell out of the door and into my arms.

"Wait!" Lena bellowed out in distress. "I want my Blu Tack girl!"

I could hear the spinning chair being pushed back from out of the desk and the glass shutter of the reception shafted up. A blob of blue gunk was dumped on the side without a word or a smile, and the shutter was slammed shut in a millisecond. It made me question what had just happened and how bad things had *really* been in the reception to be met with such hostility?

"School is a prison full of meanies!" Lena declared as she stuck her tongue out at the receptionist (who grimaced in utter disgust behind her jailing screen). The lady's lips were taut and her nostrils flared so much it was a miracle a fly didn't buzz up them.

"So, what happened today?" I enquired, still none the wiser. It would have been nice to have been given some information at least from the school so that I didn't feel the need to piece together the broken segments of information that I could retrieve from a five-year-old child.

"Nothing!" Lena declared, trying to pull on the handle of Charlie's pram to cause a deflection and barked, "It's my turn to push!" I continued to battle over the ownership of the vehicle, with Lena's small hands jostling for direction. I looked like a drunk driver as I clunked the pram up and down into many kerbs. I could sense the subject of school was off-topic and I decided to drop it there. It was the school's responsibility to tell me what had happened. Besides, surely, I should have had something in writing to at least make it official?

"I liked your Blu Tack girl," I offered as a change of focus.

She looked down at her feet and mumbled, "Thanks."

"You're welcome." I started to cool down a little. "Will you teach me how to make one?"

"You don't have Blu Tack," Lena said bluntly.

"That's a good point. I'll have to buy some." I took a moment to think of a new plan. "How about we take a trip to the park?"

"I'm sorry," she suddenly blurted out, "I tried to be good." Her face looked pale and her lips creased downwards just as much as her entire being.

"It's okay," I consoled, wrapping my biggest bear hug around her shoulders in the middle of the street. "I understand." I used my softest, maternal touch to remove her broken tear. "Just remember, Mummy always loves you." I was starting to make a parenting stride and it felt empowering.

"I knew how to write CAT, it's easy – C-A-T." Lena started with the false conception I had a clue what she was talking about. She often did that – assumed my knowledge on what she was saying as if I had witnessed it too. She always forgot that she needed to explain the parts that lead up to the story.

In true Lena fashion, she carried straight on: "I wanted to write the answer on the whiteboard and they picked Amy to do it instead. It's not fair! I knew the answer first!" Lena cried in a sing-song, childlike fashion. "It should have been my turn!" She screamed as if she was reliving the moment in front of my very eyes. "So, I rubbed out her smelly writing and wrote it much better. Then they took me out the class. They got the *Mrs Samsaroundabottom* because she's the headmistress. Then she said I was naughty. I said 'I don't care!' and I told her she was a 'poo poo bum'. I stuck my tongue out, Mummy, *because* she was a meanie and she deserved it!"

I looked at Lena as she stopped mid-flow, desperately searching for my reaction, in deep fear she had let me down.

"I'm sorry *because* you tell me I shouldn't do that anymore *because* I'm a big girl, but it was her fault not mine. Then the teacher that followed me took me to the red room and she held me down. So I pinched her arm to let me go. But she didn't. Then I bit her arm and she screamed, then I ran all the way round and round and round *because* I had my superhero pup legs on which make me run really, really fast, just like this..."

After the longest monologue known to man, Lena halted to demonstrate how she had escaped from the member of staff. She took off at full speed and ran in mini circles along the pavement. She continued rabbiting on, but I was unable to catch the end of her speech.

We headed to the park as a circuit breaker, and after some much-needed play time, we made the quiet walk home – just the three of us.

Outside the house, I could hear the car engine revving twice, before the sound of the ignition clicked as the car switched off. I knew who it was before the handle even turned. The thud of those bulky builder boots (I wasn't even sure why they were needed, I liked to remind him daily that he didn't go to work on a construction site) could be heard echoing along the garden path. The car alarm sensor clicked. Twice. Like some crazy ritual that my brain had become used to. I thought I'd go as far as to call the police if I didn't hear the second click.

In Nick walked, glancing at the toys strewn down the hallway, as if it was a war-torn bombsite, the sides of his mouth grimacing as he kicked off his tan boots. I always wondered why he bothered – his boots were more at risk of being contaminated by walking through the house, rather than the chance he had of bringing in any unwanted germs.

I knew what conversation we would be having and I was dreading it.

"Been one of those days, has it?" Nick uttered with one eyebrow raised in judgement.

"Every day is one of those days!" I snapped. "After the issue with them blaming me about yesterday – then today I had a phone call to collect Lena because they've decided to exclude her!"

"I don't know what you think I can do about it whilst I'm at work all day!" Nick disappeared into the kitchen as his words ricocheted from the walls, as though they were twisting the knife even further. Was that all he could say?

I could feel hot tears rising. I tried to hold them back; I didn't want him to see that his response had affected me. It hadn't always been like that, although lately, we seemed to be at war with each other.

I could hear Charlie murmuring in the living room and the distorted echo of Lena chanting sounds. I peered through the door, I saw her hanging upside-down over the sofa in just her underwear (her *Paw Patrol* pants, that she had refused to let me wash for the past three days, were dangling around her hips). As she saw me, she giggled and sprung to her feet. Charlie's murmurs soon turned into an assailant's assault and I skulked over to pick him up. Slowly stroking his back, he began to calm.

Lena took her favourite position in the middle of the living room and kicked Charlie's chair into the chipped wall. She started spinning in circles whilst gibbering made-up words on repeat – like some awful techno song, heightening with excitement until she made such a crescendo that she fell straight into Charlie's chair – which made an even bigger dent in the newly-painted wall.

Nick had to come in at that point, of course, like a bird of prey ready to devour his killings. "Are you *just* going to let her do that?" He belted out the words faster than a punch from a world heavyweight boxer. Of course everything had to be my fault, if a meteor fell out of the air and smashed into his darling car then that would be my fault too.

"*Accidents happen*," I uttered. I could taste lava in the air with the intuition any mother has when her cub is in danger. "They just happen."

"It's not myyy faultt!" Lena hurled at me with all her might.

"I didn't say it was, my darling." I offered my vocal cotton wool, but it was too late; the tipping point had already happened. "Remember, accidents happen," I reassured as best I could, like some negotiator disarming a terrorist.

"You just said it was MY fault!" Lena bellowed at me as she launched Charlie's rubber giraffe at the TV (I thanked my lucky stars it was a soft object that was closest to her).

A memory popped into my mind from the dreaded day Lena threw the TV remote. I could still see it skimming past Charlie's chair as my heart skipped what felt like its last beat. It was almost as if that moment was replaying the same millisecond of action through my brain. I could see the remote, paused in space, like some scene from a sci-fi movie. My voice gurgled in slow motion: "Nooo!" as we all twisted and bent aimlessly in the air (whilst Charlie still had a smile glued into place by the rush of wind). Nobody could get to the remote in time. The scene played torturously over and over in my mind. I felt so helpless, and the fear of what could have happened if the remote actually hit him, churned my stomach.

"I said accidents happen." I spoke as cheerily as possible but Lena wasn't going to be fooled.

"It *was* her fault! I don't know why you sugar-coat it all the time!" Nick said venomously as he slithered back into the room. "She would have had a firm hand if it was left to me to deal with it."

"Well, you never deal with it!" I screamed before I'd thought about the kids being in the same room. I took a deep breath and tried to recalibrate my feelings. My 'Mummy' hat firmly back on, I needed to steer this ship before we sunk completely. This situation wasn't foreign to me, I had been living it daily, and I knew too well how ugly this would play out if it was not brought under control.

"Daddy said it was my fault too!" Lena bellowed – the noise released in stages of pressure like some unwanted birthday balloon that had just been popped by an unhappy child.

"He didn't mean it, my darling, he just didn't see what happened properly," I tried to soothe.

I knew that her reaction could last for hours if she continued to think she had been told off. I had tried punishments in the past and they always made each situation worse. I'd spent weeks doing the same consequence of putting Lena on the 'thinking step' which would lead to her trying to decimate the house – throwing items across the room in some frenzied, object-killing massacre. Each day it got worse until one day her frustration got so intense that she began hitting her head against the stair banister, uncontrollably, until she bled. That night I cried so much and the confusion was all-consuming. Why didn't the traditional parenting route work for me? What was I doing so wrong? I started to feel like I was despising my own child and I hated myself even more for feeling like that.

"You should have picked a better daddy. One whose eyes work!" Lena shouted.

"Shh!" I started to giggle and she joined in. "Daddy might get upset."

"You could throw Daddy in the bin and find me a new one?" she suggested.

"Daddy doesn't mean it," I reassured. "He just got cross."

The mood was starting to lift and I could feel a heavy weight easing from my shoulders as I was beginning to contain the situation.

"Daddy needs to go outside into the blue recycling bin, then the bin men can come and pick him up and give him to another family. Then we say 'recycle, recycle, recycle' like *Peppa* and *George*!"

She ran like a whirlwind upstairs, suddenly rushing back down with a clanking and a thudding, until a heap of *Peppa Pig* figures and a house landed with a bang in a pile on the floor.

"Let's play!" Lena shouted animatedly.

I could never quite get over her mood swings; it was like she was puddle-jumping from one emotion to another within seconds, and I was constantly chasing her in catch-up mode. Whilst I was recovering from the earlier missile hitting our house, by trying to regroup my thoughts, Lena rabbited on nonchalantly about *Peppa Pig* finding some replacement brown marbles for *Daddy Pig* so he could recycle them into new eyes. My own internalised trajectory was heading onto the same pathway. How could I get Nick to change so that he could help - instead of making situations worse? More importantly, would he ever be able to change? There was also the school meeting to get through, and I wondered how I could stop Nick from showing his disapproval of my parenting decisions.

"Mummy!" Lena screeched as if sensing my mind had gone elsewhere. "I can't do my teeth anymore. And I won't be able to get dressed. AND..."

"I don't understand?" I tried to offer my support but was confused about why there was a sudden panic and need in her voice. We were supposed to be playing, I didn't know what had changed.

"I can't go to sleep tonight," Lena declared wildly, her eyes frantic, "without my controller pad to help me feel better! I need to press the buttons and hear Ryder's voice and... and... and..."

Lena burst into uncontrollable floods of tears and I put my arm around her to soothe. I remembered that she had accidentally broken her *Paw Patrol* toy control pad and I knew how much she relied on it to do all of the daily tasks that many people would have taken for granted. To Lena the pad was not just a toy but a lifeline. A way of communicating and absorbing into a fantasy world so she could perform the simplest of tasks. Now I understood where the panic had come from.

"Don't worry," I consoled. "We can try to find a replacement one.

How about I play the phrases on my phone until we can find the same thing?"

"Yes," she said through the sobs, "you're the best superhero mummy in the world!"

Just as I felt happy in the moment that I was doing what my child needed, I realised that Nick would not be happy with my decision. How would he react when he found out I had done something else without consulting him?

I would just have to keep it quiet, I told myself.

"Shall we carry on with the game?" I asked in an attempt to put us both back on-track and be distracted from our anxious thoughts.

We continued playing the *Peppa Pig* game, whilst the worry about how I would find a way for Lena to cope through the usual routines, and the fallout that was about to follow, rested beneath my skin.

"Peppa has broken her favourite toy," Lena began, back in fantasy world. "Let's pretend she is angry with herself and tries to run away, then Mummy Pig helps to make her feel better. Okay?"

"Sure."

We picked the figures up and re-enacted our reality into a creative fantasy which made it easier to process.

5

The Empty Chair

T he next few days passed relatively quietly, I guess you could call it the calm after the storm. It was almost as though the electricity that was in the air, crashed with such thunderous velocity, that it had nowhere else to go but to slowly disperse back into peace and serenity once again. I glanced outside, moving the velvety venetian blind, to see what time of day it was. I knew it was early, but I wanted to check, using the primeval method of estimation from the amount of daylight. The sun was still ignoring me with only its tip peaking over the horizon through a very foggy haze.

I knew I should shut my eyes and switch off again to get some well-needed extra hours of sleep, but my brain was invaded by an eclectic mix of hyperactivity and anxious thoughts about the day ahead. Instead, I lay there, restless. The fact that it was Thursday and I had to meet with the school was enough to send my mind into overdrive.

I couldn't face speaking up in front of them in the school meeting without any makeup on, but trying to find the extra time to fix my appearance was going to be an extra burden on what felt like an already uphill battle. How was I going to get through the morning routine and get to the meeting on time?

I checked my phone curiously to see if it was a reasonable time to rise. Oh no, 5.15am! *This is ridiculous*, I told myself, *if you get to sleep now that's at least another few hours until you really have to get up.* But then I tried to reason with myself, I mean, if I got up now I had plenty of time to get myself in order and would have no reason whatsoever to be late for the morning meeting. There was no point trying to get back to sleep, I'd only feel worse for it.

My mind raced, thinking about what I should wear to the meeting, what I was going to say, how I would keep my professional hat on if they said something that upset me. Then I started to worry about how Nick would come across in the meeting and if he would belittle me in front of them. I started to worry that the teachers would think it was down to our disconnected parenting that was causing issues for Lena... Extreme fear gripped me; what if Lena was taken off of us? I needed a coffee to calm my nerves and reorder my thoughts.

I looked back at my phone, it was now 5:30am – that definitely signalled an acceptable time to go downstairs and prepare myself with the most influential cup of caffeine of the day!

I spent the next few hours being non-productive. I was no nearer to my goal of being prepared for the day ahead. I scrolled through *Facebook* and kept refreshing my newsfeed as if I did it enough times the next status would read like I'd just won the lottery or something. I knew that I was procrastinating and that there were far more stimulating and productive things that I should be doing, but once again, I found myself refreshing the newsfeed like a hapless victim eager for more.

The sound of Nick's alarm interrupted my social navigational addiction and I quickly closed down *Facebook* (which was a blessing in disguise or I'd have lost even more minutes of the day reading trashy news posts).

As my thoughts went onto the day ahead, I soon jumped onto

another topic. I remembered that I needed to replace Lena's *Paw Patrol* controller pad. As I scrolled through the shopping options on Google, I learnt that the item Lena had was now updated, by a newer, improved version of the toy. Of course, Lena wouldn't see it like that, she would never see a change as an improvement. She would be devastated – what could I do to fix it? I continued scrolling frantically, hoping to find an older version somewhere. Finally, one popped up on *Ebay*. Phew, at last! I paid an extra five pounds for an old, second-hand toy (that I couldn't even guarantee would work) over a shiny wrapped new edition in a box (without any grubby fingermarks on either!). That pretty much summed up the parenting experience of my life.

The heavy oak door swung open and Nick entered the room to prepare himself for the day.

"You're up early?" He seemed confused as he glanced over at me on the laptop.

I just shrugged. It often felt hard these days to get the words out to Nick about how I was feeling, so it seemed the only option I had left was to keep my thoughts locked deep inside.

"Would you like a refill?" Nick waltzed over to the kitchen island to pick up my coffee cup.

"Yes, please."

I tried to subtly conceal the screen but it was no use as Nick had already clocked what I was looking at.

"I hope you're not thinking of replacing that stupid toy?" Nick remarked accusingly. "Lena needs to learn the hard way that if she breaks something then she can't just get a new one – money doesn't grow on trees!"

"Well, technically it does," I retorted. I knew my sarcasm wasn't going to win the argument but his lack of empathy towards Lena, coupled with his unhelpful parenting advice, always rubbed me up the wrong way. I knew that she needed to learn the value of money but in this context it wasn't appropriate. What was the point in pushing the consequence card on something that she didn't mean to do?

It always came back to the same issue – Nick felt that Lena needed to learn how to behave better (by following the rules that he was brought up with and firmly believed were rooted in discipline and control), whereas I felt that Lena couldn't control her episodes and punishing her for them was a fruitless exercise. Not only that, they made her worse. She always felt wrongly blamed for something she couldn't change. Of course, Nick thought that I was weak, which he reminded me about regularly. His comment about money was laden with so many more words and the true intention hit my nerve. I sighed deeply and Nick shot me a look of disdain.

"Maybe money doesn't seem to worry you whilst you swan around and I work hard to keep you all," he spat. "Perhaps you can think about using it so freely when you finally go back to work!"

I was speechless, there were no words to even explain how angry and upset he made me feel. It was like he was slowly finding ways to erode away my self-esteem. He knew that I had always paid my way, but right now I was on maternity leave after having Charlie, the original plan was to have a year off and to return to my job. But how did he expect me to do that whilst I was being called constantly about Lena and picking up the pieces of her not being in school? If anything, dealing with meetings and school, as well as managing the conflict at home, my whole life had become a full-time job. Then adding to that, Lena being excluded temporarily for one day, how would I have managed that if I would have been at work? Everything was feeling impossible to solve.

"I have always worked," I retorted. "Don't forget I have been an arts education officer for over twenty years. I have worked non-stop since I left university. That's not someone who has had to rely on others for money."

I couldn't help myself, he had sucked me back into another one of the same arguments we always had, with Nick trying to make me feel inferior to his being. It was another pressure to deal with, and the financial burden that Nick kept bringing up made me feel that I was having to be submissive and subservient to be kept. This was not what I had envisaged when I'd thought we would be having children together.

We continued on as two bodies, in the same room, in silence.

I ploughed my raging energy into unloading the dishwasher and had to calm myself down as I could feel that I was slamming the cupboards in angst. It was still only six in the morning and I didn't want to wake Lena or Charlie up just yet. I still hadn't made any headway on getting myself prepared for the day ahead and needed to run a bath before they roused. Perhaps I could lie in the bath and enjoy having a calm, peaceful soak for a while. Nick banged around in the kitchen some more. Sometimes I wondered if it was actually lonelier living with someone who you didn't see eye-to-eye with than it was to just be on your own.

"One cappuccino, just how you like it!" Nick passed me my coffee and it felt like a peace offering. He grabbed his lunch and coffee and picked up his boots – that were neatly set by the welcome mat at the front door. I followed him into the hallway and intercepted his routine.

"Don't forget the school meeting starts at nine-thirty this morning," I reminded him. He put his high-vis jacket over his shirt and seemed to take a while to process what I had just said.

"I have a busy day," he stated. *Oh great here it comes.* "I have a meeting to run first thing and then once all the drivers have their first loads set up, I'll make my way over to the school."

"You won't be late, will you?" I tried to question softly, but panic and frustration were hard to camouflage.

"I told you already that I'll be there. Don't put pressure on me, I don't know how long these things take!" he snapped.

There was silence again.

"Look," Nick began, trying to soften his tone, "I'm usually all set by nine o' clock once the fleet of drivers leave. So today shouldn't be any different. You just go as normal and I'll go to the reception and meet you there."

I knew I was forcing him to do something he didn't want to do, but did he not realise that I didn't want to have to do this either?

The door slammed and I was left with invisible words circling the empty house.

New sounds filled the house like a domino effect. Lena's small feet jumping out of bed onto the wooden floorboards, a cry from Charlie. Then, before I knew it, the whirlwind of the morning routine had firmly begun.

"Mummy," Lena's voice called out, "can I watch *Paw Patrol,* please?"

"We can only have two episodes because we need to get to school on time." I tried to prepare her so she knew what was expected.

I switched the TV on for Lena who sat with her legs up on the sofa and her head dangling upside-down. She giggled and flapped animatedly whatever direction she was laying in.

I warmed Charlie's first milk bottle of the day and fed him on my lap with one extra hand over the crown of his head to protect him from Lena's excited kicks. I located his safari rocking seat to carry it upstairs whilst dangling him on my other hip. Parenthood was always a delicate balance and I was never prepared enough for the next move.

I checked the time – it was nearly seven, the dreaded panic was sweeping through. My idealistic image from earlier about having a luxurious soak in the bath had firmly gone out of the window. Instead, I switched on the electric shower and jumped in at lightning speed – only managing to flick off my socks as a last realisation they were about to get soaked.

"Mummmyyy!" hollered Lena as she bashed up the stairs. "I want the episode where the pups save the white wolf!"

"I'm just in the shower, darling," I told her. "Let me get out and we can put it on in a moment."

"I want it on now!" Lena began screaming impatiently.

"Just wait." I was losing my shit.

"I can't wait, it hurts my brain." Lena barged into the bathroom leaving the door gaping. Any desire for privacy or warmth had soon evaporated the minute I chose to have my beautiful body invaders. It should have been Charlie who was more demanding – I'd hoped that Lena would have been able to occupy herself when I stepped out of the room. In fact, it was the complete opposite – the more destructive and clingier she became.

"Why did you get in the shower without telling me?" Lena's frown was firmly etched on her brow. "I needed your help first, Mummy!"

I could feel my pulse rising as I tried to keep a lid on my frustration of the moment. I raced around my wardrobe to throw on some clothes – which had none of the detail or effort my brain was planning on in the small hours of the morning. My hair was dripping wet and had made a nice dark puddle on the top of my t-shirt.

I continued to play catch-up for the rest of the morning – despite having been awake so early it beggared belief that I was about to be late yet again, and I hadn't had time to do my makeup.

There was a tension between Lena and I as we made the dreaded journey to school. We both felt the anticipation of what lay ahead. I kissed her forehead and hugged her goodbye in the class queue, then made my way to the reception. It was the first day back since Lena's exclusion and I was concerned about how she would be received when she went back into class. Would they forget about it and not hold it against her?

I sat in the deserted lobby for quite some time until my favourite receptionist entered.

"Follow me, please." She instructed me in a very unfriendly tone.

We walked robotically through the corridors in hostile silence until we had left the labyrinth that was the first building.

As we reached the second building and the receptionist swiped her staff badge to let us in, I noticed a small boy screaming as he wrapped himself around his caregiver's legs.

"He's *fine* when he's inside," the class teacher informed. "He forgets all about it soon enough!"

The lady's face was struggling to smile back as she said nothing. I knew that kind of silence, that solitude you have in your brain, when you want to say so much more but you become frightened to. Eventually the boy was dragged away from his safety blanket and led away screaming. My arm hairs raised; it was almost as if I felt that pain for both of them. What did *fine* actually mean? Did they ask the boy if he felt *fine* as he bawled through his tears of discomfort? It made me wonder if the school actually understood what it was like for a child to feel scared. I felt uncomfortable, I could see that kid was anything but fine!

Once inside building two, the receptionist guided me to a room the shape of a cuboid that was made entirely of glass. She stated: "The meeting is in the cube."

The Cube! What was this? Was I a contestant on a TV game show or had I actually arrived in some outer galactic experience? I took a tentative step into the room, fearing what was going to be expected of me.

I could see children glancing through the glass to have a look inside and I couldn't help but wish that I was on the other side of this.

There were two tables pushed together and on the central piece was a tall plastic jug on a tray that I thought may have been stolen from the school kitchen. There were a few glasses evenly spaced around, with a set of printed notes and a pen with the Sunnybank School logo printed on adjacent to each seat. Someone had spent more time laying out the meeting preparations than I did setting the table at home for dinner.

Mrs Ramsbottom, the broad headteacher with a frizzy bouffant, got the meeting underway.

"Thank you for coming this morning, Mrs Forte." Her poisonous perfume was stifling the already oxygen-starved air. I glanced around the meeting table and noticed there was an empty chair which was clearly indicative that somebody was not there.

"I thought we were expecting Mr Forte too?" Mrs Ramsbottom had a hint of sarcasm to her voice.

"He's on his way." I tried to not let my voice wobble as I concocted an excuse on Nick's behalf. "He's running late at work."

"Well we better get started and Mr Forte can join when, *or if*, he arrives," Mrs Ramsbottom cut in.

Where was he? I needed him. I couldn't face doing this alone.

"So, as you know, M*um*..."

I hated it when she did that. I wasn't her mum! It felt so patronising and I'd heard her do it before which irked me. I had a name, a title (and although I was on maternity leave), I did have a job too! It was like she had mixed all three of those things up to label me as just *Mum*. Could they imagine if I did the same and called them by their job titles instead?

"We have called this meeting because we have *grave* concerns about Lena." Mrs Ramsbottom didn't mince her words. "It might be best if Miss Orchard starts with outlining Lena's current PSED."

"What is PSED?" I asked. I disliked that she used educational jargon that made no sense to me and prevented me from keeping up with the conversation.

"Personal, Social and Emotional Development," whispered Miss Orchard.

"I've printed you a copy of the assessment that I have been doing for Lena. If there are any parts that you would like to discuss, or are a bit unclear, then please do stop me, Mrs Forte." I was starting to feel a little relieved that she was in the room. It seemed ironic that the junior of the two staff members was the more professional.

"It might be worth *Mum* taking this away to look over in her own time then we can save any questions for later." Mrs Ramsbottom contradicted. It felt like she was closing ranks before she had even started. Why had she called a meeting if I was not going to be given the opportunity to contribute?

"For the last few weeks," Miss Orchard calmly started, "I have been trying to get a clearer picture of the areas where we think Lena might be struggling."

I nodded.

"There are definitely some areas of learning where Lena meets the targets for her age group and can excel our estimations," the teacher paused, "I really do think she is a bright little thing."

Miss Orchard seemed to show some genuine affection for Lena.

"However," she continued, "there are concerns that Lena does not behave like the other children."

I could feel my walls go up trying to safeguard my vulnerable emotions. *Oh great*, I thought, *now her teacher is saying the same thing about Lena too.*

"That's right," interrupted Mrs Ramsbottom. "We are not happy that Lena doesn't obey school rules! She has to be reminded time and time again of what is expected of her here at Sunnybank."

"Maybe she just needs more help than other children?" I responded, hurt in my voice.

"We have noticed that she is better when she has an adult supervising," Miss Orchard agreed.

"So, why can't she have an adult with her if she's struggling so badly?" I was impatient. It felt like they were telling me there was a problem but lacked any solutions for the issue to be resolved.

"Oh no." Mrs Ramsbottom rocked forwards so fast she nearly fell off the plastic chair. "We don't have the resources to give Lena a one-to-one teaching assistant!"

"There must be something that can be done?" I could feel a scratchy sensation at the back of my throat.

"There have been far too many incidents this term which have involved hurting other children. So, it's for that reason that we feel it best for Lena's time in school to be reduced," Mrs Ramsbottom declared.

I couldn't believe it. Were they even allowed to do that? I felt out of my depth. The realisation hit me that the headteacher didn't want Lena in her school because she felt like she was just a nuisance – a bad child who nobody wanted.

"But doesn't this contradict your email about Lena's attendance if you're going to cut her time in school?"

"We are hoping that it might actually mean she attends more – the shorter days might be more accessible." It felt like Miss Orchard was trying to work with me.

"I think it would be the right time, with your consent, to refer out to services so that we can start getting some funding if we are ever going to be thinking about having Lena back in school full-time." Mrs Ramsbottom wasn't even looking at me as she continued her attack.

I looked at the empty chair and had a sudden reminder that Nick had not made it in time, any last-minute flutters of hope were washed away that he would be there, metaphorically, to hold my hand. If he'd opened the door then I would have thrown my entire being over him with pure joy and relief. The need to share the responsibility of Lena was stronger than ever. The tears continued to flow as the empty chair was symbolic of a much bigger void that was happening in my life.

"Do you need a moment?" Miss Orchard offered me a tissue and I took it gratefully. "I can imagine this must be quite a lot to take in."

"But..." I blurted out through tears. "I took Lena to the GP and he said that her behaviour was just typical for her age."

"I think you need to go back to your GP because her behaviour is far from typical," Mrs Ramsbottom instructed. "He can refer Lena to the paediatric service to get to the bottom of it. Usually they can offer you a parenting course too."

I wanted to scream. The blame always fell firmly at my feet, and no matter what I said, or how I acted, there was no way of changing that judgement. I did have boundaries. I wasn't weak. I kept consistent with my parenting consequences – lord knows how many times I had read parenting manuals but it didn't make Lena alter her behaviour. In fact, if anything, it seemed to make her worse. I had tried everything from sand-timers to weekly reward charts. All of the things they were going to tell me to do on a parenting course. I finally plucked up the courage to speak my mind.

"I don't need a parenting course," I shocked myself as my small voice squeaked out. "There are gaps in Lena's social understanding which are the problem. and they are not rooted in my parenting skills."

"Oh, of course, we are not saying that for one moment!" Mrs Ramsbottom was defensive. "I was merely suggesting that a parenting course *may* just bring up some ideas you might not yet have tried." Her sing-song headteacher voice didn't wash with me and her intonation on selected words in every sentence was starting to drive me up the wall.

"There are a couple of things that I have found work well at the moment," Miss Orchard offered to break the silent warfare that was in the cubic glass battleground. "Such as choices. But not too many options or Lena cannot choose! Oh, and if I give her a job or a responsibility to look after something, she really likes that. It does seem she's more comfortable with adult company too."

"That's because she often sees herself like another adult," I explained.

"She needs to learn to respond to authority and there won't be too much room for choices when she moves up to year one." Mrs Ramsbottom's face resembled a dog chewing a cracked bone with every extra lingering gesture to emphasise her point. "The learning expectations do increase and she must learn to work independently."

I wondered if she realised that we were talking about a five-year-old child? Surely kids needed to still be playing? I was sure I had missed some of the conversation because my consciousness was soon slapped into place.

"Lena could be at *risk* of permanent exclusion if she continues along the same path," Mrs Ramsbottom dropped unemotionally. "That's why we thought it might be in her own interest if we made a referral to the local Pupil Referral Unit."

"Why does she need to go to a unit?" A huge amount of fear was stinging in waves all over my body. "What even is it?"

"I think it's best if our SENCO gives you a call to discuss it further." I could feel the headteacher attempting to close the conversation down and end the meeting. They couldn't leave me like this, with no answers. I felt worse and further confused than if I hadn't attended the meeting whatsoever.

"What's the SENCO?" I queried.

"It's the co-ordinator who looks after students that have special educational needs and disabilities," Mrs Ramsbottom answered. "Mrs Webb is our designated SENCO and she will explain how the Pupil Referral Unit operates for children who may need to move on to a new provision that is more suitable."

I looked over at Miss Orchard in desperate hope (the Early Years Goddess was like my divine chance in the meeting who could have possibly stepped in) as I pleaded in my mind that she would say something different. She remained muted and clearly was keeping with the direction from her leader. I had made all of the preparations to come to this meeting and yet I felt like I had got nowhere but a dose of parental blame. Did nobody care about Lena and what she needed? Did they really think just moving her somewhere else would solve the problem?

My phone beeped with the ill-timing of a text just as the meeting had come to a close and a few ending pleasantries were being made.

It was Nick. I couldn't believe it.

> **Nick**
> Sorry darling, the system was down when I got to work. How did it go? Also, don't forget I've got training so I will be home late x

I felt just as empty as the chair that should have had my husband seated upon it. The tears took a whole different course of their own.

6

The Olive Branch

I tried to compose myself and put some concealer over the broken veins that were prominent on my red cheeks. It was hard to think rationally and strategically about how I could fix the mess that was becoming my life. I didn't know where or whom to turn to.

Oh shit! I remembered that I was supposed to have joined a virtual call with my two best friends yesterday! I quickly sent a message to apologise to the girls for letting them down, again. How long would they put up with this? If I wasn't cancelling plans, I was missing the arrangements completely. It was another worry on top of my existing ones. Of course the girls replied that they understood, but did they really? My family already made comments that I made silly excuses every time I cancelled a get-together and then when I did turn up, it went hideously wrong. I felt trapped by everything.

We arranged to do the call a day later than usual and I hoped the girls would let me move past my error. Having our 'Gin O' Clock' call (as we'd nicknamed it) was needed more than ever after the events that had unfolded. It was the time of the week that I usually looked forward to – a piece of me time amongst all the chaos.

We got to chat, laugh and put the world to rights. The girls were fine, as usual, that we were running a day late. I had to hand it to them – they were always flexible and supportive whenever life got in the way. They put no pressure on me and that naturally made maintaining their friendship easier than any other relationship in my life. Although, that niggling feeling that I was too often a disappointment was not easy to shake off.

My phone rang and I suddenly realised it had reached eight o'clock. Shelley and Vic were online and my brain had been scattered as usual trying to organise my time and by getting through the battlefield that was the bedtime routine.

"I got the key!" buzzed Shelley in her old-school singing voice.

"I got the secret!" chanted Vic.

"I got the key to another liiiife!" I joined in with them on the third line of the chorus. It was a custom that we always did when we were together. I couldn't even remember when or where it had become our tradition, but I had some vague recollection of being in Tenerife with the girls for a trashy drinking holiday, when we had lost the key to our apartment. It was a story we liked to repeat about how we had to smuggle ourselves in through the balcony of a boys' apartment next door, over the top, into ours and squeeze through the sliding doors, only to find the key stuck to our bottle of *Sourz*. The song lived on more legendarily than the drunken act itself, and we sung it with the camaraderie of those that would continue doing it until we were little old ladies and our bosoms were reaching the floor.

"Right, come on then, Sarah. Hit us with it. I can tell by your upside-down smile that your jelly's slipped off the plate!" Shelley was as direct as always.

"I don't have any jelly, unless you are referring to the extra wobbles on my belly!" I smirked.

"Yes, and I don't have any roses on my whiskers, so that makes two of us!" Shelley contorted.

"What the fuck!" screamed Vic, looking baffled. "I've got no idea what on earth is going on. This conversation doesn't even make sense!"

"It's the gin," I joined in (a few seconds with those two and my worries seemed to melt away almost instantly). "It takes you to a magical place – with jelly bellies, roses and whiskers."

"I'm pouring another one, I'm not on the same level as you two!" Vic replied playfully.

As friends we couldn't have looked more different to one another, and our personalities matched our appearances. For as much as Shelley was vibrant and strong, with a worked-out body that drew most eyes to her as soon as we were out, Vic was passive and quietly introverted. Vic, like me, was also struggling with her weight after we'd both had kids. In contrast to Shelley's curls, Vic had a strawberry-blonde, straight bob which neatly stopped just before her shoulders. Her pronounced glasses usually matched the colour of her outfit (which, nine out of ten times, housed the colour purple). I fell somewhere in the middle and my clothes choices had become far more conservative on account of Nick's jibing and my post-natal curves.

We skirted around the edges for a while, but once the first drinks kicked in with their lethal potions, we all started to get better acquainted again underneath the surface pleasantries. Shelley and Vic were the type of friends who you didn't need to do small-talk with and the juicier, deeper connections were what we did better. Whatever we talked about stayed in our small circle and there was a deep, respectful trust which sealed our unity. I had lost the friends that only asked questions where the answers would be recycled into gossip.

"What do you mean Nick was a no-show?" Shelley had concern in her voice.

I tried to make an excuse for him as I relayed the story, but I knew deep down that I was overcompensating. If it wasn't this it would have been something else. I could try as much as I wanted to put a brave face on, but when your friends look and see inside you, they know. They know that hurt and bitter disappointment, they see it in your eyes and your crumbling expression. No matter how high the facade goes up, your weeping soul always breaks through.

"When will he ever realise he needs to support you?" Vic asked gently.

"I guess he thinks I should be able to just deal with it, you know, he has quite old-fashioned views. He says the parenting part should be a mother's job." I confessed ashamedly. No matter what I felt about Nick, there was still an inner glimmer of attachment that I had towards him. It was one thing for me to feel things about him, but I felt strangely protective to hear anyone else putting him down. I was going out of my comfort zone talking about him in this kind of way. If I opened up about all of the grievances I felt towards him, I was scared there would be no going back.

"Does he not realise it takes two to tango!" Shelley urged. "There are two parents in this equation."

"All of the responsibility is resting on your shoulders. He needs to man-up and take some of that weight away from you." Vic joined in, "We aren't living in the Dark Ages – men and women don't have separate roles!"

I could feel myself no longer talking, I was backing away into a den like a frightened animal.

"He's been doing this for far too long and you have been picking up the pieces," I could hear Shelley consoling.

"You can't keep doing this all by yourself," added Vic. "I'm scared one day you're going to break."

"Sarah, you're so quiet these days," Shelley confessed. "It's like a part of you is being silenced."

I could hear them talking and the words were there, circling around my distorted brain. I had said them to myself for so long but it felt sadder hearing it expressed by people whose views were important to me. It meant I had to face up to the feelings that had been suppressed for so long. I just didn't know how to access them or what to even do about them.

Eventually I plucked up the courage and located a central thought in my hyperactive brain.

"He just doesn't get it. He always sees Lena like this wilful child we need to reign in." The tears began to flow. "He's just like everybody else. I've tried for so long to get him to understand, but we just seem to be walking separate paths, and, well I guess it's lonelier than if I was actually in this solo."

"Oh, Sarah," they both chorused. "I wish there was something we could do."

"Give him an ultimatum?" Vic suggested. "You could suggest that he helps you with the parenting side or else things can't carry on. You're only human, Sarah. And for the record, you have been doing the most amazing job single-handedly, better than anyone else I know. I don't think you give yourself enough credit. Shelley will vouch for me when I say we are both in awe of you."

"I certainly second that!" Shelley agreed warmly.

"Thank you." I had so few words left but their kindness was just what I needed.

"How about offering him an olive branch?" Shelley suggested. "You know men, they're not always good when you go into battle mode, but if you were to dangle a carrot it might just help."

"Yep," agreed Vic, "that's a great idea."

"That way you are guiding him to the place you want him to be. It's worth a try if nothing else, I mean, you've been going around in circles for ages and like you said yourself, he still just doesn't get it." It felt like Shelley was offering a solution that could possibly work, I just had to think about how I could do it. Nick wasn't the easiest of people to approach and he was difficult to budge when he had a closed opinion on something. His thinking had always been rigid and he saw things as black or white. I was always desperate for him to see the grey in-between.

"So, what do you think Nick needs to do so that he can understand Lena better?" Vic questioned supportively.

"He needs to spend more time with her so that he can see the difference when she is struggling and that she's not just choosing to do the opposite of what we ask of her," I expressed thoughtfully.

"And that's your olive branch, right there," Vic said. "How about they have an opportunity each week to spend time together? To start building that bridge that he needs to form a better relationship with Lena?"

"Bingo!" I squealed, "That's a perfect idea!"

"Message us and keep us updated," Vic told me. "It's a no-lose situation for Nick, surely!"

The conversation soon moved on to Shelley's latest dating exploits and we all giggled as per usual, especially as the gin was flowing. Shelley's disastrous dating exploits were always tainted with sadness, as the elephant in the room Shelley never liked talking about was her desire to have kids. With every relationship fail she grieved the loss of the child that she had never had and the cruel fate that her biological clock was ticking.

Vic added a few anecdotal stories about parenting her brood, but they were typical stories of messy bedrooms and the difficulty of getting her kids to do their homework. I couldn't help but envy the normal struggles that other parents had. Trying to navigate life with Lena was anything but conventional. It made me feel different all over again.

Then we returned to reminiscing about our school days – from the PE teacher who had random hairy patches sticking out from under his T-shirt, to the awful Office Technology tutor with his long fingernails and drainpipe trousers, and the croaky dinner lady who actually locked the tearaway kids in the utility cupboard. The memories flowed just as fast as the gin, and we soon realised we had made it past midnight as the door to the kitchen swung open and Nick stumbled in.

"Looks like I've walked into a party!" Nick squeezed in front of the camera. "Evening, ladies, I hope you are both well?" He seemed friendlier than usual and I wondered if it was his guilt for not turning up to the meeting with school.

"Hey, Nick!" they both echoed back, no doubt the alcohol was keeping their true feelings at bay.

"I'm off to bed now." He gestured animatedly. "Some of us need our beauty sleep at least. Sarah, can you try not to be too much longer, please? I need you for something." And with that, the door shut and I could hear the trail of his footsteps discreetly going up the stairs in order to not rouse the kids. There was a brief pause on the call and I wondered what my friends thought about Nick's subtle direction to end the call.

We carried on, defying Nick's last statement, and all agreed to have one more drink for the road – I didn't know where we thought we were heading (although it was certainly on a one-way ticket to a hangover in the morning). My head was getting foggy and I knew I would pay the price for enjoying myself the next day, but for that moment and in their company, I actually felt free.

We eventually wrapped up the call and I practically fell up the stairs whilst spilling the contents of the lonely glass of water I was carrying, in my drastic attempt to reach sobriety once again. I had that warm tingly feeling that spread through every layer of skin. It numbed the negativity that I had felt over the past week.

Nick collared me at the top of the stairs and it made me jump.

"I need my gym kit ready for tomorrow," he commanded. "If you can sober yourself up in the morning to get it sorted?"

"I didn't drink that much," I defended. "Besides, you've not given me much notice to get it ready in time."

"Well it's been in the washing basket for like a week." Nick's face contorted. "I should have a spare kit when one has been used. I can't exactly wear this dirty set again, can I?" Nick held up the used sportswear to emphasise his point and his stare felt malicious.

I so desperately wanted to say more but couldn't. Instead, I talked myself down and reasoned with what he had asked of me. I made a mental note to remember to do it first thing in the morning. I didn't need what he'd call my 'inability to keep on top of the house chores' adding to our already tempestuous marriage. I kept telling myself that it equalised itself out. I mean, I took control of the house and the children, whilst he worked and did the odd jobs and DIY. Maybe we were just falling into the areas where our strengths lay and that was what happens in all families? Besides, I did forget to do lots of things, maybe he had a point.

My heart was still not convinced as I relived the sensation of being alone in the school meeting room without my partner by my side.

"Perhaps, if you spent less time talking to your friends and more time getting on with being a wife, we wouldn't have these disagreements?!" Nick slunk off into Lena's room and threw himself under her superhero cover, signalling the end of our conversation.

My friends were the only people in my life who were holding me up. There was no way I was going to let them go, no matter how many digs Nick made in private. I was feeling ostracised from any familiarity I had from my earlier life. How had it changed so badly? How could he encourage me to cut my time down with the only two people who were keeping me sane? He had already chipped away enough so that my time with them was limited – what if he continued to the point they disappeared out of my life?

I fell into a light sleep, alone in our marital bed, tossing and turning, with recurring dreams of walking along a moonlit path all by myself with an aching desire to be rescued by somebody. Anybody. Or anything to ease the isolated and discombobulated oppressive reality I found myself living.

A few weeks rolled by and we were nearing the onset of the summer holidays. I still hadn't offered an olive branch to Nick. It was something I kept putting off for a moment that never came. The sunny days were filled with playing in the garden and inevitably staying awake late at night to catch up on all of the chores I wasn't able to do during the daytime. It felt exhausting but it seemed to be what we all needed. The less input from school and more time to enjoy each other's company seemed to do us all the world of good. Left to our own devices we found ways to explore the outdoors and teach ourselves new skills. If only this style of learning could be replicated in school, then my daughter might not have found it so difficult. I thought back to my warning letter that I'd received about Lena's attendance a few months ago and sighed. The holidays would help me forget those problems ever existed.

Forms had been sent home for me to sign to get the ball moving with asking for outside help from professionals to see Lena. As we were nearing the end of term, it would be as she entered Year One before anyone could come and assess her. I had asked our GP to send a referral so that she could be assessed by the local paediatric service – just like Mrs Ramsbottom had told me to do. I'd pleaded with my doctor that it was necessary because the school was only allowing Lena to be in school for a limited time and she was missing a huge part of her education. I managed to push through and she was put on a waiting list for an initial assessment.

School began arranging for an educational psychologist to come and observe Lena's behaviours so they could be advised further. Signing the documents to agree for the referral was like I was being detonated by a nuclear bomb – the wording written depicted the most insolent, stubborn and obtuse child imaginable. They couldn't see the Lena that squeezed my hand, or rubbed her rabbit's label to get to sleep at night, or the girl who really did have a heart of gold. I stuffed the paperwork behind the breadboard, hidden amongst the crumbs – this was my makeshift office space. Out of sight and out of mind, for now.

I thought long and hard about what to do about my hostile feelings towards Nick, the gap between us was becoming so significant that it was hard to penetrate the space. I also tried to plan a way for him to understand Lena better and how I could finally offer him that olive branch discreetly.

I found the opportunity one evening when I had the laptop powered up on the kitchen island. I had watched a short *YouTube* video with a man called Doctor Ross Greene who had written a book called *The Explosive Child* (I made a mental note to look the book up on Amazon as it was the first time I had heard of it and it sounded worthwhile). I watched it by myself. The American guy explained that children do well if they *can*, not if they *want to*. He talked about flipping the narrative and reframing our understanding towards challenging kids. I was absorbed. I felt like he was talking to me personally. Every single word made so much sense. It confirmed my belief that there was a reason behind Lena's behaviour.

"Why would kids not want to do well?" His words struck a chord. He continued explaining about helping a child so they can do something – which he said was more powerful than thinking the child was not willing to do it. His theory of 'Collaborative Problem Solving' was the exact thing I had been doing naturally with Lena. Not only that, she achieved more learning with me at home than she seemed to at school. It felt like a eureka moment. I had a tingly sensation in the pit of my stomach which soon turned sour. The fact I had been placed as the major part of the problem was fuelling a deep, inner beast that had been silent for so long.

So, with the preparations made, I sat next to the laptop, staged as if I was watching it for the first time. In fact, I watched it twice, as the first time Nick just walked into the kitchen and ignored the fact that I was even there. So I repeated it in the vain hope he might return. To my relief he came back in to pour himself a cold beer from the fridge.

"What's that you're watching?"

"It's a guy called Doctor Ross Greene," I answered. "He's an expert on helping explosive children."

"My word, he's got an annoying voice if ever I heard one: 'kids do well if they wannnaaa!!' he keeps repeating that same bloody bit."

"I think that's the point," I interjected, trying to remain calm. I paused the video. "Kids do well if they want to... what kid *wouldn't want to do well*? It's better to think that kids *would do well* if they *could*."

"Well they should at least try, we shouldn't keep making excuses for them, or they will never learn to do things by themselves." Nick just wasn't getting it and I could feel my blood starting to boil. I had to try to remain calm before a splurge of insults came flying off my tongue like a group of anti-aircraft.

"It's like labelling your child – it just gives them an excuse for being naughty. They make the most ridiculous things up these days." And with that last remark, Nick took his ignorant ass out of the kitchen at speed, doing his usual obligatory dramatic exit.

I was left reeling. I was so frustrated that beads of sweat accumulated all over my forehead. They rolled down my face so fast it was as if they were doing the head, shoulders, knees and toes dance. How was I supposed to get through to Nick when he was nothing but a pig-eared neanderthal? It took every ounce of my energy to not chase him up the stairs and tell him what a bozo I thought he was. As much as I was trying to remain logical and tactical, it felt like an impossible reality when my husband was acting like a primate. I knew he didn't cope well with conflict, but trying to refrain from saying what I thought all of the time just to keep the peace, was starting to kill me from the inside out.

I picked up my phone and pulled up the girls' *WhatsApp* group in a last-ditch effort to stay calm.

> Help is required, please ladies!! Just tried to get Nick to watch a video about kids being defiant and he's gone and walked out the room! I was trying to offer that bridge but it really is impossible. Shall I just confront him? Send help (or failing that – copious amounts of gin!) Love you both x x

A message pinged back.

> **Shelley**
>
> He's a man! Your olive branch needs to be more direct. Just make it clear he needs to spend time with Lena to make the relationship work. I would go that way first and then find a way to introduce ideas about parenting afterwards when he is ready to hear them! Keep your chin up, beaut. x

Shortly afterwards Vic was online and joined the conversation.

> **Vic**
>
> Yep! Deffo what Shell said. Think of it more like a trunk rather than a branch and you might be on the right track?? You've got this and don't forget – we've got you x

I still had my phone in my hand as Nick came back into the room and shot me an accusatory look.

"Who are you busy texting?" he directed sternly.

"Nobody," I responded. "Just Vic and Shelley."

"Let me see!" Nick snatched the phone out of my hands. "You're acting suspicious."

I panicked about the conversation I was having about him with my friends. He brazenly scrolled through, skim-reading the collection of chats that I had on my *WhatsApp* feed. He didn't focus on the chat that I had with my friends; he seemed more preoccupied looking if there were any text messages of importance.

"I told you already it was Vic and Shelley!" I was getting frustrated with being treated unfairly like I had done something terrible. "I can text my two best friends, you know."

"Maybe it's about time you found new friends." Nick rolled his eyes. "Shelley is always on the pull – desperately trying to find any man that will have her. And I wouldn't trust Vic as far as I could throw her! She's after something."

"They're not like that!" I defended. "My friends are decent."

"Perhaps you can stop wasting your time talking to them, and keep the house in order instead," Nick suggested. "You'll be back at work in no time and you need to prioritise stuff a bit better. January – *and the end of your maternity leave* – can't come soon enough!"

Did he really think that I was at home doing nothing? And why did he make these things up about my friends? They were nothing like he was painting them out to be. It was almost like he was jealous of me for spending time with them. The pressure of returning to my office job was piled on me by Nick. I had no idea how I would juggle that too. I actually felt like giving everything up and running away, living on a street somewhere where nobody could find me. Away from the life that was consuming me. Then I had a pang of guilt for imagining deserting my own children.

***

I busied myself making the dinner and doing the bedtime routine, settling the children down for the night. I was on a mission and nothing was going to stop me. I hastily unscrewed the next bottle of red that was resting, invitingly on the splash-backed windowsill, and poured a large amount into my glass. I swirled it around in preparation and, as the rich and fruity aromas shot into the air, I could taste the serenity it was going to bring without even having a sip.

The stools were neatly arranged under the island and I had already laid the cutlery out. I placed the open bottle of wine neatly in the centre, as if it were playing piggy-in-the-middle between two high-rise wine glasses. The wine had no chance of winning the game of remaining in the bottle. I pretty much slugged the first glass down before it could even make a lasting mark on the rim. *Heck, I may as well just carry on with the bottle and put an unopened one there instead.*

The plates were set either side and I felt nervous – it was very rare these days that Nick and I sat down to a meal together. I knew that his face was going to be shocked when he walked in. The anticipation of waiting was making me restless. I couldn't cope with the unwanted energy, it was limitless, like a huge mound of sickly-sweet popping candy. Finally, the door swung open (I was starting to feel like this was groundhog day and the only place in the entire house we engaged in conversation was after Nick flung himself into the kitchen).

I mean, we were certainly not making any polite contact in the bedroom, it was rare these days we even slept in the same bed. I usually found the tell-tale signs of Nick's previous evening en-gagements discarded on the un-hoovered carpet (these consisted of a PlayStation Four remote, an empty bag of tortilla chips and a scooped-dry pot of salsa, laid next to a solitary bottle of beer).

If he did make it up to bed and slinked in next to me, it wouldn't be long until we would have Lena's little fidgety body nestling between us. He always huffed and puffed about having to share the bed and how he needed his sleep as he had important work to do the next day. I mean, didn't we all? It had resulted many times in him plodding off into Lena's bright red superhero room and his feet could always be seen protruding outside the end of her cover. After a while, he stopped getting in with me at all. The bed felt just as uninhabited as my emotions were towards my own husband, and the untenanted bed felt as deserted as the non-existent drive I had to do anything anymore.

The second and third glasses of red had gone down so smoothly that I was starting to relax. I even asked Alexa to play me some happy songs. The numbing sensation of the alcohol took away the resentment that was always at the forefront of my being. Just as I poured the remaining contents of the bottle into my own glass, of course, Nick picked his optimum moment to enter the vicinity. He had actually made it an art, he did it so often.

"Woah, easy tiger!" he jested. "Don't tell me you've drunk that whole bottle to yourself! Are you on a mission or something?"

"It's Saturday night." I drunkenly retorted, "I'm allowed a night off!" I could feel my lips twitching, dancing to their own intoxicated rhythm, albeit delayed as if they were operating a different system to that of the rest of my face.

"Every night is a night off for you!" He laughed at his own poor joke. "You'll be booking into rehab soon." The last aside was uttered quietly under his breath as he tugged at the corkscrew on the second wine bottle, which finally popped a release as if it was fighting for its own freedom.

"Piss off, Nick." I was letting my guard down fast. This wasn't the way it was supposed to go.

"Not before I've eaten." A hint of sarcasm was buried in his voice. "I was only joking, will there ever be a time when you're not so sensitive? You take everything to heart." He changed the subject without a regret that his words may have hurt me further. "So, what's for dinner?"

"Fajitas," I practically spat out the word as I opened the fridge to get the new packet of Tex Mex dips I had bought earlier that day, and plonked them on the island.

"Does the service come with a smile?" He beamed. His beautiful face was without any imperfections, yet it seemed so unappealing as time was passing.

"You could help. I've been getting it all ready by myself, whilst you swan around entertaining yourself." I was like a jailer and I wasn't letting any prisoners past. Flying around the kitchen, trying to get the last few preparations done, whilst he was just standing doing nothing was starting to really irk me. The happy juice couldn't even stop the feeling of resentment from creeping back into my pores. I knocked the spatula out of the pan and flicked a whole portion of nearly-burnt spicy chicken and peppers onto the floor.

"I'll help by eating the bits you've thrown away." Nick grinned, picking up a chunk of chicken and throwing it from one hand to another whilst it singed his fingers. "Three second rule after all."

I accidentally kneed him with my befuddled leg and I may have actually felt a pang of guilt had I not been under the influence. My inebriated brain was laughing inside at what felt like a mini comeback.

"I see you've laid the table. I was going to suggest just plating up and watching the TV. There's a big tennis match I recorded earlier and I wanted to watch it on catch-up."

He had that desperate look of avoidance as if he had a magnet that was pulling him towards the door. His eyes spoke with impatience that something more interesting was enticing him.

"You can do that anytime." I was trying to not be downtrodden. "I've gone to a lot of effort to prepare this meal." I paused a little before I said: "I thought it would make a nice difference."

"Fine! No problem at all." But his face was telling a different story.

"It's ready now, anyway. I'm dishing up." I picked up the breadboard to lay down as a heat absorber and piled on top the wok with the fajita ingredients. I grabbed the wraps from the oven and put them onto the table, slightly undoing the foil parcel and leaving the warmth in the metal covering to keep the heat. I pretty much flung the bowl of grated cheese down on the worktop as the pièce de résistance – scraps of cheddar falling all over the unit. I tipsily spilled the words: "Bon appetit."

I poured us both a glass of wine. His looked far more appealing in his crystal clear, sparkling glass. Mine, on the other hand, was cloudy, full of smears and a spicy hand mark that was etched mistily onto one side. If a glass could symbolise a person, then this one would definitely have been me; I felt just as hazy as the glass. Needless to say, my drink disappeared in a matter of seconds, whilst Nick's glass still had plenty of wine.

I found a moment in the fractious conversation to bring up what had been troubling me. "Listen, Nick. Things need to change." I took a courageous breath before I said the last part, "I feel like I'm doing this all on my own."

"Oh, Sarah. Please stop being a drama queen like usual. You only made one dinner. Now, I'm not being ungrateful, it's good and I appreciate it, but if you're suggesting I don't do anything around the house then you really are quite mistaken." Nick was on a rant and I wasn't in any form of sobriety to articulate my point and explain myself better.

"I'm not talking about dinner," I confessed and could feel myself nearing the axis. "I'm not talking about who does what, or whether you wash up now and again, or even take the bins out. I'm not sweating the small stuff."

"So what are you referring to? I know it's something that you are implying *I don't do*, so let's just cut the bullshit and get on with it." Nick was getting flustered, I could tell because his pupils always dilated when he was cross.

"I'm talking about not supporting me." There, I said it. At last, I had said what had been troubling me for weeks. It felt like a heavy weight had lifted from my shoulders, the burden of concealing my emotions had been taking its toll.

"Not supporting you! Are you for real?!" Just as I expected – this conversation was not going to end well and had been the reason that I had avoided the conflict for so long. "I do stuff *for you* in the house! I work full-time! I go to your bloody nephew's christening when you ask me to! I take you on holidays abroad... what more do you bloody want from me?!?" Nick always did this. His voice went up to such a level and carried such anger and animosity that it became impossible to ever say what I wanted. It was always easier to just keep the peace. But doing that was breaking me.

"I'm not saying you don't do all of those things, but the house, well it's not *for me* you do it, it's for all of us. And, well, Lena... the kids... they're not just my responsibility. There are two of us." My speech was as broken as my thoughts and were as incoherent as my troubled worries.

"Oh right, so *now* I'm not a good father, is that what you're saying?" He was leaning across the table and I felt threatened by his aura invading mine. Within a second, he picked up his empty plate and threw it into the sink, spilling his leftovers down the drain, and charged out of the room.

I picked myself up with as much courage as I could find, I had come this far, I couldn't back down.

"I think it would be good if you and Lena spent some special time together. She needs it and so do I." I had followed him with my mucky glass of wine into the living room. I sat down on the opposite couch.

"You're pissed," he uttered with venom hidden in his smirk. "We'll talk about this tomorrow when you're sober again."

"That just means you're fobbing me off." I didn't know where this new person had come from but I felt empowered now that the lid had come off.

"No I'm fucking not!" Nick's swearing had increased and I knew that he was completely rattled by what I was saying. I think deep down he knew he wasn't putting the time in with any of us, and the part of him that did actually care was experiencing some kind of guilt. Instead of admitting it, his voice grew louder and louder. "I have no problem spending time with my own daughter, any time she wants me, I'll be there."

"Well how about you have a time in the week when it's just you and her? You could do something fun together, and if it was every week, she would look forward to it." I had found that olive branch and was dangling it right in front of him. All I needed him to do was say yes and it could be the start of him seeing Lena the way I did.

"I don't know what I'm doing from week to week, you know I have work." Nick looked stressed and I knew I was putting him out of his comfort zone.

"You have weekends that you could set aside. Even if it's just for an hour, that's all I'm asking for." I felt the stakes turn and the conversation tipped into my winning field.

"Nobody has to tell me when I should spend time with my own child," he retorted, almost childlike now. He was trapped and he knew it. "Oh, for fuck's sake, yes, I'll do it every Sunday after my training session. Are you bloody happy now? Can I just watch the match in peace?"

I walked out the room smiling, a spring in my step, well a drunken stumble more like. I had achieved what I'd set out to do. But then the niggling feeling returned. Should I have even needed to ask a father to make an effort with his own child?

7

Slides Have Rules

It was the second week of the summer holidays and we were fortunate to have some high pressure that created a joyous heatwave. As I reclined on the tartan picnic blanket crunching down the shiny blades of grass in our small garden, I looked up at the sky and discussed the rolling pattern of cloud formations with Lena, whilst Charlie kicked his soft legs in enjoyment. We spotted a grumpy elephant that looked like Daddy, a game of noughts and crosses, and the cloud we liked the most resembled a love heart. As we took in each breath of serene, humid air and saw the leaves dancing in the sunshine, we were unshackled from the demands of a fast-paced society. The rays tickled and caressed our skin as if to whisper a renaissance of play that we no longer remembered, and tempted our minds away from being the educational rejects.

A letter had arrived in the post to say that we were on a waiting list for Lena's first appointment with the local paediatrician. They said they were working through a backlog of referrals but we would hear in due course. A leaflet was included about what to expect at the first appointment. It was fairly generic and said we would need to bring Lena's red book with us and that she would have her height and weight checked at the clinic. Included with the letter were two social communication questionnaires to fill out (one for the parents and one to be completed by school), which we should return ahead of the first appointment. I popped the school's form in the post (despite it still being the summer holidays – I wanted to be ahead for the next school year).

I managed to get Nick to sit down with me to fill out our parental part of the questionnaire. Some questions were easy to answer, for instance did Lena use short phrases or sentences? We ticked yes automatically. But, as the form continued, we began to dispute our answers.

"Can she or he have a 'to' and 'fro' conversation?" Nick impatiently read out loud. "Yes of course she can. Now, move onto the next question or we will be here all day! I don't see how this is relevant to Lena."

"Hold on a minute, you're rushing me and I'm trying to think!" I exclaimed.

"Well, it's either a yes or no answer, she either does or she doesn't! You don't really need to spend an age thinking about that." Nick jumped up to put his empty coffee cup into the sink. "I've got things to get on with!"

"There needs to be a 'sometimes' box," I mused, "because she doesn't *always* do it. There are times that she asks questions and she seems like she is listening, but then she asks the question again like she didn't remember asking it the first time. I don't think she always understands the answer no matter how many times you give it to her. Besides, she is far more comfortable talking about something that interests her than reciprocating a back-and-forth conversation."

"You could be talking about the entire human race!" Nick snorted as he laughed at his own joke. "We could all talk about the subjects that interest us all day long, but we soon realise we wouldn't get very far in the world if we do just that."

"You're not being objective here," the words squeezed past my

95

lips with the exhale of breath that needed to be released. "What if it's something she *can't* do?"

"Oh goodness, there you go again. Making excuses. Sugar-coating things. When will you ever wake up to see that Lena just needs a firm hand and some boundaries, and then she won't have these 'invented' problems you keep pinning on her?" Nick picked up his phone to look at the time and let out a big huff.

"Just forget it!" The tears were rolling down my sorrowful cheeks as I shoved the paperwork, crumpled up, back into the envelope and started busying myself, as usual, at the kitchen sink.

"Look, I said I'd meet Alan for a drink before we go for a kick around with the lads. We can take a look at it tomorrow when I have more time." With his last words, he rushed over to me and put his arm around my shoulders almost as if he were hugging an acquaintance for a staged photo. He leant in and kissed my cheek, the pressure of his wet lips stung my vulnerable skin.

Nick's suggestion of 'tomorrow' came and went, as did the days that followed. Of course, he never mentioned the questionnaire again and I couldn't face reminding him. In fact, the demand to face the anticipatory form alone was now so big that it stayed wedged in the envelope for another fortnight. My confidence in my own judgement was completely shattered, and the fear of my emotions rising for another time prevented me from even trying to do it again.

And then I had a chance meeting with a stranger in the park which catapulted me into gear.

We had been stuck at home all day and were feeling stir-crazy, but to every suggestion I made I was met with an automatic 'no' from Lena.

"Okay," I finally suggested as my last idea, "how about we scoot to Queen's Field and you can go on the monkey swing AND we can play the *Paw Patrol* game where they are flying through the air to another emergency?"

"Maybe," Lena said unconvincingly, but the mere mention of the word nearly made me wet myself in excitement that I had made a breakthrough. "Only if I can be *Chase* and you are *Ryder,* then it's a deal!"

"Deal!" I said, giving a high-five to her little palm. There was no way I was going to say anything else as the chance to leave the prison of the four walls was a ticket better than winning the lottery.

As we arrived at the park, Lena flung open the gate to the floodlit groups of families. I could sense that it was going to be a challenging visit. The sheer volume of people on a hot, summer's day was a recipe for disaster in Lena's books. I could smell the busyness and the sweat of a multitude of people as the sound bounced from one park item to another. It was like I was doing the vetting and putting myself in her shoes – as if I were able to feel her emotions like they were my own.

"It's too busy!" Lena stopped in her tracks to shoot me an accusatory look of blame. My gut feeling had been right about her reaction. I could see there were no spaces on any of the park equipment which indicated that Lena would have to wait her turn and I knew how that would pan out. *Oh geez, please let us survive this unscathed.*

"The monkey swing is taken!" she bellowed as she threw her arms disappointingly towards the rubber floor.

I surveyed the park for the least busy area and spotted the see-saw which had three children balancing along the plank of wood – and they didn't look much older than Lena. They had to be our best bet. Who knew, maybe Lena would make some friends and that would help her relax into the park visit more?

"How about we try the see-saw?" I suggested.

I could see that Lena had spotted the children and was looking over to them curiously. After a while she started to move so slowly that it seemed as if her legs weren't taking steps and she was hovering magically towards the action.

By the time she finally arrived, she didn't seem to have an awareness of proximity (or how to give people personal space) as she encroached their territory and was tapping one of the children on the knee.

"What?" the young girl said to Lena, looking confused.

"You're not following the rules," Lena said matter-of-factly. "There should only be two people on the see-saw at once."

Oh no! If that was the first thing she said to the children, I knew there would be a point of no return.

"If two of you get off, then I could be the person who goes on with one and then it would be fair," Lena informed them as if she was a juridical leader to the infantile ears.

"We are playing a game," the little girl replied, "you have to find something else to play on."

Lena ran back to me and flung her arms around me with tears in her eyes.

"They didn't want me to play!" Lena hollered, sticking her tongue out for the group of children to see.

"Maybe you needed to start with just asking if you could play and try to adapt to their game?" I suggested softly. "Rather than telling them the rules straight away. Other children might find that hard to understand."

"What's hard to understand?" Lena asked rhetorically. "Rules are rules!"

My heart felt broken for her with the social rejection she continuously experienced. Her style of communication was just as hard for them to understand as it was for her to understand them. Lena darted off. I had a pang of worry that the earlier disappointment would impact on her ability to become irrational. I just hoped she wouldn't explode whilst we were there.

Eventually, Lena was busy on the climbing frame and repeating the action of going up the red tattered staircase and flying down the curvy orange slide. I decided to go over to her and remind her there were other pieces of play equipment in the park. I don't know why I did it really, she was having so much fun on the one slide but there were two different coloured ones either side. My interfering maternal voice was pushing me to direct her enjoyment more. I had the continuous thought that she was missing out on all of the other choices by narrowly focussing on just one thing.

"Lena, why don't you try the blue slide next? It looks like super fun!" I directed (I was unconscious in my behaviour, but I felt that as her parent I could be a better judge of what she needed).

"Slides don't like to be blue." She scrunched up her face and she stuck her tongue out at me.

Lena threw herself down at the top of the slide, with her arms crossed, frowning her most uncompromising upside-down smile. As the minutes passed a queue of impatient children formed behind her, eager for their chance to slide down a spiral-spin of euphoria.

I could hear the children shouting the words out: "Go down!" She was not budging – like a cork stuck in a defiant bottle of champagne – no matter how much she was prodded or pulled, she was neatly wedged, blocking the route.

A stuffy lady, with a neat outfit and a false smile, interrupted my thoughts and tapped me on the shoulder. "Excuse me, your child is blocking the slide."

Was she for real? Did she not think I could bloody see?

"Lena." I tried to cover my tone of feeling uncertain whilst my cheeks flushed as pink as if they were trying to acclimatise on a brisk summer's day. "Come down the slide, darling, because the other children can't get past."

I had adopted that perfect parenting style that people do when they want to ensure they seem the one in control of the situation. There was no movement from Lena as the children kicked and screamed behind her like bubbles of carbonated gas building behind a cork. She was so still and serene as if having an out-of-body experience. That energy was going to go somewhere. My fears were soon realised as Lena turned around and hit a toddler behind her who had their hands placed upon her back and was trying to push her manually down the slide.

"Get off me!" Lena screamed.

The queue of children erupted wildly. They tried to escape back down the stairs whilst the injured child screamed like a beacon signalling danger to any other vessel. The children who could move faster were bumping past the ones who took each step securely as they relied upon the railings for support. It looked like carnage, as if I was watching a free-for-all of passengers trying to escape from a sinking liner, ruthless in their pursuit to save their own bacon. At the epicentre of the drama Lena was still sitting, territorially blocking the slide, as the screaming victim refused to move. They were determined to get down the orange slide no matter what.

Now there was a clear pathway up, I managed to squeeze my overly large frame up the winding staircase to manage the situation. I tried to talk to Lena but she seemed as though she was ignoring me, until I got so close she quickly slid away. I looked behind me at the staircase and forwards to the claustrophobic orange tubing ahead. I knew whichever path I chose was going to be a risky choice. Down on the ground was a terrorising mob of preying parents, eager to watch me enter my gauntlet of doom.

I needed the fastest exit possible; I was concerned that there were other potential infantile victims and I was conscious Lena was in the middle of her red rage. I pushed my wobbly backside onto the slide and had to lever myself down in stages as my weight was acting like a stopper. With every squeak and thud it took,

I suddenly found myself trapped halfway down. I knew I had taken the wrong option but was already committed to my bad exit choice. I looked up the slide behind me and knew that I could not get back to the top. I had no other option but to keep unpeeling myself down the shiny metal. The sweat was pouring down me like I was an unfit contestant on an obstacle course, ready to be booed by my unsympathetic spectators. I was frustrated at myself for all of the overeating I had been doing lately.

I jumped off the bottom of the slide and glanced around the park equipment, desperately trying to locate my offspring. She had been watching me and was already one step ahead.

"Lena, come back here!" I shouted.

We continued with our usual cat-and-mouse style chase. This, of course, gave the crowd even more to gawp at. It was one of the things that put me off going anywhere publicly with Lena. We were fine whilst we were having fun, but there could always be an eventuality that I couldn't predict and prepare her for. It was always the reactions of others that made me panic more. It prevented me from being the decent parent I was at home without preying eyes upon us. With my heightened state of emergency, the more Lena didn't listen then the outcomes would always be worse. I always felt like I was moments away from some kind of social disaster.

Out of nowhere, a man stepped away from the crowd and took control of the playground carnival that was keeping everyone entertained.

"Does she like bubbles?" he asked.

The man had a giant bubble kit in his hand that he must have brought to entertain the boy (who I assumed could have been his son) standing by his side. The guy was ruggedly dressed with shorts and a t-shirt that looked like they had seen better times, and a warm smile that I rarely saw of late. I was momentarily stunned by his words; it felt like it was the first time anyone at any time had ever asked me a question that wasn't an accusation about my child or my parenting skills.

"She does." I nodded.

With that, he was off, making his way to the climbing tunnel that Lena had barricaded herself underneath. He kept his distance from the makeshift burrow that she was using to protect herself from the dangers of the park, and quietly positioned himself onto his knees. Silently, he poured the mixture into a tray and dipped in a large bubble wand whilst delicately balancing each handle of a rope, proceeding to lift it magically into the air. The bubbles floated, almost still in the moment, hoping to capture the imagination of a child who desperately needed their help.

I took a deep sigh, relieved to have been given a chance to take in the oxygen that my body had been starved of in the latest showdown. Lena, slowly but surely, came out of the metal den, curiously, to marvel at the joyous wonders of beauty that were enticing her into their reach. After some time of revelling, she took her tiny finger out nervously and looked at him, waiting for affirmation that it was okay, before she took almighty enjoyment in popping a giant bubble. Her face lit up with the biggest crescent grin that was possibly ever seen on a child.

"More?" Lena asked the man inquisitively.

"Oh, you would like some more?" he asked gently, still not moving from the lowly position on his knees. She looked at him warmly, directly in his eyes as she was at the same level. And she nodded in agreement.

"How about you give me a hand to make the next one?" he offered.

"Yes, please." She flapped her arms hysterically in excitement. He helped her to dip the wand, delicately, into the mixture in order to spread the solution everywhere equally. They held onto the handles of the rope together, her small hands were a little shaky, and proceeded to lift the mixture into the sky and compress the air into a gigantic, shiny bubble.

"I did it! I did it!" Her arms were giddy now with joy as if those propellers were about to lift her off onto a limitless flight. She spun around, her eyes frantic, as she suddenly scanned the park, hunting for her mother again. I knew that she was unable to see me, so I pushed myself closer to her and nearer to the bubble action.

"There you are, Mummy. Did you see that? I did it all by myself!" She plunged the wand back into the mixture as she squealed: "Watch me! I'll do it again to show you!"

Lena focused her attention to produce another fine example of a giant bubble for all to marvel at. The guy smiled at me and seemed to enjoy watching her pure enjoyment just as much as I did.

"Thank you very much." I gestured towards Lena. "She absolutely loves bubbles."

"I can see." His generous smile beamed genuinely. "Who doesn't?"

Lena continued with dipping the wand back in and out to make the game of bubble blowing and popping last as long as she possibly could.

"I think we had better give it back now and say thank you for sharing it with us." I was conscious that we could be taking up the man's time.

"Just one more go?" Lena's voice had a hint of insistence to it. "Please?"

"Be my guest," the guy answered. "I brought them for Oscar here, but he said he's too old for bubbles, so it's very lucky that I bumped into you."

A boy was standing next to him, he had the looks of a rapidly growing teenager. Oscar had dyed black hair and it fell loosely over his face, covering one eye. He laughed and signalled a L for loser to which we all started laughing.

"The monkey swing is free. See yaaa!" The sound of his last word echoed as Oscar darted off at an excited speed.

"Please excuse my son – he's not so great at making conversation with new people." The man turned the conversation back to Lena as if she was the most important person in the world. "So, what's your name, young lady?"

"Am I allowed to tell him, Mummy? He's not a stranger anymore. Is he?" Lena asked me, looking up doe-eyed for reassurance as the tops of her shiny shoes tapped nervously in excitement.

"Yes, of course, darling, you can tell him your name." It was a strange situation when you found yourself more comfortable making conversation through your child, as it was too scary to make eye contact yourself.

"I'm Lena, but I prefer to be called *Chase!*" she declared then turned towards him to continue the conversation. "What's your name?"

"I'm Timothy and it's a pleasure to meet you!" He winked. "I actually spotted your scooter over there so I guessed you like *Paw Patrol*. Now this is a secret, I don't tell many people, but I like watching it too!"

It struck me that Timothy must have had us on his radar long before he was on ours. I started to flush red with nervousness.

"Which pup do you like the best?" Lena asked, comfortably talking about the subject that she loved the most.

"I like *Marshall*," Timothy answered.

"*Marshall* is the bravest pup. He's a firefighter," Lena said in a voice of seniority.

"I work for the fire service too!" Timothy replied. "Now you know why I like being Marshall, what a clever pup you are!"

I was in shock, nobody else had ever engaged in Lena's fantasy talk before, apart from me.

"You get to fight fires!" Lena looked up in admiration. "When the pups get into adventures, we sometimes pretend there's a fire and we have to put it out to save the day." She was offering more about herself than I had ever seen her do before. "Do you want to come on the slide with me?" Lena asked as if she was making her first friendship and her life depended on it. "It can be our lookout tower."

In direct contrast to how she had struggled to interact with children her own age, she was displaying a more obvious comfort in being able to communicate with an understanding adult.

"Sure." He smiled. "Can I leave this bubble kit with you...?" Timothy paused for a moment to choose the right word. "Oh, I'm sorry, how very rude of me. I never asked your name too. Too busy talking *Paw Patrol* to remember my manners!"

Timothy smiled at Lena and she mirrored another one of her infectious smiles.

"Of course. Yes, I mean," I was blundering without using Lena to talk through as my crutch. "Sorry, yes, I'm Sarah. Nice to meet you."

Timothy held his hand out to shake mine. The moment my skin touched his I felt like it was electrocuting me with shock.

"Lovely to meet you too." I felt his eyes linger on me for an extra second and I felt awakened through the nerves.

Heat rose in my body at the social exchange that I hadn't had for over fifteen years. In fact, I had gone beyond feeling like a lonely sunflower, I was more like a slinking, creeping area of ragwort. My pulse was just as alarmed as the butterflies that were doing circles in my stomach.

"Okay, Lena. Just one go and then we had better let the man, I mean Timothy, go. I have to, I have to... urm... get back to feed Charlie soon." It was always at moments like this that I got verbal diarrhoea and felt the need to over-talk.

"He's not crying yet, Mum," Lena innocently began, "you only go to him when he cries."

Oh shit. Not only was I looking like a social buffoon, I now was also looking like an unfit mother (as if the slide fiasco earlier hadn't done that already). I remained speechless, trying to rescue myself from the hole I'd dug. I didn't know why this stranger was having such a magnetic effect on me. Maybe it was because it was the first time in a long while that I actually felt seen. Not as Lena's mum, or wife, or cleaner, or cook. But as an adult in her own right, as a woman.

Lena took her trusting hand and put it into the masculine palm of her chosen subject and led him to her favourite piece of play equipment. I could see the two of them chatting away and Lena's arms and body jolting excitely. It was incredible to watch because Lena normally didn't take too well to strangers. More often than not adults talked over her head to me, and Lena usually intercepted their conversation to ensure they knew she was there. She lacked the usual understanding most kids naturally had of knowing when it was okay to interrupt.

I suddenly had a flashback from a few months earlier when an elderly lady poked her broken fingernail over Charlie's pram and under his chin as she cajoled me, "Oh isn't he adorable!"

"You should know better at *your age* to ask before you touch," Lena had scolded. The woman's finger recoiled as quickly as it had poked itself out, and with a huff, she retreated.

"I'd have had my mouth washed out with soap and water if I talked like that!" the elderly lady snarled.

"Did they have soap in the olden times?" Lena asked. "Or had they only invented water?"

The lady rammed her four-wheeled, rustic shopping trolley over the cracks of the pavement with as much speed as her tired legs could carry her. If I could say anything about Lena, she had a natural flair for dispersing people.

"Let's kick the tyres and fight some fires!" Lena called out from the top of the equipment. I was brought back to reality in the park.

I rested a while, looking after the bubble mixture, whilst Lena and Timothy took turns looking out of an imaginary telescope. My heart started to race further with realisation that when Lena was having this much enjoyment, it was like flogging a dead horse to try and get her to come away. I was starting to worry how it would pan-out and whether another showdown would happen. This was the biggest paradox about Lena; it was the hardest mission to get her to go somewhere but it was equally uncompromising to get her to leave the activity once she had started it.

"We had better go soon!" I called up to Lena on the tower.

After some time Timothy and Lena glided down the orange chute roaring with laughter (also without the adult getting rammed halfway down). I made a mental note to start my diet again tomorrow.

"Can we have a playdate with Marshall soon?" Lena balled over to ask.

"I'm not sure," I stumbled. I desperately needed to deflect the conversation as I was feeling awkward. "We do have to go home now."

"Nooo!" Lena screamed as she threw her head up into the air allowing her tonsils to see daylight.

At that moment Oscar came running back from the monkey swing and play-punched Timothy's arm.

"Dad!" Oscar demanded. "Can we go now? My friends are already gaming online and they're waiting for me. I'm missing out!"

"I have to go now too," Timothy stated as he smiled and nodded his head towards his son. "But we come to this park all the time. How about next time we see each other we get to carry on the game again?"

Lena had stopped screaming to hear if his offer was satisfactory enough but she wasn't committing an answer any further. She also took a moment to look Oscar up and down and I wondered what she made of him.

"Why do you have so many chains on your clothes?" Lena asked Oscar. "Have you been to prison like the meanies?"

"I will be going to prison soon if my dad doesn't stop chatting!"

Oscar joked. "Dad! I'm going ahead without you, my friends are already in a rich server without me."

He ran out of the park alone and made his way down the pathway without turning around.

"Teenagers for you!" Timothy rolled his eyes and we all laughed (even Lena, although I'm not quite sure she understood the context of the joke).

"How about we leave the park at the same time? That way no pup gets left behind." Timothy was very proficient at making his voice sound inviting. Was it his job as a firefighter which made him so driven to help people or was it something else? Either way, he seemed better at this stuff than anyone else I'd ever met. He just seemed to 'get it'.

Still no answer. Lena was literally frozen to the spot.

"Shall we have a superhero race out of the park? We could see if *Chase* is faster than *Marshall*?" Timothy was inventive with using different tactics and I was taking this all in. He did it with such ease that I felt like I was learning at the same time.

"Okayyy!" Lena squealed excitedly. "*Chase* is always the fastest!"

Timothy had to gather his belongings before he could even manage to catch up from her.

"Ahh, I'm losing!" I could hear Timothy exclaim.

Lena's giggles were dispersing into the air just like the bubbles that Timothy had used to calm her earlier. Eventually we all caught up with Lena. I was balancing her scooter on top of the buggy.

"Okay, you win, fair and square." Timothy exaggerated wiping sweat off his brow.

"I don't like squares. I like circles." Lena was so literal in her response, I didn't think she'd understood his idiom; her innocence was something I cherished about her.

"Okay, you win, fair and *circle*. A big, orange circle. Here is an invisible one you can wear with pride!" Timothy leant down to her level and pretended to put the imaginary prize into the palm of her hand. She beamed her wonky smile that she did when she was bursting full of happiness.

"Thank you." I expressed gratitude towards someone who had shown us such kindness and humanity – it felt that we had been lifted to a place of pure belonging.

"Well, it was lovely to meet you, Sarah, *and* it was even more lovely to meet you, *Chase*. I'll be keeping my *Marshall* eyes wide open every time I come to the park so we can carry on the adventure. Can you give me a paw-five?"

Timothy punched a final high-five with Lena, and she was left in an unusually calm place. I wasn't used to Lena leaving an activity and still having a smile on her face. She yanked the scooter from the top of the buggy, narrowly missing Charlie's face in her fumbling excitement, and scooted off down the hill.

"Talking is boring!!" she sang as her voice jutted to the sound of the rocky pavement descending.

That left me, nervously, to make a farewell exchange. It was that awkward feeling you have when you meet someone randomly and wonder if they want to ever see you again.

"Sorry about that. She's not very patient when it comes to talking," I explained.

"No need to apologise," he replied softly. "My guess is that she probably is intolerant of saying goodbye. Who wants to ever say goodbye? It's far too final!" He laughed which I thought was rooted in nerves as I could see his leg tapping.

"That's exactly what she is like!" I replied. "It's not often someone else understands her. Most people think she seems rude."

"Oh, she's not rude, quite the contrary," Timothy reassured with that velvet tone that was even more calming than the gallons of wine I was drinking of late. "She's being herself and nobody should ever try to change that." He looked to the ground, almost lamenting if there was more but he couldn't share.

"I wish her school had the same feeling as you." I glanced over at Lena freely scooting around the path and picking wildflowers along the way. She just needed a red hood to protect her from the danger of being misunderstood by the rest of the world.

"She's not made to go down a blue slide; her path needs to curve more. If they try to make her go in a straight line, then she can't ever begin to be herself."

His words shook me and it was a simple analogy that I knew in my heart was the root of the problem.

"Maybe blue slides have too many rules!" I laughed at the absurdity of the conversation, but despite us talking about inanimate objects, this chat was making more sense than anything else in my chaotic life. It was strange because Lena liked making her own rules but could not cope with abiding by other rules that didn't make sense to her.

"Now that I agree with!" Timothy joined in chuckling.

"Mummyyyy! Hurry up! You're taking toooo long!" Her screams halted our giggling and I knew that I needed to make a move before my ticking bomb went off.

"Looks like I've been summoned! Hah! Well, it really was lovely to meet you. Thanks again, I don't think you will ever realise how much that has meant to us today."

I waved as I quickly rushed towards Lena in anticipation that another meltdown could happen.

"No problem at all, it was my pleasure," Timothy said warmly.

I couldn't turn around in case he saw my flushed face, but my step certainly felt a little lighter. I had that eerie sense that his eyes were still resting upon us as we departed, but I was too scared to take a second look back. My thoughts were soon interjected by Lena's ramblings on how much she had enjoyed having someone to play with at the park.

"Mummy, do you think Daddy can bring me here on Sunday?" Lena stopped on her scooter as she looked up at me to ask the question. "I wonder if he might like to play *Paw Patrol* with me like

Marshall did!"

I had prepared Lena about her special father-daughter bonding time, when they would get to do something alone, and she had been talking non-stop about it ever since. Strangely, Nick hadn't really talked to her much about it, nor had he given an indication of a plan for what they would be doing ahead of time.

I could taste her excitement – maybe this would be the moment we had been waiting for? Perhaps meeting a stranger would help to put things right between us all. I convinced myself that things happened for a reason and that at last a solution could be found out of this mess. What if Timothy had shown us a way to find a link that could work for Nick too? I wanted desperately to tell Nick all about it, but something blocked my ability to proceed. How would he feel about the fact that I had spoken to another man in the park?

I remembered his jealous streak and decided to keep it quiet as if it hadn't happened at all. Everything was always so complicated and I had to double-think every part of my life in fear of the ramifications. If only Nick could have seen how another adult interacted with Lena calmly and with understanding, maybe he could believe what I had been saying all along.

8

Yes the Superhero

C harlie started howling for his milk on the way home. It was almost as if he had an in-built alarm that would go off as soon as we were about to reach the vicinity of home. I let us in through the back gate to the garden, it was always the access path I used, whilst Nick preferred to enter the house from the front door. I wasn't able to consult a relationship doctor, but that simple difference had to mean we were living on completely different planets. They say men are from Mars and women are from Venus, well on days when Nick had upset me, I liked to think he was actually from Uranus.

I opened the changing bag and threw a ready-made milk carton into an empty bottle, and Charlie began sucking on it like he'd never seen food. It only dawned on me after he was fully pulling on the teat, and as I tried to regain control of the bottle, that I had forgotten to put his bib on before his feed. The regurgitated milk dripped back down his chin and made a messy puddle on his t-shirt. He wasn't giving up the teat as much as I wouldn't be prepared to pass over a glass of my cherished wine. *That's my boy,* I thought, amused. He continued to try and suck on thin air as we embarked on full-on warfare with me trying to get the empty bottle from his jaws. I tried to tickle his toes as a last resort, and although it did the trick, it made the space for a gigantic belch that shook the calm blades of grass.

I located a sensory baby blanket and laid it in the shade so Charlie could wriggle on his tummy. He was pulling faces in the shiny reflective material and cooing to sound like he was making a theme tune to his own TV show. With my baby occupied for a moment, I left Lena to entertain herself on the garden swing, whilst my mind drifted away with the fairies. I couldn't stop reliving the experience earlier at the park, over-analysing what I had said to Timothy, or the error I had made trying to force Lena to do something that she didn't need to do. My guilt was berating my conscience.

I couldn't help but notice a procession of ants crossing my patio. It astonished me that they were not deviating from their set path. They just knew what they should be doing without a leader interfering. It wasn't as if they were telling each other where the scraps of food were or where they needed to be stored. We could learn a lot from ants. In fact, we could learn a great deal from the entire eco-system.

My random daydreaming was moving intermittently from subject to subject without any linear pattern. I often tended to space out when my thoughts were becoming overwhelming. It was easier to retreat into a fantasy world than face the reality of day-to-day living. I was soon jolted back to reality as Lena had managed to climb on top of the recycling bin and was dangling half off to pull herself up on the fence.

"Come down, sweetie," I pleaded, realising that I needed to put myself into the present and leave my worries at the back of my mind to deal with at another time.

"How many days until Sunday?" Lena quizzed, looking diagonally up to the sky.

"One more sleep," I confirmed. I was already trying to think ahead to my next planned move if she refused to climb down.

"Can we go upstairs and play the part where the pups go with Lena and Daddy to the park and fight an emergency?" she asked in anticipation.

"Of course we can, sweetie." I held my hands up towards the top of the bin and she jumped into my arms, nearly knocking me onto my bum on the grassy lawn.

We traipsed back inside and I propped Charlie up to join in with the action. I thought about the fact that Lena was getting impatient about the first session with her dad and hoped that it would give them both the opportunity to enjoy spending time with one another.

My phone rang and interrupted our playing. It was my sister Julie and I could feel myself panic. We still hadn't got over the time when Lena stuffed the christening cake into her mouth and I knew Julie was perturbed because I hadn't sent my apologies about it either. Julie was trying to repair the silence between us, which made me feel happier about the whole thing, however in that moment I just didn't feel able to talk about our issues.

"I was wondering if you wanted to come to a baby group with me soon?" Julie offered. "There is a Singing Hands group that I've heard about. Perhaps Charlie would like to try a first session with Andrew?"

"Hmm," I mused. "I would need to get Lena covered and that's difficult as it's the summer holidays." It felt like Julie was only offering to meet up with the babies without Lena. It wasn't exactly an activity that included her. Was she trying to repair our relationship and was I just being overly-sensitive? Or did Julie prefer to cut Lena out of the equation?

"You could always ask Mum to have her for you?" Julie suggested.

"I'll look into it," I replied. "Look, I better go. I'll call you back when things are a bit quieter, okay?"

"Sure," Julie responded, although I could hear the disappointment in her voice. I really wanted to get back on-track but I found it so hard when I knew that she wasn't willing to budge her opinions on Lena. It often felt like my whole life was conflicted. I felt too hurt that my daughter was not liked to be able to find a way to be normal with my sister again.

By evening, I had managed to do a reasonably successful bedtime despite the thuds and the delaying tactics from Lena. Nick remained absent, watching a box set on TV. My resentment was stewing even further.

"You know it's your bonding time with Lena tomorrow, don't you?" I reminded him, trying to get his attention away from the TV.

"I'm trying to watch this," Nick replied without even taking his eyes off the screen.

"Well I was thinking of joining a running club." I carried on talking to the oblivion. "So I might do some digging online tomorrow to see if I can find a local one for beginners."

"You? Running!" Nick laughed loudly. He had suddenly tuned into what I was saying because he had an opinion about it. "You wouldn't even make it to the next lamppost without falling to the ground. I don't think they take that type of beginner!"

I stormed back out of the room as Nick's eyes returned to their glued position watching the screen again.

With Nick's ill-timed joke and his inability to plan the one time he was supposed to spend with Lena the next day, I needed to plough myself into an activity to distract my feeling of frustration. I thought about the form that had been wedged behind the breadboard earlier and went to retrieve it. With an enlightened burst of energy, I went through each of the questions with tenacity and zeal. I was determined to pour my frustration into something that could change what people thought of Lena. I had to double question myself at every answer. Had I got them right? Were they a true reflection of Lena's challenges? Knowing that I might lose my drive to post the form the next day, I sealed the envelope up so that I was powerless to go back and cross-examine my answers. The continual amount of confidence-stripping from my family and the school were hindering my ability to have faith in myself anymore.

It still took a few days to send it. There were many times when I looked at the envelope and felt paralysed. What if it had information that wasn't correct? I started to feel like an imposter in my own decision-making. I delayed sending the completed form (despite it having a first-class stamp already glued on the front). I was stuck in limbo, knowing the form had taken a lot of energy to complete, but the fear of the unknown by sending it off was disarming me. What would come of it? Was it just better not knowing and living in ignorance?

Sunday arrived and it was supposed to be Nick and Lena's fun time together, but Nick didn't seem to show that he was getting ready for it. I decided to give him a nudge.

"Have you decided where you're going with Lena this morning?" I softly opened up the conversation.

"Oh shit," Nick muttered, "I forgot it was today. I've made plans to play golf with my friends. I'll do it next week instead. It will have to wait."

That was it! How could he let her down like that and be so selfish? And how could he just *forget*? Lena and I had reminded him all week, there was no way he could have just forgotten.

"Nooo!" Lena screamed from just outside the door. She must have been listening.

I went to retrieve Lena who was wrapped underneath her blanket and snuggled up with Chicken Pox. Lena stroked and twisted the tattered label of her plush toy which managed to bring the comfort that she required. Although it was an inanimate object, to Lena it was very real. Chicken Pox was also a girl and I was corrected if I ever made the mistake of calling her by the wrong pronoun. I once called her 'it' but paid the price by having the house turned upside-down in a Lena tsunami kind of way. Needless to say, I learnt from my mistake.

It was a shame that Nick didn't have the ability to reflect on his mistakes or decision-making processes. If he had taken the time to see his daughter shutdown under her blanket because of his actions, maybe he could have reconsidered. Instead, he shouted out his goodbyes as the front door slammed shut with an abandoned bang. How could he just walk out of the door when she was in the middle of a humungous meltdown? Either he didn't realise what carnage he'd caused or he didn't care enough to stay and help resolve it.

The ripple of the sound waves must have broken Lena's sanctuary as she bolted to the front door. She was screaming the word 'no' at the top of her lungs and her body became feral as she scratched and slammed at the door. I scooped her up in my arms and felt the raining down of her small limbs. I could feel her pain as if it were my own – I had always been in sync with other people and had a deep empathy radar that ensured I experienced the emotions of others as if I were having them first-hand. It was a blessing and a curse. At best, I could understand and show compassion to others by my superhero sense of feeling so strongly. At worst, I couldn't shake the feeling or the memory of something that somebody else was going through, to the point I would often take their problem on as if it were one of my own.

It was the latter experience right now as my heart was weeping for my beautiful infant – who was crumpled up in an emotional mess due to the ignorance of her father. My sadness thermometer was soon changing into the lava of anger. Why was he not able to see the ramifications of his actions? He was supposed to be a grown man – an adult!

"How about we go to the zoo?" I offered, trying to distract her from the anguish of her disappointment.

"NO!" Lena shouted back.

"Maybe Rex would like it if we took him for a walk by the canal?" I attempted again.

"NO!" The intensity of her reply was growing. I started to panic, how was I going to turn this situation around?

I decided to take a step back and just let her be; to process how she was feeling. And then her words completely bawled me over.

"Mummy, I want to do things but I can't," she cried.

"What do you mean 'you can't'?" I questioned, confused. "If it's because Daddy isn't here then you know Mummy can take you instead?"

"No! This happens to me all the time. I can't put my shoes on!" Lena stood still and looked towards the floor as she held Blanket in one hand and Chicken Pox in the other.

"Oh, darling," I reassured, "would you like Mummy to help?"

"My brain always tells me NO even when I want it to say YES," Lena explained. "YES *never* wins the superhero battle."

I looked at her, stunned. Surely a child of five couldn't think up something so abstract like this all by themselves?

"I want to put my shoes on but I can't," she continued.

"Has somebody told you about that? Maybe at school or something?" I enquired, pushing for an answer to ease my uncertainty in unchartered waters.

"No!" she shouted infuriated. "They can't see what I am thinking. I think these things all by myself."

I was at risk of losing this conversation even though she had given me an invitation into her thoughts. I needed to keep it open. I thought on my feet and tried the option of empowering her to a higher position to see if that would salvage her ability to keep talking.

"I wish I could think those things all by myself." I looked on glumly. "I don't think my brain is as clever as yours!"

If ever there were an award for bad acting, I deserved it right there. It didn't matter though, my plan did the trick.

"Well, I could show you, if you like?" Lena offered sweetly, almost forgetting the see-sawing emotions she had gone through leading up to this point.

"Oh, yes please!" I said eagerly. "Now, if only I knew what it was like to have a superhero in my brain trying to say yes..."

"Wait!" she squealed with excitement. "I could draw it for you?" The intonation at the end of the question came with a taste of apprehension.

"That's so kind of you, thank you, darling," I reassured her instantly with my maternal bandage. I bent down and kissed her cheek and she held out Chicken Pox and Blanket for me to embrace with the same equal sentiment. I hugged Poxy and gave her a big slobbery kiss and then moved onto Blanket to keep with the fairness that she was indicating of me.

"Poxy told me you have to kiss without getting her wet next time," Lena informed matter-of-factly.

"Oh sorry, Poxy, I am silly." I pretended to shake her paw as an attempt at an apology. If anyone were a fly on the wall... well I think they would have had me locked away. I would never have predicted in my life that I would be apologising to a soft rabbit who had been given a name like Chicken Pox.

"Poxy said that it's alright, but you have to try better next time."

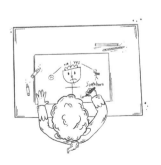

Lena rushed around the room as she had scattered all the cushions and was bouncing from one side to another. Her boundless energy never ceased to amaze me. She bounced from the last cushion onto the chair – which was placed under the dining room table – as she spread all of her stationery across the top and scribbled away.

Eventually she held up her drawing and exhaled with glee. "Quick, Mummy, look!"

I was speechless, I had to remind myself to give Lena some praise, because I was completely transfixed by the complexity of her drawing. The infantile strokes of a wobbly pencil (of a typical stick person) was juxtaposed by the incongruous detailed concept of the mind. I continued to study it in awe. Lena had drawn a big circle for the head with two dots for the eyes, a slither for the nose and a curve down for an unhappy smile. Above the facial features was a line splitting the head in two. On one side of the head was scribbled the word 'no' and the other compartment held the word 'yes'.

Then there was a line pointing out of the yes part of the brain with another stick person and a triangle attached (which she pointed out was a red cape). The poignancy of the word 'Soopa heero' made my throat tense up. On the opposite side, sprouting out from the no, was a small, unhappy face.

Lena described the picture at length to me and then wrote her name on the top of the page.

"I can be your teacher, if you like?" She passed the drawing to me and I tucked it away into a safe space until I could send it over to the school to see what they thought about it. Surely they wouldn't palm me off when they saw this?

"I would love that, darling." I planted a kiss on her hair, knowing that the earlier situation had been not only diffused, but had led to a connected piece of learning between us.

I had barely spent any time with Nick over the weekend and yet we had been home for most of it. I sighed deeply – the gap between us was widening and I didn't know how to put it right. Was it even reparable?

I'd read articles in magazines and watched scenes in films when families were separated and the other parent promised to turn up but they never did. It was the sort of thing that I expected to only happen in broken families – to the abstract family units that I assumed were all dysfunctional. Not to mine. I never would have imagined that the person I chose to go on the journey of parenting with, who joined me in unison to make the most precious gifts in the world, would be so neglectful and absent.

It was driving a bigger wedge between us than any other marital argument we could have ever possibly had. We would argue about who unloaded the dishwasher, or who did more than the other partner, and even dispute that only one of us cleaned the bath after using it. But when we were talking about innocent children feeling disappointment and sadness through no fault of their own, well there was no way we could carry on as if nothing had happened. It would only make the emotionally-charged parent need one small spark to ignite and explode with their bottled-up rage.

I spent the remainder of the day locked into my own thoughts. How could it be that a complete stranger in a park could have understood my daughter better than anyone else I had met? Why couldn't Nick change his approach and be with me on this, instead of against me? It was with a heavy heart that I realised a decision needed to be made because we couldn't carry on like this anymore. If I was honest with myself, I had given him enough chances to get on board and improve the situation.

This was now beyond my control.

When Nick returned home that evening, I couldn't mask it any longer. I was so furious that he had let Lena down and hadn't even considered the consequences. He went straight into the living room as if nothing had happened in the day and swung Charlie up into the air.

"Hello, tiger," Nick said energetically as he kissed Charlie's cheek.

"He's just been fed," my words cut through.

"I'm just saying hello to him." He shrugged noncommittally, placing Charlie into his seat.

"Dinner will be ready soon," my words were loaded with venom, "you might need to focus on talking to Lena. She was very upset about her routine change."

I wondered if he actually felt a wave of guilt, because it wasn't often he followed the instructions or advice I gave. I could hear him calling her name up the stairs.

"Go away, meanie!" Lena replied curtly.

"I'm sorry, Spitfire," it was the nickname he had called her since she was a toddler – aptly given on account of her fiery temperament, "I'll make sure we do our Sunday time next week." I listened intently but she wasn't buying his poor attempt at an apology. There simply wasn't an excuse for being selfish and kids saw through bullshit every time.

"Fine," he retorted immaturely, "next week I'll go on my own if you don't want to come!"

Lena suddenly appeared, Blanket positioned over her brow with a tiny opening held by her hands so she could still spy out. Through the gap, Chicken Pox was keeping the coast clear. No matter what happened, children could always bounce back when they were threatened with losing something. I wanted to shout to her not to engage with him, he was only playing with her emotions, but who would have seemed the childish one then? He pulled her past the blanket and began tickling her and throwing her up in the air like our living room was a gravity-free playground. The excitement and adrenaline worked; she was giggling and back to her warm self. Nick smirked as if to say that was how you did it.

Of course, it didn't last long, he soon lost interest and Lena went to find another game alone with her *Paw Patrol* figures.

I held myself through dinner and managed to get the children down to bed like I always did. I felt on high-alert as I knew what I was going to do and there was no going back. I joined Nick in the living room, opting to sit on a different sofa.

"We need a break," I blurted.

"A break?" Nick's eyes looked at me in confusion. "What are you talking about, Sarah?"

"I can't do this anymore," I braved, my stomach churning.

"Don't be silly." Nick came over and tried to offer his arm around me, I brushed it off. He had no idea that my defensive walls were up and I was long past wanting his support.

"All couples go through their ups and downs. That's just normal marriage!" Nick barked at the uncertainty of where this conversation was heading.

"You let her down today and you didn't even care," I explained.

"I know and I'm sorry. I'll make it up to her next week." Nick added, "Stop making it a big deal!"

My rage was mounting now. I had put up with the transfer of blame for far too long. There was no stopping me.

"You don't try to understand Lena," I stated. "I can't see that you're even willing to change."

"Oh, so now it's *my* fault?" Nick's voice was enraged. "Because you won't use discipline, it's my fault?"

"She needs support and understanding," I retaliated, "not bloody discipline."

"So *you* want to break our family unit up just because I tell her off here or there and I didn't spend one day at the park with her?" Nick shouted. "You're just being over-sensitive! No doubt you've been drinking again?"

I could sense my anger rising as he was trying to gaslight me as the problem. I wondered if this was always his escape route – turning it onto me? Maybe this was why I had never been able to use my voice. I had been beaten down for so long I no longer knew how or why I had become so subservient.

"Perhaps I have been drinking too much," I screamed. "But maybe it's been an escape route from a neglected marriage!"

It was the final straw that he didn't want to hear. Nick bombed upstairs and threw some items into a bag before taking one last menacing look towards me. He spat out the words: "You won't be anything without me! You'll be begging me to give it another go, and don't think you'll have a second chance. Do you hear me?"

His last words assaulted me as he slammed the front door on his way out. I didn't have time to think about how far I had pushed him or whether I had made the right choice. Without hesitation, I picked up the phone and called my two best friends.

"I've done it," I wept, "my marriage has ended!"

"Oh, Sarah," they consoled, "we will help you get through this. We promise."

"Listen," Shelley said softly, "I'll jump in the car now and come and stay with you for a few days whilst you get back on your feet."

"Thank you," I replied.

The tears streamed as my friends scooped me up, over the phone, into their arms to give me that support I desperately required.

Within minutes, as promised, Shelley was waiting at my door.

"You've got this," she reassured as she gave me a watery embrace. "You were doing this alone anyway, Sarah. It won't be that much different. In fact, it might be easier. Like we always say, we've got you too."

I couldn't answer as I continued to sob deep-rooted tears of grief.

"Anyway, how about tomorrow, when I finish work, we go out for dinner?" Shelley offered. "Lena can have one of her favourite ice cream sundaes with all the sprinkles!"

I laughed through the tears. I had to give it to her, she knew what we needed in the face of adversity – who could say no to ice cream?

"I need to get my pyjamas on," I sighed. "I feel exhausted and can't think. Sorry, Shel. I don't think I'll be good company tonight."

"Don't be silly, sweetie," Shelley said warmly. "I don't need entertaining. I'm here if, or when, you need me, you got that?"

"I owe you," I confessed.

"You'd do the same for Vic or me." Shelley hugged me and I disappeared upstairs to get changed.

Once I reached the bathroom, I slumped onto the toilet with my faded underwear hanging sadly by my feet. I held my head in my hands and sobbed the deepest cries that my body could cater for. I lost time in that position, my tears carrying all of the toxicity from the last few months. If there had been a drought, then no doubt my mourning would have come to its aid. With my eyes blotchy red and the veins protruding, through my limp, dangling hair, I could see the reflection of a woman who had been lost. I realised that I'd needed to hit that point before I could make any changes. I had to be rendered blind before I could have the capacity to see again. I needed this moment, I told myself, so that I could find a way to live again.

Memories flooded my brain from the first time Nick and I had met. The moment he bought my favourite perfume for our second date, without asking what it was, but turning up with it gift-wrapped had bowled me over instantly. He had been so thoughtful and attentive. He had made me feel special. I used to feel so proud to be with him. When we stepped out he towered above me and held my hand delicately in his as if he wanted to protect me from the rest of the world. I was so young and giddy with the overpowering rush I'd felt being around him. There was a magnetic force between us and we were inseparable. My body used to ache with longing when we had to wait a few days to see each other again. It was addictive, he was a drug to me. He gave me the feeling that I was somebody, I felt needed, important, wanted. I felt like he was the most beautiful being I had ever laid my eyes on. I was the luckiest person because he had chosen me.

How had our relationship ended up like this? The tears came back for a repeated round as if they were trying to torment me further. It wasn't just about Nick's inability to understand Lena, it was as much about his neglect to treat me as an equal partner.

I started to reflect and turn it onto myself. I mean, I didn't even love myself anymore, how could I expect him to? If I was honest with myself, since having the kids, it had been a slow decline into the depths of despair without any time to put myself first.

Time was always a struggle so it seemed there was very little point in making myself look pretty with makeup, or to dress in swag clothes, or dig out the perfume in order for my scent to be noticed. I felt bedraggled and had lost any purpose in myself and the things that made me happy. I no longer shone. My fun-searching smile had vanished.

I couldn't contemplate what the future might look like or how I would cope with the children all on my own. Nor could I dwell on what it would mean to be a single-parent family and survive financially.

I could only take one step at a time, and in that moment, I hoped that I would be able to move forwards.

Would I be able to find a way to start all over again, or had I just made the biggest mistake of my life?

9

Black Rainbow

The month of August was rolling by, and the realisation that school was approaching fast, brought some uncertainty. Hard work as it was being at home all day with two small children (without any other adult to break up the time), it was nowhere near as difficult as what I had been living up until this point in time. Nothing could be as bad as having to communicate daily with a wall of educational staff who saw me as the problem. Nor could it be as lonely and demoralising as living with a partner who was not on the same page as me. I had shut down everything – ignoring calls from pretty much everyone with the main intention of just surviving and focusing on Lena, Charlie and myself.

It was funny, all of my procrastination with getting the ball rolling for Lena's school issues had suddenly disappeared after having a breakdown. I was now able to blast through it with re-newed force. I had managed to send the social communication questionnaire in the post and I'd made a diary of what was hap-pening at home and how difficult daily routines were for Lena to manage. Then I charted all of Lena's history and the areas where I thought she found things tough. I was finding a blurry escape through the fog, and although the direction felt faint, I was starting to clear a path that was at least becoming visible. Creating the paperwork and setting myself targets to focus on seemed to be working, and it was lightening the heaviness of my emotional burden.

It felt like no time had passed and it was suddenly the first week back to school. I had to find a way to help Lena manage her own strategies to cope so that the return to school could be easier.

"You can choose the order of the morning routine for tomorrow," I began gently, "if you prefer to eat breakfast before getting dressed then we can do it that way?"

"I'm scared, Mummy." Lena's eyes were wide. "What if I don't like it?"

"I'm sure the teachers will try to help you." I wanted to believe myself, but I wasn't sure that my statement was true. I tried to pull it together – I couldn't show any doubt or it would add to her anxiety about going.

There was silence from Lena as she processed her thoughts.

"Can you think of anything that could help you in the day?" I invited her to be part of the process.

"Maybe *Yes the Superhero* could help me tomorrow?" Lena said apprehensively.

"That's a great idea," I comforted as I tucked her into bed.

Yet, by the morning her superhero disguise seemed to slip away into the depths of anxiety and fear. I'd even sent Lena's picture to school hoping it would create a bridge between home and school, but I hadn't received any communication back. It seemed like they weren't really interested in looking at why she found school hard, and my gut feeling was that they viewed her as a burden. Why did they not see that if they followed my lead, then we could help her together? Lena's dread of all the changes she would have to get used to was overshadowing her ability to put her school uniform on.

"I don't want to be in a new classroom!" Lena cried as she hid in the wardrobe with Chicken Pox and Blanket.

"I understand, sweetie, facing any change is hard. But what if your new classroom has more interesting things in it?"

"It doesn't!" she screamed. "It's scary."

"I can talk to the new teacher to explain how you feel," I reassured.

"I don't like the new teacher," Lena answered. "I only want Miss Orchard."

"Miss Orchard will still be there. You'll be able to see her at school."

"I'm not going!" Lena yelled as she flung the door open and caught me in the tummy with an angry blow. She was unaware of her own strength when she hit a state of red mist. It was an emotion she accelerated into at speed, but only after the hurdles of being scared, sad or frightened had been jumped over first. She fell into a heap on my lap, sucking her thumb whilst stroking Chicken Pox's ears. I knew there was no point forcing her any more.

I was surprised the next morning, when by pure fate, I managed to get Lena into school for the first time since the term had begun. I wasn't sure what had changed in her mind, but she exceeded my expectations by coming downstairs ready and dressed in her uniform. I was that shocked I almost looked past her to see if she was real or not. I mean, how could she just do it all of a sudden? Was I imagining the struggles that I thought she had? Surely she couldn't just be miraculously dressed and ready to start the day like nothing had ever been a problem?

My over-analytical assessment of the situation was soon brought back to reality by the time I retrieved Lena at the end of the school day. It was like I was smacked in the face with the realisation that the struggles were glaringly there.

"I quit school!" Lena declared as she ransacked the living room, frenziedly throwing every item she could lay her hands on. "You were wrong, Mummy – the new teacher isn't nice!"

Lena's Year One teacher was the longest serving staff member at Sunnybank and was known for her strict, authoritarian approach. I often heard from other parents that she was great at getting results and the children all behaved better for her as a result. The other parents always felt that it was more beneficial to have a strict teacher so that their children could reach the potential that they expected of them. I felt so differently to the mass of parents – my single wish for Lena was just that she would be a happy little girl. I had let go of any expectations that she should be reaching specified academic levels or age-related milestones. Learning to be able to exist around others, and to be a likeable person, seemed fairly healthy outcomes to me.

"What happened?" I asked, concerned, but there was no answer from Lena – she had gone to find some calm time in her safe-place, deep inside her wardrobe.

After Lena anxiously avoiding school on Monday, to Tuesday's challenges when she finally did make it into school, we were back to square one with repeated days at home and an inability to leave the house. It was a continuous battle. If only the school were on the same page and could make this transition easier? For the next two weeks her attendance continued to plummet even further. It was clear the implementation of the reduced timetable (from reception year that was still in place) was not having the success the headteacher had suggested.

As her mum, I knew that small changes would be too much for Lena to adapt to, especially right after going through the change of her parents splitting up. Although, it was a bit surreal because she was coping with the breakup as if nothing had happened. It started to make me wonder how little input her father was really contributing if her reaction was so nonplussed? Or maybe she was just holding herself together? I couldn't tell. Contrary to the belief of school (when they found out that our marriage had broken down they assumed the conflict must have been causing the difficulties in Lena), the actual main challenge was how Lena felt about being at school. How was I going to get them to understand it?

Even my mum had said the same thing in her last phone call with me. I could still hear her words ringing out when I told her that Nick and I had separated:

"Marriage is supposed to be a lifelong commitment. You can't just give up when you hit a rough patch."

"We have tried to work through it for so long, Mum," I explained. "Nick just won't change and it's lonelier being with someone when you are disconnected than it is if you were physically by yourself."

"Listen, love," Mum said softly, like she knew everything there was to know about relationships. "Lena's behaviour is probably the way it is because you were fighting for so long. If you fix things in your marriage then she will be right as rain again! You need to stick together over this and not let the problem split you up."

I sighed. She just didn't understand that I had tried all of those things and actually, if anything, Lena was better with me when Nick was not around. We sailed the ship smoother. There was nobody coming in to undo my parenting strategies that were creative and relied on thinking outside the box. I also felt like a weight had finally been lifted off my shoulders. Nick had nit-picked every single aspect of my life for so long that I was no longer able to think freely. There were so many things I could have told my mother, but the only way I could manage was to opt for silence.

My phone beeped and interrupted my thoughts. It was a text message from the man in question.

Nick

Am I still having the kids today?!?? It would be nice if you could liaise with me once in a while, I don't bite!

Did he really need to start an argument? It wasn't like I was stopping him from seeing the kids or anything. In true Nick fashion he was trying to make a mountain out of a molehill. I took a deep breath and tried to remain calm, I wasn't going to be taking his bait. I could see he was still angry with me for calling our relationship a day.

> Yes, the kids are all yours. They should be dropped off about 4pm.

Nick was bunking at his mate Alan's flat and would be looking for a more permanent solution soon. I hadn't physically seen him because my mum had been liaising between us and ferrying the kids over to him for their own time. It was desperate times when I had to rely on my own mother for support, but I felt trapped like there wasn't any other option. It was that or face Nick in person and everything was still feeling too raw for that. It was just something I had to do so that the children could maintain contact sessions with their father. I had to admit it was a relief when he had them as I could switch off for a change. It was strange that I had more of a break now that we were separated than I ever did when we were still living in a partnership.

The weekend rolled around fast and my mum arrived to do the kiddie handover. I had forgotten to conceal the envelope and I could have kicked myself for not doing it because I knew that the assassination of questions would soon follow.

"What's that?" Mum quizzed. "It looks very formal to be addressed to Lena!"

"It's a letter about Lena from CAMHS. They're inviting us to a family choice appointment," I answered, anticipating a discussion I wasn't sure I wanted to have.

"What's CAMHS?" Her face contorted in confusion.

"The Child and Mental Health Service," I answered shortly.

"Oh goodness me!" Mum's eyes widened as if she had just witnessed the Prime Minister stripping naked and doing the hokey-cokey right in front of her. "I did think there was something peculiar about her behaviour. You do realise this will be forever on her health record now that she's got mental health problems?"

"But you have said yourself you think there could be something... different... about her." I was struggling to find the words to explain to my own mother that her response had contradicted EVERY-THING she had been saying to me for so long!

"I did! But I don't think it's something to be written on her record forever! It's best to keep information like this to ourselves – without having judgements made or being tarnished as social rejects... and even worse getting stigmatised as being an out of control mother!"

I sighed. There was absolutely no hope talking to my mother. Her ignorance and narrow-minded views never ceased to shock me. I wondered how we could be mother and daughter when our outlooks were so different.

"I'm thinking about changing schools for Lena too," I added. "It might be the environment that is making things worse for her."

"Oh no!" Mum screamed with panic. "Don't do that, Sarah! You will be jumping out of the frying pan into the fire! Sunnybank is already working with you so why would you think about moving her elsewhere? The problems we have in life always follow us. She will still be Lena just in another classroom. You need to fix how she behaves around people rather than thinking the grass is greener somewhere else."

I had to change the subject before we had a heated debate. I wanted to scream at her that the school was not understanding and that they could be doing more to accommodate Lena, but I couldn't upset her now when she was a vital part of the transport and logistical process in a broken marriage. I made another mental note to avoid discussing anything related to Lena in future as it only got me riled. I needed to just have a regular conversation offering a few pleasantries and no further information.

The CAMHS appointment arrived two weeks later and I was pinning all my hopes that this would provide the answer that I was looking for. The particular morning was extra chaotic and Lena was in full refusal mode – it was so difficult to get her past any routines when she got this oppositional.

"I'm not going to a stupid appointment," Lena declared.

"I promise it will be alright when we get there," I pleaded. She always sensed my mood when I had the urgency to get somewhere, it was as if she was on a mission to disarm me to prevent us from going.

"Chicken Pox thinks you're telling fibs," Lena insisted, placing her toy rabbit in front of her face. "Tell Poxy the truth!"

"It is the truth, Poxy!" I softly stroked her cotton nose to show I was genuine.

"Why does she have to go?" Lena made Poxy's voice full of accusation. I couldn't believe I was explaining myself and cutting a deal with a plushy.

"Because..." I started whilst I thought of a plan, "Lena gets to have a secret treat after the appointment!"

"Can it be ice cream?" Poxy shook with excitement as Lena's hand exaggerated up and down.

"It might just be!" I winked and tickled Lena and Poxy under their chins.

We managed to arrive at the appointment five minutes late, but if I was honest, I was actually relieved that we had made it there at all (which, in my books, was a result in itself). The session got underway with a comment from the psychotherapist, who introduced herself as Theresa, that irked me.

"I did notice that we are missing Lena's father and baby sibling. Were you made aware that this is a choice appointment and it is supposed to include the whole family unit?" I ignored the intent and attempted to settle Lena who was beginning to pace the room.

"We have recently separated," I admitted.

"My apologies," she whispered as she glanced over to Lena, "that must be tough." She pushed her hands together and smiled at me with a look of sympathy.

"How are you feeling this morning?" Theresa enquired, her eyes resting in Lena's direction. There was no answer. Another question soon fired over.

"Do you know why Mummy has brought you here today?"

I took in Theresa; she was dressed in a sharp trouser suit finished off with pointy high heels. Untainted curls smothered her shoulders. Her skin looked pinkish and warm as if she took time and care looking after herself. She stood up and used a sponge to clean away what looked like a child's writing on the whiteboard.

Lena moved like a master at work and swiftly took the lady's chair. Lena looked at her directly, with one eye squinted up interrogatively.

"How are YOU feeling this morning? And do YOU know why you're here?!" Lena's voice boomed across the room, shocking both of us adults at once.

The psychotherapist seemed bemused by the sudden action and introduced herself.

"My name is Theresa. And you must be... Lena?"

Lena looked around, her eyes transfixed on the furniture in the room, which she went to investigate curiously as she rejected the conversation. She went to the window and touched the white plastic sill in multiple areas – I wasn't sure what she was expecting it to do in return. I almost thought with every tap it would answer back to say it wasn't about to fall. She placed her face against the window, used her warm breath to steam up the glass and drew a squiggly stick face in the condensation. I looked at Theresa, concerned that she might tell Lena off, but she remained quiet.

"That order is wrong!" Lena criticised as she perused the bookcase, yanked a couple of items off a shelf and then replaced them in the opposite direction.

This hadn't provided enough entertainment, so after just a few seconds she ran off to the small coffee table, which had a piece of paper and some decaying crayons left upon it.

Lena picked up the crayons and scribbled over the page, making circles in different colours – I noticed these were picked up and performed in repeated patterns.

"I like the pattern you're making!" Theresa called over to her.

Instantly, Lena stumped each of the crayons furiously into the paper, snapping each of them in unison as if she had been reprimanded. She quickly left the small desk, flinging the child's red seat over.

Lena continued to peruse the room fiercely and at speed, as if she were a wild animal rummaging and escaping as if their life depended on it. She finally halted at a small doll's house which had an assortment of unloved wooden dolls thrown into a washed-out ice cream tub. Lena started tidying the items and created a sense of maternal presence on the tattered home. Each item was put into a line, neatly and with precision, then assigned to a more befitting location in the house. It was starting to look like a woman's touch had invigorated the dusty place. Theresa, performing her role as psychotherapist, used the opportunity to try and draw out some information from Lena. She approached with caution.

"I needed someone to make the house look better, I'm afraid I never know how to decorate it."

Lena pointed to some discarded items on the floor.

"You had the animals inside the house. They shouldn't go there. They have to sleep outside," Lena answered directly.

"Oh. Right."

"Why did you put them in the beds? Don't you know anything?" Lena's tone was blunt, and if misconstrued, would be taken for insolent or rude. She couldn't help herself; she seemed to have no awareness of how someone else would take her conversational style.

"It seems that is the case," Theresa replied without any hidden emotion that could be detected from her underlying words. I was starting to warm to her.

The dolls and animals were once again thrown down and left, dispersed, over the carpeted office floor. I could see the therapist sit back into her chair.

I was starting to get impatient. I wanted to know what would be the outcome from this and if Theresa would be helping us.

Lena bumbled over to the noticeboard which had a selection of self-help mantras and NHS pamphlets affixed to it. One of the leaflets grabbed her attention and she reached up to unpin it from the board.

"This has a rain cloud and a plus sign next to the sunshine. That's stupid," Lena stated.

"*You can't have a rainbow without a little rain,*" Theresa paused then questioned Lena: "Now, what do you think that means?"

"A sunshine plus a rain cloud equals a rainbow. But maths is not about rainbows! It's stupid!" Lena exclaimed.

Theresa looked up and attempted to articulate an answer in her consistently expert intonation.

"A rainbow only happens when sunlight beams through water at the same time and disperses into colours." She paused after every interaction, watching and observing how each bit of information was being processed and responded to. Theresa's mannerism of nodding whilst clearing her throat, just as she raised one eyebrow every time, was looking to be a sensory attack on Lena. She hated any unnecessary human noise at the best of times.

"Rainbows are mean!" Lena blurted out of nowhere. "Why are they being so unfair to the rest of the colours?"

"I've never thought of it like that before. Could you explain to me why you think they're mean?"

"Because I like black. And rainbows NEVER have black in them." Lena looked up sideways as she continued to think then carried on her one-sided observations. "I wonder, where are all the dark colours in a rainbow?!"

Once again, my daughter had astonished me with her curiosity and greater depth of thinking. I wasn't trying to feel biased but it made me question would other children of the same age look at the world like she did?

I could see Theresa's pencil eagerly scratching at the paper, writing an abundance of notes, no doubt having a child as enigmatic as Lena was like a field day for anyone working in the field of psychology. I tried to lean over to sneakily read what was being written about my child, but the psychotherapist looked up and I was caught in the act. My eyes quickly glanced away like a child being scolded, caught red-handed with a fistful of stolen sweets. I couldn't help but empathise deeply with Lena's feelings, after all, in her perceived sense of reality the injustice that her favourite colour was not in the rainbow was no doubt painful. I wondered if Lena actually felt very dark in an overly colourful, intensely stimulating and complicated world.

"You can't really 'see' the colour black just as much as you can't really 'hear' silence," Theresa said. "When we see black, what we are actually missing is light. It's the same for silence too, then we are just missing sound. It's very confusing. It's more about what our mind *thinks* we can see or hear than the thing itself."

"Nobody sees me. I'm a black rainbow." Lena scuffed her shoes together and began picking at her lip.

It was like a golden moment. Both of us adults glanced over at one another, joining ranks, marvelling at the perplexity of such a conflicting and profound declaration.

"Thank you for explaining that to me, it helps me to understand how you feel." Theresa was delicate in her response. "Do you feel like a black rainbow all of the time? Or just at certain times?"

"School!" Lena confessed as her lips contorted and her brow narrowed. "I don't feel like a black rainbow when I go down the orange slide," she declared, which must have sounded very random for Theresa. But I immediately had a visual image of the place that she'd found sanctuary at the park at Queen's Field.

Lena suddenly lunged towards the door, yanked it open and sped off down the corridor.

"I'm bored now. Adults talk too much!" Lena shouted. "They just say *blah, blah, blah!*"

I frantically hurried after the last set of words as they ping-ponged from wall to wall. I was grateful for the sound as it was a way of leading me to her. I was never quick enough and at the moment when Lena needed to abscond from any situation, I repeatedly lost pace, not knowing which direction she would have gone in. It frightened me and I worried that one day I might lose her completely.

When I reached Lena, I put my arms around her to stop her from continuing.

"We don't have to stay any longer." I stroked her face and used a soothing tone. "But my bag with Chicken Pox is still in the room so I have to get that and say goodbye."

There was a moment of silence and I waited earnestly in the hope that she would comply. I was no longer worried about completing the session at CAMHS, but I didn't know what to do – I needed to prevent Lena from entering a big overload but I had to collect my belongings. What was the priority of the two? My senses were heightened.

"I'm not going back in the room." Lena looked up at me with a meaningful stare. Her mood had changed. There was no light or laughter; her static and rigid body was signalling danger.

"That's okay," I replied. "Mummy can go in the room and grab our things, and you can wait by the door. Is that a deal?"

She took a while, then finally nodded. We walked silently back down the corridor, hand-in-hand, her small footsteps sounded like they were struggling. I knew the last conversation we'd had in Theresa's room had been too painful for her to process and the only way she knew how to deal with her emotions was to run away from them.

I ran into the office at the speed of light and made a few pleasantries as Lena remained at the clunky door. I pointed towards Lena and tried to explain that she was in a bad place and that I would phone back. I knew if I openly communicated now, it could be the ignition to the biggest emotional bomb seen on land. Reducing conversation was not a choice but a survival tactic at moments like this.

"We will need to do another few sessions to gather some further information," Theresa explained. "Then we can decide if we are able to offer any plans moving forwards."

"Do you have enough information now? Have you seen what she's like to be able to help us?" I fired the questions, desperately hoping that there could be a way of making things better for Lena and all of us.

"I will be in touch in time." Theresa was shutting down the conversation without anything concrete to give me. I shut the door with a sigh of disappointment that I was still being left with no answers after all this time.

We scurried away from the bleak medical building and found some raised cement posts, which Lena stopped to climb on. With my support she found enjoyment leaping from one to the other. I started to process my frustration that I was no further forward and this waiting game was too much. Did nobody care about Lena and how she felt? Did she not deserve support now rather than later? I didn't want to get an ill-feeling about Theresa, but my disappointment was flooding in that we were not making any progress. When would I find help for Lena?

My anxious thoughts were soon disrupted by the sound of a pressing child. "Can we get an ice cream, please?" Lena looked up angelically, without any further discussion about where we had been or why she had felt the need to run out. I knew she needed a distraction to process some of the big feelings she had opened up about. I had to park my own feelings and absorb myself into her world.

"Of course we can," I said warmly. "Let's get one by the skate park and you can have a turn on the ramps. We'll have to be quick before Shelley brings Charlie home."

"Yayy!" Lena squealed and pulled me by the hand in the direction of the car. We had secured a deal and both of us needed the recovery time, and the rhythmic sensation of scooting up and down always seemed to help her recalibrate.

***

Shelley arrived just after dinner with the car seat and Charlie's tiny feet sticking over the edge of them. It reminded me that he was growing at an alarming pace and he really needed to transition to a bigger seat that stayed in the car. I made another mental note to remember to sort it out soon.

"There you go, Charlie," Shelley said, untying his straps. "You can see your big sister now after doing all that moaning for her!"

Lena was in like a shot, snatching him from Shelley and lifting him up in her arms.

"I missed you, Charlie. I'm sorry I had ice cream without you."

Innocence spilled out in her words.

My mothering hands rested over the top of Lena's to give her the foundation she needed to keep her baby brother safe.

"I think Charlie would love to play *Paw Patrol* with you," I suggested.

Lena bombed up the stairs and then crashed down, one stair at a time, with a thud. I placed Charlie in the centre of the living room, with an obligatory cushion rested behind his back, so that he had a good view of the action. Lena proceeded to wheel the cars and vehicles animatedly in front of him and, just on cue, he cooed and giggled to each one. This gave Lena great pleasure and I quickly snapped a photo of the event on my phone to print at a later date.

There was a knock at the door and Shelley went to answer it. I found her a few moments later in the kitchen, chatting earnestly with Vic, who was carrying a plastic carrier full of jangling bottles. Vic dumped them on the kitchen island and lifted out a giant bag of *Doritos* and a tub of sour cream and chive dip.

"I brought the snacks. It had to be done!"

Shelley and I both burst into laughter at the memory this invoked. It was always our chosen food when we'd had teenage sleepovers and we rammed ourselves with as much junk food as humanly possible. I often longed for the days when we all seemed so free and the world felt limitless. I think we all agreed that this new life of adulting was far more restrictive and we would give anything to spend a night together without the worries we had now. A night with music and talking about our adolescent crushes seemed a million miles away from the reality of today. "Seeing as we are going old-school tonight, I also brought these along!" Shelley declared as she rummaged through her oversized handbag and placed a pair of crimpers on the side.

"No way!" Vic and I screamed, having not seen a crimping machine for over two decades.

"My parents were having a clear out of their loft and found these bad boys. I couldn't wait to show you both!" Shelley smiled and pretended to use them on her own hair.

"What's that?" questioned Lena, who had suddenly appeared in the room and lifted the unidentified, electronic object. Then, with her usual speedy change of topic: "Oooh, crispies! I want some!"

"Of course you can," said Vic as she proceeded to open the bag and lower them down to Lena's tiny level. Lena pulled out a handful and stashed them like an animal hibernating for winter.

Shelley located a plug socket and switched on the machine.

"They take an eternity to warm up – you forget how much time we spent waiting for anything to load back in the day." She giggled.

After some time a light appeared on the side of the crimping machine, and Shelley sat Lena down on the stool to create a makeshift hairdressers. The female camaraderie and chit-chat lit up and filled the room with the energy that was needed after a tense day. Finally the hairstyling was finished and Shelley helped Lena to stand up on the stool to show off her childlike mannequin.

"Ta daaa!" Shelley declared. "How does she look?"

"Look at my curly hair!" Lena squealed. "They are so tiny!"

We all looked and touched Lena's hair to feel the puffed ball that had been created. With squeals of excitement and adoration given to Lena, she jumped down and ran around the room, bouncing her puffy beehive up and down as if it were an entirely separate being.

"Now I really am Spitfire like Daddy calls me!" Lena squealed, touching her bouffant. "My hair looks like it's so big it's on fire!"

Shelley and Vic looked at me but I couldn't update any conversation on Nick whilst Lena was still in the room.

We cracked open a bottle of Vic's wine from the kitchen island and poured a generous glass for each of us. I popped away to do Lena's bedtime and Shelley took over the reins so that Charlie's routine was taken care of too.

"Thank you," I said warmly, once both children were asleep in their beds. "It's such a relief to have help so that the bedtime routine goes smoothly."

"Teamwork makes the dream work!" declared Shelley as she shook out her arms. "Isn't that what they put on those stupid hashtags! Oh no, the best one is *'Making Memories,'* that just makes me wanna puke every time I see it!"

Vic and I both cackled loudly at Shelley's observation.

"I think I should change our *WhatsApp* group from *The Dream Team* to *Making Fucking Memories*!" Vic burst out, a dribble of wine drooling down her chin. "What do you think?"

"Yess!" we screamed in unison.

"That's hilarious!" I beamed. "It'll make us smile every time a message pops up."

The night soon got underway and after an hour we had had enough wine between us that the karaoke game had come out on Nick's discarded gaming device, and we were shrieking the words to multiple nineties tunes. Vic was always the more in control out of the three of us and she sneakily started recording Shelley and I as we performed another unforgettable duo. I knew the evidence would appear in our newly named *WhatsApp* group the next morning, but for the moment, I was revelling in the warmth of friendship and fun.

I was conscious that I could only have a few drinks because I was the sole person in charge of the children. It didn't matter that I had to stop drinking early, I was just high on letting my hair down in person with my friends, and my lifted state was mostly through laughter. After a while our energy levels burnt out and we crashed down on the sofa together.

It was an ideal moment to talk about the day's earlier events. I began to confess to the girls about the appointment and how dark it had gone. It felt like I was delivering a deeply bottled-up monologue that had been bursting to escape.

"So," I finally reached, "you can't have a rainbow without a little rain."

"Woah!" Shelley exclaimed. "My brain is too sozzled, I need you to repeat that again!"

"It's a metaphor," I declared, "think about how beautiful a rainbow is – you wouldn't see one without the process of rain now would you?"

"Oh, I see, but where are you going with this?" Shelley asked, her marbles slowly circulating on catch-up mode.

"I can't help but think about the fair share of rain I've had in one bloody year." I was talking to myself more than anyone else. "In fact, I feel so flooded with negativity most of the time, I wonder if I'll ever be able to see the sun shine properly again!"

"Of course you will!"

"Maybe you had to experience this amount of rain to make an even bigger rainbow?" Vic offered with her sweet tone. "Think of it like an act of enlightenment and maybe life will be richer as a result."

I took a moment to compose myself, my throat was scratchy. I felt like I might cry. I needed to confide my worries and my best friends were the only people I could talk to.

"Lena told the therapist today that she was like a black rainbow," I admitted. "She said that nobody could see her."

A solitary tear escaped the prison of my eyes and strode defiantly down my cheek.

The girls both reached across the sofa and gave me a three-way squeeze. Shelley spoke to break the silence, "You're dealing with so much on your own. Never forget that you are Lena's rock and she is lucky to have you." They both joined me with the tears falling equally.

I wanted an answer. I needed a direction to be given. This wasn't what I was expecting from being a parent and I didn't know how to deal with it.

"If you could wave a magic wand to make something better in

your life, what would it be?" It was a good question from Vic.

"To know how I can help Lena to fit into the world a bit better," I replied thoughtfully.

"You need to take a different angle on it," Vic said. "Like how can you change *the world* to make it better for Lena?!"

"That's right," echoed Shelley. "Lena doesn't need to change. The environment needs fixing around her. If a flower doesn't grow, would you blame the flower?"

"I hadn't really ever thought of it that way," I admitted.

"Maybe it might be time to start thinking about school as her soil and how it might not be giving her the roots that she needs to thrive." Vic was considerate with her delivery but confident with the point she wanted to make.

"I agree," said Shelley, "I'm afraid those fuckwits can't see who Lena is or what she needs. No wonder she feels like a black rainbow!"

"But how do I make the school change things to help her feel able to be herself?" I broke down – sobs and snot galore. "She's missing so much education, and at the end of the meeting, I was left with no answers. It feels like Lena's childhood is slowly disappearing away and nobody but me cares about it."

"You'll find a way," reassured Vic.

"We have faith in you." Shelley backed her up with bristling energy.

"I think I feel like a black rainbow too!" I cried. "I can't believe my child can work it out better than I can."

"When we are in a situation and we can't find a way out," Shelley said philosophically, "we need to be able to take ourselves out of the equation and look down with a helicopter view of it. To see the situation from a different perspective."

"I think the only viewpoint I can see it from is through an alcoholic, fog-induced haze and it looks pretty desperate, I'm not gonna lie!" I tried to make light of the situation as talking this deeply was making me feel petrified.

"Maybe you need to focus on rebuilding the layers of colour again?" Vic suggested.

"Yup!" Shelley nodded. "That's a fabulous idea."

"You need to find a way to gain control back of the situation for both of you." Vic advised, "The greatest gift you will ever give to Lena is to teach her to be happy in her own skin. If you manage that, you've succeeded. Being happy, now that's the ultimate goal."

"What the fuck has got into you two? You both sound like spiritual gurus all of a sudden!" I shrieked, spitting out my mouthful of recovery water in a very unladylike fashion.

"That's what happens when you approach forty," declared Shelley. "You slow down, wear knitted cardigans and reassess life."

"Or... you go away for a weekend with your besties and learn to live again. You prevent the aging process with fun!" Vic laughed.

"Are we letting the cat out the bag now then?" Squealed Shelly. "Fuck it, let's do it!"

My brain cells were not doing what they were supposed to because I didn't have the foggiest what my two mates were on about. "What?!"

"WE are taking YOU away for your birthday at the end of the month and we're going to make it mega!"

"But, what? Wait a minute! I can't... I mean... what about the kids?" I flustered.

"We've sorted that out already. We've contacted Nick and he has agreed to have the kids longer as it's his weekend to have them anyway," reassured Vic.

"There was no way he could say no to us. How could he say no to looking after his *own* children?" Shelley interjected in her usual bolshy fashion. "You didn't think you were getting out of celebrating your fortieth, did you?"

"You know I don't like a fuss! I was hoping it would pass incognito!" I whimpered.

"Let's just say we will get you trying things you've never tried before." Vic winked. "It will be a milestone to remember!"

We soon called it a night and the girls grabbed a taxi home. I tossed and turned that night, half in excitement and half in dread, at the uncertainty of the plans that lay ahead of me. In my dreams I saw visions of abstract rainbows.

10

Circular Sofas

I had hoped the appointment at CAMHS would have given me a magic wand to fix everything, but I was still left in limbo, desperately waiting to find an answer to the mess we were in. I felt like I was unsuccessfully begging for help whilst being trapped by a system that was ostracising us. What could I do to get us out of this situation? The fallout from Lena's frustration had an impact on my ability to concentrate or think positively. Her meltdowns at home were increasing, and the darker the hole, the more we were all disappearing down it. I was sure Charlie had stopped his daily gurgling and even Rex preferred to hide under the kitchen island. Lena's mood always seemed to dictate the household's day.

Friday was upon us and I had a sudden panic in the morning as I remembered it was the scheduled date for the educational psychologist to observe Lena in school. The only information I had been given was that the lady was called Kimberley and she would be writing a report to give some recommendations to the school about supporting Lena. The job title sounded intimidating, I didn't even know these kinds of people existed to work with children. I was learning about a whole new world that was foreign to me. Maybe this would give us the answers that we needed to help Lena at last.

I tried to push through with the morning routine and used every trick in my bag to get Lena into her school uniform and out past the front door, but they all failed. I looked up at the clock in the kitchen – the small hand had moved past the nine defiantly, at which point I started to panic that it was going to be too late. I picked up the phone and got through to my favourite receptionist who said that she would pass the message on. As she hung up, I was left with the ghostly sound of the dialling tone. I felt like I had to give up hope of ever getting the right support for Lena to be understood. I tried to remind myself to be patient. The school didn't call back to offer any support or strategies to help me get Lena in for the appointment that we needed to improve things. It was like nobody cared and we were in this void all alone.

I picked up my phone to call Shelley. My tears flooded through our call. She reassured me that she would drive over before work and have a quick coffee to help me calm down so we could think of the next steps. As I hung up the phone, I felt a sense of relief just by talking about the problem and opening up to someone.

"Listen, Sarah," Shelley began as we sat at the kitchen island over our cuppas. "They must get this all of the time. I mean, Lena can't be the only child who struggles to attend or these professionals would be out of a job now, wouldn't they?"

"Well, yes," I agreed, "when you put it like that."

I felt more grounded and my irrational thoughts were dissolving. I had to give it to Shelley, she really had the ability to help me think straight and put my life in order. Sometimes, I wondered why I couldn't just do that by myself.

As if by magic, the phone abruptly intercepted our conversation and reaffirmed Shelley's advice.

"Hello, am I speaking to Ms Forte?" a mysterious voice began.

"Yes, speaking," I responded.

"Oh, hi there," the voice started to warm up, "my name is Kimberley and I'm the educational psychologist who was scheduled to visit Lena at school today."

"I'm so sorry. I tried my best but she struggled to get to school today," I apologised. "I hope that we haven't wasted your time?"

"Of course not," Kimberley reassured. "In fact, as Lena struggles to attend, I was wondering if I could do the visit at home instead? I should have suggested it before so that she felt more comfortable, after all, the last thing I would want to do is add any more distress!"

"I'd be fine with that," I encouraged with a sudden hope that the situation could be resolved. "We're at home so we're available whenever."

There was an extra snippet of information that threw me off-course before she politely ended the call.

"I would like to bring my colleague Joanne with me," Kimberley told me. "She's the autism advisory teacher and I would value her input so that we can write a joint report to support Lena in school."

"Sure, that would be fine," I pretended to sound cool as the call concluded.

I held the phone in my hand and looked up at Shelley with a look of disdain. I was completely stumped.

"What's wrong? You look like you've seen a ghost!" Shelley observed. "I thought I heard that the lady was going to come here instead, so what's the problem?"

"She's bringing someone with her," I began, my thoughts racing, "an autism advisory teacher!"

"Is that *not* a good thing?" Shelley enquired confused.

"Autism...?" It didn't make sense. "Do you think Lena has autism?"

"Well, I don't think it's something you *have* as such. It's not like having a sickness bug or a bag you carry around with you all day!" Shelley corrected as she laughed. "It's about the way your brain works and Lena does think a bit differently, so yes, it could be a possibility. There is nothing wrong if she is autistic."

"Yes, but autism?" I repeated the word again like it was foreign. "I thought that was people who can't make eye contact or they can't talk to others. Lena's not like that. She's funny, clever *and* mischievous. Defiant, yes. Strong-willed, yes – but not like a child locked in their own world. She is more sociable than that! She's not obsessed with trains or dinosaurs or any other inanimate object either. She would make people be her toys if she had half the chance."

"I know," Shelley agreed, "but what if it goes a bit deeper than that?"

My brain was being ransacked by explanations as to why this was still all wrong, my thoughts were on a one-track route. Lena loved being with people, I told myself. It was as if she was drawn to other kids like a bee to nectar. It was just when children didn't play a game the way she wanted to, or if they changed the rules without telling her, then she didn't become sociable. But I was starting to doubt myself. I thought about how much more comfortable she was in the park with Timothy than she had been with the other children.

"What if we try searching online? It might make more sense." Shelley gently began to lead me out of the deep chasm.

Maybe Shelley was right? Oh god, what if my views on autism were outdated? So, I Googled the word and found a page with some generic information and a picture of a young boy looking away holding a toy car.

"Hmm..." I began, "this doesn't seem to tell me anything. I still can't see it resonating with how Lena is."

"I wonder if you search with the keywords 'autism in girls' to see if it pulls up anything different?" Shelley suggested.

So I opened a new search and I was directed instantly to the *NHS* website where the information was widening, and suddenly I became aware that the discourse was looking different to what I had initially thought. It started to change my perspective about what the word autism actually meant.

"Wait a minute, look at that!" I spotted a quote that struck a chord and read it to Shelley, "**Autism** *can sometimes be different in* **girls** *and boys. For example,* **autistic girls** *may be quieter, may hide their feelings and may appear to cope better with social situations. This means* **autism** *can be harder to spot in* **girls**."

I was starting to realise that my assumptions were off the mark entirely. If I was honest, my knowledge on the subject had not just been limited, it was actually completely misinformed.

"What's that?" Shelley pointed to an infographic at the bottom of the web results. "*Signs of Autism in Girls* – that could be interesting? Can you click on it?"

"'*Passionate, restricted and having specific interests...*' now that could be talking about Lena," I admitted.

"'*Difficulty moderating feelings when frustrated,*' now that could be her too?" Shelley joined.

"And definitely this one – '*Unusual depression, anxiety or mood changes!*' That describes what it's like, walking on eggshells around her because her mood changes in a flash of light!" I put my head in my hands to over-emphasise the point to Shelley who laughed knowing what it was like for me to parent Lena.

The more I was reading and starting to think about it, the more it seemed like these were some of the challenges Lena had. Even the features that I thought at first were not like Lena, such as 'difficulty with social communication', I started to dwell on, and the more I thought about it, the more I realised that she did struggle with. It was masked by the fact that her speech was clear and she could talk ten to the dozen. When I thought about it deeply, did she actually ask appropriate questions and listen for those replies back? She controlled conversations as much as she did when she was playing games, but so cleverly that it concealed her inability to take in the other person's views or opinions.

"You've always said her moods are like *Jekyll and Hyde*!" Shelley rolled her eyes.

"What if I search 'autism' and 'Jekyll and Hyde' – do you think it would bring anything up?" I was smiling at the ludicrous search term and the impossibility it would provide any results. It was hard to pinpoint Lena but the best way I could describe her mood swings were like a sudden personality change.

"Go on," Shelley urged. "Worth a shot!"

I remembered my mum's words after the christening about Lena reminding her of the patients on the ward and she was concerned my daughter could be a psychopath – I was suddenly apprehensive in case I read something I didn't want to see. I was frightened by the unknown.

I took a brave breath in and looked at the words as the search results began to load. The first item grabbed my attention as if I wasn't allowed to have any freedom of my own.

"Oh my goodness, it's brought something up!" My eyes widened. *"Jekyll and Hyde or Pathological Demand Avoidance Syndrome?"*

"I wonder what that means?" Shelley queried so I clicked on the link curiously.

"Pathological Demand Avoidance is understood to be a profile on the autism spectrum; the central feature being the avoidance of everyday demands, which centres from an 'anxiety-driven need to be in control'. Children are often labelled or referred to as 'naughty', 'wilful' or 'oppositional', and the fact that they are actually autistic is often misunderstood," I stopped reading as I felt like I was having a lightbulb moment! The sudden realisation that these words were summing up everything I had been saying about my daughter for so long - including to her closest family who had not believed me – was beginning to set in. It was her, right there in black and white. My body was shaking with a mixture of excitement and anger. Why had nobody told me about this sooner?

"'Pathological Demand Avoidance is often described by parents as if their child has a Jekyll and Hyde personality,'" Shelley read as she

pointed to the last bit of text. "*Which identifies one of the key features – a tendency of mood swings.*"

"I can't believe it!" I exclaimed. "I've been saying that phrase for so long. I can't believe it's unlocked a part of the bigger picture!"

The article had a link to a charity webpage for more information and I eagerly navigated to read further. There was a list of key features of this thing they called the 'PDA profile' and, having read it all, I used my cursor to copy and paste it into an email:

To: headteacher

From: sarahforte

Subject: Pathological Demand Avoidance

Dear Mrs Ramsbottom

I have just stumbled across a profile on the autism spectrum called 'Pathological Demand Avoidance', or PDA for short, which centres around a child who has an anxiety-based need to be in control. I think this could really be describing Lena. It also says some of the key features are having a surface sociability (but lacking depth to their understanding), resisting and avoiding the everyday tasks or demands of life, and that they can be comfortable in role-play. It also said the child can have obsessive behaviour (often around key individuals).

I'd be really keen to hear what you think? It often feels that Lena can't do something when it is asked of her, just like she drew in her 'Yes the Superhero'.

I scurried around the house, throwing toys into any crevice that I could find, in the vain attempt to tidy up the house before our visitors came. I wasn't sure why but I felt better by chucking some bleach down the toilet and scrubbing the sink to make it shine in an attempt to appear falsely perfect. If I'd thought about it, the toilet was probably the only place they were not likely to take a look at, yet it felt vital to make it look clean. With that one holy chore done, I was able to carry on getting ready for our visitors. Shelley made a prompt exit before they arrived.

The doorbell rang and Lena pushed past me to be the first to see who was at the door. I unlocked the door, by finding the key from its hiding place in the unit, as it had to be locked away at all times to prevent Lena from doing a runner. The jolt of sunlight flooded the room as the sight of the outdoors became visible from our safe cocoon.

"Hello," I said politely, "come on in."

"Can you just stand on the door mat only?" a small but masterful voice popped up behind me, taking the power. "Please!"

"You must be Lena," said a brunette lady with a pinstripe suit and high heels. "My name is Kimberley and this is my colleague, Joanne. We've been very excited to come and meet you."

"Is that *Paw Patrol* on your t-shirt?" asked Joanne as she remained safely glued to the spot. Joanne was dressed far more casually in loose cotton-style pants, a collared polo shirt and flat pumps. The two ladies looked about the same age, but Joanne seemed the nimbler of the two. They both wore smiles that matched their individual attires. Joanne bent down on her knees and reduced her presence with an open body.

Lena nodded without uttering a word to her direct question. It must have made a shift in her thought pattern because she took a step back into the house.

"You can come in and go straight into the living room," Lena interjected, "and then you can sit anywhere *but* my favourite sofa."

"Which one is that?" Joanne asked softly.

"The circular seat, of course!" Lena said, matter-of-factly. "I would never sit on a rectangle shaped sofa. The sides are too straight."

"If you are kind enough to let me into your lovely house, I will respect your wish to not sit on your favourite sofa. Is that a deal?" Joanne was bargaining like a pro and I could sense that she was the expert with getting mistrustful kids aligned on her side.

I was watching on, smiling nervously, as the conversation unfolded. I hoped that Lena wouldn't shout or stick her tongue out at anyone – I was so used to people being shocked by her behaviour that I was always in a hyper-vigilant mode. *Please just let this go smoothly,* I thought.

Lena rambled on but most of her words were incoherent as she had her back to the visitors she was leading into the living room. As the two ladies went past and I shut the door behind them, Kimberley gave me a quick wink and a smile to ensure I knew that they were fully engaging at Lena's speed. They seemed to be working well as a team and the communication style was clearly developed and planned for a reason. I started to let my fears subside.

"Miss Orchard has a circle face and she's pretty. The Year One teacher has an oval face and it doesn't look right." We all smiled at one another discreetly at the directness of Lena's observations. "I don't like oval faces."

The room fell quiet, I'm sure we were all checking each other out in fear of seeing any of us had oval faces that Lena would be pointing out next.

"Is Miss Orchard your favourite teacher?" asked Joanne, surveying the room, making sure to avoid sitting on any circular couches.

"I don't have favourite teachers," Lena declared brazenly. "I don't *hate* Miss Orchard *as much*."

The visitors sat across from Lena, on the sofa that lined the shape of the wall, and they put their handbags and some of the papers they had been carrying in their hands down by their shoes. Joanne had an extra drawstring bag which she opened a touch so that the contents could be seen curiously by anyone interested in exploring further. Lena was still too apprehensive of the strangers to allow her curiosity to get the better of her.

"Are there any parts of school that you like the best?" Joanne asked enthusiastically.

"Why are you here anyway?" A masterful conversation change indicated that the subject of school was clearly off topic. "This is my house! You see that bag you carried in and those papers and that toy car hanging out of your bag? Well they are all your things. But these walls..." Lena indicated with her finger whilst spinning around. "They belong to me!"

"Okay, well I'm glad we got that straight," said Joanne. "The walls and the circular sofa?"

"Good," retorted Lena. "Now we can get on with it." Lena's manner was strange for her age and she always performed as if she was the adult in the room.

The visit continued on pretty harmoniously and most of the engagement happened between Joanne and Lena. It was lovely to see her open up to a stranger that she hadn't met before. It had taken some time to warm up, but her true personality was visibly on show. Kimberley moved across the room and sat at the small dining room table with me whilst Joanne played with Lena. She asked me some questions and took as much information as she could on all of the things that Lena was good at, as well as the things that she struggled with. It was fairly informal, and for once, it felt nice to have a cup of coffee with an adult who seemed to understand the situation better than most.

"So..." Kimberley began as we sat alone at the table. "I wanted to get an update on things from you, if you don't mind, Sarah?"

"Of course," I answered, taking a sip of coffee.

"I can see school has introduced a part-time timetable but Lena is still struggling to attend," Kimberley summarised. "I'd like to know what you think Lena needs?"

I was taken aback. It felt strange that she was asking me what I thought was needed. I was so used to being treated as just *the mum* that I couldn't believe my opinion would be asked.

"More understanding and support," I began. "Anyone working with her needs to be aware that she isn't choosing to be defiant. She can't help how she responds."

"That's a very strong point," Kimberley agreed. "Remaining neutral is key to calming her down."

"I stumbled on a thing called Pathological Demand Avoidance today and I had this kind of lightbulb moment as it felt like it described Lena," I blurted out, feeling more comfortable around this professional to speak freely.

"I'm glad you're well-versed in PDA because I have seen lots of indicators of the profile in my visit," Kimberley said enthusiastically. "So my report will be very in-line with strategies that work with a demand avoidant child... like being non-confrontational when they can't cope with a demand, for example."

"Wow," I sighed. "It feels like a weight has lifted off my shoulders having you here this morning."

"That's very kind," Kimberley said modestly. "We're just here to try and support in any way we can. Lena is quite a character, that's for sure!"

"I've been to the GP before, but my concerns were dismissed," I confessed. "I think I'll go back to the doctor showing them the paperwork on PDA this time."

"Just to pre-warn you," Kimberley began tentatively. "PDA is very contentious amongst professionals – many people still think it doesn't exist."

"How can it not exist?" I exclaimed. "I just found details about it online and it matches my daughter – I think I have living-proof it exists, right here!"

I was fighting back my emotions. How could I have just found something that finally made sense and then be told I faced an uphill battle getting the thing recognised? Why was trying to go forward so bloody hard?

"Try not to worry about the exact wording, because Lena's needs have to be addressed and provided for no matter what they get labelled as. Services will catch up one day, it's a relatively new diagnosis and these things take time to be embedded," Kimberley tried to reassure me, but my brain was back in alarm-mode.

"I see." I couldn't find the words through the panic.

My attention moved over to Joanne, the autism advisory teacher, who was perched on the floor and sitting right next to Lena. Her body language was non-threatening and it reminded me of the guy that we'd met in the park who'd used his bubbles to calm her down. There was a way in with my daughter, you just had to get down to her level and treat her with understanding. It made me wonder if we would ever bump into him again. I hoped I would be a bit more together if the chance ever arose, and I'd tell him he was influential in this whole process.

"It's empty! I'm bored now!" Lena's attention span was often very short unless it was an interest that she chose. She had already investigated the contents of the drawstring bag, which included a colourful array of fidget items and moving, mechanical toys – which Lena had enjoyed figuring out how they worked. Joanne moved at the pace Lena required and moved on to the next activity.

"I wonder if we could draw a picture together of all the things you need to make school better?" Joanne invited.

"That's easy," Lena responded freely as she grabbed a pencil to make lots of speedy marks on some paper. I was surprised; the subject of school had been vetoed earlier on.

You couldn't fault Lena for her imagination as the creation of her utopian dream school couldn't have been any more inventive. The stick men and objects ranged from a blob that was Rex, to a cluster of circled squiggles which were her *Paw Patrol* toys. Then there was a swimming pool, a cinema to watch films with popcorn, and the appearance of a giant ant which turned out to be a pair of headphones to block out the horrible noise at school.

"That's a table to eat lunch at on my own. That's a fluffy cushion because the carpet is itchy and smelly!" Lena laughed as she cupped her hands innocently over her mouth, thinking she had said a naughty word. Then she drew a number sum and said, "I only want to do maths when I want to and not when the teacher tells me I have to do it because it's boring."

"I think you've given me a lot already," Joanne praised non-directly.

"There's too many people in the classroom," Lena said sadly, drawing windows in her castle-like school with two blobs in each. "I don't like it. I want it to be one teacher and one child in every class."

"So smaller class sizes would help you, I think," Joanne acknowledged and I saw Kimberley jot a note down on her pad.

Listening in on everything Lena was saying gave me a pang of guilt. Had I been forcing her into school without realising how intolerable it really was for her? Why hadn't I listened to my gut and done something about it sooner?

"I can imagine it's too much for you. I think you're so brave sharing these thoughts with me," Joanne expressed. "Is there anywhere you can go to when all these things get too much?"

Lena didn't directly answer but instead proceeded to draw a stick lady outside of the school.

"Who is that you've drawn?" Joanne continued.

"That's my mummy." Lena was concise and her voice sounded fearful all of a sudden. "I want my mummy to be at school. It's scary when she's not there."

"Do you have any safe people you can go to when you feel scared?" Joanne asked in a soft voice. "They might be teachers, children or even the dinner ladies? Just anyone who would make you feel better?"

"I'm alone when I'm at school." Lena began scratching at her *Paw Patrol* top as she did when she was nervous in situations. "They don't care when I'm scared. They just move my name down to the thunder cloud in front of everyone. I'm a black rainbow at Sunnybank School."

There was complete silence as the visual analogy was so emotive for all of us adults in the room.

"So that's something that we could change to make school a little easier for you?" Joanne replied thoughtfully. "We need your voice to be heard."

Lena nodded a traumatised yes to the question.

The two visitors began collecting their things together and moved towards the front door to say their goodbyes. Lena pushed past them and threw her body weight against the front door to create a barricade to stop them leaving. Her demeanour changed; a frown reappeared upon her brow and her lips crinkled downwards sternly.

"You're not leaving yet. We haven't finished playing." Her anger was building. I wondered if the assessment had brought up some bad feelings in her. I felt even more parental guilt.

Joanne bent down and untied her drawstring bag. She opened it up in front of Lena who reluctantly unfolded her arms to peer inside, growling as she did.

"I don't like leaving either. I think we have a lot in common." Joanne was artful in her ability to get down to a child's wavelength.

"I want you to play *Paw Patrol* with me. We didn't get time!" Lena barked in reply.

"How about you choose one of the toys from the bag and you can teach Mummy how it works like you taught me?" Joanne enquired softly and without pressure.

Lena paused for a while and then dug her hand into the bag. She pulled out a wind-up unicorn and used her usual, overly loud voice, to instruct me further.

"Come on, Mummy, let's put it on the floor to make it work!" she squealed. Lena had brushed past the visitors and was pulling me by the loose material of my t-shirt into the other room. It gave me the chance to unlock the door, whisper goodbye to the two ladies and thank them for their visit.

"You can coommeeee back again!" Lena hollered from the next room as the sound of the front door shut behind them. "But next time you have to play *Paw Patrol* with me!"

"It's a deal!"

I tried my best to listen to Lena's explanation about the wind-up motor but my mind was elsewhere as I was staring into space. I felt that empty feeling of waiting yet again. What would be the outcome of the visit? Would we finally get some answers about Lena? I was torn by the desire to push forward and the fear that I was doing something wrong by making her still try to go to school if she found it so bad. Why was parenting Lena so confusing? Even scarier, what if I was doing more harm than good to her? It wasn't like I even had time to grieve over my relationship breakdown, or have time to miss some of the earlier memories I'd made with Nick either – trying to advocate for Lena was a full-time job.

I had an idea to channel my anxiety and inform the school of an idea that could potentially work. I fired up my laptop and sent over an email to the school.

```
To: headteacher
From: sarahforte
Subject: Today's Visit

Dear Mrs Ramsbottom

I hope that my email from earlier found you well as I
did not receive a reply?

As I discussed, the educational psychologist and the
autism advisory teacher both came to the house and
were able to engage Lena with some activities around
school. She opened up to them about what she felt she
needed for it to be more accessible.

One of the issues she described was the carpet being
```

```
too itchy and she said she would prefer a cushion to
sit on.

I am wondering if we can find a way to accommodate
this adjustment before we get the full report of rec-
ommendations from the two professionals who visited?
It would seem beneficial to make the necessary changes
so that we can find a way for her school experience
to be improved.

Kind regards,


Sarah Forte
(Lena's Mum)
```

I didn't receive an email back, but it was late. Maybe the head-teacher would reply tomorrow to see how she could work with me on the issue. Although, I still hadn't received an email back from when I'd provided her with the information on PDA and asked for it to be shared with everyone in school. I wasn't convinced that my words would be actioned, because, as far as the school were concerned, I was just 'the mum'.

11

Red is for Tribe

"I don't like my new teacher," Lena declared one morning as I was trying to support her anxiety-based avoidance of school. "I'm allergic to her!"

I had to give Lena the acclaim she deserved for being inventive; the information she conveyed was always graphic. She was adamant that her new Year One teacher, Mrs Carter, was mean and ugly. I think she was still upset that she wasn't the old teacher, Miss Orchard, and she was finding it hard to let somebody new in. I had heard a conversation (at the end of last term) between the parents in the class queue, at pick-up time, that Mrs Carter was stricter and she would do wonders at helping the class achieve. The snippet of information was already like a forewarning to me, because Lena didn't cope with strict too well. If anything, the sterner someone was, the more she was driven to rebel. It was strange how my hopes and desires for Lena were so different to the masses. I knew they would never understand what milestones my aims for her really were.

As autumn was laying her finest, coloured canopy on the floor, Lena used the season to her advantage to delay our walk to the gates by shuffling clumps of leaves into the air and watching them fall to the ground. The fine mist in the air was cleansing the atmosphere, creating a sharp feeling with every inhalation we took.

"It's the month of Halloween!" Lena declared randomly.

"We still have another thirty days to get through first." I tried to ground her before she got too excited and her impatience for the event would overtake the enjoyment of the occasion. It wasn't working and she continued on obliviously.

"I'm going to dress as a vampire pup." Lena's mind was preoccupied, no doubt so that she didn't have to think about the separation at the gates. Just like her, I was starting to dread the moment that we parted when I had to trust someone else to help Lena like I did. I was torn by the instinct I had to keep her home where she was safe, and the fear of the consequence or proceedings that could happen if I did go against the status quo. I felt like we were in a no-win situation. I continued with the rhythm, robotically, unsure what the answer really needed to be.

I was expecting a showdown at the reception, but Lena just froze instead. My favourite receptionist, who was still undeserving of being referred to by her actual name, smiled falsely as her words condescendingly fell off her tongue, "Come on, Lena, you're not in nursery or reception anymore. You're a big girl now!"

I'm not sure if she actually believed that was going to work or whether she just found enjoyment creating havoc for a bit of entertainment. Lena clearly wasn't moving, so the receptionist went off to fetch the class teaching assistant from Year One.

"Miss Young is here," the receptionist stated, "off you go, Lena." I could tell by her tone that we were always viewed as an inconvenience to her day. Lena didn't budge and the receptionist sighed loudly. I felt even more pressure that Lena wasn't conforming.

The teaching assistant crouched down to talk in a soft voice. "Would you like to come and help with some of the morning jobs, Lena?"

There was still no reply from Lena who was stuck like a statue.

"I need an assistant to collect the class registers and the lunch bands." Miss Young tried again. "Do you think you could help me?"

Lena nodded. The teaching assistant held her small, quivering hand and they set off through the reception office together. I had the usual butterflies not knowing how the morning would go, and more importantly, how Lena would be coping.

I walked home briskly, doing the same route we had earlier, but cutting the time in half. My mum arrived to pick Charlie up just as I reached the back door and set foot in the house – I had asked her earlier to babysit as I had intentions of trying something new.

"So, where is it you're heading off to, Sarah dear?" Mum asked with a puzzled look.

"Erm," I stalled as I thought carefully about how I was going to word this. "Just to a social group."

I had to avoid the actual details of the type of social group it was going to be, as I didn't want to reignite another subject with her that simply got me cross. It was so difficult biting my tongue when I needed her support to have the children, whilst balancing my own internal dialogue at the same time.

"Did you ask Julie to go with you?" Mum had a frown that was getting deeper as she continued. "I did hear that she asked you to go to a baby group with her and you closed down her attempt to repair your relationship. You know, Sarah, this is a two-way street. One day, she might give up on you if you keep giving her the cold shoulder. I mean, she didn't even know that you and Nick had separated until I told her. She wasn't happy to hear it second-hand."

I could feel the injustice rise inside. I mean, it wasn't like I was just doing this all on purpose. Could my mum not see any of the underlying problems at play between her daughters? As always in our family, any conflict was swept under the carpet.

"I'd better go, Mum, or I'll be late." I picked my car keys up and grabbed my just-in-case bag to make a well-needed exit out of the back door.

"Maybe you could give Julie a little tinkle on the journey and see if she wants to join next time?" Crikey – would she ever give up?

"Uh huh," I replied in a non-committed tone (ready to superimpose the truth better than a politician). "I'll check to see if it's up Julie's street first."

"Poor you," Mum said with an overly sympathetic tone, which made me shoot her a last glance back to see what she was going to say next. "Sarah, there is no shame in asking Nick to give things another try. I mean, you really don't want to be approaching forty and having to go to social groups for a bit of interaction. Being a woman at *your age* on your own can be extremely lonely, don't forget. Next thing you know, you'll feel that desperate you'll be turning to one of those rabbits for company."

As much as I had tried to contain my feelings, I couldn't help but slam the back door in response to her words (not that it would have made a difference – my mother seemed to lack the ability to read my emotions). I jumped into the car and drove to the town centre, then parked up, before walking through the old part of the town that led to the church.

I wasn't on the prowl for another man! I was actually heading to a support group for parents of children or young people who were autistic, and I hadn't wanted to discuss this with my mum when I didn't even have a diagnosis for Lena as yet. It was also the reason that I knew Julie wouldn't be able to go – because she wasn't a parent in the same category. The flyer stated that a diagnosis wasn't necessary; if the child or young person was waiting on a diagnostic pathway, then this was sufficient. I felt nervous and like an imposter going somewhere that I probably shouldn't be going. Okay, so Lena wasn't on a waiting list as yet, but even the professionals who came to the house had seen indicators, so I knew I wasn't just imagining these things. I wavered as I climbed the church steps. I took a deep breath before opening the large door to see a group of strangers that I didn't know. I tried to calm myself down, after all, what was the worst that could happen?

The room was set up with a banner for the support network and some bullet points with rules about being in the group. It was being run by an older guy, with a walking stick and limited mobility. He had a pony tail and a smile that was as welcoming as the sun. He spotted me trembling as I walked into the room and stopped before the circle of seated adults.

"Would you like a tea or a coffee?" His warm voice was all I needed to hear to put my worries at bay.

"Oh, a coffee, please. That's very kind," I replied.

"How do you take it?" He beamed as he limped over to the side table where there was an out-dated urn and some cups.

"Just white and no sugar, thank you." I smiled and felt the weight on my shoulders starting to lift.

"I'm Jacob," he said softly, pouring the water and stirring in the milk to finish the coffee. "Welcome to the group and thank you for joining us."

"I'm Sarah," I directed my speech towards him. It was too frightening to look at the individuals in the group.

"Have a seat, Sarah. And here's your coffee." I sat down as I took a warm mug of inviting coffee in my shaky hands.

Jacob sat in his seat in the neatly-assembled circle of chairs, and got the group underway. He asked to go around the circle and do a brief introduction of who everyone was and the child/young person that they were there for. My heart stopped in my throat. I found it difficult to listen to everyone else's situations because my mind was preoccupied about having to speak out in front of the group. What would I say? Would they think I didn't belong?

Some of the people's stories hit a chord with me and I was momentarily distracted from my social anxiety and imposter syndrome (and the earlier frustration with dealing with my well-meaning mother). A couple of the parents were also dealing with schools who thought that their children were fine, and they felt that their parenting was always being criticised or blamed.

"Hi, I'm Susanna," the next lady spoke out, "I have three children who all have complex needs." I only had one to contemplate and that felt stressful enough, I was a little in awe of her strength as she spoke so confidently with a smile on her face. As I continued to listen to the struggles from other parents, I realised that I was in exactly the right place. Could I learn to be as knowledgeable as these parents who seemed like they were strides ahead of me? I was starting to feel empowered and inspired by the resilience of people I had only just met. It didn't feel like I was an outsider anymore.

Jacob even introduced his own family as we reached the half-way mark of the group.

"So, you all know, I'm Jacob," he began brightly. "Some of you might not know that I was brought into this journey by my son, Alfie, who is now not quite as young as many of your young people."

We all smiled back at Jacob and I was curious to hear more.

"We had an interesting route through education," Jacob continued. "With many exclusions, risk-taking and truanting, which eventually led to a dark underworld of drink and drugs. Alfie found himself facing a small jail sentence, but it was actually a blessing in disguise. He found a way to self-educate himself whilst he was inside, where a diagnosis of ADHD also became apparent. A trial of medication helped him in many ways, and once stable, he finally found he could make sense of who he really is. The rest is history, but you could say it inspired me to run this group to empower other families like we needed in those early days."

I felt humbled just listening to what Jacob had been through. I felt a deep appreciation and awe of the group leader already and inspired by the journey he had been on. If he could turn a bad situation around, then why couldn't I? I tried to make myself feel better about Lena as well, I mean, if we were on a pathway towards a diagnosis at this age, perhaps it would prevent the long-term damage of being misunderstood all her life. The realisation that Lena could end up like Alfie and be locked away scared me, but I was able to reassure myself that it wouldn't be our situation because I was making the steps this early. I couldn't bear the pain of knowing what Jacob's son had been through. It also made me think about the types of people who were locked up in prison or in mental health units – were many of them undiagnosed from earlier needs and had fallen down slippery paths?

It was finally my turn to talk. My heart began to beat heavily as I began an introduction.

"Hi everyone, I'm Sarah," I stumbled. "I'm so sorry. I'm a little nervous... but I'll try to give it a go."

Jacob leant forward and winked at me reassuringly. I took a deep breath in and continued.

"I'm here because my five-year-old daughter, Lena, is extremely spirited and determined, to say the least." I rolled my eyes with exaggerated humour. "She struggles with school and refuses to go a lot! In fact, sometimes she refuses the things that she does like doing like going to the park."

"That's tough," Jacob acknowledged.

"It really is," I paused, "I also recently split up from my husband and now have two children alone. That's a story for another day I'm sure, but if I'm honest, half of the reason we broke up was because we were at loggerheads at the way we needed to parent Lena. Her father is deep-rooted in discipline, but I feel that Lena's challenges are much more complex than that. She's on an assessment waiting list for social communication challenges, but I have recently dis-covered something called Pathological Demand Avoidance and I think this could explain my daughter."

"I think my son Luca is PDA too!" a lady with a softly-cut bob said. "We can chat in the break as it's good to know another parent in the same boat. I'm Flick by the way." She smiled, her eyes were friendly. I began to feel a bit more relaxed now I had finally beaten my fears to talk in front of the group of strangers.

"What is PDA?" one of the other ladies, who was named Jamiliah, asked towards my direction.

"I'm not that knowledgeable with it yet," I said hesitantly. "It's sort of when someone needs to be in control, but it actually stems from anxiety. The PDA part means they struggle with the everyday demands of life."

"So are they autistic or not?" Jamiliah queried. My fears of being an imposter in a group where I didn't belong were rising back up to the surface. I felt under pressure because the spotlight was on me and I was fearful of saying something wrong. I didn't want to answer a question about something I barely knew anything about.

Jacob must have sensed it; he politely intercepted the question for me. "That's a great question, and if you don't mind, Sarah, I'll continue." He seemed intuitive as if he could actually read my thoughts.

I smiled, relieved. "No, please, go ahead."

"This might be something for everyone as it's the first time it's been mentioned in this group, so I'm glad Sarah has kickstarted the subject." Jacob smiled at me. I had to hand it to him, he knew how to make a group feel comfortable.

"Pathological Demand Avoidance," he continued confidently, "or PDA as it is often labelled, is a lesser-known profile on the autism spectrum. It was only discovered by Professor Elizabeth Newson in the 1980's. She was researching a group of children who seemed like they were autistic, but yet they almost seemed *different*. Through her research she noticed that they had an underlying need to be in control which was rooted in anxiety. These children were often very sociable and used their skills to avoid demands that were placed upon them. The problem with PDA is that it is still very under-researched and challenged by various professionals. This has led to it being like a postcode lottery trying to get the profile recognised and getting the right support and strategies in place to support our young people."

"You're the first person I've spoken to who really knows about it," I confessed to Jacob. I had tears welling up in my eyes at the sheer feeling of being understood.

"It's something I've researched a lot over the last few years. I believe Alfie could be undiagnosed PDA as a lot of it fits him too," Jacob explained.

"Wow!" I felt connected to this stranger more than I was to most of my own family.

"I think it can be quite common to have comorbid presentations alongside diagnoses such as ADHD," Jacob explained. "Although not all of the time." I realised right then that I knew nothing about ADHD either – I wondered if it could be something adding to Lena's challenges too.

We had soon completed all of the introductions, and then Jacob went around the circle and used his hands as indicators to shift us into three smaller groups. We were given some scrap paper and a pen as we waited patiently to hear the instructions for the task ahead.

"I would like you all to brainstorm ways you can advocate for your young people as they transition into a new year group," Jacob instructed.

This was a real eye-opener because I learnt that there were so many 'legal' adjustments we could ask for in order to help our children cope with starting a new academic year. I pulled my old diary from my just-in-case bag and jotted down some notes for myself. I learnt that I could ask for things like a 'soft start' where Lena could take her time to come in and start an activity that was low-demanding to decrease her anxiety. There were other ideas like being met by a key adult each morning so that she started to build trust with the new teachers. I could also ask for her to have more sensory movement breaks when she was struggling, and maybe to not be sitting down in order for her to listen. So many ideas. My brain was starting to feel alive with the passion and confidence that I could help my daughter access school a little easier.

It was soon the break and Flick tapped me on the arm and asked: "Would you like another coffee? There are some chunky cookies on offer today, I think Jacob has spoilt us!"

"Yes, please." I nodded eagerly like I was in a nursery class and desperately wanted to make a best friend. Flick could have taken me to watch a group of pigs be slaughtered and I would have still followed along, nodding my head excitedly.

"It's so nice to have someone else here who understands PDA," Flick began confidently. "You know it's a nightmare getting a diagnosis in this county – they say it doesn't exist. I can't tell you how many paediatricians I've argued with, eventually they gave me the words 'Autism with Significant Demand Avoidance' just to shut me up!"

I laughed on cue. I think my lips were still going like a caricature – part with nerves and part with childlike relief that I thought I was being accepted and liked. There was a nervous silence and I realised it was my turn to reciprocate the conversation, but I hadn't fully concentrated.

"So, have you been to this group before?" I quickly asked.

"Oh yeah, plenty of times." Flick was trying to pin her flyaway bob behind her ears whilst she held her coffee cup under the urn. "I think I had Jacob on speed dial for quite some time. He's such a lovely man, most people would have told me to jog-on after the first few calls! He just helped me to be calm and was there for me, better than my own family."

"I can relate to that," I commiserated, "if it wasn't for my two best friends and our gin o' clock calls I don't know where I would be."

"They sound like my kind of people!" Flick laughed and I joined in.

"They are amazing." I could feel my face tingling with pride. "They say you can pick your friends but you can't pick your family." I paused as I gathered my thoughts. "I can't talk about this with my family because they make some wise crack that I'm trying to put a label on my child. They claim people who label their children are just trying to make excuses for them being naughty and they need a good spanking!"

Flick half coughed and half laughed. "Excuse me!" She tapped her chest. "Woah, that last nugget just shocked me!"

"I know." I rolled my eyes. "The ignorance is shocking."

"Oh my! Sometimes we just can't get others to see past their outdated views," Flick comforted. "I don't think my family are quite so outright with their opinions, but then I have to face the silences and hidden judgements. The looks on their faces give it away, anyway. I tend to ignore it now. I've changed how I go about it too. Besides, we don't visit family anymore if we can help it. I go by the philosophy that when they want to see us, then they can come to our house and they have to adjust to the way our individual family operates. If they don't like it, then they know where the door is. Simple."

"I think I need to adopt your approach." I confessed. "Honestly, Lena is always worse when she's around my family. I'm sure they kind of set her off. I think I've been trying to make her fit into what everyone needs her to be for far too long."

"Don't be so hard on yourself," Flick said sympathetically. "We all get pushed into this until we finally see the light."

"It's just so hard when everyone tells you that you're doing it wrong and you're the reason behind the problem." I was confiding more to my newly-acquired friend than I had done to people I had known for years. "You start to doubt yourself and eventually you end up believing what they say."

"Yep, I know that all too well," she replied. "I just tell myself to FTS – Fuck That Shit! Sorry if you don't like swearing, but it's kind of my new mantra and it seems to be working."

I laughed loudly. "I think I need to hear that on repeat every time I have to cope with someone telling me how I should be parenting Lena! Don't worry, I'm not easily offended. I must say, this parenting malarkey has made me a terrible swearer myself."

Flick continued to make light-hearted conversation about her son, who was fourteen, and had finally found a coach at boxing that was helping him to channel his energy. "James, the coach, just gets it. I think he was a bit of a tearaway himself when he was a youngster, that's why he's so good at understanding and meeting Luca where he is at. I think they just need someone who treats them with respect and they get it back in abundance."

We were soon called back to bring ourselves together into a group. It was hard for Jacob to get us all to stop nattering and to re-focus – like a group of kids who had been interrupted during a sugar rush. You could definitely feel the tension had lifted and we were all warmly lubricated enough to socialise.

"Before you all go," Jacob concluded, "I'd like to set you a small task to do at home before the next group session. It's often so hard for parents and carers to find any 'me time' but it's essential to our wellbeing. You know, it's just like that analogy on an aeroplane – you have to put your own oxygen mask on before you can put on your child's."

"I like that one," said Flick, "I need to remember that next time I'm being pestered when I'm in the shower!"

The whole group laughed together and we felt even closer.

"So, the task to take away home from today is this..." Jacob smiled. "...Can you find ten minutes every day to do something for you?"

"I can't fly abroad to lie on a beach in ten minutes!" Flick added with a bit of jest that gave rise to another communal giggle.

"I think we all wish we could do that!" Jacob laughed and his pony tail almost joined in with the rhythm. "Actually, it's good you made light of that because it also hits an important point. Often, we have goals that are unreachable and then we feel more frustrated that we can't do them. We also then compare ourselves to what we believe other adults are doing too. It just becomes a cycle of negativity. Now, I'm not saying Flick can't whizz off on a flight to a tropical holiday, I sincerely hope you can."

"Cheers, Jacob." Flick smiled. "I think I owe you a plane ticket just for the sheer volume of calls I've made to you over the last year!"

Everyone laughed again and the atmosphere felt more like a party than a support group with a room full of strangers who barely knew each other. I sat there quietly in my own solitude for a moment. I felt a pang of apprehension that my friends were taking me away on a weekend break soon and I was stepping away from it all. I felt embarrassed; the joke in the group was about to be my reality. I feared that maybe I was letting the children down by going. I kept it to myself and tried to tune back into the group's conversation.

"I'd come anytime!" Jacob replied, then recaptured his discussion ahead of the next session. "So, by next time, it would be great if we could all give feedback on something we made the time for in our day that was just for ourselves. It doesn't have to be elaborate, I mean it could be taking ten minutes to sit in our own thoughts with a cuppa, or time to read, listen to music, have a bath, a walk around the block maybe. I think you all get the picture. Just something you enjoy, to not be Mum or Dad, or Grandparent or Carer. Not to be writing an email or cooking dinner. Just being you."

We all made our goodbyes and Flick gave me her number as I

left the room. "Remember," she said on parting, "FTS!"

I was still laughing as I walked back home to get a few chores done before it was time to pick up Lena. I thought about what I would enjoy doing that would make me feel a little like my old self. I remembered when I was younger and how much I used to get from doing sports, although that made me feel even more frustrated knowing how much I had let it slip. Instead of doing anything about it, I just fuelled the problem even more by over-eating and drinking too much alcohol, meaning that I felt even more unable to return to feeling fit again. I remembered that feeling of having energy and the adrenaline that used to surge through me when I would compete at sport. I felt like I was invincible.

I fired up the laptop, and with Rex jumping up my leg for a cuddle, I had one hand stroking his ears and the other typing out with a wobble the keyword search: 'Couch to 5k'. Instantly I logged onto the NHS website and found a weekly plan of running for beginners and printed the details off. I found a magnet of myself with the kids on the fridge, and pinned it up, knowing that if I saw the plan every day it might just motivate me to eat and drink a little less. I remembered Nick's words about me trying to run again and how he had brought me down poking fun at my unfitness. *I'll show him.*

I reflected on the support session and how rejuvenated I felt having been around people who were in a similar situation. It was almost euphoric – as if my body had been pumped with endorphins, just like the energy I used to have when I was doing sport when I was younger. I remembered the conversation with the girls about feeling like I was living in a black rainbow and how they had made the suggestion to find ways to fill layers of colour back again. It prompted me to text them and touch base.

I picked up my phone to send a message to my girlfriends.

> Hey ladies. I plucked up the courage and went to an autism support group this morning. I feel like I've finally found my people (other than you two) – they totally understood! I think I've taken your advice and found the first colour for my rainbow. Red is for tribe! I feel like I have some control back, there is a plan. I have you guys to thank xx

I didn't have a chance to wait for a reply as my phone started ringing more or less straight away. It was my favourite receptionist who was about to zap away those endorphins I had only just experienced.

"Ms Forte," penetrated the voice, "you need to come to school straight away."

"Why?" I was confused.

"Lena has absconded from the premises!" she responded without any sensitivity in her voice. She didn't care what impact her words had on my emotions.

"Where has she gone?" I demanded. "Are you saying you've lost her?!"

"If we knew that then we wouldn't be calling you." I could detect a hint of defence in her voice.

"How on earth do you NOT know where she is?" I could hear myself screeching.

"We've called the police and they're out searching for her," the receptionist retorted.

"The police!" I yelled. "This cannot be happening!"

I hung up the phone wildly. She was just my baby. Where the hell was she? *Please don't tell me something bad has happened to my baby!*

12

Camels Avoid Sand

My legs were pumped and my eyes were wild. I could feel shards of pain piercing through my breaking heart. Where were my keys? I couldn't think straight. What did I need? I didn't need anything. I just needed to get there as fast as I could.

I jumped into the car and revved up the engine, forgetting to put my seatbelt on in the process. My thoughts were jumbled, it was like my body was going into operative mode but I wasn't sure who was in control of the actions. My driving felt erratic but I was unable to do anything about it. I could smell the taste of heat in the air and my breath was misting up the window screen. There wasn't a second to balance myself or feel any emotion. I was driven by a force that was cursing through my entire body – as if there was a puppeteer above my head and I wasn't in control of the situation at all.

Waves of nausea were enveloping my body and permeating into the atmosphere. I couldn't look straight ahead at the oncoming traffic; I was frantically looking out of each window, desperately hoping to see a glimpse of Lena's green uniform and her strawberry blonde hair. My whole being was shaking in horror, desperately fearing to see an image I would never forget. Where was my little baby? What if something terrible happened to her? She could be run over. A stranger could have taken her. What if I never saw her beautiful, freckly face again?

I couldn't bear the thought of the tragic possibilities that could lie ahead of me. The more images that popped into my brain, the more I felt like I was suffocating. My breath was getting shorter. My legs felt like the blood had gathered in my calves as the muscles were tight and full of adrenaline.

I jumped out of the car, leaving the door open. I didn't give two hoots about any part of my reality, I was driven purely by survival instinct to rescue my infant.

I buzzed the button at the school gate and the receptionist let me in without speaking. I sprinted down the pathway that led to the office, my keys jangling frantically in my hands. Mrs Ramsbottom was in the office with the new teacher – Mrs Carter – and the receptionist.

They all stood still in silence as if they were defendants in a courtroom.

"Have you found her yet?" I screamed in an animalistic voice that even I didn't know I was capable of. It shocked them and I'm sure the vibrations of my anger continued to shake them.

"I'm afraid we haven't. We were waiting for you to get here in order to join the search effort." Mrs Ramsbottom attempted to take control of the situation.

"You should have been out there looking for her!" I was not the quiet, amenable walk-over that they had been so used to dealing with.

"Please be assured, Ms Forte, that we are dealing with it." Mrs Ramsbottom was not holding my eye contact. "We already have four police patrols searching for her. There was talk from an officer that they will get a helicopter out if she is not located very soon."

"What if she goes home and I'm not there?" I cried, tears were starting to roll down my flaming cheeks.

"Could you ask somebody to be there, just in case?" Mrs Carter interjected strategically.

I picked out my phone and reluctantly made the dreaded call to Nick. Each ring that was not answered felt like an eternity. He finally picked up.

"Nick, it's me. There's an emergency. Lena's run away from school. I'm out looking for her and I need someone to go back to the house in case she goes home first," I rushed through the snippets of information in haste so as not to lose any precious time.

"What the fuck, Sarah!" Nick bellowed so loudly that I was pretty sure the staff in the entire school could hear. "How could they lose a kid?!?"

I wasn't ready to answer the question in front of them. More importantly, I was, for once, on the same page as Nick, thinking the exact same thing.

I soon put the phone down and shouted to the school staff, "I'm going to start looking. You need to call me if there's any news."

"Of course," Mrs Ramsbottom assured in a squeaky-clean voice. "Do you have any idea where she could have gone?"

"Knowing Lena she could be anywhere!" I cried.

As I left the school, a police car was driving up the path. It parked in front of the office.

"Have you found her yet?" I shouted over to the two officers.

"We're still searching," they replied apologetically. "We've been over to Queen's Field and are now moving a bit further out."

I ran out of the gate and began pacing the streets in a desperate mission to bring my baby back home.

My phone rung and I picked up hoping there was some good news. It was just Nick who had arrived at the house. Nobody was there. He asked if there was any more news.

"I need to keep the line free," I uttered, "I'll call you if we find her."

As I hung up, I looked across at some of the hedges blocking off the school's border and wondered if they'd searched them proper-ly. Could she still be hidden in the border playing hide-and-seek? Or was she trying to rescue some wildlife and been so concealed that they didn't spot her?

It felt like I was looking for a needle in a haystack; the more I looked at my surroundings, the more places she could be were popping into my mind.

Minutes were beginning to feel like hours of intense pain. With every impending second the situation was feeling graver. I had visions of newspaper headlines shooting across my mind and im-ages of a child being abducted by a masked individual and pushed against their will through the side door of some unknown van. I was so cross with the school for not doing their job properly. If she had felt safe, then she would never have felt the need to run away!

My stomach was in my throat with waves of uncontrollable sick-ness, my legs were feeling like they were moving in some strange extra-terrestrial world that I was estranged from. The thoughts were chopping in front of my eyes and it was impossible to have a coherent conversation with myself. *Try to think straight, Sarah. Where could she have gone?*

I suddenly had a memory about the park at Queen's Field, where we often visited, and her obsession with the orange slide. Was it a possibility she could have gone there? It was on the way home – maybe she had seen it and stopped to play. But the officers had already checked there, what if I was wasting valuable time?

I took the plunge and ran along the pavement, trying to get there as fast as I could. The adrenaline was kicking me into action and I didn't even need to stop for breath. I was a fierce mama bear desperately searching for her helpless cub in the most dangerous of worlds.

I finally reached Queen's Field and could see the playground at the far side of the common. I carried out a speedy search, frantically scanning the surroundings in the hope of a possible sign. As I swung the gate open to the park, I saw a green cardigan on the soft tarmac and felt an instant surge of relief. I looked up towards the top of the orange slide. Lena was positioned, solemnly still, blocking the path of the slide.

"Lena!" I called, barely able to recognise my own voice.

"Mummy!" Her face told a deep story of relief. "Why did you take so long?" Lena slid down the meandering slide and I was there at the bottom to swing her into my arms and kiss her tear-strained, rosy cheek.

She nestled her head deep into my clothes and collapsed into the biggest sobbing breaths her small body could chamber. I picked my phone out of my pocket and called Nick.

"It's okay," I told him, relief flooding my voice. "I've found her."

"Thank fucking hell!" Nick cried. I could hear the tension releasing from his voice. "Something needs to be done about this!"

I rang school to tell them the news too. I was immediately transferred to Mrs Ramsbottom who adopted her usual voice of superiority.

"I think it is in everybody's interests that you take Lena home today and we will be in touch when we feel that we can have her back in school," she instructed.

I hung up the phone. I wasn't in any place to think straight or to be able to articulate any answer. I made a mental note – yes, another one – to email her once I was back home to hold her to account and to ask how on earth they had managed to lose my little girl.

We turned around and started walking back towards Sunnybank School. Lena froze to the spot, refusing to take one more step. I crouched down to her eye level and softly whispered to her that she wouldn't be going back to school today. I explained that my car had been abandoned outside the front gate and I needed to drive it home. She reluctantly agreed to continue with the journey and we walked silently together, her little hand in mine.

Her small voice eventually broke the solitude, "They shouted and put me on the sad cloud because I didn't sit on the carpet."

How could they do that? To be reprimanded and shamed in front of the class when I had already informed them that this was something that caused her discomfort. The information had clearly not been communicated to all of the staff members working with Lena or they could have done something about it (no doubt they knew nothing about the PDA profile and strategies I had asked them to read about). No wonder she took flight after that! I didn't know what had ignited in me, but the fuel of fire was deep inside my core and there was no turning back. I had put up with too much of their nonsense for far too long. The dreaded fear whilst Lena was missing was beginning to subside, and in place of it was the greatest surge of anger and frustration.

It was at that moment that I realised it was never Lena that was the problem, she was perfectly being herself, it was Sunnybank that had been causing the problem. She had told them what she couldn't do, I had told them how they could support her, but they'd carried on punishing her regardless. Why was her voice not seen as important as an adult's one? Did they think this was teaching her to be a respectful child?

It was the straw that had broken the camel's back. It had been building for so long and yet something so simple like making an adjustment to not sitting on the carpet they couldn't just do it. I felt infused with knowledge from the support group I'd just attended. Surely the school had to weigh up the outcome from not being flexible enough?

"I hate sitting on the carpet, Mummy!" My rambling internal dialogue was interrupted by Lena's defiant voice. "It's itchy! They make me cross my legs! It hurts! And the bobbly bits stink worse than Rex's farts."

We both laughed together with some much-needed relief.

"I told them NO when they told me to sit down! The other

children were all sitting on there and were looking at me. I didn't like it. Then Mrs Carter pulled me by my arm..." she trailed off as she hurriedly stood up to re-enact the tale of events (as she often resorted to when trying to rely on being able to explain something to me).

As she held her twisted arm up, she continued "...And she pushed me on the carpet and it hurt even more. So I stood up." She jumped back up from the cold pavement. "And told her she's not the boss of me. I stuck my tongue out and ran out the door."

With that, Lena ran off and turned to show me her tongue-sticking finale.

"Mrs Ramsbottom was chasing me around the playground like this," as she spun in circles, "she's like the mean *Mayor Humdinger* in *Paw Patrol*. So I told her she was a smelly humdinger in the land of *Foggy Bottom*."

My eyes widened as Lena continued her one-way story.

"She screamed at me saying I was a very rude, little girl!"

"Maybe she isn't quite so well versed in *Paw Patrol*?" I offered neutrally. "She might not have understood that they live in *Foggy Bottom*? Or who *Humdinger* is, for that matter?"

"Well, she's an adult," Lena retorted angrily. "She should know these things already!"

I changed the subject: "Would you like to play *Paw Patrol* when we get home?" I tried to use the most nurturing and supportive tone of voice to show Lena I was on her side. It was a strategic move to throw her off-course as I was trying to prevent the onset of a meltdown from exploding.

I was not going to put up with it any longer, I meant business and I felt empowered remembering Flick's words (from the support group) that I needed to 'Fuck that Shit!' I had the swear words circling my brain and I couldn't quite believe myself – it was like I was having a complete change of personality. I wasn't sure if that was a good thing or a bad thing, but I could no longer control my submissive nature any longer.

Once home, I picked up my phone and sent my first message to Flick.

> Hi Flick, this is Sarah from the Spectrum Support Group, I hope you are well? I just wanted to tell you that I used your slogan today and it felt good! Can you believe the school lost Lena today?! I found her in a park and they had the cheek to say not to bring her back! Looks like I'll be needing to say FTS for quite some time! I hope to see you at the next support group x

My phone rang shortly afterwards and it was Flick. I was so glad I had chosen to reach out to her. I reeled off the events of the day and she was flabbergasted by what had happened. To be listened to and to feel a sense of connection was just what I needed. I cried and I apologised through the tears. I felt like a mess and my embarrassment was seeping through.

"Don't be silly," Flick comforted. "I'm a safe space for you any time."

"That's very kind of you," I expressed through the tears.

"It's a pleasure to help," Flick replied. "I can't imagine what you went through today, that's pretty traumatic for any parent."

"I was so scared I'd never see her again!" I wept. "It was completely avoidable as well. I had already told the school what was triggering her and they didn't share the information or even acknowledge my bloody emails!"

"This really needs to be sorted." Flick took control positively. "Can you request a meeting at school to discuss it?"

"Yes, I'll do that," I answered gratefully.

"Keep me updated, won't you?" Flick suggested.

"Yes of course."

After a few days of recuperation at home, and an email chasing Mrs Ramsbottom about what the school were going to be doing in the long-term situation and to organise a meeting, the phone suddenly rang. The contact number for Sunnybank popped up on my phone and I had the suspicion that they were trying to avoid putting any details down in writing. Maybe it was a sign of guilt or maybe it was just a sign that they were trying to plot something by being underhand. Either way, my trust in them and the system as a whole, was completely shattered.

"Oh, hello there, Ms Forte," drawled the voice on the other end of the receiver. She had a twang of an American accent. "If you will, please let me start by introducing myself. My name is Veronica Webb and I am the Special Educational Needs Co-ordinator at Sunnybank – or SENCO as it's abbreviated to. My apologies, it has taken so long for me to make contact. As I'm sure you can imagine, we have a lot of children in our school with additional needs and we have to prioritise those who need more support."

"Lena has needed support for quite some time," I spoke coldly. I wasn't ready to be sweet-talked by any more of these un-committing professionals.

"Oh yes," she quickly backtracked. "Lena has been high on our list for a while. I try to get around all of the children that need my support and so forth."

"Yes, but this is the first time you're phoning me. Lena should have been top of your priority when you put her on a reduced timetable, and not after the moment you lost her from school."

She cleared her throat and took a moment of silence. She was clearly rattled. Even from the silence over the receiver, I could picture her face looking like she had just bitten a lemon.

"If you will, Mrs Ramsbottom and I have been discussing how we can find a way to have Lena back in school and we're quite concerned about the risks she poses. Not just to herself, but to the other children too."

"And... ?" I prompted.

"We have drafted a risk assessment that we will be sending over to you so that you can read through it and sign if you're in agreement." She was using a soft approach and it made me wonder what was going to be written on this paperwork.

"What will be on the risk assessment?" I enquired sharply.

"Oh, well, um." She hesitated a while. "Just a list of the risks that could potentially happen with Lena and an agreed plan to cope if they happen."

"I will have to read through it before I agree to it," I concluded.

"Yes, of course," Mrs Webb reassured. "We would never ask a parent to sign something that they hadn't seen or they were not comfortable with."

"Okay," I muttered. I had no ability to say more than that.

"We were also going to suggest to you, Ms Forte, that we're considering the idea of applying for your family to be put on a plan with the support from the 0-25 Together Team at Social Services."

"What's that?" I asked, feeling alarmed. Social services?

"It's not as frightening as you might think. We can refer Lena to be placed on a plan called a TAC – which stands for the Team Around a Child. It is simply a way of bringing all professionals around the table and agreeing the right outcomes for our young people who need that extra support and so forth." Her constant adding 'if you will' and 'so forth' into her utterances was beginning to rile me.

"I'll have to research and look at what it entails," I said, still alarmed by the dreaded social services suggestion. I wasn't ready to accept that anything Sunnybank offered would actually be in Lena's, or our family's, interests.

"Actually, it might come with some funding so we can put more in place for Lena and to help you as a family," the SENCO finished.

Oh here we go, I thought, it was a way for the school to claim money and avoid using their own budget to put in provision for a child that was going to cost them extra. That was their tactic. I said nothing. I knew I was being hard work and probably not very co-operative, but seeing as they had the lack of ability to keep my daughter safe, or to understand the adjustments she needed to feel better at school, or to even respond to my emails, they were therefore being treated to my awkward approach.

"Also, we thought that we could put in a referral to the local Pupil Referral Unit, or the PRU as you might hear us refer to it as, so that we get one of their outreach workers to come and do a bit of work with Lena."

"What would be the purpose of that?" I asked curiously. "I don't think being sent into a unit is actually in Lena's best interests, do you?"

"If you will, the PRU can share their practices with staff and they might be able to unpick a bit of Lena's behaviour issues in school," she explained in an arrogant manner. "They come to see the child and deliver a weekly session with them. Lena doesn't need to go into their unit as such."

"Are they trained to work with autistic children?" I questioned. I knew I was being oppositional but I had lost faith that bringing someone new in would make any difference. What if they were just the same as the school?

"They're the local experts and work with a range of children with social, emotional and educational needs." Mrs Webb paused. "Incorporated in that will be many children with autism. However, we don't have a diagnosis of autism at present so we can't put the provision in place until we know that for sure. I mean, I've worked with kids with autism and it doesn't strike me that Lena fits the bill."

"That's not what the professionals have said who came to my home," I declared. "And besides, what will happen in the mean-time? Will you be putting Lena with a one-to-one teaching assistant to make sure she is looked after at all times?"

There was a long pause. I could feel the tension on the call; this was going to be the bit that they obviously didn't want documented. "We think it is in Lena's best interests if she just attends those outreach sessions to start, Ms Forte. After all, we don't want a reoccurrence of the day she ran away. We can start building her time back up from there."

I was in utter shock. It felt like their actions were showing their desire to get rid of Lena from the school for good.

"So, if you're in agreement, we will require you to pop into school to sign the referral for the PRU? We can get you to complete the form to set up the TAC and then acknowledge receipt of the risk assessment and so forth?"

"Fine!" I concluded. My decisiveness shook the call reception and it echoed through the radio waves. My goodness I was on fire – I had been extra fuelled by her irritating phrases on repeat.

"The sooner the better, as I'm sure you are aware, these processes often take time." There was a hint of an agenda behind her words, I was sure.

I muttered a response and then pretty much hung up the call without making any further pleasantries. How could they have her in school only once a week? How could they not see they were failing her? It felt so unfair. My anger towards a system of inequality for children who needed extra support, but were not receiving it, was propelling me at force. Then there was the added pressure that I was due to go back to work in a few months' time. How on earth was I going to manage that? I mean, how were parents supposed to cope when they had a child who was only allowed in school for one session a week? How could this even be legal? What about the financial pressure...? How was I expected to earn a wage whilst navigating this? There were so many questions exploding in my brain about the sheer complexity of having a child not in school and balancing the needs of my own life at the same time.

My brain stilled. Just three words: 'fuck that shit' were able to appear. They followed their own pattern – like a marble run along my neural pathways – until they had finally run out of their own force to roll any further.

I made a call to Shelley to see if she was free some time to babysit the children for me so that I could go into school and sign the dreaded paperwork. We made a plan for Friday afternoon, as Shelley was able to take half a day annual leave, and she said she could have the two of them over for a play date with their favourite adult who knew how to have fun! I reminded myself once again how lucky I was to have such solid and altruistic friendships when every other relationship in my life had gone to pot.

Friday arrived and I had decided to walk to school because I knew that I needed the fresh air and the exercise to start improving my mental health. Who was I kidding? The number one reason for opting to walk was actually because, in my mind, it delayed the arrival time to the school grounds. The need to avoid the vicinity of this particular educational establishment was stronger than a negative magnetic force. I started to wonder if this was how Lena felt. I was a fully grown adult and the school had the ability to give me the shakes. I never expected, as a new parent who was starting out their journey into parenthood, that the worst time of my life would be the simplest of acts like taking my daughter to school.

I buzzed through the gate and entered the reception. I didn't even need to look up to know my favourite receptionist was there, grimacing, because I could actually smell her through the glass screen. She had a stifled odour of out-dated poisoned perfume. She couldn't even give me the luxury of a greeting as she directed the instruction: "Sign in!"

I picked up the pen and, using the heaviest imprint to diffuse my frustration, I etched my name and the time I'd arrived in school. I tickled myself as I had the genius idea to sign myself as a funny prank name like 'Sarah person in'. The internal humour helped to fulfil the task, particularly as I had been spoken to so disparagingly.

The SENCO, Mrs Webb, was notified that I was there by an

internal walkie-talkie system, and seconds later she opened the locked door. It must have been something about the fact that I was now back on school grounds, because Mrs Webb altered her manner and said, "Oh, hi, Mum. Do you want to follow me?"

"I am not your mum," I said coldly. "Please could you refer to me as Ms Forte?"

Well that told her! I needed to be assertive to feel colours in my life, even if they felt as far away as finding a rainbow.

"Yes, sorry, of course," Mrs Webb stuttered, not meeting my gaze. "Not everyone has the same preference, so we err on the side of caution."

The walk to Mrs Webb's office was pretty boring; avoiding small talk was treacherously difficult to say the least. I was opting to remain silent as opposed to being unable to find the words to speak.

As we took the journey through the lunch hall, we got stuck at the exit door of the first building. Mrs Webb seemed to be having a fight with the lock. It amused me that the door was winning.

As she finally opened the door, exasperated, she gave a false smile and was having a one-way conversation with herself as she purported to be sweet. "Oh, crumbs, would you look at that! I can't even get out the door properly!" She squealed, "I really am so *special* sometimes."

She was guffawing at her own joke without having any realisation that she could have said something offensive. I couldn't believe she had just said *that* word. If this was the kind of terminology the special needs co-ordinator used, then what chance did the rest of the staff have with this person as their example?

I watched on like a viewer from another perspective. I had a tendency to be present but to be passively processing things instead of being active in the moment. It was like I had a superpower at absorbing every single piece of information in my environment and decoding it for future reference.

Crossing down the corridor into the second building, we passed the ever-appealing headteacher.

"Good afternoon, Mrs Webb," Mrs Ramsbottom sing-songed along with her usual sneer-like frown. "I'm pleased to see you have made contact with Lena's Mum."

"Good afternoon, Mrs Ramsbottom," echoed back Mrs Webb, responding robotically like a congregation of children in a school assembly. I wouldn't mind, but they probably had only just slurped down their fiftieth cup of tea for the day together in some locked-up room (where they buried innocent young bodies who couldn't complete their times tables), and yet their voices gave the indication of surprise as if they hadn't seen one another for a good year or more. It was clearly for my benefit.

Finally, we reached the office that was snuggled away next to the cube meeting room with a sign that said 'SLT' dangling from the top.

What could it stand for? I wondered. It made me giggle to myself when I spotted that if a U was added it could look quite inappropriate. I questioned why I had the ability to think the strangest of things at the most random of times, and was momentarily distracted. I saw a list of three names under the heading 'Senior Leadership Team' which then made sense of the SLT abbreviation.

Mrs Webb was pretty fast at passing me the relevant paperwork and asking me to sign in agreement. I took a while to read through the information in enough detail so that I could be sure of what I was agreeing to. I then asked Mrs Webb if it was possible for copies of what I had signed to keep a record of them at home. She was very compliant and left the room within seconds. I sat for a while, just waiting with my hands crossed neatly on the desk. I glanced around at some of the notices pinned onto the board and spotted a note about Lena, which was half-heartedly concealed under a list of children needing pupil plans.

I stood up and quietly lifted the cover to reveal a handmade poster that had the title '<u>Lena Forte</u>' boldly scribbled, in what looked like a Sharpie, and some ticked bullet points underneath. They read as follows:

- Please be vigilant if dealing with Lena's parent – Mum is anxious!

- Any concerns in behaviour please report to safeguarding lead

- Under no circumstances will her behaviour be tolerated

- We are looking at alternative options

- If another parent complains, ask them to put it in writing

- We need to build our evidence for a PE!

I had no time to take a screenshot on my phone, or to capture it perfectly in my memory, because the door swung open and Mrs Webb walked in carrying the papers. I quickly sat down, hoping she hadn't noticed. What did PE mean? Mrs Webb gave me a confused stare. It didn't matter; I knew what I had seen and I knew that my instinct had always been right – they were not approaching this in the right way and they were too busy with parental blame instead of assisting me with Lena's struggles. I had a sudden panic as the realisation hit me that they were plotting against us.

My eyes darted far away from the board and I tried to keep myself together until we walked back down the dull corridor, out through the walkway to the dining room, and out of the reception door. It only dawned on me as I was practically running down the pathway, that I had forgotten to sign back out of the reception, but there was no way I was going anywhere near it for quite some time.

How dare they label me as anxious! I was in my rights to be worried about my child – after all, it was the school that was supposed to be safeguarding Lena and they had bloody well lost her! The police had been called as a result and yet this got turned around on me as if I were the problem – an anxious parent! I felt powerless in my pursuit to stop these atrocities happening to my vulnerable family. The whole notice on the board was being used to pre-warn all of the staff in the school that, as Lena's parent, I was the root cause of the difficulties. This was like a witch hunt. A parenting trial based on ignorance and bias. I was so livid that my anger could not be contained.

I got home and made a call to Flick. Just as I was relaying the hidden information I burst into tears. I wasn't making a good impression on her as I couldn't hold myself together whenever we made contact. My anger had nowhere else to burn, so I was left with no alternative but to cathartically shed the heat as tears.

Flick had the ability to reassure me. "Remember, Sarah, they shouldn't be doing any of this stuff. You do realise it's illegal?"

"I didn't understand what a PE stood for but there wasn't enough time to look at it in detail." I exhaled deeply.

"It's short term for a 'Permanent Exclusion'. I've been here before with Luca, so I know the process from experience." Her voice was full of compassion and was just what I needed.

"Oh, jeez!" I exclaimed, in shock that I was facing the reality that my tiny five-year-old was likely to be expelled from school. How was that even possible? My mother's warnings were actually right for once.

"What they are doing is against the code of practice and the family legislation that is set in law too," Flick explained with confidence. "When a child has unmet needs, school should be making adjustments, putting in extra support or suggesting to apply for an EHCP – not asking parents to log bloody complaints! An exclusion should be a last resort, not as a method of evidence-building to get rid of a child who has unmet needs. That's without openly fabricating that you're anxious!"

"Hold on a minute," I interrupted, "can I ask, what is an EHCP?"

"An Educational Health Care Plan. They are given to children who might need more support than is typically provided in a school." I was feeling out of my depth. There was so much I didn't know. "Actually, they can stay in place until the individual is twenty-five so they're supported into adulthood, when needed."

"They've never even mentioned that to me!" I declared. "Which you would think they should have when they have a child who is hardly at school?!"

"Exactly!" Flick's voice was animated now. "They shouldn't just ask staff to document evidence for an exclusion when they've not gone down any advisory routes! Oh this is literally making my blood boil!"

"Yours and mine!" I felt so relieved to be talking to someone who could lead me in the right direction. It had always been in my gut, knowing that Lena wasn't being helped how she should be, but without the ability to act upon it.

"Sarah, I would definitely urge you to put this into an email confirming for the record the information you saw. Factually, of course. You could start with: 'Just to make you aware that some information on Lena was on the noticeboard compromising her personal data and it was of some concern. To summarise it said etc, etc...' and then reel off what they said they were doing. It will keep everything documented and you may need this further down the line. If nothing else, it shows their utter incompetence and tells them that you mean business!"

"I will do, thank you." I took a deep breath as if I were about to write the email in my mind instantly.

"Remember, keep to the facts and leave it with a question so they should respond. We both know they will try to get out of it, but it almost holds them accountable and ensures they reply. Or rather, it acknowledges that it's been seen."

I listened quietly, taking it all in.

Flick continued assuredly, "They can't exactly say you've made it up; they know it's the truth and they will be panic-stricken that you may have taken a photo of it and will share it all over social media to make a mockery of their unlawful shenanigans. Sorry, I'm on a rant now!"

"Thank you, again, so much." I was repeating myself and words could not do justice to how grateful I was for her invaluable advice.

"You're welcome."

"One last thing," I said, "they want me to sign a referral to the local PRU for an outreach worker and they also suggested applying to go on a TAC or something. I have agreed, I hope I've done the right thing?"

"I know the local PRU well and they're very clued up. I think it will be a support for both of you," she reassured me. "And the TAC? Well, they can be useful as they bring all of the professionals together which is something you've been lacking. It might just backfire on school and hold them more accountable. No doubt they probably think it's an easy way to get a bit of funding so they don't have to use their own budget that they get assigned for their students with additional needs!"

I was starting to admire Flick even more – she sounded like a lawyer.

"That's exactly what I thought too!" I replied in female unity. "But I kind of did it because I wanted to comply and seem like I'm working with them, if you know what I mean?"

"Yes, of course I do," Flick agreed. "Although, it shouldn't be like this and you shouldn't feel forced just to get them off their backsides to safeguard your child!"

"I know right!" I said. "I feel like I'm often in a no-win situation."

"I hear you," she said softly. "It's the reality of being a parent-carer in the UK, I'm afraid. But listen, when they set the meeting up, give me a shout. I can be there as a friend and an advocate. I might not be able to talk on your behalf, but I can be a pair of ears, or write you notes and can take minutes for you too. If nothing else, I'll be there to make sure the things that are being said are actually legit."

"That would be lovely," I said gratefully. "You're so generous, Flick."

"It's the least I can do." She began philosophically, "Remember, if you fall into a black hole it will always be another parent of an autistic young person that pulls you back out. Trust me, you will be there for the next parent who needs that person to lean on. We do it because we understand how screwed up the system is and we have deeper empathy levels because we just get it. Raising a child with any challenges helps you to appreciate the world from a much better vantage point."

"I won't ever forget it." I sighed. "One day I would love to give back to other parents too. Just like Jacob does and just like you're doing for me."

"That next parent who reaches out to you will be a very lucky one," Flick complimented me. "I knew instantly you were a caring, warrior kind of parent the moment you entered the Spectrum Support Group."

"Thank you," I muttered, "the parent-blaming has been such a confidence-stripping experience that I feel like it will take a long time to believe in myself. I need to take a leaf out of your book. I'm so scared of what they're trying to pin on me. I don't want them to take Lena off me!"

"Trust me, they don't have a chance." Flick jollied me up. "Never forget, you are Lena's rock and she is one lucky little lady to have you in her corner."

My face went a shade of crimson. Despite not being with Flick in person, I sensed she knew I wasn't able to take praise very well. Was that in-built in me like it was for Lena? Or was it just a case that it had been stamped out of me? It also felt bittersweet because my guilt was seeping in about my weekend away with my friends and whether I should really be going under the circumstances.

"I hope so," I eventually responded. "I don't feel like such a good parent right now. You see, my two best friends are taking me away for the weekend for my fortieth birthday, but I feel guilty about going away to have fun when Lena is struggling so much."

"Self-care is important," Flick reassured me. "Lena needs you to have positive mental health or she won't flourish, anyway. So think of it as doing it for her benefit!"

"Thank you. I guess you're right." I could feel that niggling sensation that I was getting uncomfortable as the conversation had gone a little deeper. "Look, I best go and relieve my friend Shelley. She's been looking after the kids for me and is no doubt pulling her hair out now! Hah!"

I always did this; I often made a quick humorous aside in order to distract away from the conversation as a breaker to find a quick exit. It wasn't that I didn't enjoy the phone call or talking to Flick, it was just the anticipation of the silence that you have to break whilst remaining polite because you had other things to do and didn't want to upset the other person or be labelled as rude. I always over-thought aspects of typical social interactions, I didn't know why, but they seemed to play over in my mind and I liked to script them ahead of time. It especially freaked me out if I had an unexpected call from an unknown number and there was an uncertainty of who would be calling and what it was they wanted. More often than not, I let the phone ring off, as the blind panic was too much to deal with. I preferred to see if they left a voice message so that I could take control of the anxious feeling it provoked. This would be catapulted to a different level if no message was left and I had no idea who the unknown caller had been.

"Oh yes, you'd better go!" Flick agreed harmoniously after all that. "Please don't hasten to call me at any time if you need anything."

"I will do," I concluded and sighed with relief. "Thank you for helping me, I know that I made the right call."

"You certainly did! Take care and speak soon."

I busied myself by emptying the washing machine that was laden with more *Paw Patrol* clothes than you would find on a merchandising website. I needed to take the reins back from Shelley, but my mind was jumbled as always, especially as I processed what I had just discovered from the school.

It wasn't long before the door came crashing open and Lena steamrolled past me as if she were a diva leading her entourage of Rex behind her. As soon as she was in my presence, I couldn't help but smile. She had an essence of a personality that was so strong you could almost taste it; it was unique, something you couldn't quite describe as it wasn't tangible enough to formulate into words.

Shelley passed Charlie to me and waved goodbye from the garden path. I indicated that I would give her a call later on.

Lena came back into the kitchen with Rex by her side. "I know something you don't know!" She teased me as if she were the parent and I the young infant.

"Is that right?" I replied playfully.

"Yes!" she screamed and her hands flapped as if she was about to take off. "You don't know how camels keep sand out of their eyes!"

I laughed at the unusual topic.

"The sand slides down their humps?" I guessed, sending Lena into hysterical squeals which were too infectious to not join in with.

"Wrong!" she shouted abruptly.

I read the situation and I knew that she wanted me to entertain her by being unintelligent, so I guessed another ludicrous attempt: "They use sand umbrellas?"

"Hahahaha! No, Mummy, you are silly." She told me in an adopted adult voice, "Guess again!"

"Okay, I got it." I could feel the corners of my mouth raising upwards in anticipation that the next guess was going to hit the mark. "They use camel karate moves?"

Lena fell to the floor clutching her small tummy. Every time she tried to move she set off again into further bouts of uncontrollable laughter.

"Okay," I interjected joyfully. "You just have to tell me the answer as I'll never get it right."

"Camels have three sets of eyelids AND they have two rows of eyelashes to keep the sand out of their eyes!" She was smiling gleefully and relishing the knowledge that she had taught me, an adult, something I didn't know. What she didn't realise was there was a lot I didn't actually know. She really was my teacher about life, about parenting, and about the kind of person I really wanted to be.

Lena lost interest in our conversation and left the teaching academy to go and source a game of *Paw Patrol* in the living room. Of course the lesson only ever involved a subject of her choice, and the opportunity to learn always had to be on Lena's terms. She avoided the opportunity to be led just as much as camels probably found the chance to avoid getting sand in their eyes.

I thought about her fact on camels and it struck me that they had either been designed to live in a hot, sandy environment or that they had adapted over time to cope in this hostile habitat. It was quite mind-blowing to get my head around. Avoiding had been long ingrained in our physical evolution before we could even call it a thing, thinking about it, that was just a little bit like Lena too. She had the art of avoiding something she felt needed avoiding.

Maybe that was what I needed to do; if I modified my behaviour, I could adapt to cope with the hostile world around me. I had been protecting the notion that as a family we needed to fit in for far too long, and I had been keeping out of conflict for an even greater length of time. I needed to grow myself a few pairs of eyelids and a few extra rows of eyelashes (not quite like the tacky ones you'd see plastered on the girls with fish lips in the beauty parlours), so that I could bat away any of the challenges the school threw at me. It made me smile as I pictured myself rocking back up to the next school meeting dressed as a camel with extra pairs of false eyelashes. I certainly had a grumpy hump to act the part.

13

The Weekender

It was Thursday night and it was my last Gin O' Clock with the girls before their surprise plans for my fortieth birthday. I kept trying to quiz them about what I needed but they weren't giving anything away. The only thing I knew was that they had borrowed my passport for the last couple of weeks so I had the sneakiest feeling that they were intending to go abroad.

"You're on a one-day countdown to your birthday, don't forget. Welcome to the big four-zero! The naughty forties and all that!" Vic giggled. "We're not giving anything away before you try either!"

"That's right," Shelley agreed enthusiastically. "Plus, the celebrations start right now! This is going to be the most hardcore weekend of your life."

"I'm dreading it already," I joked, rolling my eyes during our weekly video call. "What should I pack?"

"Nothing!" They both screamed with laughter.

"Come on, you two, how can I go away with no luggage?" I pleaded.

"You'll have luggage," Shelley confessed. "You see, the other day, when I had the kids, we sneaked into your room and packed your stuff for you!"

"That shows either how unobservant you are, Sarah," Vic teased, "or that you must wear the same loose comfy clothes every day, because you didn't notice your best articles of clothing were missing!"

"You two are really enjoying this!" I grimaced as I took the phone with me and searched my wardrobe whilst they were still on the call. I switched the angle of the phone around to face the unit. "Come on, fess up, you pair! What did you take?!"

"Finders keepers!" Shelly taunted. "Who knew you owned such luxurious items? Your underwear drawer hid the best surprises!"

Luckily the gin was starting to lubricate me before the full feeling of panic seeped in.

"Enough about that anyway," conducted Shelley, "let's talk logistics. You need your mum to pick the kids up at seven in the morning – sorry I know it's early! Then it's hasta la vista to the little people! We're going to give you a taste of freedom, albeit for only a weekend, but beggars can't be choosers!"

"Looks like I have no say in this." I surrendered to their game.

"Absolutely, and you're going to feel all the better for it," soothed Vic. "What other reason do you have besties for anyway?"

"To take me for a cream tea and be respectable for my ripened age. Just like the more 'mumsy' type of mums I see at the school with their long, flowing skirts and flowery bags." I was smiling as I jested with them.

"You'll never fall into that category, Sarah dear," Shelley gushed. "You are far too fabulous for that."

"I'll take that as a compliment," I muttered. "So, let me get this right, I don't know where I'm going. I don't have anything to take. I don't know what we will be doing for the next few days, AND you want me to be relaxed!?"

"We're not answering that!" Vic was grinning. "That's why we're cutting the call early tonight because we know exactly what you're like and you won't stop digging until you find out."

"On that note, Vic, shall we say goodbye now then?!" Shelley winked.

"I think that's wise, Shell!" Vic agreed.

They both had smiles like cats as they chorused in unison: "See you in the morning, Sarah!!"

"Oh, jeez." I exhaled. A cacophony of fear and adrenaline pulsed through me as I replied, "See you in the morning."

I barely slept a wink that night. I tossed and turned with some trepidation, apprehensive about what the weekend that lay ahead of me could involve.

It was hard the next morning to kiss the children and leave them behind as my mum picked them up to drop at Nick's. I tried to stay silent as I knew that if I spoke any more than I had to I would be too choked and could potentially bail out of going. The separation anxiety was intense and I had this huge fear of having an accident and my children being left without a mummy. The thought was too difficult to bear and I tried to kick my brain into gear and to erase the negative thought out of it. I focused on my breathing like some reinvented yoga guru – only with every deep breath I could feel my cellulite rippling in effect on my buttocks. It made me smile and at least helped to disseminate the intrusive thoughts. Fat butt won the day!

"So, are you going to tell me NOW where we are going?" I probed, desperate to know something about the weekend.

"Of course not," my friends both answered.

"You'll find out when we get there!" added Vic.

"Yes, but *where* is *there*?" I insisted.

"There!" they screamed and howled at my confused reaction.

We drove along the motorway and I could see the signs coming up to junction ten on the M1 – the turning for Luton Airport!

"Oh shit," I uttered. It was like I was blindfolded but with a different gag to confuse my senses. "We *are* going on an aeroplane?"

"That's right!"

We parked Vic's car in the mid-stay car park and left the keys in the car. "Are we just going to leave the keys in the ignition?!" I queried fretfully as a new, mysterious bag was passed into my hands.

"Don't worry," reassured Vic, "it's all sorted and booked in. An attendant will move the car for us and return it back to the collection point when our plane arrives Sunday evening."

"We know how to travel in style," Shelley oozed as if she was a vlogger for some kind of travel channel. She was just missing a glass of Prosecco in her hand and a shimmering sunset to complete the look.

We marched down the pedestrianised walkway and followed the travellers who, for some reason, walked in silence – which made the reverberating sound of the squeaking trolley wheels bumping over the raised tarmac cracks even more dastardly. Considering the airport had received a regeneration project, the walkways were still pretty dire.

"I hope I've not been duped as a drug mule?" I laughed as I glanced down at my mini holiday bag that I was towing along on wheels.

Shelley and Vic cackled and signed their fingers over their lips to one another, pretending they were warning not to tell me the truth.

"I'll take that as a yes then." I laughed at their juvenile game and couldn't help but absorb the feeling of excitement too.

We walked up the raised ramp that led to the terminal and followed the sign for the departures. There was a young guy, with tousled brown waves and very skinny jeans, gyrating with a boombox to some foreign, wailing tune.

"I'll be arrested in customs with that young lad," I exclaimed. "It looks like he's taken some of the stuff he has been couriering!"

"At least you'll get a chance to do some birthday moves with someone of the opposite sex," howled Shelley. We all laughed at that one.

I followed the girls to the departures sign and eventually we arrived at the queue for a very cheap budget airline; so cost-effective that they only had one assistant to book in every flight going around Europe for that day. It also meant that no information was given away about the end destination as there were too many airports to write on the sign. As we finally approached the desk, the girls unzipped my luggage and handed me a small, leather handbag which they said had my belongings in. Our passports and boarding passes were given to the passenger check-in officer with our items of luggage. I had to hand it to the girls – this was one of their best-kept secrets they had ever managed to manoeuvre.

We passed through security with little disruption and headed into the departure lounge for a greasy fry-up in one of the extortionately priced airport cafes. The lounge was frenzied with sweaty bodies racing into different shops before their flights were called. We joined the chaos to buy bottles of water, some chewing gum ahead of the flight pressure with the likelihood of our ears popping, and some very vital trashy magazines for in-flight entertainment.

It seemed we were in a race against time, I wasn't sure why airports made you feel like that, but it never seemed like there was time to sit back and just take it all in. I wondered if school for Lena felt like a noisy, overly-chaotic, fluorescent airport lounge. I could feel panic rising in me that I needed to go to the toilet before take-off in case my life depended on it. I had just about finished using the complicated sinks when an announcement was called over the Tannoy:

"Please can the last passengers travelling on flight PGY2221 to Alicante please make their way to gate 2. *"Por favor, los últimos pasajeros que viajan en el vuelo PGY2221 a Alicante, diríjanse a la puerta 2."*

"Oh shit, that's our final call!" Vic screamed. "How did we miss it?"

"Pissy knickers here was too worried about finding a loo," mocked Shelley. "It's her old age, bless her!"

We raced through the long corridors, hazily and out of breath, past the ticket collector, along the walkways to the flight and fastened up in our seats.

I was so exhausted from the sleepless night and the built-up fear of leaving the children and venturing into the unknown, that I slept like a baby for the entire flight. I awoke with the crash of the wheel hitting tarmac at the Spanish airport of Alicante. As I glanced outside, I could see palm trees and a crystal blue sky. It didn't matter that it was the end of October, just looking out of the small window, it was clear that the temperature was going to be mild and moderate which lifted my spirit naturally.

"Welcome to Benidorm, Señorita!" exclaimed Shelley. "This will be your birthday weekend to remember!"

We boarded a coach to the resort. It took about half an hour to arrive. We were dropped off outside the Hotel Casa Blanca which was a high-rise, white concrete block with a stamp-sized swimming pool to the rear and a medium-sized terraced garden jutting out of the first floor of the hotel. The brass hotel name sign was hanging slightly and the last three letters were trailing down the side of the building. If first impressions were anything to go by, I was starting to wonder what state the interior was going to be in. I had visions of a kitchen full of cockroaches like off some awful hotel inspection programme on TV.

We made our way through the lobby and checked in at reception to find out that our room was on the sixth floor and the lift was temporarily out of order. We traipsed our bags and tired selves up flight after flight of stairs – all three of us making deep breathing sounds that could only be made if a pig was mating a horse. We each collapsed at the door as we tried to hold ourselves up to put the electric card into the lock to open the door. We didn't even have the breath to talk about the fact that our card wasn't working. I looked at my two friends, with drops of sweat line-dancing down their brows, and indicated that I would go back to sort it out. Their faces spoke relief.

I rushed down the stairs as quickly as I could, ran to the reception, replaced the card and made it back up the stairs to find my resting friends sitting in the doorway to our room. The non-starter to get in was almost like a sign to leave straight away. We threw the door open and found ourselves in an outdated, ivory-tiled room with murky-brown furniture. Shelley threw herself down on the single bed and pointed over to the double bed.

"You guys will have to share. You know I need to sleep in just my knickers at night because I always overheat."

Vic and I rolled our eyes as we laughed.

"I certainly would prefer to spoon you, Sarah, I hope YOU wear PJ's!" Vic said.

We cackled as we threw our bags on our beds and Shelley opened her case. She flung a t-shirt at me which I caught just in the nick of time. I unravelled it and pleaded with them, "Oh god, no!?"

The t-shirt had a photo printed of the three of us with our school uniforms on and bold writing that said on the front: 'Sarah's 40th' and on the rear of the shirt: 'Girls on Tour!' Shelley had her iconic crimped hair, Vic was sporting an awful bowl haircut and I looked terrible – wearing a cropped top with a Spice Girls logo on, my hair scraped back with so much hairspray it looked rock hard, and two little strands hanging down either side of my face.

"Don't worry," reassured Shelley, "we'll be wearing one too – for moral support."

"That's right and the plan is that we all need to put them on now as we're going downstairs for a cocktail by the pool!" squealed Vic.

"If you undo your luggage, you'll find your swimsuit in there," directed Shelley. "Which I noticed all you had was one of those pull-me in types, so I dug deeper through your drawers and found this bad boy!"

Shelley ruffled past me in my suitcase to find a plunging, solid red swimsuit that she held up. It had the tiniest of strings to hold my mid-drift together. I screamed in shock!

"Oh no, not that!" I held my hands over my mouth in protest. "Nick bought me that about ten years ago when he wanted me to look raunchy for our family holiday and I threw it in the back of the drawer hoping he would forget about it. I just pretended I had forgotten to pack it at the time!"

"Well YOU, Sarah, are going to start as you mean to go on." Vic was smiling at me as she grabbed the costume from Shelley and flung it at my tummy. "There is no way you're going to be *unnoticeable* from here on in."

"I'll just swim in the t-shirt!" I declared.

We made our way down to the swimming pool and grabbed a sunbed each to relax on. If anything else, just not being on parenting duty was a relief in itself. That wasn't to say I didn't miss the kids or didn't want to be a parent, but just being free with my friends felt uplifting and something I probably needed more of to replenish my depleted energies.

Vic went to fetch us all a cocktail.

"Three sex-on-the-beach for three sexy senoritas!" she declared, passing us the peach-like substances with a slice of pineapple on one side of the glass and a cherry on the other. I slurped on the straw and twirled the glass. The sound of ice cubes clinking against the glass added to the sensation of feeling refreshed. Considering we were booked in an all-inclusive hotel, the alcohol element was still surprisingly strong.

The sun was resting its positive rays onto my skin. The small hairs on my arms were glistening white, swaying in the light breeze. It was a brick-built, high-rise version of paradise – one that I was grateful to be relaxing in!

"Come on, ladies," ushered Shelley. "Let's swim!" The girls pulled their t-shirts off to show their vibrant costumes as I stood awkwardly as if my sunbed would protect me from being on show. They both grabbed my t-shirt, heaved it off and led me by my arm to the pool. I didn't dare protest in case that drew more attention to my over-sized and very mottled white body. There was an olive-skinned local guy who was working in the drinks hut next to the pool. He winked over to us and I felt even more mortified that we were visible.

Vic and Shelley jumped in and I didn't want to waste any time standing there so I straight-jumped in as quickly as possible. The external ripples highlighted my dietary issues for any other holiday makers to see. It was actually what I needed and quite elevating; the natural relaxation of water had a holistic effect. We all swam around, giggling as if we were the only holidaymakers there, and played some racing games (which shocked both of the girls, as I still had the technique enough to fly past them even with a protruding booby line).

After some time we made it back to our towels and laughed as we walked together to the drinks kiosk to replenish our fluids (like we had lost any!) with another cocktail.

"Another drinks of sex-on-beach comin' up," the bartender said with a grin. His ability to miss a consonant here or there, or add them when not needed, made the feeling of being abroad even more theatrical. As he passed us our drinks he took an extra moment to pass me mine. His eyes lingered down my plunging cleavage. We locked eyes and he knew I had visually apprehended him, so he brazenly winked at me. I smiled, partly out of nervousness and partly out of shock.

"My name is Carlos. Welcome to Hotel Casa Blanca. What your name?" he asked, not taking his eyes off me. His intensity was making me feel queasy and I wanted to sprint away.

"Our names are Shelley and Vic," indicated Shelley, and then, pointing in my direction: "AND that is our lovely friend Sarah. It's lovely to meet you, Carlos."

"The pleasure is all mine." He lunged forwards against the wicker kiosk charismatically and intercepted my hand to kiss it.

I could feel my face burning red. It might have been easier if I could have taken flight. I tried to smile, but the heat was preventing me from having the elasticity of fresh skin. Well, that and my forty-year-old aged body, to be precise.

We made a quick exit and my two friends rammed into my waist, giggling all the way back to the sunbeds as if we were love-sick teenagers again, desperate for a bit of male attention. Vic gestured back towards the bar and jested, "Think Carlos wants to get into your knickers, Sarah!"

"Oh, come off it," I denied. "He's probably after anything that moves, that's why he does this job – so he can have his pickings of the wasted women for a quick fix."

"Don't underestimate your attractiveness," continued Vic, "know your worth!"

"That's right, Sarah," consolidated Shelley. "Any man would be lucky to woo you."

Our conversation was intercepted by Carlos, who had moved rhythmically, weaving in and out of the sunbeds enroute, to arrive before us. Raising one leg up (the protruding sight of his crotch was on full display), he broke our conversation as he began to do a Spanish dance with a red cloth in his mouth, which, having watched enough episodes of dancing competitions on TV, led me to believe he was trying to re-enact a dramatic version of the Paso Doble. He stamped his feet in unison and flung his hands up as if he was some erotic bull fighter. We looked on, slightly baffled by the display in front of us.

"You like?" Carlos quizzed me.

"Uh-huh," was the best answer I could give as the girls were screaming hysterically in laughter. In fact, the rest of the sunbathers had all stopped to watch the commotion.

"You come dance with me, tonight?" he asked confidently, as he masterfully swung the red material around his shoulder in some random act of manliness.

"I have... um... plans." I tried to squirm out of his proposition.

"Mañana?" he pushed. I didn't have the foggiest what he'd said.

"Uh-huh," I repeated like I was a frozen robot on repeat.

"I come here pick you up mañana!" He disappeared back to his kiosk and did a few extra dancing toe taps as he left.

"Oh shit!" I screamed to the girls. "What did I just say? My mind went blank!"

"You agreed to go out dancing with him tomorrow!" The girls were beside themselves with giggles that wouldn't stop.

"Oh god," I pleaded. "You'll have to come up with an excuse for me tomorrow!?"

"How do you know you don't like Mediterranean until you've tried?" Shelley was shameless with her banter. She knew how timid I really was.

Luckily for me it was the end of Carlos' shift and he swapped over with a young girl who seemed more professional at her job. He blew a kiss over in my direction as he waved to say goodbye, which of course gave the girls even more material to find humorous.

"I meet you here at seven? Okay?" Carlos called over to me.

"Okay," I agreed. I had no idea what was coming over me but something inside was telling me to let go for a change.

The girls threw me around pretending to be a Spanish dancer laughing at the situation even more.

"I may as well try," I said to them. "Fuck that shit! It's my new mantra."

"We love the new mantra." Shelley grinned. "Sounds like the words of a wise woman to me!"

"Fuck that shit indeed!" Vic declared as she held her glass out to us both for joint cheers.

We slugged the remainder of our beverages, then ended our afternoon shenanigans, retiring back to our room to get washed for the evening. I opened my case and found a raunchy leopard-print dress with a pair of black heels and a push-up bra laid neatly at the top. I couldn't even remember purchasing these items!

"You've found your outfit for this evening," Vic told me. "You are gonna be one hot mama hitting the Benidorm seafront!"

Either the drink had hit me or I had mellowed in their company as I didn't even flinch at the fact that I was being made to wear something more revealing than I had been seen in for the past few decades.

We left the hotel and made our way along the seafront into the port area where the complex of bars, restaurants and clubs were situated. As we arrived, there were multiple same-sex gangs of drunkards swaying along with beer dripping down their chins onto their stained t-shirts. I had a little panic attack, was this the life as a middle-aged singleton that I had to look forward to? Even more depressing, what if I had already turned into a female version of one of them?

The fear was drowned out by too much alcohol and I wasn't really sure of the order of events for the rest of the night because my memory was hazy. I fell asleep in my bed, and as I rolled onto Vic, I had a strange dream of Shelley talking to a young local boy on the beach, disappearing behind a parked pedalo...

***

The sunlight was shining through the balcony and the glass patio door to wake us up with a prod. We all rolled over, with a few aches and pains, and a few extra sighs, we lifted our heads off the plain white pillows to see if each other were still alive. I took a deep breath in and could feel the alcohol seeping from my pores and escaping in waves from my mouth. I needed to brush my teeth and go to the toilet in the desperate hope that it would help me to feel refreshed. There was always a sense of relief when your friends felt as rough as you did, so that you knew you were not the only bad apple. *You shouldn't have got so drunk,* I berated myself.

We each got showered and changed, then made the trip to breakfast in the dining hall before going for a snooze on the sunbeds by the pool. Quite a few hours had passed and finally we roused ourselves back up, not wanting to waste the weekend away.

"Come on, ladies." Vic jumped up. "Let's have the hair of the dog?"

I felt apprehensive. I knew I had overdone it the night before and that I should give my body a rest, but the idea that we were only away once, and this wouldn't happen regularly, swayed my thought pattern.

"What's got into you, Vic?" Shelley asked. "You're usually the sensible one out of us three!"

"Well, we don't want to go home regretting that we didn't make the most of it, do we?" Vic joked as we jumped back up and made the sorry walk back to the kiosk to pick ourselves a drink. I was relieved that Carlos wasn't on shift as the realisation hit me once again that I had agreed to go out with him that evening, and it filled me with fear.

We spent a few hours topping our alcohol levels back up and drenching ourselves in the glorious Mediterranean sunshine. We chatted and gossiped until there was no air left in our lungs to keep on nattering. Shelley jumped up, a mischievous twinkle in her eye.

"I've got the best idea," she quipped, "let's go to the beach and rent a pedalo."

"A pedalo?" I questioned. "Isn't that something you do with kids?" I laughed at the ludicrous situation I was about to get myself into.

"Come on," joined Vic, "don't be boring! There's not an age limit on having fun, you know, Sarah. You can't start changing on us now you've hit forty!"

"Piss off, you two!" I screamed. "You will literally be joining me in a few months!"

"Well, you don't want to be acting like a grandma, do you?" Shelley jested. She looked at Vic as if they had an in-joke going on. I knew that I was being stitched up but the alcohol was making me a little more fearless, and I could see that I was going to be fair game no matter what it was going to involve.

"Oh fine," I pretended to protest, "come on before I change my mind."

We crossed the swimming pool complex and followed the narrow path that led straight to the beach. We were lucky that the Hotel Casa Blanca was just a stone's throw from the sea and the amenities on offer (it had to have some perks at least). We took off our flip-flops and traipsed over the sand, which was warm and comfortable, instead of the blistering heat that it held in the summer months. The feeling of the dusty sand falling in-between my toes was a luxurious sensation – I wondered why it was with age that you suddenly appreciated such small things that made you feel good. We located the counter for the water-sports activities and paid for an hour session on a pedalo with a very broken slide erupting from the top of it.

Walking towards us, whilst striding effortlessly over the sand – as if he were a heavenly gift – was the most jaw-droppingly, *beautiful* Spanish man I had ever encountered. Clearly, the girls thought the same as they were both slyly grinning, which was overtly confirmed by Shelley giving our group an exaggerated eyeroll.

"*Buenos dias,*" the Latin stranger said confidently – although in my mind his husky tone was saying a whole lot more than hello! With his dark sunglasses and baseball cap shielding the bright October sun, I momentarily forgot I was a forty-something mother of two. My lip turned down to the left side, shamefully drooling at his perfection.

"*Buenos dias!*" we all harmonised back in reply.

I didn't need to work hard to mentally undress him as the only piece of clothing he had on was a teeny pair of black swimming trunks, which clung to his toned and tanned thighs as if they were sprayed on. His macho body entered the sea in a strapping fashion to locate our pedalo effortlessly, and as he returned to us, my brain entered a teenage fantasy world as if my 90's dreams had come true and he was a real life Peter Andre.

Oh, oh, oh, oh, oh, oh... mys-teer-iousssss girl, I wanna get close to you... my subconsious was serenading my mind as I had memories of stacking up my parents' phone bill, sitting in front of our bulky TV screen waiting for the song to finally play on *The Box* channel for the hundredth time. They never did forgive me for that faux-pas I suddenly remembered.

"*Una hora?*" Mr Andre leaned across and picked up my arm and gestured to my watch, interrupting my nostalgic memories. "*Una hora! Lo entiendes?*"

"*Sí, sí!*" Shelley saluted as she confirmed her over-the-top sign for *yes*. "*Una hora*! We understand-ay, one hour!"

"What's with the Spanish mockney accent, Shell?" Vic probed, knowing exactly what she was doing to torment her bestie. "Is that what you learnt at GCSE?"

"Fuck off!" Shelley squealed as we all looked at Mr Andre who was smiling his flawless smile at us in return.

"He understand-ay that very well!" I teased and we all erupted into a fit of middle-aged cackles. The energy of our raucous laughter was so infectious even Mr Andre joined in. I just needed him to spray the turquoise water all over his body and the reenactment would have been exactly like my music video vision.

After some time, we broke up our little rendezvous as we were aware the clock was ticking and we would have to bring the pedalo back very soon. We all entered the sea, one by one. As the cold, fresh water rose up to our thighs, it was a stark reminder that we were getting in the water in autumn and it was feeling a little more brutal. We each climbed up the ladder and I began a conversation in my brain which was like a headteacher scolding an innocent child. What was I even doing fantasizing over a foreign man probably half my age? *Damn those sex-on-the-beach cocktails!* Maybe I'd had one too many and the combination of the alcohol and the sun had made me giddy! *Okay. Focus! Just need to climb on the boat...* I told myself sternly. I always did this, my internal voice was my worse judge, criticising me and making my life so much harder than it should have been.

Couldn't inner-me have a fucking sex-on-the-beach and chill out for once? Of course there was no answer, my brain busied itself enough to cut me some slack and return to the present before it spiralled out of control.

Just as I was composing myself, Shelley hollered back to Mr Andre in her most artificial voice, "*Hasta la vista – Baby!*" I nearly died in embarrassment, but the shift in my mental focus was respite.

The Spanish Stud that was Mr Andre traipsed back into the water, probably guessing we would need extra assistance, and indicated for us to climb onto the makeshift boat whilst he held it steady.

Vic and Shelley clambered onto the boat and took the two front seats to manually work the pedals to get us moving. I rolled onto the back area and leaned back. I joked that I was going to be relaxing whilst they did all of the hard work. They told me that I was a shirker and not a team-player. We all laughed as the banter kept us propelling along the calm, undulating ripples.

As I glanced out to the misty horizon, with the sprinkle of salt laying an invisible blanket on my skin, leaving Mr Andre behind on the shore, I felt physically refreshed. "It doesn't even seem like we're moving!" I joked. "Where are your muscles, ladies?"

"You take over if you think you're any better," suggested Vic. We tried to swap places, rocked the boat and sumo-wrestled each other, holding on for dear life.

"Let's see if we can make it to that buoy." Shelley pointed over to the red plastic water-marker bobbing another fifty yards out.

We used all our energy kicking the pedals around with our feet, stopping momentarily to have a breather, then pelting them again as fast we could, eventually reaching the destination.

"Phew," we all chorused with relief as Shelley swung her sarong around the buoy in some heroic-like act, like she was a female version of a shipwrecked Robinson Crusoe, to hold the boat stationary.

We sat there for some time, just feeling the wobble of the water, rising and dropping as it hit the side of our tiny boat. The sound of the water lapping against the sea breeze was a sensory euphoria that we all seemed to be enjoying as I blurted out the lyrics of *Mysterious Girl* to the empty ocean.

After the first few lines, Vic joined in too. We began taking it in turns to sing a line each until we ended up singing together, trying to create what we hoped was the perfect harmony. We glanced at Shelley, she was shaking her head, tears streaming down her face. And that was that, we couldn't sing anymore – we burst into unmusical laughter.

Shelley suddenly dug in her bag and produced a wrapped foil and a box of matches. "So, Mysterious Girls, whose up for trying a joint?"

"A joint!" I cried. "Are you for real?! We're abroad, we could get arrested or something!"

"Don't be silly," Vic reassured me, "it goes on all the time. That's how the authorities make their money, by supplying and getting a few back-handed deals. Besides, nobody is gonna see us doing it out here!"

"Did you already know about this?" I quizzed Vic and she gave a wry smile. "And, how the heck did you get that here?" I asked Shelley, slowly on catch-up mode.

"I picked it up last night at the beach," she answered simply.

"So that's what you were up to!" I squealed. "I thought it was just a dream that I'd seen you with a young lad!"

Shelley unwrapped the foil to find one prepared joint neatly placed as if it were being delivered as a birthday present. She took out a match and tried to light it but to no avail as the wind was blowing it out. "Bloody wind!" she hollered. "You can tell I'm not used to doing this!"

We all cupped our hands together to give Shelley the wind protection she needed to light the drugged prize. Eventually, after a few fumbling attempts, she had it alight and took the biggest drag followed by exhaling a cloud of smoke. "*Pass the dutchie to the left-hand side*," she sang comically as she gave the joint to Vic who attempted, surreptitiously, to take a big lug too.

It was my turn next and I nervously took a drag of the joint as I confessed to the girls (who probably already knew me better than I knew myself): "I think I've popped my drug cherry!"

We all screamed with laughter at the craziness of the situation. The spliff must have been quite strong because we erupted into wild and unmanageable laughter. We finished the smoke and had no ability to hold ourselves up as we all leaned back against our plastic, makeshift bedding on the pedalo. It was like our bodies were glued down. Shelley confessed she was trying to hold on to the sarong with all her might to keep us from not drifting away further. I used my last zap of energy to lift my weary head up from the pedalo seat to look back to the beach. My view was psychedelic and blurry. Blurgh. Head down. Recover. How do we get back? Help!

"What if we get picked up like stoned castaways out at sea?" I asked innocently. My vision looked strange. Resting upwards, focusing on the emerald-green sky and mushroom-like sun, I felt very different.

I don't know who started it first, or who followed next, but somehow, we found ourselves laughing harder than we had ever done before. It was so unruly and disordered, if we had measured our laughter in watts it would have had enough energy to push us all the way back to England. The tears were streaming down our cheeks with the remnants of blotched mascara sliding down in unison.

We undid our temporary sarong-rope and tried our best to pedal our feet back towards the shore. It felt impossible trying to pull ourselves back together. We had only made it about a third of the way back, when Vic suggested: "How about we get in the water to wake ourselves back up?"

"That's a good idea," I agreed.

"As it's a time for firsts, how about we try skinny-dipping?" Shelley had her usual cheeky grin back on her face.

"I'm game if you both are?" Vic joined in.

"Oh fuck off, you two!" The effect of the joint was wearing off and I was already starting to come down. "You had this planned, didn't you!?"

They both giggled and nodded with joyous guilt as they watched my reaction to their continuous surprises they were throwing at me.

"You don't want to be remembered as a chicken when you're really ancient and your boobs are drooping to the ground!" Vic teased. "How will you know you don't enjoy it if you never try?"

"A life without experiencing things is a life half-lived," Shelley added, trying to be philosophical. "Besides, your tits and your fanny will be half the way down in gravity if you do it now compared to trying when you're seventy!"

I don't know what came over me, perhaps it was the taste of freedom, or the colour that was starting to inject itself slowly back into my life, but I yanked my swimsuit off and dived into the water.

The girls screamed and howled at my wild braveness. It also meant that, because I had taken the plunge, they had to follow. They threw their tops and costumes off too and, not quite so boldly, jumped into the water to join me. We all trod water, sometimes on our fronts, then rotating onto our backs, our full nudity glaring back up at the sun. There were six wobbling boobies that seemed to float to the surface as if they had actually been designed to be buoys or lifejackets if ever needed in an emergency. The water washed over our bodies, inside the orifices that never usually saw the light of day, over our rippling female tummies and caressing our joint stretch marks. It was momentarily delightful, a sensation like no other. A soothing, rocking motion came from the waves as we used our energy to float in the sea water, whilst spitting the discharge of salt out of our mouths. It felt like we had no weight. It felt like our youth again. And, most of all, it felt like freedom.

"Oh shit!" I screamed at the other two misfits, "I don't think I can pull myself back up the ladder. One of you will have to help me!"

Shelley swam to me and tried to hoist me up with her shoulders, but as she did a trickle of urine slipped down my leg. "What the fuck! You've just pissed on me!"

Vic tried to hold onto the bottom of the ladder, tears rolling down her soft cheeks. "I... can't... help... aghhhhh!"

We erupted into the biggest concoction of panic, boobs, vaginas and laughter. Our naked bodies were becoming visible to the spectators back on the shore. We were like this for quite some time, slipping back and forth, as we tried to escape the wet climbing frame.

"It's no use," I yielded, waving my arms frantically. "We need to call for help!"

We began waving our SOS signal back to the beach in the hope that someone would be able to rescue us. From our stranded position in the Mediterranean bliss, we could just about visualise a boat speeding towards us. In my utter naked despair I realised Mr Andre was on his way to save us and he was now taking on the role of action hero and going one step further than my favourite music video. When he arrived, he idled his boat, dived into the water with ease and used his muscly body to help lever us back onto the pedalo.

"*Dame la mano!*" Mr Andre shouted, holding out his hand whilst holding onto the ladder.

Is he asking for my hand in marriage? I thought as I was definitely away with the fairies in dreamland. I passed him my hand and he heaved up my ghastly weight as I slid back onto the pedalo.

The reality of our bodies crashing down with utter nakedness on show, like what could only be described as a group of beached whales, totally broke the delusional place I had escaped to. Mr Andre turned away whilst we covered our bodies once more, which was probably way more than we deserved. Even though I was absolutely mortified, I couldn't do anything but continue laughing once again knowing I had had the most unbelievable experience of my life.

"*Gracias,*" Shelley called out coyly on behalf of our shameful group – although it made me giggle even more as her awful accent sounded like she was saying he had grass on his ass!

"*Es peligroso!*" Mr Andre scolded us all, wagging his finger in the air. I could see his Spanish eyebrows rise above his sunglasses as he tried to disguise his obvious enjoyment at being the action man for the day.

"He said something about danger, I think," Shelley relayed to the group as she recalled some of her thirty-year waste of a GCSE in Spanish – that she only got a grade C in – her words for the remaining years had been she always deserved an A. *Judging from today's episode I think she was lucky to get a C grade,*

Mr Andre began dragging the pedalo back to shore. The spray from his speedboat was smacking us in the face, just as the crowds

– who were gathered in the shallow waters of the shore – were clapping and cheering at the rescue mission that had just taken place. I kept my head down, at the yellow, white and blue peeling paint from the bottom of the old pedalo, like a celebrity avoiding being papped.

"No, no, no!" Mr Andre scolded, still tutting in a sexy manner, as he tried to pass us our clothes before he began dragging our boat back to shore.

We returned to the hotel and traipsed our guilty butts back up the six staircases until we reached the sanctuary of our own room. We were now pros at working the electric key and whizzed into the bedroom to discover the maid had been in already to make the beds. It tickled us as, on top of our bed covers, neatly laid out, were three replicas of our bodies with our pyjama sets. You could picture the person who the clothes belonged to and, making us laugh even more, we saw that on Shelley's bed was the tiniest string vest and hot pant combo, which were supposed to be her PJ's! Little did they know that even those tiniest of items were discarded during the night as Shelley slept in her thong! You could tell she was still the un-birthed out of the three women as she still took effort in her sleepwear, whereas Vic and I dressed our bodies head-to-toe with more material than we cared to admit. We made an in-joke that we could tell who was the more promiscuous out of the group. Shelley retaliated by showing us her two fingers (which simply prompted even more laughter).

We didn't lounge around too long and quickly got ready, with Vic's iPhone playing some old school music anthems. Nobody wanted to walk back down the stairs to get a drink for us all, but we designated Shelley for the job and told her it was in her favour so that she looked even better in her thong for the next time she had one of her Tinder dates.

Shelley slammed the door and arrived back about ten minutes later with three cocktails in her hands, and with no hands spare, she had to use her foot to bang on the door. We opened up just as Vic and I were gyrating our bodies to some awful reggae tune. Shelley fell in with her eyes rolling at our busted dance moves.

"Guess who I bumped into downstairs looking all dressed up with a rose in his mouth?" Shelley taunted.

"Oh god," I replied, holding my head in shame. "So it wasn't a prank?!"

"Of course not, Sarah," Shelley informed. "Carlos knows he is lucky to have the chance to take out a glamorous woman like you. Looks like he's pulled out all the stops."

"Ahhh!" I grimaced at the thought of trying something new.

"You'll be fine," Vic insisted. "How about we play a song to get you in the mood?"

"In the mood..." Shelley grinned, "for love!"

"Hah hah!" They both began laughing again.

"*Alexa*!" shouted Vic. "Play *Mr Bombastic* by *Shaggy*!"

The lyrics '*Mr Lover Lover*' from the song began blaring over the speaker, shaking our hotel room with a bit of nineties nostalgia. I couldn't help but feel like I was a teenager all over again with the prospect of going on a date with a guy, not knowing where the night would take me. A pang of excitement hit my tummy and my body felt so alive.

Out of nowhere my phone rang and I had a panic that it could be something about the children. I picked up without checking who the caller was.

"Hi, Sarah," a voice I recognised began, "wait a minute! Are you abroad? I just dialled your number and got the strange ringtone. Nobody told me."

"Hi, Julie." I widened my eyes, signalling to my friends that I was receiving an awkward call. "Erm, yes I am. Shelley and Vic have taken me for a weekend away to Benidorm as a surprise for my fortieth."

There was a difficult silence. My sister didn't need to say anything; I could sense she was hurt and disappointed. We hadn't spoken for so long that she had no idea this was even planned. Not only that, she hadn't been included in any of the birthday preparations (which, once upon a time, she would have been involved in one way or another). No doubt she felt very overlooked. I began to feel guilty. Were my actions wrong? I tried to justify to myself that I was away with my friends and we both had always had different friendship groups. The uneasy feeling of guilt was not subsiding.

"Oh, I'm sorry," Julie stumbled. "I can hear you're busy, so I'll catch up with you another time."

And with that I was left with the dial tone and the image of my pained sister etched onto my mind. I had to get rid of it before my anxious thoughts created a dip in the mood for my two best friends who had made lengthy efforts to create such a special event.

"Shall we down these and get going?" I swallowed my emotions as I sung the last of the lyrics to the Shaggy song in an attempt to mask the truth.

We necked the glasses of drink down, and whilst the girls went off to hit the town again, I took the stairs carefully in a black figure-hugging dress and strapped up high heels ready for a night of freedom with a man I barely knew.

I spotted Carlos waiting at a table near the drinks kiosk. As soon as he saw me, he jumped out of his seat and sped over.

There was no going back. I took a deep breath, bracing myself to move out of my comfort zone.

Carlos wrapped an arm around my body and kissed me on the cheek.

"I am so happy you come dance with me," Carlos caressed the words as he candidly took a look at my outfit. Up and down.

"It's my pleasure," I answered.

The evening was calmer this time, we saw fewer raucous gangs of wasted revellers, so I was able to enjoy the sight of the moon leaking onto the night-time shoreline with such beauty and elegance, and for that moment, I forgot we were in a beer-shovelling resort with ex-pats. The palm trees were spaced out along the promenade with such precision and the light reflected back from the glistening ripples in the sea so beautifully, it was giving me the sense that I was in some natural, outdoor spa. There was something about being near the sea that was extremely euphoric and it brought the date into a level of relaxation.

Carlos held my hand as we walked, trying to make small talk to get to know one another a little more.

"I divorced – no wife!" Carlos shared. "And you?"

"I am separated too," I replied, "just trying to figure things out."

"He crazy!" Carlos exclaimed. "To let you go. He crazy."

His English was broken but I got the gist and my face blushed. I could see that he was trying to compliment me and it felt strange as I wasn't used to a man looking at me like that.

"Thank you." I smiled sincerely.

"I take you the big bar?" Carlos asked. "They have DJ and music, I think you like it?"

"That sounds perfect." I nodded, trying to conceal my anxiety that I didn't know where we were going.

Carlos led me into a great big American-designed bar called *Chicagos* which was coordinated with rock and roll memorabilia on the walls and on the side of the bar. It was pretty mobbed and it took a while to queue up at the counter to order our drinks.

We found high stools and perched. We tried to have some form of a conversation over the power ballads that were pouring through the speakers. It seemed a strange place to be having a first date, but I felt some relief it was such a busy, public place for my own safety. After some time I looked across at the dance floor (which had steadily been building since we'd arrived) and noticed Vic and Shelley, dancing animatedly, surrounded by groups of guys. I could see their handbags on the floor – along with Shelley's rigid high heels. They boogied as if they had no worries in the world.

"Oh look!" I signalled over to where they were dancing. "My friends have come here too!"

"They look like they have fun!" Carlos smiled as he shifted his stool a little bit closer towards mine. I tried to not pull back; it was my instinct to make more space between us as I wasn't used to being so close to another man after having been married for so many years.

"They're the best friends anyone could wish for," I told him with pride.

"Want to dance?" Carlos picked up our drinks in one hand and offered his other to guide me to the dance floor. Touching his hand felt like my insides were on fire. I couldn't remember my skin touching someone else's and feeling so shocked.

We joined the girls on the cramped dance floor and they shot us a look feigning confusion that we were there too.

"What are you guys doing here?" Vic asked overenthusiastically.

"We wanted to ask you the same question!" I laughed as I leant in to deliver my answer so they could hear me over the din.

"You probably think we're spying on you?" Shelley asked. "But honestly it was a fluke we ended up at the same bar!"

"Hmmm!" I answered suspiciously. "You were probably keeping tabs to check I was safe!"

They both smiled, their lack of words said everything. It made me feel even more affection towards my loyal friends; we would do anything for one another.

We busied ourselves dancing and Carlos didn't seem one bit bothered by the girls muscling in, in fact, he looked quite excited at the thought of getting three-for-the-price-of-one! He eagerly asked everyone what they would like to drink and ferried off to the bar to generously buy us all a drink each. When he returned, I'd almost forgotten that I'd come with Carlos. I joined a line with my two besties and tried to recreate the *Steps* song *5,6,7,8*. As usual, we were standing in Vic's shadow; she'd always had the best rhythm out of the three of us and was the one who could remember any move or lyric to a song.

"Here you go, ladies," Carlos said as he passed us each a sex-on-the-beach cocktail. "Enjoy!"

"Thank you, Carlos," we said in unison, clanking our glasses together with his.

A natural break occurred as the girls moved more into the mass of bodies dancing, whilst Carlos and I hung back at the edge of the dance floor. He moved in closer towards me as we danced. I tried to shake off the feeling that people around me were watching my moves and judging my behaviour. Nobody knew who I was or that I was recently separated. I tried to tell myself that I could be who I wanted to be tonight and it didn't matter.

Out of nowhere, Carlos lunged towards me, placing his hand around my back and pulling me even closer to him. Tingly sensations like waves over my body made me shudder. They were enjoyable and I was drawn in wanting more. I looked into his deep-set brown eyes as he took a moment to slow down before he pushed his lips onto mine and forcefully opened them with his tongue. He started slowly and softly, almost like a soft whisper, but it began to build with more passion as he explored my mouth. I felt a lust that I hadn't experienced for so long that I'd forgotten the feeling of desire.

We kissed for quite some time, unaware of being in a public arena, because in the moment we were romantically entwined, everyone and everything else ceased to exist. I could feel his hand move onto my leg as he slowly tickled over my dress and the sensation lifted my newly-shaved hairs back out of their pores in kindred anticipation. Carlos' hand reached up to my top and brushed over my breast, it was no mistake or accident – he was clearly pushing towards a clothed version of foreplay. I conceded, involuntarily, motivated in the moment by the feeling of being caressed and by being awoken by the opposite sex. I moved my hand towards his inner-thigh, lightly placed it on his jeans and rubbed gently. The gnawing sensation of being inappropriate with someone I had just met was being suppressed by the overwhelming feeling of desire, but yet it was not something I could act on further.

I had to suddenly pull away as the fear became a block that I could not get past.

"I'm sorry, Carlos," I apologised. "I can't do this."

"You not like it?" he asked, confused. "But you kiss me back?"

"I liked the kissing," I explained. "I just can't do this. I'm not ready."

"I understand," Carlos said. "So you not want me make love with you tonight?"

"I'm not comfortable with that, I'm afraid," I confessed. "I have to check on my friends... I'm sorry!" I ran off to grab the girls to see if they would leave with me. Carlos seemed to take the rejection on the chin as he moved like a piranha through the dance floor to find a new match.

"I don't get you." Shelley frowned. "If you kissed him, you must have liked him, so why are we leaving?"

"Because he wanted more and I got spooked," I explained.

"One night of fun might have done you good, Sarah!" Shelley shrieked.

I fell silent, left in my own solitude. It was hard to explain what had gotten into me.

"When you're with someone for so long who controls every aspect of your life, it's hard to imagine letting anyone new in," I admitted. "Plus, the thought of someone seeing me naked is too much to think about right now."

"But we saw you naked," Vic pointed out. "And from my angle, it looked pretty darn good!"

"You're different," I said with a sigh. "You would like me just the way I am."

"And so should any man worthy of spending time with you," Shelley replied. "The man you married was not deserving enough, he doesn't know how lucky he was. And by the sounds of it he was overshadowing your ability to be free."

"Trust me." Vic joined in. "One day Nick will come to a realisation of how he messed up and he will kick himself."

"Every single thing I ever did, I was told I was wrong. Every item I wore, was wrong. Every phone call I made, every time I spoke, every moment I tried to do something that might better myself, just every time. All of it. He pulled me down and made me feel worthless. It's hard to pick up the pieces of your worn-down esteem when you've been oppressed for so long," I confided. It was difficult to talk about because it wasn't like Nick had been physically abusive to me, but the feeling of being controlled emotionally had been just as much to cope with.

I cried deep, soul-destroying tears as I tried to process the emotional rollercoaster that I was on. I knew I was still broken by the breakdown of my marriage and that I wasn't ready to go anywhere near a man again, no matter how much lust or drive was guiding me underneath. My friends squeezed their arms around me and we walked, the three of us, arm-in-arm all the way back to our hotel.

"One day you'll be ready, sweetie," Shelley reassured me. "Don't ever pressure yourself until it comes. But always know, we will be right here by your side, every step of the way."

I was locked in my own thoughts as I reassessed my marriage and started to wonder whether I had experienced a covert form of domestic abuse over the years. Nick had overpowered me masterfully for so long that it was taking longer to rethink how I viewed myself. It wasn't something I was ready to talk about. I pushed my worries to the back of my mind.

We returned to our apartment and followed Shelley onto the

balcony so she could have a pre-bedtime fix on her vape, but when we looked diagonally down, we could see three elderly ladies out on their balcony. They were giggling as they called out for help. Apparently, they had been getting a bit too lubricated in an Irish bar, jumping out of their seats to have a go at an Irish jig. When they decided to retire to bed they didn't realise how drunk they were and had managed to get locked out on their balcony. They were in room 407 and needed one of the staff to unlock the door. We picked up our room phone and dialled 'six' to speak to the receptionist who sent somebody up as an emergency. They all waved and cheered up to our balcony to thank our efforts for saving the day.

"That reminds me of our situation in Tenerife when we were younger and why we sing our tune about it," I reminisced. "That could be us in a few years' time!" We all laughed at the coincidence and the imaginary situation of us repeating the same kind of holiday when we were elderly, just like them.

"I love so much how they're still making every day count," Vic spoke softly. "And that their friendship is still vibrant and strong."

"So true," Shelley agreed. "We can only hope to replicate the same at their age."

"Love is not always about finding a partner, it's about finding the right kind of friendships too," I reasoned with deep affection.

"So what you're saying is that you love us?" concluded Vic. "Let's cut to the point without the soppy shit."

"Abso-fucking-lutely!" I declared.

"And, lucky for you, we love you right back!" Shelley declared as we all went in for a three-way hug that signalled the end of a very eventful and memorable weekend away.

14

Flaming Orange

When you've been away and you return home, it almost feels like you never even left in the first place. The children were upset with me when I got home, but only one of them could vocalise that feeling. Charlie, on the other hand, just whinged a little bit extra as if he needed feeding all day. It didn't take long for us to fall into our natural rhythm when we were reunited together. I knew I was back to being Mummy again. Something had ignited in me since the weekend away and it felt like a small flicker of light was slowly glowing and giving me that injection of passion I needed to approach our life a little bit differently.

A phone call interrupted my thoughts. The person on the phone introduced herself as Betty, our allocated Family Support Practitioner from the social care team. She made arrangements to hold our first TAC meeting in the third week of November, so that we had enough time to coordinate a free diary for all of the professionals involved. She proposed a date and said she would send a follow up email to invite everyone once I gave her the say so. She asked me to keep an eye out for an email invitation and for me to reply with my acceptance so that it was definitely confirmed. I thought it was a bit overkill as I had already agreed, but

I reluctantly obliged as I wanted to be seen as being co-operative once again.

As I replied to her electronic invite, waiting in my inbox was an email from the school SENCO. I wondered if she had finally answered my last email about the note they had pinned to the noticeboard about trying to exclude Lena.

From: senco
To: sarahforte
Subject: Outreach Worker

Dear Ms Forte

The Centre of Visionary Education (COVE) have made contact and Lena has been allocated an outreach worker.

The COVE have been commissioned to run ten sessions for an hour every Wednesday between 10-11am. They have said you are quite welcome to stay with her for the first session or until she is ready to attend independently. We have expressed our concern that as you are not a member of staff (and not DBS checked), that we can't have you in school for safeguarding reasons. We did suggest that the outreach worker runs the session outdoors in the school grounds. I have enclosed some further information from their website.

Kind regards
Mrs Webb

Okay, so it wasn't a receipt about the previous conversation, but seeing as they weren't answering my acknowledgement about what I had seen, it was proving their guilt. If nothing else, at least they knew I was now one step ahead of their antics.

I took a look at the alternative provision from this pupil referral unit, and I was sold. I replied instantly to accept the session for Lena; I was desperate to re-engage her into something as it seemed like the longer she was staying at home, the harder it was to leave the safety of her confined walls. Reading the information from the COVE was sounding promising; just the way it was worded gave me the impression that they cared. That orange light was flickering even brighter with the hope that a solution was on the horizon. I beavered away to get things ready so that I could prepare Lena and encourage her back to school.

The session was booked in for ten in the morning, which gave me the ability to give Lena a slow start. I left her playing in her pyjamas for a bit longer than usual so that she had built up enough calm time to face leaving the house. The frosty, glistening pavement had mostly thawed out in the late autumnal sunshine, leaving untouched, frozen patches in the lowly shaded areas. The air felt piercing and our cheeks were burning a shade of red from the glow of the wind. I had my gloves and hat on in preparation for being outdoors for the hour. Lena did her usual act of throwing layer after layer of clothing off the self-warming boiling system that was, in fact, her body. I always tried to encourage her to put the clothes back on, feeling the pain of the cold on her behalf, but she always had none of it. The purer the cold temperature, the more calibrated she felt. It was something I'd learned to live with – despite the regular stares and judgements from the typical bystander walking down the street.

We reached the gate to school and buzzed to be let in. Our favourite receptionist growled the words: "Come in."

I lifted the big steel gate and Lena squeezed past me and ran up the path with one arm protruding ahead of her (clearly in full role-play as a superhero for me to follow). The gate slammed rudely as if to say we weren't really welcome there. The loud thud unnerved me enough to feel like we were trapped with nowhere to escape. I trotted as quickly as my legs could so that Lena didn't run too far ahead without me.

As we neared the reception, Mrs Ramsbottom and Mrs Webb were situated by the door, their arms crossed and lips tensely pouted. They had a regal and ordered look about them, which was enough to make me (let alone Lena) feel intimidated by their presence. I doubted they could ever put themselves into Lena's shoes to see how unsafe they made her feel by just standing with their body language like it was.

Both of the dragons altered their frames, their faces sickeningly softened into smiles as a male 'outsider' walked along the school path just behind us. It was his footsteps that made both Lena and I turn around as they were more playful and flexible than the rigid taps from the adults we were in touch with. His clothing was smart and yet it had an air of looking casual at the same time, which emphasised his worked-out physique as he strode sportily with energy towards the two women. His dark hair was slicked down neatly, his bushy beard cut with precision that lined his glowing, Asian skin. He had an understated use of any external decoration except for a thin, gold ring securely wrapped on his wedding finger. He was collared at the front of the reception by the two cronies who had had an instant personality change. They ushered him into the school to sign in. We, on the other hand, were left like unwanted refugees on the other side of the glass door.

Shortly afterwards, the door opened, with Mrs Ramsbottom making an announcement as if she was a foghorn warning of any navigational hazards to boats out at sea.

"This is our pupil, Lena." She pointed her finger towards Lena.

"And this is her mum."

I took a breath in as Mrs Ramsbottom rolled her eyes over towards me – it was the only way I could prevent myself from reacting.

"Mr Hussein is from the COVE and has kindly come to visit you both." The smile of pretence was still painted on her taut face as she patronised us both with her insincere introduction.

"Nice to meet you," the man said as he held his hand out to enthusiastically shake mine. "Please do call me Tariq. I think it helps to just use first names. I didn't quite catch yours?"

"Sarah," I responded, already feeling an instant like for this man in just how he conducted himself. "Nice to meet you too."

He nodded ever so minimally, and although he didn't contradict the headteacher, I had a gut feeling that his response was insinuating he had seen right through her pretence.

His eyes warmed towards me and then he looked down inclusively to Lena. "Nice to meet you, Lena."

"Talking is boring," Lena replied indignantly as she abandoned the conversation and began kicking and chasing a pinecone over the grass.

"I agree," Tariq answered, unnerved. He swiftly followed in Lena's footsteps. "I like your game. Can I join you?" His actions were demonstrating that he was not taking Lena's direct style of speech too personally.

Lena stopped in her tracks. "How old are you?"

"How old do you think?" he replied.

"Old," she said directly.

"Right answer!" He smiled and craned his leg over to the right to swing another pinecone back onto his path. He copied Lena's game but kicked the cone away and chased it to repeat the action again. She observed, stopped her game and left her cone discarded to chase after him.

"You have a face like a baby." She was dissecting him from top to toe with her eyes to find some much-needed information. "So I'm going to call you Baby Face." Her conversation was jolting from one viewpoint to another, and her inability to pitch an appropriate conversation to a male adult that she had just met, spoke volumes of her vulnerability. She seemed to be trying to make sense of him in her own, abstract, way.

"Are you married?" Lena asked bluntly.

"Yes, I am."

"Do you have kids?"

"No, not yet," Tariq replied once more.

"What kind of man are you?" Lena continued to demand. In Lena's world, men and women had to follow set paradigms on gender that were constructed from overly-used stereotypes in media and society. Tariq was no escapee from the unsettling experience of being thrown under an intense inquisition. I felt mortified and far too embarrassed to intervene.

Lena watched on, twiddling on her green cardigan sleeve. Tariq picked a few sticks, stones and leaves up and began to make a happy face out of his natural materials.

"Can you make a face too?" Tariq offered without a hint of threat to his tone.

"Babies can't talk," Lena stated. This was always Lena's style – to throw a few insults to test the battleground. She proceeded to focus intently as she gathered some crude materials and began designing her own work of art on the ground. Tariq remained quiet, in a passive, unassuming role. His approach was different to the way staff handled Lena; who instantly tried to snatch the control back from Lena with the emphasis that she was unruly and disobedient. Tariq's interactions suddenly reminded me of the skill that I'd noticed Timothy, the guy from the park, had all those months ago with the bubble kit and the ability to calm Lena down. It was strange that I often found myself referring back to that chance meeting.

Lena was perfecting the task from Tariq and she pointed to where two stones were missing.

"The Tooth Fairy took those ones to build her castle made of teeth," she stated straightforwardly.

I could see Tariq stifling a giggle that he managed to hold under his breath as Lena continued on in her child-like way, "I don't give the Tooth Fairy my teeth. She's not the boss of me, she should use her own teeth and not mine for her castle."

"Your face is much better than mine," Tariq commented with genuine awe as he pointed to the two stick-like faces on the floor. "You were right, my creation looks like a baby face!" He feigned horror as he playfully annihilated his own piece of art and Lena laughed at his overdramatic expression.

"I think we'll be fine now." Tariq looked back to the two members of staff standing tense like stiff, foreboding statues. "Thank you for the introduction and I'll come back into the reception at the end of the session." Tariq caught my expression and smiled reassuringly. He said nothing to me, but in that moment, I had the sense he knew their formality and lack of flexibility were the problem.

Lena used her extra excitable energy to do a few laps of the early years' exploring area at full pelt. She darted in and out of the wooden painted hut, and then jumped from the protruding steps neatly spaced in a line. Next, she ran to a wooden bench and balanced along it, descending into a star jump at the end to dismount. She lost interest with her self-led circuit training and went to bang a few hanging saucepans with a discarded stick before her finale, where she ran to the horizontal bar and remained hanging upside-down with her infant arms dangling freely down. Lena made you feel tired just watching her.

"Do you want me to show you the fun bits, Baby Face?" her voice was now quite inviting and being the wrong way up seemed to bring out a softer side to the cheeky monkey.

"I thought they were the fun bits?" Tariq said joyfully. "Are you telling me there's MORE?"

She nodded as she muttered, "Uh huh," but not looking anywhere in his direction. She ran over to him and pulled on his jacket, not remotely shy or socially aware, as she made physical contact with someone she had just met.

"Come," she instructed. I stood, silently, hoping she would continue to bond with him. At last, someone was seeing Lena's true colours, it was giving me hope.

Tariq was led to a part of the playground which had a circle of giant tyres cemented in the ground, creating a circuit of rubber springboards.

"You have to jump from one tyre to the other tyre – just like this." As Lena demonstrated bouncing energetically, her voice was playing catch up to her sudden movements.

"Looks like fun!" Tariq replied enthusiastically.

"It is! Let's play the floor is lava!"

"What are the rules?" He looked up at her, cleverly giving her the reins.

"You have to follow me and you can't touch the floor or you die in the lava. Ready?" she told him with no time to lose so she could begin the game. "Go!"

Lena bounced over the tyres with such flexibility and ease that there was no chance she would be landing accidentally into the lava. Tariq pulled himself up onto the first tyre and began following her leaps. After a few jumps he stumbled and used his hands to steady himself back onto the tyre as if his life depended on it.

"Cheater! You can't use your hands!" Lena declared joyfully. "I win!"

"Can I have another try?" Tariq asked tentatively. He was clearly enabling Lena to go at her own pace.

"Okay," Lena agreed. "One more turn, only!"

Tariq clambered back up onto the first tyre to replay the assault-course-style game one more time. He seemed to be putting all of his effort into staying afloat. In this position, he was able to strike up a conversation far easier with Lena. As they bounced and spring-boarded from one tyre to another they had snippets of discussions such as how she liked to play *Paw Patrol*, that she thought school would be better if it was made of animals, and how she thought the teachers were too mean trapping her inside when she liked being outside.

I tried to slip into the distance and found a bench that was located by the ramp adjacent to the reception. Tariq glanced and saw me giving them the space. He winked with a thumbs up. The relief was creeping over me, in tickling waves, that finally someone had come in to work with Lena and was using an approach that could support her. The conversation I could hear was slowly disappearing into the wind as I let them get better acquainted.

After some time sitting in solitude on the bench, my mindfulness was interrupted by two sets of footsteps approaching me with excitement. There were lots of smiles and laughter as they busied away chatting until they reached my spot.

"Mummy!" Lena gave me the biggest baby cub hug. "Baby Face said I could bring my pups next time!"

I could feel my face glistening a shade of red like it always did when Lena broke down social barriers that anticipated a parenting intervention from me. The divide of being pulled to do what was expected versus what I knew worked for her were always at odds with one another. I needn't have worried; Tariq broke the awkwardness, "I love my nickname. I think I'll ask the rest of my colleagues to call me it at the COVE!" He laughed as he playfully pulled on his cheeks to insinuate the compliment that he looked good for his age.

"That was one of Lena's more complimentary nicknames." I laughed in agreement.

"I've already noticed that Lena's use of vocabulary is pretty advanced for her years."

"She loves watching videos about animals on *YouTube*," I explained. "She teaches me things I never knew."

"Boring!" Lena interrupted. "It's time to go!" She started skipping towards the gate.

"Yes!" I called after her so she could hear me still. "Adults talk too much... blah, blah, blah!"

Lena turned around and stuck her tongue out. "Hey! That's what I say, you copied me!"

Tariq and I laughed as I made my apologies for the quick exit. He reminded me that transitions of starting and finishing were probably hard for her and he understood. "Let's just try to make her feel more comfortable. There is never a demand to say hello or goodbye or please or thank you. She will do things when she's ready."

"That's so refreshing to hear you say that," I uttered. "Thank you so much."

"Next week..." he began, "would you be alright to stay again so that she feels happy and secure getting to know me? They want me to do the sessions in the cube, but she's not ready for that yet."

"Of course," I replied. "I'll do anything to help Lena feel better about school."

"That's clear already." Tariq smiled warmly. "Just remember, the problem doesn't lie with you."

I looked up, momentarily shocked from being vindicated of parent blame for the first time by a professional. There was an air about Tariq that made me feel like he wanted to say more but was stopping himself, so I gestured a quick thank you before I left.

As we walked down the path to get back in the car to go home, I suddenly realised what he had said: *the problem doesn't lie with you.* It made me think about what else he meant. Did he know more? What was happening to Lena when she was inside the building? It was one thing to feel oppressed for so long but it was an even scarier sensation to realise that I was right and there was a chance that truth might come to light.

The next week passed smoothly, and apart from my Thursday Gin O' Clock call with the girls, I had very little other social communication with anyone else. I hadn't heard any more from Julie since she'd called me and found out I was in Benidorm. I hadn't tried to make any contact with her. She must have felt that she was the one trying to make all of the effort between us. If I was honest with myself, she was probably right. I didn't know how to deal with the awkwardness and resentment I felt about our relationship; I only knew how to avoid it. In fact, it was a relief that she had stopped making contact as I didn't know what to say. My frustration was muddied with a pang of guilt and yet I didn't know what to do about it. Maybe I could try and tell Julie what it was that had upset me? Surely it couldn't be that hard? I just didn't know how to do it, so I left the thought at the back of my mind.

Wednesday was suddenly upon us and this time Lena was ferrying a bag of *Paw Patrol* toys into her school reading bag.

"Baby Face doesn't know the pups so I'm going to teach him!" Lena declared.

The usual challenges of getting ready, or putting her shoes and coat on were side-lined by the distraction of excitement. It was heart-warming to watch.

The second session went in much the same manner, except I was instructed to stay seated on the bench by Lena for the duration of the session. We were going at her pace and she felt in control; it was working.

It was reported afterwards that they had been playing *Paw Patrol* on the outdoor equipment and Lena was full of boundless energy for the following week.

Again, it was agreed to do the third session outside and for me to start on the bench and possibly go for a walk around the block when she was ready for me to leave. Lena instructed me to go for the whole hour. As I walked away smiling, I felt glad I was able to trust that she was in safe hands.

Tariq beckoned me over at the end of the third session after Lena had skipped over to the gate to avoid saying goodbye – as was her usual routine.

"Did it go well?" I enquired nervously. I had that apprehension that something might have gone wrong as it was the first time I had been relaxed enough to leave.

"Absolutely," Tariq reassured me, "she's doing so well and I'm really proud of her."

"That's fantastic to hear." I was holding back tears of joy.

"I just wanted to arrange to meet you here early tomorrow, before the first TAC meeting," he explained.

"The TAC!" I looked bewildered. "Of course, yes. Sorry I forgot it was booked for tomorrow. What time should I come?"

"I have preliminarily booked the cube for a session with you at 10am so that will give us an hour to go through things before the meeting. I said I had some paperwork for you to sign, but I also just want to give you the opportunity to collect your thoughts and have some support before the meeting begins."

"That's very kind, thank you." I was overwhelmed by his genuine care and support.

When I got home I sent a quick text to Flick from the support group to say I had forgotten to remind her, but that the first TAC meeting was at 11am the next day. She replied to say she would juggle a few things around and try her best to come. I said that I understood if she couldn't and there was no pressure as I hadn't given her much notice. By the end of the evening another text popped through.

Flick

Hi Sarah. All sorted for tomorrow. Please can you text me the postcode for the school? See you in the reception. Remember to FTS when you're there! x

I sent Flick a Google link to the location and focused on getting prepared for the next morning.

The school never asked me how or if I was able to manage to get childcare for meetings or appointments – it was just expected of me. I was fortunate that Shelley had offered to have the children or I would not have been able to attend (which, of course, would go against me). I made a mental note to prepare myself better and to mark in my diary any future meetings. I didn't know how managing adult life could be so complicated, but I needed to be more organised. My brain felt frazzled most of the time.

The next morning I dropped the children at Shelley's house and made my way to meet Tariq ahead of the meeting. He was waiting patiently in the reception for my arrival. We were promptly led, by my favourite receptionist (who made no small talk enroute), to the cube. Tariq and I chatted away merrily enough to fill the silence.

"The receptionist is such a joy-sponge," I commented as we turned into our designated room and the door was shut firmly behind us. "She sucks the life out of everything! I know she's been grumpy with me since word go when Lena stuck her tongue out at her!"

"I can only imagine," Tariq began, "the problem is you just can't change people. They have to be willing to see things from a different perspective."

"How come you're so good at understanding this stuff?" I was curious.

"My wife seems to think I have ADHD," he shared. "I think she could be right because I've always thought outside the box and been drawn to those who can't quite fit."

"It's a relief," I confided, "that you understand."

"It can be just as frustrating from a professional viewpoint too," Tariq admitted. "I left my teaching role because I couldn't cope with watching on powerlessly, as the children struggled, and not be able to change things. So I decided to do outreach work instead to build bridges with those children in a way that I could help them. I try to do this by empowering their parents too; it's the best way to improve their outcomes because they have the tools then to advocate for what they need. I guess I had to take a different route. It happens when things are static."

"That's exactly the problem I've had because school can't see Lena's struggles." I could feel the heat rising in me. "It makes me so angry that she's so misunderstood."

"You've been in passive mode, holding everything in and complying," Tariq began seriously, "now the difficulty is when you have that knowledge you may suddenly be propelled into acceleration state. It's good that you've moved out of your seat of allowing these procedures to happen, but what we don't want is for you to move in the opposite direction fuelled by anger or aggression, because then you won't be able to advocate for Lena. We need you on a dial that fits somewhere in the middle, with the knowledge and desire to push forwards, but with the ability to remain professional so that you can achieve the desired goals. Does that make sense?"

"You've hit the nail on the head," I confessed. "My feelings on everything have been side-lined for far too long. They just think *the mum* has nothing to contribute, that it's my bad parenting."

"In my experience, it's only the parents who are able to become their children's voice that get anywhere," Tariq admitted. "It's so wrong but sadly that's how things are."

"I really am dreading this meeting," I spoke as though I were talking to my best friends and not a person who I barely knew. He had that ability to put me at ease.

"I will do my best to support you and I will try to ask the right questions in the meeting. But... I'm paid by the same county who employ the people who are in the room with me. My ability to speak is limited. I can only say so much without risking my job, and then the way I see it, I won't be able to have an inside route into schools to change things. I can, however, take notes and prepare you like we're doing now."

"I really am so grateful." I felt indebted to him for giving me the strength to face the upcoming battle.

"It's nearly eleven," he said, showing his watch. "So I'll prop the door back open and we can be ready for when everyone joins us, okay?"

"Okay." I took a deep breath in. A flame was burning stronger in my soul, I was not going to be a voice unheard. It dawned on me that the feeling of fire could be visualised into a new colour. Had I created an orange hue for my rainbow of colours? Or perhaps it was a transition from red and I was fiercely heading towards yellow. I could see all three colours at once in my fire. I knew I had ignited the fuel and the light was burning brightly again. My flame was lit and this time I was not prepared to back down. I meant business.

15

Bin Bananas

The flow of attendees meandered into the room and I felt frozen to the spot as the TAC meeting was about to get underway. Although I was there in body, my mind was elsewhere as if observing the action as a separate entity. I was so scared and overwhelmed. All of the people in the room were about to be analysing me and my child. It felt so intrusive. Why was I having to go through this? What was normal parenting like? I just hoped it would finally help us.

Flick slipped in quietly as the first attendee and tactically positioned herself adjacent to my seat (so that I was in a sandwich between my two allies). Then came Theresa who Lena had visited a little while ago and whom we hadn't seen since Lena bolted out of the choice assessment.

Mrs Carter and Mrs Webb, the designated school representatives, came into the meeting room together as if they were the same animal tribe embarking onto Noah's Ark. They looked at me and half-smiled in offer of a greeting. A petite lady, with mousy coloured hair and a wonky fringe, who I'd never met before, came in and seated herself alone with a few extra centimetres of personal space added. I wondered who she was.

Last, but not least, Kimberley and Joanne, who had come to do the home visit a few months before, entered the meeting room. Images of them being told to not sit on the circular sofa in my house appeared in my mind. I was quite relieved to see them and a hope flickered that they would be able to help the school find a way to work with Lena.

Mrs Ramsbottom slammed the door. The windowpanes that made up the entire cube shook in nervous anticipation; mirroring my own feelings towards the infamous headteacher.

"Shall we get things started by introducing ourselves?" instructed Mrs Ramsbottom, starting the clockwork motion of passing the opportunity to speak around the table from her authoritative chair.

"So, I'm Deborah and I'm headteacher at Sunnybank," Mrs Ramsbottom began.

"Hello, I'm Veronica, school SENCO." Mrs Webb smiled.

"Hi, I'm Trudy, Lena's Year One class teacher," Mrs Carter added flatly.

"Good morning, everyone! I'm Tariq..." a much warmer voice changed the board of baseline introductions, "and I'm Lena's outreach worker from the COVE. Nice to meet you all."

"Hi, everyone," I began timidly, "I'm Sarah and I'm Lena's mum." My heart was racing as all eyes fell on me. I had to tell myself to calm down. *You can do this.*

"Hello, I'm Felicity," Flick started with strength and continued, "I'm Sarah's friend and supporter for today. I'll also be taking minutes on her behalf." There was a silence that hit the room followed by incremental body shuffles that signalled some bigger feelings were being suppressed.

"Are you from a professional body?" Mrs Ramsbottom enquired, a few wrinkles of uncertainty fell across her brow.

"Not for the purpose of this meeting." Flick omitted any further information to disarm Mrs Ramsbottom.

"Thank you for clarifying." The headteacher smiled reluctantly and moved on to her next victim.

"Good morning, all," a squeaky voice popped up, "I'm Betty and I'm the designated family practitioner from the 0-25 service for Hertfordshire. Nice to meet you all."

So that was who she was! I wondered if she would be on the 'for' or 'against' side of the room.

"Most of you won't have met me before," the next female voice interjected, "I'm Theresa and I'm a psychotherapist from CAMHS." I worried about the assessment we'd left so abruptly; would this professional also see me as the person to blame? What if she told them that I had no control of Lena and it was my fault? I tried to push the concern out of my mind to refocus on the introductions.

"Hi, I'm Kimberley," the next voice introduced, "I'm the educational psychologist, also from the 0-25 service, working with Lena."

"And hello too," Joanna joined calmly, "I'm the autism advisory teacher also from the same service."

"That's great." Mrs Ramsbottom charged ahead with leading the meeting. "And Ms Forte..." All eyes were now back on me. "I'm assuming your ex-husband won't be attending again?"

"He's at work," I explained directly, "however, I will be relaying the information from today back to him."

I knew that we were going back to the hint towards the family breakup as being the major issue at play, and my answer was to shut it down by showing them we were still operating as a united family – even if it was a slight exaggeration.

"Okay. Great. So let's get started." Mrs Ramsbottom's expression told a different story as to what she really thought about the situation. "As a brief summary, we have had Lena here at Sunnybank since she started with us in nursery, although she didn't particularly hit our radar until she started reception class. Of course we did have a few behavioural incidents logged by the nursery manager, but they were fairly minor."

The square of robotic faces around the table nodded, waiting patiently for the next instalment. The sound of Tariq shuffling his pen up and down, rhythmically to his own beat, was the only distraction to the group's concentration.

"But by reception class we noticed a spike in Lena's behaviour and her inability to listen to instructions. She also started to have incidents with other pupils and was routinely running out of class. We agreed to reduce her hours to a part-time timetable to see if this would improve things, but Lena still remained the same. Mum reports that she refuses to come to school regularly and her attendance is now very poor. We haven't had her in unsupervised since October when she absconded from school, at which point we sought expert advice from the COVE. Perhaps, Tariq, it might be a good starting place to hear from you about where you are at with your sessions?"

"Of course." Tariq confidently took the lead rope. "So I'm here as an outreach worker. The way that we work is to establish a relationship with the young person so that we can ascertain their profile and what we feel may suit them individually. We then use an approach that transfers our skills into school by modelling how that looks to staff so that it can be replicated across the setting. This works usually like a buddy who will then support the rest of the teaching staff by being the model of how it works best."

We all nodded once again, giving him the capacity to continue. "Lena has completed three sessions with me and I have moved away from the remit to bring her back into school. The onus needs not to be about Lena hitting imposed milestones, but rather to work at her level so that she feels enough trust and safety to reintegrate back into the classroom at her own speed."

"Which is understandable," Mrs Ramsbottom uttered with an air that felt condescending, "but Lena does need to understand that it is expected of her to eventually be doing work like the other children and that school is not just about play."

I could see Tariq and Flick take a joint intake of breath of disbelief, whilst the school staff looked from one to the other, uncertainly, as if they were watching a game of ping pong and were waiting to see who would be crowned the winner.

"Lena needs to not feel forced," Tariq explained, "in order to feel more in control of her anxiety in the environment. I have seen it written in paperwork that she is waiting for an autism assessment and there is potential of a PDA profile."

"Yes, but we can only work on that information if there is a diagnosis," Mrs Ramsbottom defended, "and PDA is also not recognised in our county."

It was like hitting a wall. Why couldn't she just be open and then things would be easier? I felt angry, I wanted to knock some sense into her.

"We don't need a diagnosis to put the provision in place." Tariq was clearly rattled and was trying hard to camouflage it. "Any special educational needs that are identified should be supported appropriately – as is set out by the guidelines in the SEND Code of Practice. It's a needs-based, outcome-focused approach and is a legal requirement for all schools to use it."

I think I could have heard a pin drop as the room fell into inhospitable silence. The energy was shifting and Tariq's shoulders lifted up and down before he leaned back into his chair. Betty, the family practitioner, shot him a look, signalling him to not speak any further. He didn't need to, my fire was burning, I was able to take over where he had left off.

"So, if it's supposed to be a needs-based approach, can I ask how you intend to make changes so that Lena is supported in school?" I asked. "There are also statutory guidelines on the dispute of PDA not being a reason why the appropriate provision is delivered. As a school, I'm sure you are aware of this?"

I was losing the embarrassment of speaking up in front of everyone, as my passion and knowledge drove my flow. Mrs Ramsbottom looked completely shocked and I saw a flicker of panic as she realised I had done my research and wasn't the walkover she had expected me to be.

"It was already in my plan to assess staffing levels," the head-teacher stuttered, "that's why we are here today – to put the provision in place."

She was backtracking. This wasn't what she had been saying for all the months before, but only with a jury surrounding her, she was finally about to follow the protocols. It made me realise that it was working and I felt empowered.

My eyes averted to Flick who was scribbling a message for me on a Post-it Note.

"All children of compulsory school age are entitled to a full-time education," I repeated confidently. "It is not legal to exclude a child with additional needs because of staffing levels."

"Oh no," Mrs Ramsbottom defended quickly, "we aren't excluding Lena, not at all. She can't manage the school day or we would, of course, permit her to attend."

The first of many fluorescent notes were passed discreetly onto my notebook from Flick. I read the next one and attempted to deliver it as if they were my own thoughts.

"Where is the paperwork from the day that Lena was excluded?" I questioned confidently. "Just sending a child home without written advice is actually an illegal exclusion."

"Well, yes..." Mrs Ramsbottom had beads of sweat appearing on her brow. "We do have the paperwork. Perhaps we forgot to pass it on. We do apologise."

There was silence in the room and I think everyone knew she was lying. The shift of energy was tipping into my corner.

Another orange note was passed to me from Flick who smiled as I continued my advocacy line.

"Also, what reasonable adjustments will be made to accommodate Lena's needs?"

"We will, um..." Mrs Ramsbottom was stumbling with her reply. "We will give her extra support with the class teaching assistant."

"The same thing I asked for in our last meeting but you said was not possible?" I queried. I had to hold myself back, just like Tariq had advised me to do before, or I could sound aggressive. It was just so frustrating that she was saying the complete opposite now others were there to witness the truth.

"I can't quite recall that," Mrs Ramsbottom defended dishonestly.

"Have you looked at the things that were triggering her? Have you thought about what led to her running away that day so that it doesn't happen again?" I was on a roll and I wasn't about to wait for any flimsy answers. "Have you also looked at the information I gave about PDA and the website on strategies for schools? I emailed ahead of time to make the suggestion that Lena could be given a pillow to sit on as she found the carpet too itchy, but nothing was done about it. Instead she was forced to do it and was put on the sad cloud as punishment when she couldn't, so it's not any surprise that she ran away."

"Well, yes, um..." Mrs Ramsbottom struggled. "But I can assure you that we have had our autism training as a school and we are all consistently using the STEPS approach to diffuse incidents." She was waffling and clearly trying to cover her tracks. I knew she hadn't even read the information I had emailed through, because if she had she  would have seen that the approaches for children with PDA could be different to those you would typically use for other autistic children.

"Perhaps we could pass over to Kimberley and Joanne, I'm sure their expertise might help at this point," Betty intervened, clearly attempting to chair the meeting professionally. The headteacher looked relieved. I got the sense that Betty was trying to protect her. I put my guard up about her instantly. "Perhaps you could update us with your assessments?"

I took a deep breath as I knew that I was getting too overheated and my emotions were driving me. I tried to remember Tariq's advice once again, about keeping my dial in the middle, but it was so hard to do when I knew that the school was at fault. There was also a fear that the professionals had broken the direction of the meeting because they didn't like me. I needed to ground myself fast or my tears would flow. Things were getting very serious and I knew that conversations had taken place before I had even entered their vicinity. This was becoming a cutthroat game and I needed to keep my performance cool, calm and professional.

"Joanne and I did a joint home visit back in September because Lena hadn't been able to attend that day due to her school anxiety." Kimberley sitting up straighter. "So we thought it best to observe her in a place where she would be more comfortable. Joanne managed to work her magic and she seemed to bring Lena out of herself and capture a lot of information which really helped us to build a bigger picture of what Lena finds challenging around school."

Everyone was listening carefully.

"Lena is such a character." Joanne was beaming as she relayed the information across the room. "When we arrived you could really see that she needed to take the driving seat because her intolerance to uncertainty was so high. But once she starts to build your trust, she can show her vibrant colours. She is an incredibly intelligent child, with a creative imagination and is wildly humorous. It was a pleasure to be around her."

The divide in the room was becoming quite obvious as Tariq, Flick and I smiled gratefully at Joanne for defending Lena's honour and seeing what a wonderful child she was underneath. I started to lose the panic that was still etched on me from the verbal assault I had overloaded on the headteacher.

Joanne opened her file and presented a hand drawn picture to the board of attendees and laughed as she began. "So, Lena did request that she bring her dog Rex into school, and that her dream school has a cinema and a swimming pool in it too."

The childlike animation was bringing a sense of warmth to the table.

"But, digging deeper, she did express that she needed her mum because she felt scared and she didn't identify an adult that she could go to in school. She also picked out lots of sensory triggers such as the noise in the classroom and sitting on the itchy carpet. Maths is also a key area that she finds hard and I would imagine is quite demanding for her. Also, the use of the cloud system, which is a positive behaviour system, seems to be triggering for her."

"That's right," added Kimberley, "the use of a punishment and reward system for a child who is unable to understand the social expectations, or control their impulsive reactions, is probably quite futile. As you can see from the sad face that she has drawn, this is quite upsetting for Lena; she would be taking this quite literally that she is a bad child, which just fuels a negative cycle. I think it needs scrapping in order to be a far more inclusive environment."

"We have both finished our reports with our recommendations in finer detail." Joanne passed a few copies onto the centre of the table. "They might need duplicating so that everyone can have a copy to take away and read at their own leisure. However, in essence, the key message is that Lena needs to feel safe in order to manage her day in school. Building trust with key adults and having a safe place to go is key for her to cope."

Tariq was smiling, they had come up trumps and were simply backing up his ethos.

"It's great that Tariq has been making some progress with Lena in his sessions," Kimberley added. "Could there be capacity for school to use the same model and to start building the steps to have Lena back?"

"Yes, of course." Mrs Ramsbottom was almost animalistic as she squawked her response. "We want her back in school and would have her any time."

We all looked at her with confusion, hadn't she been saying the complete opposite a few moments ago?

"I have a space tomorrow morning in my diary as I had a late cancellation today," Tariq said. "Perhaps it would be beneficial if I came in to do another session outside with Lena and an allocated staff member so they can begin to replicate these sessions and build her trust?"

"Well, um," Mrs Ramsbottom stuttered once again, "we might need a bit more notice than that to allocate staff."

"I think Sarah did remind us that Lena is entitled to a full-time education," Tariq spoke confidently. "With all due respect, funding issues should not be a reason to not be providing appropriate support. Her needs *have* been on the radar for quite some time."

"I will see what I can juggle," Mrs Ramsbottom said through gritted teeth. "We can release the class teaching assistant for the session."

"Great." Tariq beamed.

"I shall put that down as one of the action points from this meeting then," Betty declared. "It would be appropriate now to record any other actions from today. So, I'll start by noting that school will be looking at the recommendations from Joanne and Kimberley's reports and incorporating them to support Lena."

"Thank you," they both agreed.

"And for Lena to start attending outdoor sessions in the playground each day, starting with a handover from Tariq?" Betty continued.

"Sounds great to me." Tariq nodded.

"Sarah," Betty called me out and I feared what she was going to say. "I was wondering if you could get Lena to go through some child profile work and see if she would like to put any of her views down? She can draw them or you can annotate them. It's just simple things about Lena, what does she like, what is important to her, what would she like to do in the future... If she doesn't engage that's fine, but if you could have a go that would be great. I'll pop that down as another action. We like to have the child's voice at the centre of what we do."

The stapled worksheet was passed across the table to me and I stashed it underneath my notebook. It was like a sudden jolt back to reality as I realised that the school had never once asked Lena anything about her opinions or what she needed.

"I was also going to suggest that we put in a referral to see if we could get Sarah onto the Triple-P Parenting Programme," Betty spoke over the table and was met by a deathly silence.

That was that?! After all the time and effort to get so far, they wanted to offer me a course to learn how to be a better parent? If I said no I knew they would note down that I was not being compliant. I felt like turning it around and suggesting she should go on a programme to be a better practitioner to see how she would like it.

"I think that Sarah's time is already stretched," Tariq intervened, "perhaps she can take her time to think on that one and, if necessary, apply to do it at a later date."

"Yes, of course," Betty replied. "It must be quite strenuous with how much you're balancing. We can think about this later on, but at least give it some thought as these things do take a while to process."

I nearly jumped out of my seat to give Tariq the biggest kiss on his face for saving my bacon. He smiled at me as if I had done it invisibly. He'd known I was being backed into a corner that I wouldn't have been able to get out of.

"So if there is no other business...?" Betty asked.

"I'd just like to share some details from my initial assessment time with Lena," Theresa said quickly. "The appointment was quite exhausting for Lena. She struggled to stay in the room for the whole session and her anxiety was clearly over-spilling, which I would imagine is a usual state of being for her. She also made a very profound statement, one that we would typically expect of a much older child."

The room was silent.

"Lena talked about the injustice of not having the colour black included in a rainbow. That all colours should be seen. She said she felt like she was the colour black because nobody was able to see her." Theresa's words echoed around the room.

"I completely agree with you," Joanne piped up, passion oozing from her. "Kimberley and I both felt that Lena had been forced to mask her authentic self until she was no longer able to do so. That's why she is constantly in fight or flight mode. She needs to build trust with those around her so that school is no longer scary without her mum, who is clearly doing a wonderful job with her."

"Could we ensure that the last comments are included in the meeting minutes, please?" Flick spoke up and nobody questioned that she was voicing her opinion. "I have recorded it in my notes but it will be important that those details are documented. We can check the professional minutes once they are formally distributed and Sarah can make sure that nothing has been missed."

Flick smiled at me and I knew right then that she was trying to keep an evidence trail to safeguard me. It was even more clarification that she knew too well the narrative that was being fed behind the scenes with some professionals purporting that it was still a parenting problem. It was a tactical move from my advocate, one I would absorb for future reference.

There were quite a few vocalised agreements in the room and my face transitioned to its usual red glow with the pressure that eyes were on me. I felt like my role as a parent was finally being seen, by some at least, and the bulk of blame was catapulting into another direction. The school staff remained noticeably still and quiet; a passive response that spoke more than it would have done in words.

"I'd like to book in another session with you, Sarah," Theresa called over to me. "Perhaps we could stay at the end of the meeting, just to get a date in the diary?"

"Sure."

"With more sessions in place I'll be able to unpick more to support Lena," Theresa explained to the group. "And to work out how I can best work alongside this process."

"Okay," Betty concluded. "Looks like that was the last business for the day and I'm conscious of the time. I propose that we put a new date in the diary for the end of January for the next TAC? And I will arrange to do a home visit and assessment with the family before then too."

Everyone beavered over their diaries until a date was secured. The meeting came to a close and everyone began to disperse out of the glass prison. Before making my way home, I secured a date with Theresa.

I called Flick whilst walking home.

"The meeting couldn't have gone any better," I said warmly. "You were so helpful. I can't thank you enough, Flick."

"Anytime," she responded, "but you need to give yourself a pat on the back. You bloody aced that!"

"Do you really think so?" I questioned. "When they cut me off, I had the feeling that I had gone too far into aggressive mode!"

"Remember what I told you?" Flick reminded me with a giggle.

"Fuck that shit!" I exclaimed proudly.

"One hundred percent! You've got this!"

"I really hope so," I answered. "Although I sensed that things have been happening in the background that I need to protect myself from."

"Your gut instinct is right," Flick soothed. "You'll need to stay one step ahead of this. Trust me, I've seen it before and know the game they're trying to play. Just a word of warning, please keep yourself guarded at all times; the school and Betty are not trustworthy."

I hung up after I had made arrangements that I would meet Flick for a coffee soon, and she offered to attend the next meeting in the new year. It felt like some things were finally coming together, but I wasn't out of the danger area just yet. My tribe from the colour red were helping me to push forwards and I was successfully putting the layers back into my rainbow.

***

"So, I think I may have just had the worst day of my life!" I confessed to Shelley and Vic over our weekly drinking night on *FaceTime*. We had moved our virtual meeting a day later again as I didn't have the energy to talk after yesterday's meeting.

"Wait for me," giggled Vic, "I'm just pouring my Mojito. These ones are only 99p at the moment from *Aldi*!"

"Bargain!" Shelley commented, slurping on her almighty glass of red wine. "Although I couldn't drink that shit. It's not strong enough! Hah!"

"Well you know I'm a lightweight," confessed Vic. "Not a hardened drinker like you bloody pair!"

"Haha! Too true!" I laughed. "I don't feel so bad about my continual drinking habits knowing that Shelley is just as bad!"

Shelley mimed slugging the remainder of her bottle. We all burst into the relief that we needed – laughter was always the collective medicine that cemented our deep friendship. She suddenly jolted back up. "You weren't so much of a goody two-shoes in Benidorm, Vic!"

"What happens on tour, stays on tour," Vic retaliated with a glint in her eye. We all knew that we wouldn't let our shenanigans be made public!

"So," I began, "it was one of those days when not just one thing goes wrong, but *everything* goes wrong! I had been up all night with a mixture of Charlie murmuring and then Lena saying she was a 'Superpup' and needed to fight crime."

The girls giggled as I continued my story.

"I finally drifted off in the small hours but missed my alarm. So, I was playing catch-up with the morning routine – which, in case you wondered, is virtually impossible when you're chasing a child around the house who is bellowing *'This pup's gotta fly!'*"

"I love Lena-isms, they're just classic," Shelley said lovingly.

"You wouldn't love them if you had to deal with them all day, trust me!" I smiled. "So, with all Lena's tactics, I managed to get her to school five minutes late for her first morning session outside."

"So, she's back in school now?" Vic enquired.

"I'm guessing that was the upshot of that meeting you had yesterday?" Shelley pieced together.

"Yes, it was. The new outreach worker has come up trumps. He's quite amazing actually, he really gets it." I was feeling happy to relay some good news for once. "He's organised for the school to start having sessions with her outside in the playground and she had her first one this morning. She sent me away this time and I used the opportunity to try and run with Charlie in his buggy... because I've given myself the Couch to 5K challenge and it was a..." I paused before I exaggerated the last comment: "BIG MISTAKE!"

The girls were listening, intrigued.

"So, I was running down the pavement, out of breath and sweaty, of course, and decided to take a detour towards the canal. I was trying to get the buggy over the pebbly towpath, through the muddy swamps that were in fact the puddles along the path, when I suddenly slipped on a..."

There was an eager silence on the call. I held my head in shame and uttered the words: "A banana skin!"

"A banana skin?!" The silence was broken by the biggest amount of screams and laughter that could possibly be made by two people.

"That's like something you'd see in a cartoon. I didn't think it actually happened in real life!" said Shelly.

"Yes, I know, but have you ever actually stood on one at an angle? I'm telling you – those bloody things are slippery and, well without intending to be crass, I fell arse over tit! And it was lucky that I've consumed my own body weight in wine and chocolate since the separation, because I had enough of a pad to fall onto! It was beyond mortifying. I can see myself now in slow motion, legs racing one after the other into the air – elegantly, just as you would imagine. Think of *Bambi* on bloody ice and you'll get the picture. I knocked the buggy over with me... Charlie screamed in shock. The flashbacks make me cringe, especially when Timothy came out from his thatched house to help pick me..."

"Hold on a minute!" interrupted Shelly. "What guy? From what thatchy house? Is there a more important part of the day you've missed out?"

"Nothing like that," I said quickly. "A guy came out of his property at the unfortunate moment that divvy here slipped on a banana skin. I mean, it was bad enough the first time I met him in the summer, but this just took the biscuit. If he hadn't thought I was incompetent the first time, then this would have definitely cemented the idea." I knew I was over-talking but I had to seize control of the conversation as I was starting to feel a little vulnerable. More importantly, I knew the assassination of questions that were about to follow.

"So, this *thatchy* guy, you've met him before and we didn't know about it? And he picked you up, a damsel in distress, with a rose in his mouth?" Vic piped up, soon joined by infectious giggling from Shelly.

"No! Not like that!" I blurted out. "He was insistent on making sure I hadn't broken anything. At which point I only bloody realised that I had my running leggings on inside-out with size fourteen stretched out across my ever-growing arse. How could my day get any worse?"

The girls were suddenly gripped by the story and were all ears – something they only do if either a) it involves a drama, b) the story contains some juicy bit of gossip that has wet their appetite, or c) it involves making plans for a girls' drinking night.

"So, as I stood up to try to compose myself, I quickly tried to brush the mud and leaves off my leggings in the hope that I could restore the chaotic imbalance that I hated to admit was my life. And that's when I noticed the huge rip that pretty much reached my pull-me-in briefs and exposed the unshaven beasts that are my legs. Oh my goodness, a jungle would have had less undergrowth! Plus, the briefs were now that awful grey-white colour from the amount of times I've worn them at the dreaded time-of-the-month and accidentally washed them in with the darks. The guy looked at me in disbelief, I think he could sense I was on the verge, as he softly offered to fetch a blanket to make me more comfortable. I must have had a look of disdain on my face as he said to follow him. Which I did, whilst trying to keep the blanket up and make my way past the brambles and bushes, and push an unsettled baby in a buggy."

"Through the brambles to get into his house! Who is he?" Vic questioned." Sounds like a chance meeting of Beauty and the Beast!"

"Oh my goodness, Beauty didn't shag the beast at the end of the story, did she?" Shelley cackled. "Now that would require the beast to fight back the brambles. I bet you can't even remember the last time you had sex, Sarah?!"

"Sod off, you two!" I grimaced. "I knew I shouldn't have told you!"

"Don't be getting your knickers, or should I say *pull-me-in-briefs*, in a twist. We're only having a giggle," Shelley said as she winked at me through the screen.

"That's right, babe," said Vic. "We were just getting excited. I mean, after all you've been through with Nick, we just want something positive to happen for you. We care about you, don't forget that."

"Exactly!" shouted Shelley. "You're our bestie and we only want you to be happy. Shag or no shag!"

"There is no shagging in it." My face was flushing again and it was beginning to annoy me that I was such a giveaway. I wasn't a teenager, I was supposed to be past all that stuff. My face was telling a different story, though.

"So, who is he? Come on, spill the beans?" Vic asked.

"Nobody," I said, trying to close the conversation. "Just someone Lena got chatting to in the park over the summer. She was having one of her 'moments' and he pretty much helped to distract her from it. I really don't know anything more about him than that. Honestly. Out of courtesy, I'll drop the blanket off at his house, make a few pleasantries, but that will be as far as it goes." I took a moment to breathe, but my tongue kept rolling like a steam train, desperately avoiding the silence that would enable their reactions. "Besides, he has a kid, he's probably married for all I know."

"So you've thought about it, haven't you?" Vic replied, smirking with that stench of someone who is holding something over you.

"No I haven't!" I protested.

"Keep your eyes on the path back out when you return, Sarah, those brambles could be embroiled with magic 'luuurrrvve' potions!" Shelley said with a cackle.

"I'll be busy looking on the floor for banana skins from now on," I stated and was desperate to steer them onto a different topic. "It should be a criminal offence if you throw one of those bad boys on the ground. If I'd had been an old lady, I could have come out a lot worse."

"If the words stick..." shrugged Vic, laughing at her own joke. "We are old!"

"Bananas are dangerous weapons, they should be taken care of." I was on a one-way rant like a regular bitter drinker, propped up on a stale bar in a pub, inhaling scampi fries and talking politics to nobody because my boredom had shot them all at close range. "A bin is there for a reason! Bananas should be binned, it's a duty of care for oldie-woldies like me."

"Bananas remind me of a very different situation entirely," confessed Shelley.

"Oh no, do we really need to hear this, Shel?" Vic pretended to cover her ears.

"Well, there was a time I met this guy on *Plenty of Fish*..." Shelley began.

"Ahhhh!" Vic and I squirmed at the prospect of what we were going to hear next.

"I thought you were on *Tinder*?" I asked, supressing my giggles.

"I'm getting to that bit... so we met up and went for a meal, and as soon as I saw him, I knew I couldn't go there! I knocked back my glass of wine and was looking around to see if I could order another one from the waitress – just to pluck the courage to say I had to go and had no plans meeting him again. The waitress caught my eye, she must have read my drink deprived gesture, and just as she was walking over to the table, he outrightly asked me: "Are you adventurous?"

"Did you answer him with your feminist knowledge?" I blurted.

"Yes, I *may* have shut him down quite quickly. I pretty much just said that he was repulsive and I wouldn't be having sex with him if he was the last man on earth." Shelley paused for a moment. "Okay that was a slight exaggeration. Perhaps I *could* have had sex with him if he *really* was the last man and I was desperate, but I was too enraged at his audacity at that point."

We all rolled our eyes in disgust.

"Then you will never guess what he asked me?"

"What?" I asked, wondering what it could possibly be.

"He said…" Shelley paused for a second, "would I consider getting intimate if he used a banana instead!"

"Eughh!!!" We all screeched. I quickly shut the living room door in fear that our wild and drunken antics would wake the kids up.

"That's surely not even possible," said Vic. "It would go all squishy!"

"And that, my dear ladies, is why I left *Plenty of Fish* and thought I should try *Tinder* instead. Those beef heads are far more apparent and I wouldn't waste a pain-inducing night like that ever again!" Shelley said simply.

"Fair enough!" I replied. "This is why I'm against internet dating. I couldn't cope with it all. I think I'm gonna be a born-again-nun, anyway."

"After what Shel has just told us, I think it should be a criminal offence to use a banana full stop," Vic replied wittily.

"Agreed!" I said. "We should get it written into law that bananas are only to be eaten and discarded into specially-assigned bins. I can see it written all over the Prime Minister's next manifesto: *"Bin Bananas!""*

"Ha ha ha!" Shelley guffawed. "Then, in small-print on the campaign poster – *One would recommend a courgette or aubergine for domestic use!"*

"So funny!" I screamed, feeling quite wasted by now.

"Not as funny as slipping on a banana skin in real life," Vic pointed out. "I'm still reeling over that one!"

"Hold on a minute!" Shelley's voice was so loud it practically shook the kitchen through the video call. "Bananas are yellow! I think making an idiot of yourself in public definitely constitutes hitting a new colour."

"Well, if that was what it took to tick off yellow, then there ain't no way I'll be doing that one again anytime soon!" I confessed.

"Consider your rainbow three parts more colourful now, Sarah." Vic was smiling.

After a last few exchanges of actually remembering to enquire about how each of our families were, we decided to call it a night. We all felt a bit lighter after our virtual gathering and discussion of the probability that bananas certainly didn't have any good uses. As I was falling asleep, I could still feel the burn of my rosy cheeks as my mind relived bumping into Timothy once again. I couldn't understand why I only ever met him when I was appearing such a bumbling mess. Why should I care what someone I barely knew thought of me? I couldn't shake the feeling that I was more bothered than I cared to admit. Knowing I should return the blanket and face Timothy again was making me feel uneasy. How could I get out of it?

16

A Visit to the Beast

T he weekend passed and we remained home for the whole of the duration. Lena seemed to have depleted her energy levels from her two mornings back in school, which seemed crazy as she wasn't there all day like the other children, but doing something so small seemed to monumentally affect her ability to function afterwards. The moment that I tried to suggest any ideas on Saturday or Sunday – to go to a park, or visit the skate ramps, or even to our favourite indoor ice cream parlour (where Lena normally chose her multi-coloured sprinkles for decoration), she rejected them all. She didn't have the energy to try and have fun. Instead, Lena opted to stay within the safety of the home, not even attempting to venture into the garden to let off some steam. Any hint of demand on her resulted in a full-on meltdown of kicking, screaming, biting or trashing the house. Instead, I pottered around, playing with Charlie and waiting for the storm to blow over.

By Monday morning, peace had been restored as Lena returned back to her more cheerful self.

"Miss Young wants to see my *Paw Patrol* toys," Lena informed me as we embarked on the walk to school with Charlie cooing in his buggy. "I'm taking them in my school bag."

I could almost taste the smell of freedom that the world was offering. The day had that quiet hue which occurs when the rush hour is finished and there is relief that the rest of the community can carry on with their daily chores at their own pace. We saw the odd dog walker with a wagging hound that prompted Lena to delay us further. An occasional van broke the solitude as it revved by on a delivery run. The sky mirrored the feel of the day with a few leftover plane trails across the empty blue ceiling, which was broken a few metres below by a red kite that was circling and hovering over the chimneys above us.

The ground was hard and each of our footsteps made an extra loud thump as we scurried along the pavement to reach the school for the ten o'clock start. After our peaceful journey, we soon arrived at the school gates and Lena pounced on the buzzer before I could even lift my hand away from the buggy handle. After a few rings the sound of my favourite receptionist could be heard through the speaker: "Who is it please?"

"It's me, duh!" Lena shouted back through the speaker. I could only imagine the look on the happy lady's face. Well I guess she'd asked a question and Lena did just answer it!

The gate opened and we made our way up the path with Lena skipping ahead as usual. Just as we were reaching the reception, the teaching assistant, who had been assigned the new task of bonding with Lena, appeared at the door.

"Good morning, Lena." She beamed down at her.

"Let's play!" Lena shouted gleefully as she flung her green reading bag onto the mud and opened the flap to reveal the hidden stash of characters. I smiled at the teaching assistant and nodded my head to indicate that I was leaving.

I had brought Timothy's blanket that he gave to me on the day that I'd slipped over. It was nestled in a carrier bag on the tray of Charlie's buggy. I had it all planned meticulously and ready to execute, surely it couldn't fail? It was Monday morning, so the probability was high that Timothy would be at work, meaning it was the most ideal time to go and knock; he was unlikely to be there. I could leave the wrapped bag, with the blanket concealed, on the doorstep and then rush away so that I could avoid the awkwardness of seeing him again and not knowing what to say. It would also seem that I had been polite enough to return it quickly, so he might think I was a nice person after all.

I don't know why what he thought of me bothered me so much, but it did. There was something about Timothy that was drawing me in and my response to that feeling was to avoid it further. Whenever I faced a challenge in life, it was far easier to circumvent it than to face the threat head-on. It was a default response that I couldn't get myself out of and it made me wonder whether Lena was a lot more like me than I realised. Her avoidance tactics were just as ingrained in her psychology as they were in mine.

Did I look okay? I pulled my coat down to try and cover my ever-growing bottom and used my hands to smooth my hair to smarten myself up. *Just in case I see him.*

I knew I didn't have long in the space of the hour before I needed to return to school to retrieve Lena, so I hurried my steps as fast as I could until I reached the narrow alley that led to the canal towpath. My anxious thoughts were accelerated as soon as I could see the bramble bushes that indicated Timothy's house was just over the other side. I paused, then continued with my mission as if I were on an expedition to discover the extreme epicentre of the South Pole. I knocked nervously on the front door of his ornate cottage. I was just about to retreat on my heels when the oak door swung open to reveal a man standing with casual, slouchy clothes, and a pair of slippers on his feet.

"Oh, hello there." His smile was warm. "What a pleasure to see you again."

I took a moment to take in some details about his presentation. Timothy's beard was trimmed neater than I had remembered. His eyes were dusky brown and had a glint of sadness to their surface warmth. There was something about him that drew me in. It was almost as if his soul exuded past his skin and made him attractive from the inside out.

My face flushed as the thought penetrated my mind that he was undeniably handsome and I was attracted to him.

"Hi, Timothy," I blurted, trying to regain myself. "I just wanted to return your blanket. Thank you so much for helping me out the other day. I have to say I was mortified for making an idiot of myself in public."

I laughed through my verbal diarrhoea, wishing I knew when to stop talking.

"Please call me Tim." His teeth were so clean. Oh god, why the hell was I noticing that? It was like my brain was already working out that he was a fine specimen to kiss. I was only supposed to be bringing him back a blanket. What if he could read my thoughts?

"Only my mum calls me Timothy and that's only when she has a bone to pick with me!" He laughed loudly to break down that barrier of not knowing somebody very well. "Would you like to come in?"

"Erm, yes that's very kind, but erm..." I was a rabbit caught in headlights and I hadn't anticipated this part of the story happening in my preparation for the visit. I suddenly had a random panic that I hadn't brushed my teeth and my subconscious reaction was to rub my tongue over them to check for residue. "I've just dropped Lena off at school and have to be back there for eleven."

"That's okay," he reassured. "I'm super-fast at making a cuppa! Do you prefer tea or coffee? How do you take it?" He began walking back down the hallway towards his kitchen. It was lucky that he wasn't a big man because the ceiling was looming over his head without much room to manoeuvre. I unstrapped Charlie from his buggy, put him on my hip and flipped off my shoes at the front door to follow Timothy inside. I closed the predictability of the safe world outside behind me. Tim hadn't even questioned why I had to pick Lena up early. Did he not think it strange that she was not being collected at usual school operating hours? I wondered if he sensed more about the situation (just like he had at the park) than he had let on.

"A white coffee please, no sugar." I glanced around the inside of the cottage, which was painted in an ivory-grey. The wooden, rustic beams were lined in rows along the ceilings and were also propped along the exterior of doorways, which gave the impression that I had walked into my own version of a *Brontë* novel. The lighting was soft and had the look that the electricity wasn't strong enough to make its way around the aged property.

There was a small dining room with artworks of woodland landscapes circulating a large, ornate mirror in the centre of the feature wall. The room was open-plan and there was no clear transition into the living room which featured a curvaceous, grey sofa, with a selection of cushions and blankets adorning it. The wooden mantlepiece above the fireplace had a few candles neatly placed and a photo in a frame of Tim and his son that we had met at the park. I pointed towards it and felt a bit embarrassed as I asked: "I'm so sorry, I've forgotten your son's name."

"It's Oscar." Tim smiled. "No need to apologise. It was quite a long time ago, and if it makes you feel any better, I can never remember names. When I first saw you again I also forgot your name and thought in my head 'the *Paw Patrol* lady!'"

We both laughed and it eased the air. He seemed quite direct and he didn't fluff around the edges.

"How old is Oscar?" I asked, trying to find a question to make the conversation flow.

"Thirteen. Growing up way too fast. He's bigger than me already – although that's not very hard."

I laughed. There was something about Tim that made him easy to talk to. I started to relax as I peeled off my hat and gloves and wrapped them up into my hand before doing the same for Charlie who was looking like a snow baby in his all-in-one coat. The fire was burning in the centre of the living room and the sound of cracking wood was crisping in the air. I had to give it to Tim – his small cottage was perfectly inviting on a cold, autumnal day.

"Have a seat and I'll just fix the coffee," he called out as he rushed to the kitchen. "Can I get anything for the baby?"

"That's very kind but I have Charlie's beaker here so don't worry," I replied as I fetched it out of my just-in-case bag.

A few moments later Tim had appeared and sat himself on the single pouffe that was adjacent to the sofa. He rested the drinks on the coffee table next to it. He had a small tin of biscuits that he opened and offered to us both, to which I politely declined. Charlie's eyes grew wide and his lips were drooling so much it would have been cruel for me to have said no. I dipped in the round tin and passed a chocolate digestive to Charlie who sucked merrily away, a trail of sloppy chocolate racing down his chin.

"We never did bump into each other again at the park!" Tim observed. "I've kept an eye out when it's my weekend with Oscar and on the occasions we have gone to Queen's Field."

It didn't matter what was said in the rest of the sentence as I had zoned out with the information that he only had Oscar on some weekends. I wondered if it meant he was separated from Oscar's mum. I had assumed he was married. With the realisation that he could potentially be single, it changed the direction I felt the visit could go in.

"Lena hasn't been wanting to go out very much lately, not since the day she ran away from school. I feel like we've been quite housebound since then."

"Is it just you?" Tim asked curiously. "My apologies that I'm quite direct, I was just thinking it must be quite tough if you were doing that solo."

"I'm recently separated," I confessed. "Although, if I am honest with myself, I was probably doing it alone anyway."

Had he been trying to fish for information? Was he attracted to me too?

"I'm sorry to hear that." He had an affectionate smile. "Although sometimes a change has to happen to make things work out better. It can take a long time to reach that place of contentment again. I wouldn't have said that at the beginning of my separation – I pretty much nose-dived into self-medicating as a release."

I sat quietly. His words were describing I was doing just the same, but I lacked the courage to admit it, not just to a stranger but to myself too. I guessed if I acknowledged I had a problem then it meant I had to do something about it, and my crutch of drinking through my anxious pain was an escape route that I wasn't ready to give up just yet.

"Your cottage is beautiful." I changed the conversation. "It's the first time I've ever been in one actually."

"So you're a cottage virgin!" He laughed with the inappropriateness of making a familiar joke with a stranger he barely knew. "Oh shit, did I just say that?! My apologies, I don't have much impulse control sometimes. I try to tell myself to think before I speak, but I'm useless at it. If something funny pops into my head I'm not very good at gauging whether it should be verbalised or not."

"No offence taken," I reassured. "You've summed me up pretty well after a first meeting, I think my whole life has been spent being a cottage virgin."

"I'm ADHD," Tim confessed candidly, "it's a superpower and a super-pain! It's the reason I get hyper-focused in activities that interest me, but also the reason that I've always been known as 'half-a-job' because I can't finish things when I'm not interested. I think it's why I was drawn to your daughter in the park; I seem to have a radar for my neurokin! She has the charm of someone who is far more interesting than the rest of the world."

I was right – he had sensed more about our situation. I smiled as I could relate to everything Tim had just said. I wondered if he was just as nervous as I was to be meeting again. He seemed to be over-sharing information. Did he feel just as flustered as I did?

"You could say she's a character, that's for sure." I held my hand over my forehead with an action of embarrassed shame and we both laughed.

"Oscar was quite forthright when he was younger," Tim continued, "it's what set me on a path of self-discovery. They say the apple never falls far from the tree. I often feel indebted to Oscar for so many reasons. In life he has definitely taught me to be a better version of myself."

"It's funny you should say that," I joined, "because I've started to realise that a lot of what Lena does seems similar to me. It takes a mini version of yourself to hold the mirror up to your own reflection."

"Yes!" Tim said excitedly. "Exactly that!" It was refreshingly attractive to hear a man talk so lovingly about his child and it felt the extreme opposite of what I had been used to in my relationship with Nick.

"I think it's why I understood her so early on," I explained. "And why it caused such a battle in my marriage, because her dad had the opinion that labels only exist for bad behaviour."

"Ouch!" Tim reacted. "Oh boy, you really did have your work cut out."

"I know." I was opening up very quickly. "To make it worse I feel quite awkward with my family right now because, up until recently, they've been in agreement with him."

"Jeez." Tim seemed genuinely astounded by what I was telling him. "That's so much for one person to be dealing with. I hope you won't mind me saying this, but it seems like you're a pretty resilient person."

"Thanks." I smiled, choking back my emotions. "I often just feel like I'm in survival-mode so I do appreciate the compliment."

I sipped some of my coffee in desperate need of a caffeine fix for a change of mood. I was feeling extremely vulnerable all of a sudden and the instinct to put my protective wall back up was building. To joke it away was the only method I had at my disposal.

"I didn't seem to bounce back easily when I slipped on a banana skin!" I jollied.

"Oh, is that what you did?" Tim looked shocked. "I just heard this almighty thud the other side of the bush. When I looked up I was so surprised it was you! I couldn't believe I had bumped into you again."

"I think I would've been less embarrassed if the first time you had met me I hadn't got it so wrong too!" I proclaimed.

Charlie let out a small belch right on cue and we both stifled a giggle at the spot-on timing.

"I think Charlie is trying to tell me something!" I commented.

"He's probably saying don't take me running again!" Tim chuckled softly. He clearly liked to find the humour in situations. It was a relief to be around.

"So, I signed up for this stupid Couch to 5K thing as part of a self-care task I was given from a support group," I began, "but on my first run I only went and slipped on a banana and ripped my trousers. It could only happen to me! My friends thought it was hilarious when we had our weekly call. I'll be the butt of their jokes for quite some time."

"I don't blame them," he said flirtatiously, "it was pretty epic!"

"Don't you start as well!" I played back. "I'll never live it down. I mean, can you imagine how mortified I felt facing the music giving you the blanket back?" This was going far smoother than I could ever have imagined. I felt like I was lubricated with alcohol to speak so easily. It was testament to the fact that Tim seemed to put me at ease.

"Maybe you need a running buddy so that you don't make the same mistake again? Save Charlie from the ordeal?" His face sparkled as he poked some light-hearted fun at me. "To pick you up again if you have another fall?"

"What next time?" I laughed. "I only needed a small excuse not to try again. This was off the scale."

"As a matter of fact I go running too. Notice the use of the right verb there as I didn't say I go *slipping*!"

We both laughed and were milking the joke for all it was worth.

"I hope you know I'm only joking." He looked up, almost unsure of my response. "But if you would like some company to run with, or even walk with, then I'd love to join you?"

"Sure," I replied, feeling apprehension fill my body. "That would be lovely."

"I'm on shift work until the weekend," Tim told me, "but I'm free on Saturday or Sunday if that works for you? No pressure, obviously, just off the top of my head the times that I am free. Or the week after could work too, but after that I have Oscar for his weekend with me. So I'll leave it with you. Perhaps if I gave you my number you could let me know? Equally, if you feel that it's too much, I will understand too."

"It's not too much." I smiled. "In fact, it might be the push I need to try again." I took my phone out of my pocket indicating that I was ready to take his number. He gave me the digits, I typed them into my phone and told him that I would give him a quick missed call so he could save my number. I rang the number he'd provided and his phone started beeping from the kitchen. I quickly hung up the call.

As I had my phone out I checked the time; it was ten minutes to eleven. I jumped off the sofa and started to put mine and Charlie's outer layers back on at the speed of light. "I'm so sorry, I've just seen the time and I've only left myself ten minutes to get back to school to pick Lena up!"

"Well, it was lovely to see you again – the right way up of course!" He winked as I was rushing out of the door.

"Byeee! Thanks for the coffee." I called, hurrying past the thickets and the brambles as I reached the towpath with an extra spring in my step. It felt like I could hear the rhythm of the clock ticking in my brain urgently informing me that I was late, yet again. I began running whilst pushing the buggy along the pavement, past Queen's Field playground, along the main road and over the zebra crossing to Lena's school. I was so out of breath by the time I reached the buzzer, that I gasped for air as I tried to express the one word I could manage: "Lena!"

"Come in," the cold voice replied over the speaker.

I congratulated myself for doing a second run of my Couch to 5K without even realising it – that had to be worth an extra bar of chocolate for achievement! Then it dawned on me that I had agreed to run with Tim and I had no excuse to get out of it. The greatest wave of panic hit me. What if I made a fool of myself yet again? I was so preoccupied by overthinking how I had presented myself in his cottage and if I had made any social faux-pas, followed by worrying about what I would wear if I ran with him, I didn't hear my phone notification.

It wasn't until I got home that I checked my phone. There was a message waiting for me from Nick.

> **Nick**
> Hi, how are the kids? Am I still having them for you this week-end?

Then another one.

> **Nick**
> ??

I texted back.

> I hate to remind you that they are both *our* kids. Oh and they are fine.

My phone pinged a reply instantly.

> **Nick**
> No need to keep making everything a battle! I'll come over Saturday morning and drop them back Sunday. Happy?

I couldn't help myself – his audacity and ignorance had gotten to me. Why did he feel the need to make every chance an opportunity to gaslight me?

> You made it a battle, not me. Can you be specific with a time? I have plans. I thought my mum was dealing with drop offs?

A direct reply returned from Nick.

> **Nick**
> Your mum shouldn't have to do this. Is 10 specific enough? And you have plans?!

Two can play that game, I thought.

> Yes thanks. See you then.

Nick had successfully managed to change my good mood in minutes. I tried to switch my mind back to the excitement of being with

Tim again. Was my life ever going to stop feeling so confrontational?

17

The Green Zone

I pulled on my fitted running leggings that I had only just pur-
chased online, so I had something comfortable and as attractive
as possible to wear in time for the big event with Tim. I had chosen
a pair promoted in their advertising to slim bodies because they
were plain black, with an animal print that ran along the seam
on each side of my legs to draw the eye away from my rolls. I
combined this with a long-sleeve, sweat-absorbing black t-shirt to
conceal as many wobbly bits as possible. I checked my appearance
in the long mirror in my bedroom and yanked the material on my
top down, desperately attempting to magic more length and space
in my outfit. *Try to relax*, I berated myself. It wasn't working and I
looked as fun as a dry sardine. I had to laugh – surely I couldn't
screw up this meeting again?

I felt remarkably fresh for a Saturday morning – having refrained from drinking for the previous two nights. We had delayed
our weekly Gin O' Clock call from the usual time on Thursday to
take the opportunity of having a Saturday night together seeing as
I was child-free. I hadn't told them about my arrangements in the
day with Tim, partly in case it never happened and I had to explain
that he had bowed out on me, but also because their excitement

might send me over the edge and build up the experience with even more anticipation than I had already.

I felt restless, like I was being driven by a motor; unable to stop or do one thing at a time as I charged from room to room buzzing on nervous adrenaline. At this rate I'd be ready for bed instead of having any energy left to run with. I really wanted Tim to see me looking my best but I couldn't work miracles.

I returned to the mirror, remembering I hadn't fixed my make-up which took extra fuss and procrastination to create a safety mask. I added extra layers of mascara to pump up my eyelashes and grabbed my concealer to stick plasters over the dark, yellow circles under my eyes. *Okay, that looks better,* I told myself.

Next, I worked on my barnet which I had added a new shade of cherry red onto that morning (from a quick bottle of semi-permanent dye that I'd selected from the supermarket). The colour was far more vibrant than I was used to but I decided a change was better than any. I strategically placed my hair into a loose ponytail and pulled a few whispery strands down at the front to cover the wrinkles that felt far too exposed. Okay, so it was going to have to do. I mean, it wasn't like we were going to a restaurant or a bar. I started to panic that maybe I had put too much effort in. My frantic thoughts were relentless.

I ran down into the living room where Lena was waiting with her *Paw Patrol* backpack on, her matching trainers already fastened. She had been in the same location since breakfast so I knew where to find her.

"Mummy, why does your hair look like it's bleeding?" Lena asked curiously without any hint of sarcasm in her tone. She always said the words exactly as they appeared visually in her brain without any filter.

"I put a new colour on it," I replied, treading the water cautiously. "It's supposed to look like cherry red. Do you like it?"

"No."

"It comes off after a few washes so the old colour will return soon." I cuddled her closely as her eyes looked confused and sad. I could feel her pain as if it were my own.

"I don't like it when things change," she confided as she squeezed her small arms around my running leggings and I tried to cuddle her back at arms-length, suddenly realising I didn't want any marks on my outfit.

"Me too," I empathised. "But eventually I get used to a change and then sometimes I even like the thing that's changed."

"When things change it scares me," Lena explained. She was so much older than her years. "I always want things to stay the same."

"Some things do stay the same." I softened as I stopped worrying about my outfit and pulled her into a maternal squeeze. "Mummy loves you. That stays the same."

"You have to love me. I'm a superpup!" she declared. I laughed at her beautiful integrity of spirit that just shone through in every situation.

I could hear a murmur from upstairs and went to fetch Charlie from his cot. I had put him there half in the hope he might have taken an early mid-morning nap, and half with the desperate need to put him somewhere safe whilst I got ready. He was babbling to himself and as soon as he saw me, he had the relief that he hadn't been abandoned forever. He was far too excitable and alert so I knew he hadn't had a nap.

As I went into the living room I could hear Lena having a one-way fight. "No, *Alexa*. Not that one!" she shouted. "You always get it wrong!"

"I'm sorry, I didn't quite catch that," *Alexa* began politely as if she had been designed to deal with a child as explosive as Lena. "Could you please repeat it again?"

"I SAID..." Lena screamed like she was an animal with many heads unleashed at once, "play *Paw Patrol*!"

"I have one song in my library," *Alexa* began apologetically as if her robotic voice was actually reading the situation on target, "The *Paw Patrol* movie theme tune. Would you like me to play this selection?"

"YESSS!" Lena was bouncing up and down with her arms flapping.

The song began playing and Lena started following the sequence of actions in her head that created an unusual dance in the middle of the living room floor. The dance moves she was visualising along with her energy, created a sense of incongruous moves that were so infectious to watch that I joined in – Charlie swinging on my hip. Lena squealed with excitement.

We were murdering the lyrics: "*No job's too big, no pup's too small, we're on a roll!*" I swung Charlie in a circle, through the living room air and watched him as screaming laughter blasted out like it was dispersing on a Tannoy system. Suddenly, Rex was barking and jumping up in the chaos we had created, desperate to not be forgotten as the fourth important member of our family. We howled, united in our dance moves, lost together in a unique snap-shot of family life that we had carved to be our own.

We were so engrossed that we hadn't noticed an observer slink into the room.

"Daddy!" Lena screamed excitedly and ran to be picked up.

How long had he been watching?

Nick shot me a look, and for once, it lacked the usual hostility he was armed with. There was a sad vulnerability that exuded his aura and reminded me of the stranger I was once attracted to.

"Looks like you're too busy having fun to notice me knocking on the door," he remarked, his eyes making sense of the scene in front of him. "I feel like I'm invading."

"Let's go, Daddy!" Lena jumped down from their embrace and yanked his jacket to pull him out of the room.

"Hold on a minute, sweetie," Nick said pleasantly. "I just need to get your things together." He picked up the packed duffel bag and the small *Paw Patrol* backpack and swung them over his shoulder. "I guess these are coming with us."

"Uh huh," I replied. I was having difficulty finding the words to act civilly towards Nick after his last text message had enraged me so much.

"Looks like you didn't really need me here." Nick looked at me as we passed Charlie between us. "Seems like you've been coping alright on your own."

It was a strange thing to say and I wondered if he was regretting our break up. I held my head high as I looked directly into his lost expression and firmly said, "We're doing just fine."

It felt cold being so blunt but I tried to remind myself that he'd had enough chances to change his ways and get on board to adapt with the way our family was. Trying to play the victim card was a lame attempt for some redemption on his part and it wasn't good enough.

"You going to a gym or something?" Nick was perusing my outfit with his inspective eyes. "I didn't think that was *your* thing."

"I'm getting back into it," I said guardedly. I refrained from correcting his loaded comments. My soul was secretly gloating that he had the impression that I was surrounded by other fit men. I started to wonder if I was imagining it, but it seemed as if he were lingering in the room with me on unfinished business.

"You look..." Nick paused and, uncharacteristically for him, struggled to find the next word. "Different."

"Mummy changed her hair," Lena interrupted. "She wants to look cherry red!" We turned around to see Lena clutching Poxy in her gentle, childlike clutch. It was a bolt to reality that the children were still in the room and any communication between us needed to be tailored to suit their small ears.

"She's changed a lot of things," Nick voiced towards Lena but more for my attention, "Mummy is looking very happy."

I could smell his freshly-shaved skin and his usual cashmere-wool aroma from across the room. Just the smell of his masculinity was making me feel like I was weakening. His essence, his persona and his feelings were always so strongly projected that it was hard to not be entrapped the moment you were in his company. The new life that I was carving around myself was filtering away to leave the shackles of my naivety bare. I thought I had moved past my longing to still be with Nick because of the anger and resentment I felt about his inflexibility towards our family's needs and the complete control he had over me. And yet, I was still deeply entangled in the complexity of my feelings. I felt weak and raw.

"I have to rush. I have plans." I tried to remain in control. Besides, time was ticking and I knew that Tim was waiting for me.

"What plans?" Nick's face suddenly contorted and he was back to his unvarnished tone of voice to which he corrected himself, "I'm sorry, that's none of my business anymore. I shouldn't have asked."

I was stumped. The loyal part of me wanted to answer his question openly, but I refrained with the desire to remain aloof. I kept to a non-disputable conversation to keep things secret.

"What time will you be dropping the children off tomorrow?" I enquired.

"I'll text and let you know." Nick looked perplexed. "Why, do you have plans with someone tomorrow?"

"I just have things to do," I said non-conclusively.

"I have football tomorrow morning actually," he was reversing his tactics, "so I best drop them back by ten. That okay?"

"Absolutely." I smiled with a small sense of achievement. "Bye, kids!" I lunged forwards warmly to give them a nurturing embrace and tried to keep the farewell short. Nick went to the front door to put on his tanned builder boots that were neatly positioned by the frayed matt. Just the repetition of a small habit was enough to remind me of the person I had felt trapped in a relationship with a few months ago. He gave me one last look of confusion

– or was it suspicion? I wasn't quite sure, but he definitely knew that I was preoccupied and his comment that I didn't really need him suggested he knew I was moving on. He probably had always thought I was reliant on him and could never fend for myself, a wave of pride fell over me as I firmly shut the door.

I promptly picked up my phone to text Tim.

> Hi Tim. Sorry for the delay this morning. I'm ready whenever you are? Sarah x

A reply came back quickly.

> **Tim**
> No apologies needed. That's great, shall we meet at Queen's Field in 15 mins? x

> Sounds like a plan! See you shortly x

I decided to leave straight away and walk slowly on my journey there. After all, my energy needed to be retained so that I could look at least half-presentable on my arrival.

I walked along the cracked path that dissected the two halves of the grassy field, straining to see if I could recognise Tim. There was a family with a kite earnestly attempting to get the thing off the ground on one side of my peripheral vision, and on the other side a small cluster of dog owners were having a natter in the breezy outside calm, whilst the dogs circled and wagged their tails at one another.

My heart began to bang with the onset of fear of the unknown and it was gripping my muscles tightly. How would it go? Would I be able to talk? What if I saw someone I knew? Why couldn't I just relax and be normal? Where was he and what if he didn't show up?

Suddenly I spotted a lone, hooded person jogging from the bottom of the path by the canal, heading right towards me. I waited in anticipation. The stranger arrived and unpeeled his protective hood to unveil a face that wasn't so unknown.

"Blimey it's nippy this morning." Tim smiled, gasping. "That short run here took my breath away!"

"You did better than me," I confessed sheepishly. "I cheated and walked. I thought I needed *extra* warm-up time." We both laughed quietly in order to break the ice.

"Do we even have a route planned, or shall we play it by ear?" Tim asked.

I took a moment to dissect his appearance which was pretty casual. His trainers were worn and the laces fraying as if they had seen better days. His tracksuit was loose and plain grey in colour with no branded names on display. His hair was looking un-styled as if he'd just got out of bed. His complexion gave the impression of someone who put effort in from the inside and didn't spend much time worrying about the material things in life. I felt grounded just by being around him; it was refreshing after so many years of tight control.

"I don't mind," I admitted. "Let's just see where the wind takes us? Or rather – where the wind can help roll me right back to afterwards!"

"I love your thinking." Tim laughed. "Although, I'm not a great person to listen to, I get lost doing it this way every time!"

"Ha ha!" I laughed louder and more genuinely this time as I was warming up. "Just remember, keep your eyes peeled for any banana skins! You promised you had a job to do today!"

Tim signed a salute in acceptance of his role. "I'll be on duty."

"Shall we start going down the hill first?" I indicated my finger back along the path Tim had just come from. "I need all the help I can get."

"Great idea," Tim replied and we both shuffled to find our rhythm as we ran.

We ran towards the canal and onto the towpath. Because it was dry the terrain added extra resonance to our steps. We ran by parked barges near the arena where there seemed to be a community moored there. It was picturesque; the reflection of boats mirrored in the ripples of the water. We chatted about the scenery around us and it fuelled our steps further as if the effort of running had been transferred to our legs automatically whilst we enjoyed the scenery.

We came to a stone bridge that we needed to cross as the towpath continued on the other side of the canal. The dated, arched bridge looked as if it had been restored by bright paint in an attempt to regenerate the appearance.

"I love how the sunlight bounces back from the bridge onto the water." Tim pointed, as we reached the rear of a coffee-making warehouse which was fenced off behind the path.

"That smells delicious," I commented, as the aroma of coffee beans caressed my senses.

"There's something about the smell of coffee that is so inviting," Tim agreed. "I didn't start drinking it until I was about thirty. I wanted to get on the band wagon because it smelt so good."

"I live on coffee by day and switch to alcohol at night!" I laughed as I suddenly felt awkward admitting it. "I do joke but it's on my radar to make some healthier life choices – hence the reason I pushed myself to start this running malarkey!"

"We all have our vices," Tim began apprehensively. "Although for me there was a danger when the pleasure turned into a need."

"Yeah, I hear you," I opened up. "It's a fine line and something that I need to do something about."

It was strange laying my soul bare, but I realised that being more open about the issues in my life was starting to help my emotions. I wasn't sure how a running date could actually feel more like a counselling session, but it did.

We continued to run along the path, this time leaving the smell of coffee behind. A few metres along we reached a pub named The Wharf, with a few empty tables and umbrellas reflecting in the water.

"Is it okay if we walk just a little?" I panted, embarrassed at how unfit I was probably looking. "I just need to catch my breath."

"Sure," Tim said. "I was needing a quick breather too."

I could tell that he could have kept on going because he was extremely fit. I knew he was used to running because he did it with such ease. Me, on the other hand, had sweat pouring out of every pore, cheeks that were swollen and red with disgrace, and newly-washed cherry hair plastered all over my face. I had so wanted to look attractive; I felt mortified that I was looking such a mess. *Oh no, maybe going for a run with Tim this early was not something I should have agreed to!* My internal dialogue was increasing with anxiety. As the previous chatter took a momentary pause and I was trying to not blurt out something to fill the silence, Tim took the conversation to a deeper level.

"After the divorce I spiralled out of control." His voice was sombre. "I think I had to reach rock bottom to make some changes. My desire to be a better dad to Oscar was definitely a driving factor in my recovery. I'm a big advocate for talking about positive mental health now, even more so in men, it's all too often swept under the carpet. The ability for a man to admit he feels weak is still such a taboo. That's why I started the men's shed."

"What's the men's shed?" I enquired with interest.

"It's a cabin I've set up so that men of all ages, all walks of life, can go there to find a way to connect to others. We have a construction shed and there are mini projects on the go run by a lovely carpenter who gives up his time to volunteer and share his skills." He laughed. "Us men, well, we're Neanderthals at heart! We need to be confused and do something next to each other so that we can find a way to have a simple chat!"

"That's interesting," I began, "because, as a woman, I've relied heavily on my friends and it's easy for us to natter on the phone and to forget the time because we feel better being with one another. I've never thought of it like that before."

"We need connections in life," Tim continued passionately, "therapy comes from them. We really are socially driven as human beings and our mood naturally enhances when we find those connections."

"You seem like you're well-versed in this stuff," I observed. "It's good that you put back into others who might be less fortunate."

"I always tell myself that you never know what anybody else's life is like unless you've walked in their shoes. I try not to judge but come from a place of understanding."

"I think that's why my daughter warmed to you in the park that day," I recollected. "She doesn't normally connect with strangers."

"In my experience we have a gut reaction when someone understands us."

"I'm sure Lena has a sixth sense for when people are kind," I said. "She's not been wrong yet. It's as if she has an instant like or dislike depending on the air people give off. I'm usually just playing catch-up, but she's always right."

Tim nodded.

"Shall we start running again?" I suggested out of panic that he must have been feeling frustrated running with me when we had done very little of the activity.

"Yes," Tim replied. "I do feel more refreshed now. Anyway, I think I was also drawn to your discomfort as her parent..." Tim started tentatively, "because I've been there too so I know how it feels."

"Not many people do," I declared. "I wish I could just parent the way I do at home, but when I'm out in public the stares and judgements get the better of me."

"Try not to worry what others think," Tim advised. "Even when your child has morphed into an alpaca and is jumping up and down on your car, screaming they are trying to get to the cool air at the top of a mountain!"

We both fell into a fit of giggles at the bizarre creativity that was at war with the level of distress our children found themselves in.

"That's not quite happened yet." I giggled. "But I wouldn't put it past Lena to pull that kind of manoeuvre!"

"That's actually a true story from when Oscar was eight years old and the people around us thought he should be acting more appropriately for his age." Tim held his hands out and shrugged. "Of course, in truth, he was in total distress."

"I'm always thinking on my feet." I felt animated now. "Just when I think I've mastered this parenting thing there is always another curve ball thrown at me to keep me on my toes."

A family of ducks crossed our path and they were coming closer to the pathway where a lady had unstrapped her toddler from a buggy, and they were bending down to get a closer look. The mother duck was swimming closer, followed by four small ducklings in an obedient line, who were paddling to keep up in the pursuit of scavenging some food from the humans. The smallest one at the end of the queue was making the loudest quacks to not be forgotten. Finally, as the group hit their destination, they stopped, bewildered, unsure why their usual prize of bread was not being delivered. The ducks weren't aware of the sign that said 'thank you for not feeding us bread' placed on a fence nearby. They hung around briefly for a few seconds before moving on down-stream.

"Did you see that family of ducks?" Tim began. "The mother duck didn't need to instruct her ducklings that it was dangerous to hang around any longer."

"Yes, that's so true!" I joined in. "They follow their instinct."

"We all need to learn to be a bit more like that," Tim analysed. "That way, you can do your badass parenting that you do at home all of the time, no matter who is around to pass judgement."

"I think my greatest problem so far is that I lost my way in being able to trust my own feelings," I confessed. "It's surreal, but I keep seeing elements in nature that remind me of following my instincts without being told. Seeing the ducks has just reminded me of that."

"I struggled with that too, and not that long back either," Tim reassured me, "but I found a way to start again."

"That's exactly what I'm trying to do," I said, holding back the emotion.

"Addiction would have squeezed the life out of me if not," Tim explained. "I made the choice to live again. I wasn't any braver or stronger than you are now. Just the will to make a change so that I could be the kind of role model Oscar needed me to be was enough."

The conversation fell silent and I wasn't sure what to say. I wanted to admit to him that I knew I was self-medicating my anxiety and stress levels, but it would have opened a floodgate that I wasn't ready to explore no matter how many times we were returning to it. Tim must have sensed my discomfort and slowed down his pace to point towards a passageway off the canal path.

"I'm not sure how you're doing for time." He looked up briefly before he continued, "But if we cut through here, we could run along the main road back up to Queen's Field. I'm sure there's a small coffee shop up that way too, on the corner of the parade of shops just before you reach the bottom of the field. Would you be up for grabbing a coffee? My treat?"

I smiled and agreed to his kind offer as I uttered the words: "I'm okay for time. That would be lovely."

We gave up running for the second time (which was a godsend as I had a stitch anyway) just as we reached the longest gradient ever. We decided that walking it would be the best thing to do. I sipped on my water bottle and chatted away until we reached the coffee shop.

"What's your order?" Tim gestured.

"A white coffee, no sugar, please," I replied thankfully.

"Can I tempt you into eating a Danish pastry with me?" He beamed. "We definitely deserve it after that mammoth run!"

"That's very kind, thank you." I went to get my phone that had my credit card in it, but he ushered me to put it away again.

"It's my treat, remember?" Tim said as he slipped into the shop whilst I stretched my seized-up muscles outside. "You can always return the favour next time."

Tim had said 'next time'! Did that mean he intended on seeing me again?

He returned with two coffee cups, a delicious aroma coming from them. We walked along until we found a bench and plonked ourselves down. Tim kindly passed me my coffee and a brown, greasy paper bag with the flaky cake inside. We munched on our sweetly-baked delicacies and sipped down the frothy coffee with steam rising up into the cold November air, as we took in the busy playing fields around us. The two of us gently relaxed in the crisp sun.

Hours were passing, with the regular flow of people or animals in the park, whilst we remained constant in our seated paradise. It was only as the feel of frost-bite began to set in from remaining static, that we decided it was time to call it a day.

As I reached my front door, a text appeared on my phone.

Tim

I had a lovely time. Please give me a shout if you would like to meet up again? x

Yes that would be nice. Thank you very much for the coffee and cake too – an added surprise! x

Tim

It was a pleasure. Would you like to meet again one evening? For dinner perhaps? x

I would love to, just need to sort out childcare, but can be done x

Tim

How about you let me know when suits you and we go from there? x

Sounds like a plan x

Tim

I'm off for a soak in the bath. My body is not as young as I think it should be! ;-) x

Enjoy and will be in touch soon x

Soon after I'd got my running gear off and had a shower to freshen up, Shelley and Vic arrived, banging on the front door. I opened it and they both piled in with a few rustling bags and a large gin glass each.

"Look what I picked up online!" squealed Vic, throwing a plastic glass into my ribs. It had swirly pink writing on that read 'Sarah'.

"Wow, thanks," I replied. "Is that because I'm so old I might forget my own name?"

"We've all got one," Vic replied as they both held their own versions up with their grinning faces blown up through the transparent material, their names beaming back at me.

"Nice! What are you two like!"

"We need a photo of them all together and we can change our profile picture in the *WhatsApp* group!" Vic announced, although I knew it would be shared around the rest of our social media feeds too.

The girls opened the fridge to dump their collection of alcohol bottles inside to get them chilled for the night ahead. They had to move a few things around to get space as I had wedged in some pizza boxes and buffet food onto the shelves.

"What's all this??" Shelley queried. "You didn't go to any bother did you, Sarah?"

"I just got a few bits in for our sleepover tonight," I confirmed. "I wanted to surprise you with a bit of a spread to say thank you to you both for everything you've done for me these last few months."

"Oh, Sarah," they both chorused sweetly. "You didn't need to do that!"

"I wanted to. It was just a small gesture to show my appreciation."

"For what?" Shelley asked, her eyes sparkling. "Taking you down a dodgy road of getting you stoned and skinny-dipping in public?!"

"Yeah!" Vic joined in. "What great friends we are!" We laughed as the memory of our endeavours entered our minds.

"You've both kept me going," I told them. "Even if you do push the boundaries."

"Enough soppy talk," Shelley interjected. "Let's get drinking. We have a dare for us to do tonight!"

"About that," I started apprehensively, "I thought it might be nice to just have the buffet tonight and boycott the drinking?"

"Why's that?" Shelley questioned, genuinely confused at the sudden change of direction. "Are you not feeling well, sweetie?"

"I'm fine." I took a deep breath before I opened up. "I want to cut down on my drinking and get fitter again. I need to find a more constructive way of coping."

"If that's how you feel," Shelley responded, "then we will stand by you. We don't need to have a drink to have a good time."

"Uh huh," agreed Vic. "Just being together is a treat in itself. True friendship means you go through life together, whatever the direction."

"Oh, you guys are so supportive." I beamed. "You both rock!"

The girls began by putting the bottles back into the carrier bags that they had brought with them, then filled our new glasses with mocktails of shaken, mixed juices over ice. I chucked some food into the oven and began laying out plates of ready-made food onto the island. It felt like I was finally in control of my life and it felt good.

"Even though we're choosing to stay sober," Shelley said, munching on a vegetable roll. "It doesn't mean we can't still do our planned task!"

"What planned task?" I squealed, unsure if I was going to agree to another one of their bright ideas. "What have you two been up to again?"

"We were texting each other the other night," began Vic, "and we thought it would be funny to record a *TikTok* dance!"

"You've got to be kidding me!" I cried. "I don't even know what they are!"

"I downloaded the app in the week," Vic explained. "You find a

dance trend and then record your own version. I have to admit –
I've been addicted!"

"She's found the perfect dance, if you're game?" Shelley winked.

"What dance?" I was holding my head in dramatic disbelief.

"The bestie dance." Vic added, "It's easy to follow, even for Shel
who's normally useless at putting one foot in front of the other!"

"Eh, bloody cheek!" shouted Shelley. "Although very true!" We
laughed with memories of when we were still at school and we
could never teach Shelley the *Macarena* or the *Saturday Night* dance
as she was always turning in the wrong direction with her arms
shaking loosely about.

Vic positioned her phone on the kitchen island as she began
playing the song. We stood around, bunched together in our trio,
consuming the energy of what we were about to tackle. After a few
repeated plays of the song, Vic (who was always the lead dancer
when we were younger), explained where we would be standing,
and flipped her camera into reverse mode so that we could see our
aged bodies gleaming back from the screen.

"Ouch!" I screamed. "This is torture. I can't believe I'm agreeing
to this, it's not like we look like those young toned bodies in the
video."

"That's exactly why we are doing it!!" Shelley contradicted my
thought pattern. "Because we don't look like them and we *are never*
too old to learn to try something new!"

"I'm not sure this was the best night to try and stay sober," I
cajoled.

Our feet were cumbersome and clunky as we bashed back and
forth in no set pattern and with no similarity to the thing we
were supposed to be doing. We sipped on our mocktails as we
practised again and again, eventually able to bring together some
form of a routine. It didn't look anything like the original, but just
as Vic pressed record, we created a piece of *TikTok* magic that was
probably far more entertaining than the posed, perfected routines

we had watched in the build-up.

"Right, it's going up!" Vic posted it onto her profile with a quick click as we all screamed in unison.

"It doesn't matter," joked Shelley. "We're far too old and un-eventful to feature on the 'for you page', which basically means we will have zero viewers!"

"What if we go viral?" I laughed.

"Well, you get to tick off all of your rainbow colours at once if it does!" Vic smirked. "Let's watch it on playback!"

We laughed loudly as we watched ourselves replaying on the screen; full of life, friendship and the ability to not take ourselves too seriously, no matter how old we were.

"Shel..." Vic poked the screen. "Where were you? Did you forget to listen to the beat?" We paused and repeated it again and again, bellowing with laughter and tears as Shel knocked us with her bum and fell off the edge of the screen recording.

"Right that's enough, you two!" Shelley snatched the phone and pressed the home screen to get rid of the video. "Show me it in twenty years' time and I might appreciate the fact I could still move my joints."

We threw ourselves onto the stools around the island and sipped at the hydrating liquid that had been topped up in our named glasses. We clinked and commemorated our real-life gathering with a "cheers".

"I have some news to tell you both, actually." I broke the sound of us downing the drinks.

"News?" asked Shelley. "I'm intrigued!"

"The other day I made a visit to 'the beast' to return his blanket," I admitted. "He invited me in for a coffee."

"A coffee!" Vic said, stunned. "You kept that one quiet!"

"We got chatting and he asked me to meet for a run together," I began. "After we talked about my poor start to that new pro-gramme I've started – he offered to keep me company."

"Keep you company?" repeated Vic, it was as if they had a recording and were playing back the end of every one of my sentences.

"So we went earlier on today, what with being child-free and all I thought I'd make the most of it," I spoke with apprehension, knowing I would be quizzed further.

"You went for a run as a date? Did I just hear that right?" Shelley was shocked.

"It wasn't a date as such," I said coyly.

"So you dyed your hair just in time?" Shelley demanded.

"Well, um, yes, but I was thinking of doing it anyway!"

"Did you put on mascara?" Vic was grinning.

"A little bit," I answered sheepishly, not admitting to the layers I had caked on.

"Did you take effort to select your best outfit?" Shelley asked.

"Well, I, um," I stuttered. "It was just a running outfit, so it was casual."

"Was it new?" Vic added, trying to catch me out. My face went red. Before I could make any attempt to respond she answered for me. "Yes! It was, wasn't it! Hah, we were right, it was a date! You only make that effort if it was a date."

"Who goes on a running date?" Shelley wrinkled her nose. "You don't get those arrangements on *Tinder*. Talking of which, you won't believe what happened to me the other day?"

This was typical of our group, we switched from one topic to another as if we were rushing to cover every subject known to woman.

"What happened?"

"I only went on a date with a man who was sixty-nine!" Shelley screamed with her usual adrenaline that was there whenever she delivered a story. "He had a picture on his profile from when he was forty so of course I didn't recognise him when he turned up. He told me he was turning seventy in two months! Can you believe it? The worst part is... I actually would!"

"Ewww! Gross!" Vic and I grimaced and cringed.

"Don't knock it until you've tried it is my motto!" Shelley defended. "Besides, sometimes you meet someone at a certain time in your life... you really could be soul mates. Finding a kindred spirit isn't always age-restrictive. I mean, if I had met him when he was forty, I would have been mesmerised by him. He still had a glint of something that sparked an attraction, if you know what I mean. He had nice hands! It was just a shame that we're on different paths in life."

"So, you shagged him?" I questioned. "Let's get to the crux of it!"

"Now, that would be telling!" Shelley winked.

"You did or you didn't?" Vic asked, her eyebrows raised in shock.

"We've shifted focus." Shelley smiled ruefully. "More to the point – what happened with Sarah and the Beast?"

"Nothing. We just had a coffee and a cake and sat on a bench for a while, that was it."

"Are you seeing him again?" Vic asked. "What's his name again? I've forgotten."

"Tim," I replied, "and he messaged to ask if I could be free one evening to meet again."

"See!" Shelley grinned. "It was a date. Did you snog?"

"No!"

"But he's asked to see you again," Shelley explained, "so you're moving out of the green zone."

"The green zone?" asked Vic, confused, "is this some new online dating terminology you've picked up and we know nothing about?"

"The Friend Zone." Shelley tutted at our incompetence. "Sarah doesn't want to stay in the green for too long or it becomes too awkward for him to make the next move. Think of it like a traffic light indication that he's heading to the red – love zone!" Shelley was laughing at her own baffling visualisation of dating and relationships, although her advice didn't speak for much seeing as she was forever single.

"Shit!" shouted Vic as she flapped her arms in excitement. "That means you've hit another layer of colour!"

"Yess!" Shelley screeched. "Sarah was in the green zone with a man and is heading into shagging territory. That definitely constitutes a colour of her rainbow to be ticked off."

"Fuck off, you two!" I hung my head in shame. "This is like torture having you both rebuild my life for me."

"We'll add more than just the colour, sweetie." Shelley winked. "We'll find the glitter for you too."

We carried on nattering until there was no air left in our lungs, then collapsed onto our make-shift beds in the living room. I could hear both of my friends snoring as I drifted off to sleep, a smile on my face. It had been one of the best days I could have wished for. For once, I was actually proud of myself for the decisions I had made, as well as taking authority over the direction I had chosen to go in. I fell into the first peaceful sleep I'd had in a long time.

18

Out of the Blue

I woke up locked in a jumble of feet and arms strewn all over my body (it was impossible not to be as our three blown-up beds were joined together), with the sudden realisation that my sweaty armpit was stretched out with poor Vic underneath it. I located my phone concealed neatly under my pillow. My first thought was to check there were no urgent messages about the kids. It felt so strange waking up without them. A pang of guilt crept over me.

Stop, I told myself. How could I make changes if I was continuously berating my subconscious? Self-care was important, so why did I always feel guilty for having it? My mind raced to Nick and the kids and whether they would be coping together. I had to find a new way to deal with it. I mean, after all, they were his responsibility as much as mine. Did he feel guilty when I looked after them? It was strange when I flipped the narrative.

The only way to banish the depths of anxiety was to get moving. I got myself up and went to make coffee for my guests. Once upon a time we would have been sneaking pop drinks for breakfast, just because we were driven by that desire to do something we shouldn't have been doing. Now an adult, it was my last thought to drink a fizzy can of drink to start the day.

We spent the next hour chattering away whilst we tidied up our sober party from the night before.

"We better make a move now, Sarah," Vic said. "It would be weird to pass Nick at the door and to act like nothing's happened."

"You don't need to rush," I offered. "Things may be strained in our marriage, but I have no doubt he would be polite enough."

"I'm sure he would," Shelley responded. "It's just that awkwardness of not knowing what to say. I feel like I'll put my foot in it. You know how blunt I can be."

"It's also like we're part of a grieving process with you," Vic continued.

"Nobody has died," I reminded them. "But I get what you're saying and understand that it puts you in an awkward position."

The girls gathered their belongings to make their quick exit. It was slightly surreal to be doing the walk-of-shame but with the same bottles of alcohol that we hadn't touched the night before. We definitely didn't need the booze; we'd continued to make memories together like we always had.

"Look after you," Shelley and Vic proclaimed as they stepped out of the house.

"I will." I smiled and embraced them for one last hug before they left. "If I don't talk to you before, I'll look forward to our video call later this week."

The door closed and the silence of the house without the kids engulfed me. Even Rex looked perplexed that it was randomly quiet as he lowered his chin onto the carpet and moved his eyebrows side to side. My thoughts were jumbled even more than usual, with images of Tim and how we'd sat on the bench for all of those hours. They were soon contrasted into poignant, panic-stricken images of having to see Nick once more.

I tried to potter around the house, running by my usual fast-paced motor, to rid the place of mess and clean the surface grime to make it shine. How could I make it look like I was coping without him? I had the sudden urge to prove to Nick that I was capable of being a good parent and running the house simultaneously. I grabbed the recycling bag to run it outside to the bin before Nick arrived so that he couldn't see the mountain of food containers we'd eaten. But just as I unlocked the door, he pulled up in his *BMW*.

The car door jerked open and Nick retreated to the rear to retrieve Lena – who bounced out, wittering on about one of her favourite topics to the solemn air as it was clear nobody was listening to her. Rex ran out and bounded up to Lena, giving her the biggest lick up the side of her face as she threw her arms around him for a cuddle.

"Mummy!" squealed Lena. "We had a movie and popcorn with Daddy!"

"Sounds like super fun," I said in my animated, child-friendly voice.

"Charlie laughed at the bit when the big red doggy sat down and squashed the bus!" Lena giggled.

"Did you, Charlie?" I asked, tickling under his dribbly chin.

"Da da," Charlie gurgled back on cue.

"He's saying he had fun with Daddy," Lena explained importantly.

"Oh, is that right?" I lifted my eyebrows, acting in disbelief.

"Charlie says he gets to eat more treats with Daddy!" Lena continued as she tickled under his coat. "Didn't you, Charlie?"

"Da da!" repeated Charlie. His face lit up into a merry smile as he started chuckling.

Nick, Lena and I joined in with the laughter, and for the first time in a long time, despite being separated, we actually seemed closer together as a family unit.

"I'm nicknaming Charlie 'the wind machine!' He really doesn't stop trumping!" Nick added to the humorous exchange. He smiled at me almost as though he were seeking my approval. I returned the expression and his eyes soon darted away. The air between us was starting to feel less suffocating.

"Daddy!" Lena demanded, pulling his branded sport jacket her way. "Come and play inside with me!"

"Well, I can..." he said, half-committed. "We have to ask Mummy if that's okay first, Spitfire!"

He never normally said yes to joining in with Lena, nor would he ever usually ask for my approval either, so I was momentarily dumbfounded. I didn't get a chance to reply before Lena's voice boomed over me.

"I make the rules and I say you can come and play!"

I carried Charlie inside as Lena dragged her father in by his clothes. She was almost like a female spider, entrapping her flies and wrapping them up in her web to play with at her disposal. Lena told her father the game specifics, his character, the plot and every line of his dialogue that he needed to say.

He eventually came away looking a little shell-shocked, but well, that was what happened if you really got to see the true essence of Lena. I had a pang of hope that maybe he would finally see what I had been saying for all those years.

"I feel exhausted!" Nick declared as Lena took a moment to pause and watch her favourite *Paw Patrol* episode on the TV. "She makes you petrified in case you get a word wrong. I see what you mean about how she is driven to be in control. I guess I have to say... I'm sorry that I didn't listen. It must be draining for you doing this on a daily basis."

His eyes looked into mine, full of sorrow. He seemed apprehensive as if there were more he could say but was holding back. I was in shock. It was so uncharacteristic for Nick to behave this way, that I was lost for words. I tried to not sound bitter as I admitted, "Yes, it is."

There was an awkward silence. Nick's eyes fell to the ground as if he were a young child being scolded. "I'm sorry for letting you all down. I should have listened to you more."

We stood still. I was hunched and guarded in comparison to his bodily expression of looking small and broken. We stayed like that for quite some time, embracing the silence further. There had been so much animosity between us, it was hard to remember that we were once united as a couple.

"I'm sorry too." I wasn't sure what was coming over me but I was starting to shake the anger away and seeing Nick in a crumbling, new light was having an effect on my emotions. "It takes two people for a relationship to break down. We just didn't talk to each other."

"I didn't know how to handle any of this stuff," Nick explained sorrowfully. "It's no excuse, I know. If I could turn back the hands of time I would and I'd do it differently. I should have helped you better. Been a better husband. Accepted your opinions more."

Nick broke down and started crying. Not small crocodile tears but meaningful, heartbroken sobs that were uncontrollable as they rolled down his desolate cheeks. It was discomposing to witness Nick in this position; he seemed to be a shadow of the man that I had been married to. It was almost as if he had been blinded and wounded by the reality of losing everything. I went towards him and offered some support. He pulled me in close, clasping onto my body for dear life. His head rested on my shoulder as he rubbed his hands over my lower back affectionately, patting gently as if we were platonically embracing.

Then, he lifted my head up. With his tear-strewn face, he kissed my lips so passionately as if his life depended on it. His tongue entered past my weary shields, caressed my tongue with desire, imaginatively creating foreplay in my mind. My lack of physical contact with anyone of the opposite sex was disarming me and enabling me to reciprocate his desire. He leaned against me tighter now, driven by impulse and hunger that had arisen. I could feel I was being guided to his erect penis that was prodding me through his jeans. My back was pierced by the edge of the kitchen island. Nick lifted me up and wrapped my legs around him. I couldn't even remember us being physically attracted to one another like this, because it was so that far in the past it felt like it belonged in a different lifetime.

I could feel the pulse of awakening as I continued to kiss him back, roughly and with deep yearning which was making me lose myself and any control of my actions. He pulled my hand over his jeans to contour and rub his hardening tool. I could sense him throbbing. He guided my hand gently in a caressing movement over his area of longing. His hand left mine in action as we continued to explore our mouths together, whilst his hands gently tickled the line of my tummy until he reached my breasts and crept one hand inside my bra to titillate and arouse my nipple. My whole body was starting to tingle, each touch was stimulating my sexual parts and messaging sensual shockwaves into my erogenous zones. I could feel my insides convulsing, thrilled by an awakening and pining for him to break and then enter. The need in me was aching so profusely that I had forgotten who I was, and any responsibility I had to be looking after the children in the room next door.

I unzipped his jeans to stroke his bare skin and he twitched in excitement. He reciprocated with further exploration by seizing my breast out of my laced bra as if it were his own treasure, and began to lick around the area erotically. We were experimenting like it was the first time and we wanted to taste the lechery of passion with one another. I was no longer covertly covering my stroking action as I pulled on his erection rhythmically.

I heard a sudden bang next door and I was catapulted into reality

311

about what I was doing. I quickly pushed my naked breast back into my bra and straightened up my top. Nick turned his back towards the door in prevention as he pushed his pulsating manhood back into his jeans and zipped himself back up, just in time as Lena crashed into the kitchen.

"You're still here, Daddy!" she exclaimed as our faces flushed crimson, full of guilt. She sensed she had walked into something. "Are you being nice to Mummy?"

"You could say that." Nick winked at me and I could feel myself cringing with slight regret that I had let my feelings get the better of me. "Anyway, I better be going."

Nick made a few pleasantries as he gathered himself up and kissed the kids goodbye. He shot me a last look but I struggled to make eye contact as my tears were now flowing.

I was left rattled by our encounter. What did it mean? Did I still have feelings for Nick? Was I making the biggest mistake by separating and not working it out with the person I had chosen to spend the rest of my life with? Weren't we supposed to stick with marriage through thick and thin? I started to feel vulnerable from allowing myself to fall backwards into an unprecedented place, my feelings for Nick were now compromised. I thought I was moving on. Why was I going back to something that hadn't been working, rather than taking the leap into something new?

I felt the desperate need to text him to ask him to come back and rescue me, that all could be forgiven and we could resolve our issues as a partnership. Then images of how trapped I had felt and how he had let Lena down so badly kept arising in my consciousness. The assault of emotions was too much to bear.

After doing the bedtime routine for the kids, it dawned on me that Nick's change of feelings had completely come out of the blue. Bingo! I thought. Ingrained by my friends' doctrine of injecting colour into my life, I had realised that another colour had been attained. After all, my rainbow must be working if my ex-husband was making a move to repair things! I grabbed my phone and eagerly opened the group chat to inform the girls of the recent development.

> Girls, you won't believe this but I just hit another colour today!

> **Vic**
> You figured another one out by yourself, I'm impressed!

> The colours were slow at first and now they keep coming fast

> **Vic**
> Wow! That's amazing, what's changed?

> I think I hit blue...

Shelley appeared online and joined the discussion

> **Shelley**
> Wait for me! What did I miss?

> **Vic**
> Sarah hit another colour all by herself!

Shelley
Bravo!! Prey, do tell, Sarah!?!

Nick admitted he was sorry and it came out of the blue! I think his change of heart definitely constitutes hitting another colour!

Vic
Wooaahh! Did I just read that right?

Yup!

Shelley
You see it's working. The rainbow is shaking things up!

I guess you guys were right xxx

Vic
I'm pleased for you. You were dragging the wet dirt for far too long x

Shelley
What she said!

Actually… he didn't just say sorry! He made a move on me and it kind of felt good like the power is now in my corner.

The messages ceased and there was suddenly a gap in our communication until finally a text popped up.

> **Shelley**
> I'd prefer to talk to you properly. Can I call now? x

It seemed strange; I thought the girls would be egging me on, congratulating me for having Nick back like putty in my hands. The urgency of her text was starting to make me panic.

> Sure.

There was a moment of silence as I was still looking at the message and saw that both of my friends had received and read the words. The friendly camaraderie had changed and my spider feels were indicating I was going to hear something I wasn't ready to process. My thoughts were broken by the sound of my ringtone. I took a few deep breaths before I picked up.

"Hello?" I answered tentatively. "You needed to speak to me?"

"I didn't want to do this over text message and I've been stewing for a few days about how to broach the subject with you," Shelley replied nervously. This wasn't like Shel and it was unnerving me.

"Just tell me," I instructed quite bluntly. My anxiety had risen and was making my heart race uncontrollably. I was not rational enough for my usual social fluffiness.

"The other night, you know when I was on my *Tinder* date out of town with the pensioner we laughed about?" Shelley began.

"Uh huh," I replied, not picking up the humour from the past subject matter.

"Well, I saw Nick having dinner with another woman," Shelley confessed, a heavy weight to her voice.

"Maybe it was just a friend." I felt a pang of betrayal without even knowing the facts but I tried to conceal it. "I mean, I went for a run with Tim. We're separated after all."

I could level the playing field, but still couldn't shake the feelings of jealousy and embarrassment.

"I saw them kissing," Shelley said softly. "Look, Sarah, just be careful before you make any decisions to go back. Please just take your time to process things before you decide what to do."

"I can't believe you're not happy for me?!" Anger rose in my voice.

"Of course I am," Shelley said quickly. "Try and stay calm to just think over what I'm saying."

"How the hell can I keep calm when you've basically just told me I'm a fool and that I shouldn't be going back to someone who obviously didn't respect the relationship as much as I did?" I could feel myself yelling at my best friend and it felt like I was watching somebody else do it.

"That's not what I'm saying," Shelley defended sadly.

I fell over the stool at the kitchen island and scattered the discarded junk onto the floor. The same place where I had been sitting hours before, heatedly engaged with the same person we were discussing. I'd let my guard down. What had I been thinking? My skin began to feel allergic to itself and itched with repulsion at the deed I nearly had got myself involved in.

"Why didn't you tell me earlier?!" I demanded.

"I wanted to," she explained, "I just didn't know how to."

"You should have told me!" I screamed ferociously. "I bet Vic even knew before me?"

"I... tried... to..." Shelley stumbled without a chance as I barraged another insult.

"Of course she fucking knew!" I shouted indignantly. "I was the last to find out like the moron everyone takes me for."

"We wanted to find the right time," Shelley maintained, "we couldn't do it yesterday because you were high on life and we didn't want to spoil it. Things were moving in a better direction and it was the one night you had to switch off. You even made positive changes like running and ditching the booze."

"So you left me in the dark to make a twat of myself! I bet my life is the gossip everyone needs. I'm that laughable."

"We never would do that! Give us some credit. We're proud of you, not laughing at you."

"I never thought you would keep a secret from me!" And with that, I hung up the phone.

I ransacked through the kitchen drawer to find my favourite family photograph of the four of us from last Christmas, just after Charlie was born. I'd hidden it in there a few months ago when I wasn't ready to give up on the dream of being a family unit. I shredded it into pieces and flung it into the dustbin. It wasn't providing the healing that I needed so I picked up my notebook on the side of the kitchen worktop and whacked it over my head. The thud echoed and the pain was excruciating. I began to question my own sanity for harming myself with such a random weapon. I was screaming from the inside out, with so much anger and resentment, so much turmoil that my teeth were gritted and my eyes were hazy. I lost control of any rational thought-making.

I just wanted it all to stop. I wanted to run away, but there was nowhere to go because the pain of my berating conscience was a prison shackling me to my hostile thoughts. I was trapped in my position over the kitchen island, immobilised by the shame and confusion, driven to resent myself.

I could feel a lump protruding out of my skin and rushed to get an ice block to numb it down. The sudden realisation that I needed to get a hold of myself, to not appear unbalanced, as I was supposed to be a strong mother leading her bear cubs in the world, hit me. What would my children think if they grew up seeing me in this state? The pang of knowledge that the two innocent beings upstairs in their beds were relying on me to keep them loved, nourished and safe was the only single thought I had that was keeping me going.

I had to find a way to bounce back, to find some resilience to start again; they deserved it. I decided that I'd conceal the bump with my hooded coat for the time being. The last thing I needed was for people who were already judging me as a bad parent to believe I was having a mental breakdown.

So many thoughts were jumbled in my mind about the mess I was in.

How was I going to repair my friendships?

I'd made a big mistake looking at Nick again in that way. I had moved on, I was rebuilding my life. I should have known it wasn't a good idea to go backwards in a moment of weakness.

I picked up my phone to send him a text.

> I think we should revert back to my mum helping with the contact from now on. We need to keep the boundary for the sake of everyone's feelings.

Nick
Suit yourself. Well, you weren't saying that earlier?

> It's for the best, Nick.

Nick
You won't ever get a chance again – just for the record.

> We did make some progress today. We should just try to focus on the positives.

Nick

It was all your fault anyway. Don't think I don't realise what you are doing?

Oh my goodness, I could see hints of the old Nick, he was completely playing mind games.

> And what is that exactly?

Nick

Getting yourself dressed up for my benefit, pretending you have plans to try and tease me to think I'm missing out on something.

> I don't want this to get messy.

I could feel myself backing down like I used to, trying to be submissive by diffusing his usual baiting comments.

Nick

Good luck if you think YOU can do better. You don't even work right now, how do you think you're going to pay to keep everyone? You need me more than you realise.

I decided to not reply. He knew he was dangling the financial card over me because I had been reliant on him whilst I was on maternity leave. I was self-sufficient before and an equal contributor to our family's financial situation. He knew that, and yet he was trying to manipulate me so I felt that I couldn't cope without him.

I wasn't about to feed his neglected ego or give him the power in this situation that he seemed to be craving. Nick's tactics kept changing the moment he wasn't getting what he wanted. I was determined that his game playing wasn't going to work this time. I had to remember that it was he who had made the move, not me. He who had seen me looking happier and fresher, and had tried to act upon it. Nick didn't like the fact that he was feeling rejected and he was taking his frustration out on me. This was more like the Nick that I was used to. *A leopard never changes its spots.*

Was it better to tell Nick I knew he had been seen with another woman? Did it even matter? It would have only fuelled the argument even further and Nick was determined to win no matter what. Then there was also the fact that I had met up with Tim, as well as going on a date with Carlos, a few weeks ago. It would make me hypocritical to bring up his personal meetings when I was not innocent from having them either.

It was emotional knowing that we could both be with new partners one day, maybe that was why we had been wavering at the prospect of closure. I had to remind myself that he was not the partner I'd needed him to be. No matter how many times I had tried to spell it out to him, he was never able to meet me halfway. It was a transition that we both needed to get through to reach a happier place. Mostly, above anything else, I knew that I had to find a way to release my thoughts differently. I couldn't afford to hurt myself again. What if anyone saw the lump on my head?

How could I be sure that I wouldn't ever self-harm myself again? Just as I'd thought I had been getting on track, I had been sent an even bigger curveball to get past.

19

No Shrinking Violet

A few days had passed and I hadn't replied to any of the messages from my friends in our group chat. I was cutting contact with anyone and everything, driven by the need of animalistic survival. I just didn't know what to say to my friends and I felt that I was seen as a fool in the eyes of everyone. As the anger started to fade it was soon filtering into a transition of shame. The rollercoaster of emotions was so difficult to ride that it was easier to cling on to the carriage than to address the threat head-on.

My phone beeped a few days later with a message from Tim.

> **Tim**
> Hey you! How are you? Would you be up for meeting again? Xx

It was another demand that had mounted onto my mental overload and I was unable to deal with it. What could I even say back?

The basics of feeding, cleaning and dressing the kids took the core leftovers of my energy stores. The extra requirement to get Lena to school each morning for her outdoor sessions was enough to spill me over. The rest of every day was spent vegged on the sofa.

I wasn't living; I was just existing and the ability to even eat was throwing me an extra demand to cope with. My emotions were so locked up and confused that it was debilitating knowing where to even get started.

"Mummy," Lena declared one afternoon as we sat enveloped together watching a *Paw Patrol* episode. "You've lost your smile. Did you lose it at the shops?"

I consciously forced my lips to revert the frown.

"It doesn't look right," Lena quite rightly declared.

"It's not working," I said openly. "How do you think I can get it back?"

"With a superpup tickle!" Lena declared as she pounced on top of my ribcage, poked her wiry hands onto my skin and began to tickle her fingers in an attempt to cheer me up. "It's working, you laughed!"

"It did work!" I kissed her forehead. "I knew I needed your help."

"It might work better if we go to the skate park?" Lena queried inquisitively. "We don't have to get ice cream because it's cold, but if we whizz around the ramps on my scooter, it might help your smile again." It was as if we had reversed roles and she was playing the part of the caring parent.

"Why not?" I answered. "Let's give it a try!"

I gathered my just-in-case bag, popped a warm snowsuit onto Charlie, and Lena suddenly appeared carrying my shoes.

"There you go." She passed them towards me. "The shoes are the hardest part."

I was in utter disbelief – the child who usually was unable to put her socks or shoes on and couldn't face the uncertainty of leaving the house – was switching places and replaying the same support strategies I had used with her. Lena was showing me the way to heal from the trauma I felt was so badly embedded inside. Maybe she could relate to somebody else in pain because it was something she often felt.

We left the house, chatting and cooing as a family unit, ready to improve our mood at the skate park. I knew right there that we would find a way to move forwards because I was no longer alone with my pain, I had someone who loved me back, unconditionally, to partner that process with me, just as I had done so often with her. It was a moment that made my heart warm and was an indication of something, at least, I was doing right. A smile of genuine relief appeared on my face.

By the time I returned home, I must have started to feel a bit more like my usual self, as a knot of guilt in my tummy appeared in the knowledge that I had gone cold on Tim. He hadn't done anything wrong and had been unfairly left in the dark which he didn't deserve. This was all one big mess and my brain was blank on how to even approach a conversation with him. *Oh sorry, Tim,* I thought as an imaginary text, *I've had a mental breakdown and hit myself with a notebook. Would you mind waiting to meet me until my comic-style lump goes down?*

I braced myself with a deep breath of air before I went in for the kill:

> Hi Tim, my apologies for the delay, you could say it's been a tricky week. How are things your end? X

The word 'tricky' was the best I could do.

That's so kind. I will be in touch and thanks again x

Okay so it wasn't the most in-depth conversation a man and a woman could be having, but it was a start. If nothing else, hopefully I hadn't screwed up my chance to see him again. That's if he even liked me in that way; he'd never initiated any romantic suggestions but there was a pang of hope that it could go somewhere. I wasn't attracted to him in the same way I had been to Nick, but I was attracted to something that emanated from Tim, an aura of kindness and depth that brought a desire to be around him more.

***

The morning sessions at school were running smoothly and Lena didn't want to leave when they were finishing. Tariq pulled me aside on his Wednesday session to ask for my thoughts.

We agreed that it was probably time to start increasing the length and variety in the sessions and that he would bring it up with the team around us. As promised, an email from Tariq arrived, with every member from the TAC meeting copied in:

Wow, Tariq was good at this stuff. He had the ability to say what he meant and to push forwards without it ever sounding aggressive. I was sure the staff regretted making the referral to him now that he was shaking things up a bit.

It was two whole days before the school replied, copying back the said group of spectators:

```
To: coveoutreachteam
cc: sarahforte
From: senco
Subject: re: Next Steps for LF


Dear Tariq


After some careful deliberation, we feel it better that
we increase gradually in fifteen-minute intervals, so
as to not cause any deterioration in Lena's progress.
Perhaps we can start next week for Lena to stay for
one hour and fifteen minutes and see how she copes?


Regards


Veronica Webb
```

Mrs Webb had missed out the word 'kind' from her email sign-off – omitting the word was like a secret code – admitting clearly that she was rattled and being forced to do something she was unhappy about. I smiled. She knew exactly what she was doing. She didn't like it now that I had some troops behind me, fighting the good fight. I wasn't sure how the relationship had become so fraught, it wasn't the only one in my life that had crumbled, but it was one of the crucial ones that I needed to resolve to move forwards. Lena depended on me for that.

I suddenly remembered the paperwork that Betty had passed to me in the TAC meeting and that it was my action to complete it with Lena. I went to retrieve my just-in-case bag (which regrettably wasn't as reliable as I had named it). I delved to the bottom to find the desired item buried under a mountain of nappies, fidget toys, a chewed diary (Rex was lying sheepishly in his basket as I glanced up), a tub of nappy cream with grease around the edges, and a packet of opened wet wipes that had made the paperwork soggy. It could only happen to me! I clasped the page with my fingertips, trying to not make the soft material rip, and frantically went on a search to locate my hairdryer. I finally found it – discarded in the washing basket of all places. I didn't have time to backtrack the clues to solve the mystery as to how it got there. I sat on my knees and held the damp paper upwards as if it were worth a million pounds. I desperately tried to blow away my adulting incompetence.

"Why are you drying paper, Mummy?" Lena's eyes were dilating out of confusion. "Did you forget what the hairdryer is for?"

"Mummy is silly," I confessed, trying to keep it light without revealing my inner anger at my own stupidity.

"That's okay," Lena encouraged, "I can help you fix it." She took the dryer out of my hand and spirited it around in every direction in an attempt to dry the paper but instead spread the wasted hot air on the empty bedroom.

After some time we had the paper resembling a drier form of tissue waste and I decided to call it a day. I took a moment to think that maybe I could use the disaster to my advantage to employ some kind of reverse strategy to get her to do the work with me.

"You did help me fix it, well done!" I declared, followed by an open-ended question. "I wonder if *anyone* could help me fill out the boxes so it doesn't look ruined anymore?"

"I can!" Lena proclaimed with excitement, not even knowing what she was opting in for.

I grabbed a pen and scribbled Lena's name, age and school in the first few boxes of the one-page profile form. The next question I read out loud, "Hmm, what are the things that are important to you?"

"Easy," she answered dramatically, "animals."

"Anything else?" I dangled, trying to engage her further.

"You and Charlie are important to me AND my *Paw Patrol* toys. Oh, and Poxy, how could I forget Poxy!" Lena beamed.

There was no mention of Nick in the equation and it reminded me that I was still providing emotional support for the both of us. It was also a reminder that Nick was not the father we needed him to be, and a further reason as to why I needed to keep moving on as a single parent family.

"Next it says: What are the things people like about you?"

"I'm funny and kind and silly and good at jumping!" She sprung to her feet, bouncing up and down manically, Poxy's ears flapping to-and-fro.

"Yes, you are good at all of those things," I confirmed. "And how can people help you better?"

"By leaving me alone," Lena replied without any hesitation. I stifled a giggle as she was so blunt with her answer, but it was the truth in Lena's eyes. "And not forcing me or bossing me around. They need to be quiet when I don't want them to talk either."

There was a small box for a picture of the child and I passed the pen to Lena to see if she could draw an image of herself so that the last frame made the page look pretty. She obliged and drew a big blob, with usual stick arms and legs, a smiley face and a few lines for hair. She created another shape that she informed me was Rex. I took a scan of the document on my phone and put it away in my paperwork behind the breadboard for a rainy day (waiting, as usual, to be filed when I had enough energy to hyper-focus and clear the bundle). I sent the page to Betty in a separate email. She replied with a confirmation of acceptance and said that she would be in touch in due course.

The group email conversation went back and forth a few more times with passive-aggressive disputes over the next steps, whilst I hung back allowing Tariq and a few of the other allies to perform their magic. Other than that, the rest of the week ran quietly and we finally reached the weekend. We opted to stay home, wrapped together as a unit, to recharge our batteries. I was still avoiding any communication with my inner-circle as well as preferring to wait the time out at home whilst my lump was healing. I couldn't believe I had concealed it so well for so long. My woolly hat had helped with that as well as the fact that it was hidden on my scalp by my hair. Most of all I was hugely relieved that Lena hadn't noticed; it would have been national news if she had.

Monday morning was suddenly upon us and my phone rang. I didn't recognise the voice until she introduced herself further:

"It's Theresa. From CAMHS?" she said slowly, waiting for acknowledgement to proceed.

"Oh, sorry," I apologised, "I wasn't sure who was calling as it came up with an unrecognised number."

"Yes, they're a pain, aren't they?" Theresa said softly. "All of our communication is kept confidential, it's why we don't have email addresses that go out either," she explained further. "Anyway, I was just calling really to see how things were and whether we could schedule a triage call before our next session with Lena?"

"I don't see why not," I answered, with a hint of caution.

"I just wanted to set aside the time to go through some questions about Lena's early development, the wider family tree, and gather some background information that I would prefer to ask without talking over her head. It's a bit of a bugbear of mine actually, because I am of the opinion that children absorb everything so of course they won't feel comfortable with conversations about them going on in the same room."

"I see your point," I agreed. "When would it be?"

"I have some available sessions on Tuesday morning next week," Theresa informed, "what time would suit you?"

"I drop Lena off at school for ten so I could be free then?" I answered.

"Fab stuff," Theresa replied. "You should receive an NHS text confirming the time of the appointment."

"Okay, thanks."

"Oh, and one last thing," Theresa paused, "which I hope will be off the record?"

"Of course," I replied, surprised.

"If you haven't already, then I would strongly advise you to apply for an Education Health Care assessment to see if Lena might need a plan of support," Theresa urged. "I mean, obviously that's not my place to say that she will meet the threshold, but let's just say it is clear she has identifiable educational needs and she's on a reduced timetable. That in itself indicates that she needs a little bit more support to meet her full potential. You may have a fight on your hands to get one for her, I'm afraid, but Ms Forte...?"

"Yes?" I could hear myself pleading for more advice.

"Her mental health is so important, in fact, it's the most important thing," Theresa disclosed. "She sees herself as different and unseen, so supporting her through school is key to not accumulating trauma."

"Okay," I said hesitantly, trying to take on board what she was suggesting.

"Please look after yourself too," Theresa finished. "Self-care is going to be your strongest weapon."

"I will do, that's very kind." I smiled.

"Girls who are autistic can often slip under the radar," Theresa concluded with a suggestion she was describing a bigger meaning. "They often become autistic women who learn to mask or fawn their difficulties, but hiding their identity comes at a terrible cost to their wellbeing. Knowing who they are from an early age really is key."

"You've been very helpful," I commended. "Your advice won't go any further." I understood why the call had been more complicated and the information was not put into words for her to be quoted against. I was starting to see that the heroes of the professional world were so tied up by the restraints of a flawed system, that they were frustratingly limited in their freedom to really help families like mine. It made my gratitude deeper.

We ended the call shortly afterwards. Her words played on my memory. It dawned on me that maybe she was inferring that I was one of those girls who hadn't known they were autistic. I was overanalysing the conversation and its intent to the point that my brain couldn't shake away any of it. It was almost as if the subtext of what she couldn't say was there for me to decode and make sense of and it was adding to my confusion.

Then I remembered that Lena hadn't been given a diagnosis yet and we were still waiting for a referral from the GP – which I had done for the second time and was still left in limbo. I wasn't sure where we were on the waiting list but I had read online that it could take a year, or even more, to be seen. Why was it like that? It felt like only a few people understood the significance of how serious this was and that Lena was missing the chance of an education. I knew she was falling even further behind and it pained me inside. What was happening to her innocent childhood?

Theresa had said the word *autistic*. Maybe she knew more as an experienced professional? It could have just been a slip up or maybe she had assumed it was a given already, but my thoughts were starting to believe that she was pushing me on to get Lena assessed.

I scrolled online to do some research on assessment centres who were knowledgeable in diagnosing autistic girls. I found a few and read their reviews until my eyes were drawn to an established doctor in London who was highly commended. I clicked onto her website to find out more about her clinic and what she did. The words were there in black and white that she was a leading specialist in the private sector at diagnosing Pathological Demand Avoidance as an autistic profile. She had written books about it for children and practitioners, as well as running detailed support for related mental health difficulties. Bingo! It was exactly the type of person I believed could have the knowledge to see Lena and help us finally get to the bottom of this situation.

I sent an email of interest and asked whether I could pay for the assessment and reports on an agreed payment plan. The personal assistant replied that they could be flexible to support high-need families. Then came the shock part – they had a cancellation this week in their clinic in London, which we could take or go on the waiting list for an appointment (at an estimation of three to six months waiting time). I thought back to Theresa's coded conversation and the importance of understanding identity, and pinged an email back to book the slot. Nerves hit my insides like a train tunnelling off the tracks at speed, it hit me that I would finally know, one way or another, whether my daughter really was autistic. Was I doing the right thing? For once, I was making a decision all by myself about our future and it felt like I was second-guessing myself.

With a limited amount of people to talk to, I picked up my phone to text Flick – she would be a voice of reason and knew more about these things than anyone else I'd met.

> Hi Flick, I just want to run something past you. I've booked a private assessment for Lena but I'm having a wobble. Should I go through with it? x

> **Flick**
> Absolutely! Just check on the professional's credentials and if their reports are accepted in this county. I'm so pleased you will have an answer. x

Dr Ivanna is supposed to be the leading specialist in this field. She diagnoses PDA and has even written books on it. X

Flick

I have one of her books! Yes she's fab, you have no worries then. Good luck x

I had three days to get through before judgement day. I tried to introduce the idea softly to Lena so that I could prepare her for what lay ahead.

We were playing *Paw Patrol* together and I began by taking my pup and leading Lena's pup to the top of the *Lookout Tower*.

"So, let's pretend *Skye* is meeting a doctor in a clinic to find out why she thinks differently to the other pups," I began creatively.

Unusually, Lena seemed to accept the swift change of play and curiously followed the idea.

"First, Skye," I instructed as the doctor, "we will be doing a few activities together and then we can play a game. Sound like a plan?"

"Uh huh." Lena nodded apprehensively.

"Don't be worried at all," I reassured, talking through the toys. "You are safe and you can stop at any time."

Our characters acted out a few tasks together and Lena excitedly completed all of the things that she was asked.

"Well done, Skye," I congratulated, "you were amazing. I can see your brain is very clever and you are one of the greatest superpups there ever has been."

We put the pups down the helter-skelter slide at the end of the action, content that the story had reached an appropriate climax. I wondered if Lena understood what I was trying to do, as she looked at me quietly appearing perplexed.

"Mummy." Lena sighed. "You're not very good at making up *Paw Patrol* games."

"I guess you're right." I laughed as I went in for a tickle. "But you better run away before I get you and pin you down for more tickles now!" I chased her around the house, her wild laughter flowing from room to room.

As our preparation game for the big day faded into a memory, I started to worry – had it been enough? What if she couldn't leave the house on assessment day? Would I still be charged? How would they be able to get her to engage? Worse still, what if she acted sweet and compliant (like she did sometimes unexpectedly) and they wouldn't see the real her? I tried to remember Flick's words in her text about Dr Ivanna being fab. Surely they had to be used to this kind of thing? After all, she was supposed to be the leading consultant in the field. I tried to push my doubts away and concentrate on the task at hand – getting our things together for a long day out in London.

Wednesday came and I managed to grab a quiet discussion outside the school reception with Tariq as Lena continued to play on the equipment.

"I have news to tell you," I began, "Lena has an autism assessment tomorrow in London and it's with a well-renowned specialist in PDA!"

"Oh!" Tariq said excitedly. "That's fantastic. A step in the right direction. How is Lena feeling about it?"

"I've tried to explain it to her," I told him. "We even played the story out with her toys, so I'm hoping that I've prepared her as best I can."

"It's impossible to take away the unexpected, but you've eased it," Tariq reassured me. "You've just created your own social story, which is basically an autism strategy we use, but you've tailored it to work individually!"

"Have I?" I took it for granted that all parents did what I did. I didn't think I was doing anything that special.

"Absolutely! Kudos to you, as always!" Tariq declared as he placed a hand warmly on my shoulder. "You're one of the parents who come along and we are blown away by your capability and knowledge!"

"Me?" I pointed to myself almost in disbelief. He moved his hand away but I could still feel the warm imprint of it.

"Yes, you!" Tariq said, full of glee. "We sometimes have to try and work with parents who child-blame and it's infuriating. I can't begin to tell you how hard it is when you see the child, I mean *really see the child*, but have to politely persuade the parent in the right direction because their focus is WAY off!"

"Oh crikey," I said shocked. "How can anyone blame their child and not see it from their point of view?"

"That's exactly why you rolled heads when you entered our radar," Tariq lowered his voice, trying to keep the conversation private. "You do realise that as professionals we talk amongst ourselves when we get the opportunity. You are well thought of amongst the whole team."

I instantly lowered my voice as if I were a spy trying to conceal our mission. Knowing that Tariq was taking a risk, by moving outside the paradigm of the business-like normality, was making me conscious that I wouldn't want him to get reprimanded, whilst the drive for him to open up more was pushing me to keep the conversation going.

"That's a relief to hear," I declared honestly. "I was so scared of facing any more parent blame that I dreaded any referrals being made. I'm so glad I pushed through; you guys have made all the difference."

"You really have nothing to worry about in that area. Having had the chance to liaise with the others, I was pleased to see we were all in agreement and we can see that the opinion of the school is your biggest obstacle."

"I've sensed this for so long," I confessed. "I just never had the strength behind me to know how to tackle it."

"They're too busy trying to force a square peg into a round hole," Tariq observed. "Which we know can't happen because Lena is no shrinking violet and will try her best to make them see she creates her own shape."

"That's true."

"It depends on whether they have the capability to ever see it?" Tariq asked rhetorically. "It takes flexibility of mind, and when teaching staff are set in their ways, it can be hard to get them to see a different path. The rhetoric that is passed down comes from the senior leadership team as they set the ethos of the school."

I knew it. I thought about all of the encounters that I'd had with Mrs Ramsbottom and Mrs Webb. I'd sensed so many times that their views were way off the mark and in no way inclusive. What chance did the staff underneath them have of understanding a child who needed more help if their leaders were so poor?

The school gate flew open and a woman dressed in a kitchen uniform swiftly walked past us, which gave us a natural break to our deep topic.

"Thank you," I said sincerely to Tariq, "for everything."

It was an unfinished conversation but one I felt like we would return to again when the opportunity presented itself.

"It's always a pleasure," Tariq replied supportively. "Please let me know how tomorrow goes, won't you?"

"Of course," I confirmed and waved my arms to attract Lena's attention. Eventually she spotted me and started to skip towards the gate. I sped off to meet her there first before she left ahead of me.

"Bye!" I called back as a last-minute thought that I hadn't made a pleasant farewell with my hasty exit.

I felt a glow inside; a part of my drive for justice was flickering alight and my energy stores were feeling like they were being replenished. I started to believe that I could face the obstacles that were bothering me. I thought back to Theresa's call and how women could mask their difficulties. I understood that I had been so competent at camouflaging my feelings and working hard to please others, that my own wellbeing had suffered as a result.

Maybe if I had been supported better by my own family, or I had some self-awareness to my possible identity, then I could have been more like Lena who was forthright with her need for autonomy?

Tariq's words that Lena was *no shrinking violet* echoed back into my psyche and aroused my feelings more. *Violet,* I had reached *violet.* It was another colour layer for my rainbow. My hairs rose sensitively, knowing that I was nearly at the end of the rainbow and that things were changing.

I thought about my rainbow and visualised the layer of violet being squashed and forced by all of the other overcompensating personalities in the rainbow. Nobody even thought about the colour violet. *In fact,* I thought to myself, *violet is always confused for purple.* Why hadn't I known that I was violet before? A colour who was masking as another and unable to be their true self? A tear fell down my cheek – I didn't want to have to shrink anymore. My brain felt exhausted at having its own internal marathon of a psychology session.

I made a pact with myself – I wasn't going to be a shrinking violet anymore and my direction from now on would be moving forwards and making sure Lena wouldn't have to camouflage either.

The knowledge that I had unconsciously hit a pivotal colour, but felt unable to share it with anyone, made me feel as if I were hitting the end of life and passing away on my own. I needed to face my demons and move out of my cave of safety. I picked up my phone and sent a message to my friends in our group chat:

> How are you both? x

They both saw the message and didn't respond straight away. I knew they were upset with me about my silence. I didn't know what to say next, but eventually a reply came.

> **Vic**
> Not bad thanks – being harassed for online gaming currency by the kids just as we speak x

Still no reply from Shelley. I knew she was royally pissed off with me. I felt sickly worried that I had damaged our friendship.

> Girls, I'm so sorry for taking this out on you. Will you ever forgive me? x

> **Vic**
> Don't worry about it, Sarah, we can see you just got over-whelmed. Promise me you will speak to us next time, whatever it is, then we can find a way to get through it? x

> I can handle the rest of the challenges in my life but I can never cope with not having you two as my best friends. You are like family to me x

Shelley eventually popped back online and the notification said that she was typing to the rest of the group. I felt so nervous waiting impatiently to see what she would reply. Would she forgive me?

> **Shelley**
>
> You hurt me when you said we had talked about you behind your back. If we don't have trust in our friendship then we don't have anything.

> I just overreacted. I'm so sorry and I'll try not to let it happen ever again. I know you both are loyal friends – I said it in frustration. You didn't deserve it x

> **Shelley**
>
> It's done now and we can't change the past. But we can move on from it x

Although Shelley said was prepared to move on, I wasn't so convinced. Her messages were still curt and not full of the laughter or playfulness they usually were.

> **Vic**
>
> Anyway, we haven't caught up with you. Are there any more layers to your rainbow that you've built up? x

> I kind of think we have reached violet x

> **Shelley**
>
> Tell us more! x

I explained that violet was for finding my true and authentic identity, but held off from providing the rest of the details. Things still felt too tense and I wanted to wait to tell them about booking the diagnosis assessment at a later point. Would our friendship ever go back to normal?

20

Do Labels Equal Layers?

Assessment day arrived and I took a deep breath, desperately hoping the day ahead would pan out like it needed to.

"Would you like to bring your *Paw Patrol* toys in my backpack?" I asked Lena as we prepared to go.

"They can have an adventure on the train to the big city!" Lena answered in a cartoon-style voice.

The play scenario that we had enacted a few days before seemed to have worked the trick as she was uncharacteristically flowing with the new situation. I gave myself a virtual pat on the back for having a mini parenting win.

We set off for the day, and after a long wait on the station platform, our train pulled in and we were soon chugging along on our way to Euston. Lena stole the window seat and I plonked myself down next to her. It felt like I had a strange freedom in my limbs as I was missing Charlie – whom I had asked my mum to look after for the day. When I'd asked her, it had been a difficult conversation.

"Oh, Sarah. You haven't given me much notice! I have things to do, you know!" Mum was being her usual impatient, inattentive self.

"I'm sorry, Mum," I said through gritted teeth (trying not to rock the boat because I needed her), feeling irked by her lack of compassion once again. "It was short-notice and a few things came up."

"You really do need to get better at time-keeping, Sarah!" Mum exclaimed. "I'm not sure how you think you will juggle everything when you add going back to work into the mix."

I felt so frustrated every time we tried to communicate with one another. I mean, did she honestly believe that I did nothing all day?

"I do have Lena on a reduced timetable," I counteracted, "and I'm backwards and forwards with phone calls, emails and meetings."

She changed the subject, quite clearly thinking that I was just making excuses for what she assumed to be laziness as the root cause of the issue.

"And, do you really want to spend all of your money on an assessment for Lena?" Mum began. "You need to be watching the pennies now you've decided to break up with Nick, especially whilst you're not working."

Decided to? Her words were repeating in my mind for analysis. Did she think I'd found it easy to make that decision? My mum didn't need to say it, but I could sense she wasn't happy with my decision to separate from my husband and it was still going to be a contentious subject – just as much as the suggestion that Lena may have additional needs.

"It's important," I answered, carefully choosing my exact wording, "so that Lena can get the help she needs to be back in school full-time."

"The school will still be the same," Mum responded, "her behaviour will still be the same, label or no label."

"A label is not a bad thing," I defended, "it will help with the understanding and support that she might need."

"But how can a class change for just one child?" Mum questioned. "I mean, they'd be opening a whole can of worms if they let one child get away with things. It would lead to utter anarchy."

I felt a pang of fear in my heart. Would she ever understand the situation and help me?

"Mum, those children can go to school just as it is!" I declared, trying to hold back my frustration. "Adapting the classroom to help everyone attend is called inclusion. There are laws written specifically for this reason."

"Have you discussed this with Nick before you go ahead?" Her question was loaded and it was the last bullet to trigger me.

"Just forget it!" I snapped. "I'll ask someone else to have Charlie."

I hung up the phone and put my head in my hands. I didn't cry. I had done crying over and over. There was a bolt of resilience in me that was going to plough on regardless. Lena was depending on me. I knew that I hadn't told Nick about the assessment because he wouldn't have been happy about it and would have tried everything he could to have stopped me. There was no way I was going to let him do it – I needed an answer and I was going to the assessment for Lena regardless.

A little while later my mum rang back to make the arrangements to pick Charlie up. I wondered if she had felt guilty for her reaction. I had to let it pass and move on.

The train soon pulled into our end destination and my thoughts returned to the present. We jumped onto the platform and joined the sea of passengers heading to the turntables in order to present our tickets.

"Let's go down the escalators." I pointed to the sign for the underground.

We descended, with Lena clutching Poxy, as we took an obligatory last glance back to wave goodbye to the fresh air before we hit the coal-like stench of the windy tunnel leading to the next platform.

Lena's focus was soon drawn to a formal, yet frumpy, business lady whose footsteps she was honing in on and following with her frown-like expression.

"Make her clip clops stop, NOW!" she suddenly burst out over the dusty station as she slammed her infantile hands over her ears.

The platform fell silent and all of the commuters turned around to stare at us. I took a deep breath and told myself to ignore the looks. I was going to start how I meant to go on. It reminded me of the day at the christening when I hadn't been able to be so thick-skinned about being in public when Lena had a meltdown. I was actually getting better at this stuff.

I could read the signs that Lena was heading into distress (and I knew we still had the assessment to get through), so my gut reaction was to lower some of the sensory triggers. I dug into my just-in-case bag to see what I could find. I used my woolly hat – from my own head – and discovered a pair of gloves in my bag, which I experimented with placing over Lena's ears, securely fastened by an extra layer of the hat. I hoped it would give her a temporary respite to the unwanted commotion. I dug deeper in my bag and discovered a pair of sunglasses which emphasised I hadn't cleaned out my bag since the summer. I pressed them gently over her button nose, their over-sized frames rested over the remaining freckles visible on her cheeks. I prayed it would reduce the unnecessary lights too.

My resource of handmade tricks worked and we were soon calm enough to reach Doctor Ivanna's clinic.

We debarked at Marylebone and made our short walk to Winchester Street as Lena threw the surplus accessories she felt she didn't need any more back in my bag. We reached a large row of terraced Victorian buildings that arched into a circle with a towering white-gated respite area in the middle. Lena let go of my hand and ran into the green-encased resting area to find one tree, one bench and one colourful flower bed as the central feature.

"Is that it?!" she declared, confused. "Where is the park?"

"There isn't one here, sweetie," I answered. "But after our time with Doctor Ivanna we can go to one that is the biggest you'll have ever seen!" I gently slipped my hand into hers and guided us back onto the pavement to find the right clinic (which was like locating a needle in a haystack with the rows of plaques and business signs of surgeries and medical practices).

Eventually I spotted Doctor Ivanna's office and proceeded past the iron railings and into the wraparound porch that was protecting a powerful door (which looked like it had been designed to fit a giant through it). I pressed on the small buzzer to notify the receptionist of our arrival. The Tannoy beeped and I pushed the heavy door open. Lena remained glued to the step.

"Superpups can't go inside," she said. "I'm too busy fighting crime in the city!"

"Come on, Lena." The panic of being late and missing the appointment was seeping in. "They're waiting for us."

"Who is *Lena?*" she stated with her arms up confused whilst exaggerating looking around in the smoggy air. "There are no Lenas. I'm *Chase* and you're my handler *Ryder,* don't forget!"

I suddenly twigged that she was switching to role-play and went with it in a desperate attempt to get her through the door.

"Sorry, *Chase,*" I said animatedly, "I was trying to keep our true identities secret! Let's sneak inside and see if there's an emergency that the pups can fix!"

"Yes, *Ryder,* Sir!" She saluted the side of her head, acting out the fantasy as if she truly believed it. She dropped to all fours and moved like a canine through the lift and along the corridor to a reception where I booked us in. We were guided to a seat in the waiting room. I spotted a water dispenser and fixed us both a replenishing drink

"You need to put it on the floor so I can drink it properly," Lena instructed as she licked the water out of the plastic cup.

A door opened and a pretty lady, smiling warmly at us, came over.

"Hello. My name is Doctor Ivanna. I'm pleased to meet you both." There was an Eastern European twang to her accent but it was hard to place as her command of English was so impressive. "Would you like to follow me?"

"Woof, woof!" Lena barked, jumped onto her paws and proceeded to perform her four-legged walk to the assessment room.

It took a while for Lena to be told about everything and prepared for what was going to happen. Eventually, I was behind a masked glass panel with Doctor Ivanna.

A speech and language play therapist, called Richard, engaged with Lena on the other side of the one-way screen. Lena couldn't see us and soon stopped focusing on the mirrored glass, that we were concealed behind, and began one of the most energetic shows known to the human world.

A picture book was placed in front of her by Richard and he gently requested for her to tell him the story. She could see the pictures of a cat but created her own abstract version of the tale that was incongruous with the images she could see. It was almost as if she was cleverly sabotaging the task.

"The white duck took a bath in the canal," Lena said robotically, "it ate some bread. The end."

I sensed that she was going to make Richard work to build her trust and a realisation hit me that she was being very typically herself. That had to be a good thing, surely? I carried on watching, eager to see what he would find.

Next, he opened a plastic tub with a selection of dolls and action figures and asked Lena if she would like to play. She ignored his question and proceeded to line the toys up in size order, meticulously, and studied each pair to get the adjustments just right. A few dinosaurs were thrown aggressively back into the container.

"They don't match. Dinosaurs lived millions of years ago," Lena declared.

Richard scribbled notes down on a pad of paper, Doctor Ivanna did the same through our hidden looking-glass.

"I'm bored now!" Lena proclaimed without making any eye contact with Richard. She suddenly jumped up out of her seat.

"I wondered if you could help me with this book?" Richard pointed to a make-shift, laminated resource on the table. "I need help working out the shapes."

"Help!" Lena screamed animatedly as she stole a word from his sentence. "I'm melting!" She dropped into a puddle on the floor and even I was astonished at her creativity with that one. It was definitely a new avoidance strategy I hadn't seen before. The pencils held by the two professionals beavered away merrily and it reassured me that the assessment was going well.

Richard tried again with a new task.

"Let's pretend this is a sink." He indicated to the invisible air and Lena shot him a look as if he were mad.

"There's nothing there. Are you blind?!" She seemed infuriated by his abnormal premise to try and think outside the box; she certainly was too literal for that. Doctor Ivanna laughed warmly as she scribbled yet again and smiled over to me. I felt no judgement for once, just connection and understanding.

"But let's pretend... if it *was* a sink..." Richard repeated slowly. "Could you show me how you brush your teeth?"

"No!" she screamed angrily and stuck her tongue out.

Lena ran and snatched his pad of notes and his pencil and pointed back to his creative-play space. Mimicking his exact style and tone of voice, she repeated back to him: "Let's pretend this is a sink. Can you show me how *you* brush *your* teeth?"

Richard got up, smiled and obliged with her demand – which he acted cooperatively. "Now it's your turn, can you show me how you brush yours?"

"No!" she retorted bluntly. "I don't like brushing my teeth. The sound of the brush is too yucky!"

She picked his pen up and drew squiggles all over the page. "Ha ha! Now you can't write any more stupid notes!"

"That's fine," he replied. "Writing is boring anyway."

She continued to draw a blob. "You have a poo poo on your page!"

"Eww." Richard smiled. "Does it smell?"

"Uh huh!" Lena fell into a manic heap of giggles. She was ranging from every extreme emotional state possible.

"I have to go now!" Lena dropped back onto all fours. "Ryder needs me with the other pups. I can hear him sounding the alarm, *there's an emergency!*" She screamed the last part excitedly as if she were about to take off. She let out an almighty "woof!" to the ceiling.

"There was one last thing I was just going to show you." Richard's voice had a tone to it that suggested he was still trying to hold things together. He placed a jigsaw with ten broken pieces that needed to be reassembled again onto the table. "Could you help me to fix my picture?"

Lena's eyes were fixated on the puzzle pieces as she froze on the spot, a deathly stare on her face. He repeated his instruction. It was like a stand-off, she wasn't budging.

I knew that look well, it was always a signal of danger. I could feel myself panicking but I was powerless to do anything.

Richard started to demonstrate the task by placing two of the pieces together. Lena began to slowly draw near to his alien task. She picked a piece of the puzzle, explored it with her fingers and held it up to an eye to inspect it further as though she expected it to come to life.

"These feel funny," she observed with her cool tone that was too calm compared to her stiff, intimidating body language.

Then she proceeded to group the pieces into colour-coordinated piles on her own agenda.

"That's very clever," Richard praised. My hairs went up – I knew this could be a one-way track to disaster – complimenting her when she hadn't asked for it. "It seems you like to put things into order, am I right?"

Lena bombed away from the table before anything else could make her explode as she ran, fuelled with adrenaline, around the assessment clinic with her arms spread open. "*Chase* to the rescue!"

Her speed increased, which I didn't think was possible as she was already taking a hold of the room like a tornado. She unexpectedly stopped still and cupped her hands together as she commanded the final words.

"Drone! Do your work!" Lena's arms threw an imaginary weapon across the room (which, as she had already bulldozed it with her spirit, was pretty believable and was clearly being aimed at Richard) as she screamed and forcibly threw herself onto the floor. "POW!"

Richard looked up to the glass, nodded and Doctor Ivanna jumped out of her seat and moved towards the door. I think he knew it was about to turn into an aggressive, uncontrollable meltdown if it wasn't stopped in time.

"I think we're both happy with what we have got and that's probably enough without putting Lena into distress," Doctor Ivanna politely informed me.

"Thank you," I said agreeably as I followed her back into the assessment arena and gave Lena a big hug of comfort.

"Hello, *Ryder.*" She beamed and licked my face.

"Well done, *Chase*, you were amazing!" I patted her head and both the adults in the room looked on affectionately. Lena looked at them suspiciously.

"You clearly work well as a partnership," Ivanna complimented. "Shall we let *Chase* play with this iPad whilst we have a quick catch up?" Ivanna opened a cupboard and passed Lena a rubber-proofed pad.

Lena stood frozen to the spot, looking at the electronic device and not knowing what to do.

"It has a cool liquid game which you press and it makes satisfying patterns!" Doctor Ivanna tried to offer.

"No thanks!" Lena claimed the prize and retreated onto a soft beanbag to play independently as she delved in autonomously to select her own game of interest.

I was seated with the adults. A wave of nervousness hit me. What were they about to tell me? Would the news be what I expected or was I going to be left in the void of not knowing yet again?

"So how did you think that went?" Ivanna opened the conversation.

"She was definitely being herself – especially when anyone asks her to do anything!" I exclaimed.

"I think I can say for both of us what we concluded today," Doctor Ivanna started as she looked for a nod of approval from Richard. "We tend to work in unison and I think I can confidently ascertain that we are in agreement?"

"Definitely." Richard smiled.

"There was enough we noted today to diagnose that Lena meets the threshold for an autism spectrum disorder," Ivanna informed as Richard nodded in agreement.

"I have to say," Richard began, "her use of vocabulary is exceptional for her age and her creativity is off the scale."

I beamed as I was hearing positive feedback for a change.

"Absolutely!" Ivanna agreed. "She uses her verbal skills enormously to navigate the underlying challenge of her anxiety."

"I've been saying this for so long and nobody has been listening to me," I confessed.

"We also feel that, as part of her diagnosis, she is incredibly demand avoidant so we will be adding the profile of Pathological Demand Avoidance to her diagnosis," Ivanna concluded. "I am aware from your original enquiry that you are quite well-versed, so I won't go into the details of how she marked that threshold, but we will write all of it up in a report and send it to you."

I couldn't believe I was hearing these words. Tears of relief filled my eyes. "Thank you. So much. It's such a relief to finally have an answer."

"Hopefully this will be the pathway to better support and understanding for you both," Doctor Ivanna replied sympathetically.

"Mummy!" Lena bellowed across the room, forgetting her fantasy identity from *Paw Patrol*. "I'm hungry! Why haven't you fed me?"

"Listen, you guys go get some lunch," Doctor Ivanna said softly for Lena's benefit. "*Chase* has worked super hard for it – helping with all those emergencies!"

Lena barked and we all laughed.

"Just one last thing," the doctor said as we were turning to leave and Lena had returned to her position of being on all fours. "We would definitely recommend exploring whether ADHD is also part of the bigger picture. It's not something we were testing for, but there could be some potential signs and it might support the understanding process better."

I kept myself together on the journey out of there (trying to entertain Lena in London to make the day memorable) until bedtime where the processing of the day's events began to take place.

My child is autistic, I told myself.

The realisation was sinking in. I mean, it had been on the cards, but to have this confirmed by professional opinion made the truth a reality.

I felt numb. A rollercoaster of emotions took over me.

I had known all along that Lena saw things differently, that we needed to adapt our parenting to the way that she was, but I hadn't pushed forwards enough.

Guilt was consuming me.

And what about her future? This diagnosis confirmed that Lena would be considered disabled. Would she never be like the other children in her class? Should I even feel happy about the diagnosis?

Oh goodness, how would I begin to tell people? How would I tell Nick? Would he be cross that I did this without him?

And school! The relief hit that I could finally tell them there was a reason for Lena's behaviour and they couldn't blame my parenting any longer.

Would this be a pivotal turning point? I started to feel a sense of hope again as I leant across Lena's bed, tucked up her duvet and kissed her forehead goodnight.

I remembered the last nugget of news from Doctor Ivanna – that I looked into ADHD too. There was still so much to do to support Lena and the challenges that she experienced. How would I even go about it? I made a mental note to do some research when I next had time, to see if there was a pathway for ADHD too. What if there were more diagnoses that would be added? It felt like this was just the beginning of a long journey to get to the bottom of Lena's profile and find out what she would be needing help with. How did I not realise this when she was a toddler? Had it not been glaringly obvious?

I thought about my rainbow and having this newly-acquired knowledge. Maybe it meant power? I visualised the next layer of colour in my rainbow – it was indigo. I wondered if this could mean anything. Did a label equal a layer? I didn't have the capacity to join the dots but it felt like there was a connection somewhere. I thought about messaging Shelley and Vic, but it was too fractious still and I didn't want to just drop news like this without any further information. Tiredness was beginning to consume me. Eventually, I crashed into a restless sleep as my thoughts continued to bash my brain. How could I find out the answers that I needed for us to be complete again?

21

The Arc

I woke up with brain fog from having a turbulent, chaotic sleep where my thoughts were frantically keeping me awake. I left my bed early to make myself a cup of coffee and fired up the laptop. An email had arrived late last night from Doctor Ivanna's clinic with the full report from the assessment day. That was quick, I thought. I forwarded it on to the school whilst copying all of the professionals in at the same time.

To: senco

From: sarahforte

Subject: Lena's ASD Diagnosis

Dear all,

Please find attached a private report from Dr Ivanna.

The ADOS assessment was held yesterday in her clinic by a multi-professional team and they said that Lena meets

```
the threshold for an ASD diagnosis (with a profile of
Pathological Demand Avoidance).

Details of recommendations and adaptions are included
in the report. They have also suggested for me to look
into ADHD too.

I would also like to proceed with an application
for an Educational Health Care Assessment and would
appreciate it if school could support me with this
process?

Kind regards
Sarah Forte
```

As I pinged off the email, confident in my stride that I could now communicate professionally and effectively, a sense of relief came over me. I was finally able to say the words that I had suspected for so long. There would be no more reasons why Lena should not be able to access an education and maybe the school would be more productive instead of focussing on parental blame. Nor would they be able to keep pushing to exclude her! I wondered what they would be thinking as they read those words. Would I get an apology that they had been so wrong at the start? How did they not know that Lena was autistic? Mrs Webb had said Sunnybank had many children with needs, so they must have come across this type of thing before. That was, unless, it was just easier to lay the blame within the family.

I thought about how lucky we were to have been able to find a payment plan to go private. It was so wrong that the same service could have taken years to wait for via the NHS, not only that, our local providers stated they would not use the PDA wording as part of their diagnostic outcome. It made me feel passionate about changing things for other children, after all, there would be kids suffering who were left for a long time being misunderstood. It really was a postcode lottery as to whether we were able to access help and support. That was completely unjust and discriminatory – perhaps I could find a way to campaign about it? I had to stop my mind running away with itself; I was sprinting before I had even learnt to walk.

I decided to mention it at the next Spectrum Support group for parents. I would tell them my recent news as well. I was excited already to go back to find my tribe at the group who would understand exactly how important this news was. I was grateful that I had found people who made my experience and truth feel validated. It reminded me to message Flick.

> Hey lovely lady! I have some exciting news to tell you! x

Flick
Come on then, you can't leave me hanging!? x

> Lena has her diagnosis. She's Autistic with a PDA profile! x

Flick
Congratulations! In the best possible meaning of the word. I am happy that Lena will have the information she needs to be her true self. x

Thank you. Also, for everything you've done along the way. I don't know where I would have been without you x

Flick

I have some news right back for you. I'm creating an advocacy service to support and empower other parents. Helping you has inspired me that I want to do this full time. So I have you to thank right back x

Oh Flick, that's fabulous news. I have every faith you will make it the biggest success. Any other parent you help along the way will be extremely lucky x

Flick

I'll keep you updated and once we have Lena sorted I'm hoping you may even join me! Anyway, the next scheduled support group session is next week so I will hope to see you there? X

I wouldn't miss it for the world! x

As I put my phone down, I thought about the fact that I had told Flick first before any of my other friends or family. It made me feel slightly guilty. I tried to remind myself that she was a neutral person – almost like my advocate. The most important person who needed to know about the diagnosis (before she heard it mentioned second-hand) was Lena. I pictured my daughter and thought about how far we had come together; our bond was now stronger than ever.

I tried to find an opportunity for it to happen organically, and as usual, that involved playing with her toys.

"Doctor Ivanna would like to see *Chase* at the top of the *Lookout Tower.*" I added a new direction in our game.

"Yes, *Ryder*, Sir!" Lena dragged her pup to the top of headquarters. "*What for?*"

"When you came to our clinic yesterday," I said, "we found out why you think differently to the other pups."

"Why do I?" Lena's dialogue for her chosen pup continued with the story.

"It's because you're *pawsomely* autistic!" I replied excitedly.

"What does that mean?"

"It means you understand the world much better than other pups," I explained. "It's why sometimes it's hard to get on with the other pups and why it can be too noisy or busy for you. You have a special way of understanding the world."

"Oh right," Lena answered.

I had to smile. I'd just told her life-changing news and the best she could say was 'oh right'!

"Being autistic is your superpower – if you learn to use it wisely."

"Can I tell the other pups?" Lena questioned.

"Of course you can," I confirmed.

"Guess what, pups?" Lena exclaimed. "I'm an autistic superpup!"

I felt happy that I'd begun to sow the seeds for the start of an important conversation. She was so young to be introduced to what it meant in detail, but I would buy Doctor Ivanna's book and introduce the PDA aspect slowly to add more depth. I felt pleased with myself that I had created an opportunity to present it as a positive thing. A feeling of warmth and contentment spread throughout my body. My rainbow was starting to feel like it was nearly full of every colour. Although, I still needed a way to complete the layer for indigo!

My mind raced onto a different subject as I thought about the need to tell Nick and my family of the recent developments. How could I get around it? What was going to be the best way? I couldn't exactly forward the email on and just drop a bombshell like that without any explanation. What if they saw it as a negative thing and didn't accept it? Even worse, I had to break the silence between Nick and I since our last text exchange; that felt like a task all on its own.

An idea popped up: what if I brought everyone together and told them at the same time? I was flowing with productivity and the desire to use this knowledge to implement change once and for all. I really needed my family to see that a label was not a negative thing and that it could help them understand Lena better. I picked up my phone to text my family in a copy and paste message and anxiously hit the send button.

> There is something that I need to talk about with you all. I would like to do it as soon as possible. Can everyone come to my house this evening around 8pm? Thanks, Sarah

My mum replied first that she could come over, although she was confused and checked if there was an emergency. I replied to reassure her it was nothing to worry about but it was important nevertheless. This response was soon followed by my sister who said she would swing past after her Pilates class. My dad replied that he was going to watch a football match but hopefully Mum could fill him in afterwards. Okay, that's fine, I thought, confident that two out of the three could carry the message back. There was a long delay (despite a read receipt acknowledging the text had been seen) until Nick finally replied.

> **Nick**
> Sounds a bit extreme? It's a bit awkward having a family get-together now we are separated? I'm confused?

> It's just something I need to talk about with all of you. Hopefully it won't take up too much of your time. Thanks.

> **Nick**
> Are you about to tell us you've decided to bat for the other team?

He was at it again – trying to bring me down because I wasn't budging on my decision to not give things another go. Maybe it was going to be a relief that we had others around us.

> It's a family meeting and it involves Lena but thanks for the concern.

> **Nick**
> Lighten up. It was just a joke.

> I'd appreciate it if we keep this focused. See you at 8.

As usual, asking Nick to be present or involved with something was still a contentious issue. I got busy with getting Lena ready for the morning session at school and tidying the toys away to try and gain some order to my house. All the while, my head spun thinking about and analysing how I was going to open the subject up to Nick and my family about Lena.

How would they take it? Would they be supportive? Was this going to help them to see the bigger picture? I felt bad that I hadn't included my friends to come for the group announcement, but I just wasn't sure what they were thinking about me and my recent behaviour. I was back in avoidant-mode from the discomfort of not knowing if I had ruined the two major friendships that meant so much to me.

Evening was suddenly upon us. I scurried around after putting the children to bed so that the house looked a little less of a shambles. As much as I felt like I was fretting over it, I tried to remind myself that I was striding forwards as a new person. Anyone who wanted to have a relationship with me had to accept me how I was – house mess or no house mess! I glanced around some of the items still strewn over the chairs and carpet and felt strong in the knowledge that I was choosing not to pick them up to make a false impression of my identity. My focus was always about making positive, loving relationships with my children, not living in a show home.

My sister arrived first. I took a deep breath and reminded myself that we could get past our rift and feel more connected as siblings again – only if I was open to trying.

"You're the first person here, Julie." I smiled. "I wish I could borrow your punctuality one time! I think you ended up with that better part of the gene pool!"

"Sarah, you'd arrive late to your own funeral!" Julie quipped and we both giggled as our eyes locked in a shy glance. "When we went on holiday as kids, I used to pack your bags for you just to speed you up!"

We laughed, united by earlier childhood memories. Ones that were happy and connected, without a care in the world. The air felt lighter all of a sudden. Julie had always been a protective big sister and we would spend hours on our roller skates together just roaming our cul-de-sac and tasting freedom together. She was always there like a shot if any other kid said a word to me.

"How have you been?" I enquired carefully.

"Good. Thank you," Julie answered. "How about you?"

"Things have been..." I paused, waiting to find the right word before settling with: "Interesting!"

"I'm intrigued." Julie grinned. "Well, you've changed your hair colour so something is definitely going on!"

"You could say things have been *colourful* of late," I teased as I held back any details of my latest pursuits. "How about we go for a coffee soon, just the two of us? Maybe I can fill you in properly when the time is more appropriate and without Mum about to walk in?"

"Sounds like a plan!" Julie beamed. I wondered if she was genuinely as pleased as I was that we were finding a way to communicate with one another again.

Just as I was about to suggest a time to do it, the doorbell rang and our mum was waiting at the front door, followed by Nick who was just behind her.

We all gathered around the living room – with my mum and sister strategically separating the gap between Nick and I. After what had happened between us the last time we were together, it felt safer to have a greater sense of distance from one another. Nick looked at me as he sat himself down on the sofa, but I found it difficult to meet his gaze. It was at times like these that I realised how unsafe he could make me feel sometimes. It was only the space that was helping me to see it clearly.

It was confession time and I openly told them all about paying privately for the assessment at Doctor Ivanna's clinic (which Mum already knew but kept quiet knowing it wasn't the place to let on she'd had the information before anyone else). I had a copy of the report on the coffee table and picked it up to show them the official outcome from the tests conducted.

"Lena is autistic." I could feel my shoulders tense as I pre-empted the response that could come. What were they going to say?

"Are you sure?" My mum answered. "They don't always get these things right."

"Yes, I'm sure," I responded. "It's been on the cards for a while now and has been picked up by some new professionals who have been working with us."

"What professionals?" Nick questioned suspiciously.

The ones that got involved after we had the meetings that you never turned up to! Of course I had to hold it in to keep order of the situation and to avoid getting lost in 'blames-ville'.

It made me realise that if we had pursued the rendezvous from the other day, we would have still have those underlying issues in our relationship that we hadn't been able to work through. My friends were right, yet I'd been too stubborn to hear them properly.

"We have a new team around Lena," I informed him as if he were a stranger and not an equal parent in the equation. "They're helping to try and make adjustments in school so that she can eventually go back full-time."

"So this so called 'team' told you our daughter is a *retard* and you've paid them for that piece of information?" Nick's lips were pursed and his frown lines deep. "And you believed them?"

Oh my goodness, did he just call our daughter the r-word? How could he do that? I was livid with frustration and finding it impossible to disguise.

"That word is derogatory," I chastised him. "I don't want Lena to hear harmful words like that!"

"Well what do you think the kids will say to her at school?" Nick snapped. "Having a label will make her stand out as *different*. I've told you this before, but you've ignored my wishes regardless."

It was lucky my family was there as I could sense his anger would've overspilled and we could have found ourselves in a one-sided debate.

"It's not like that anymore." I tried to disarm his ignorant views. "There isn't a stigma about autism. It's better this than everyone around her labelling her as some naughty kid all the time. We should embrace her difference rather than making her feel shameful about it."

"I have to agree with Sarah," Mum's voice popped up unexpectedly. I had a flicker of hope that she was changing her feelings on the matter. "If I had something wrong with me then I would want to be told."

Okay, so she wasn't politically correct and I had to work on her assumption that something was *wrong* with Lena, but a change was happening with my mum and it was a step in the right direction.

"Look, I'm sorry. It's just a shock!" Nick conceded. "I mean, I always thought people with autism didn't speak and they were stuck in their own world."

"I think this is a shock to everyone," Mum consoled. "Perhaps we have spent too long trying to curb her behaviour instead of looking into things in more detail. I have to admit that my understanding is definitely limited, but it looks as if Sarah may be able to enlighten us, after all, she has always said there is something there."

She really was changing her mindset and my heart was starting to swell; I couldn't remember the last time I had felt a positive emotion towards my mother. She picked up her hand and gently rested it on Nick's knee as a gesture of moral support. It was working; he was starting to be influenced by my mother's lead. We may have been separated, but she was still a motherly, respected figure in his life and one he did listen to. At last I had broken down the wall of resistance in my family and they were starting to open their minds to something new.

"Our ideas on what it means to be autistic are just outdated," I continued. "I've learnt a lot on the way and had to rethink my way of understanding it too."

Nick looked at me, bewildered. I could sense his weakness and I knew right there that I needed to find the strength to lead us all through this process.

"I think it's important to celebrate that Lena is autistic!" I tried to infuse him. "She doesn't carry her autism with her like it's a bag. It is an integral part of her identity, and now we can start to support and understand her better."

There was silence.

I just needed them all to see that Lena's journey into the future would be more enlightened by having that knowledge. If only they could see it as a positive! I had to convince them further.

"It's not a death sentence," I said, trying not to smile. "We just have to flip the focus. There are just as many strengths as there are challenges to this. In fact, society has always been neurodiverse – we've just come some way forward to recognising that. Who were the people who found new continents? Or those who made innovative inventions? Or the leaders who took risks? Many of those people in history have been neurodivergent too. With the right support, Lena may start to flourish and her mind can learn to thrive like those who have come before us."

"That's a bit deep, don't you think?" Nick remarked.

"I guess it makes sense," Julie commented and seemed to be backing the family side up. "I know I was unforgivingly cross at the christening, but Lena's behaviour shocked me. She doesn't seem to act like other children and it's a bit confusing. I had no idea... I wish I could have done better."

"Lena has a different way of communicating," I explained. "When we understand her profile, we approach how she interacts in a different light."

"I think, amongst all of the stress of organising a big event, I wasn't very understanding," Julie said forlornly.

"I have had a lot to learn too," I comforted. "There's a lot to process and it can be very difficult to challenge how we traditionally deal with things."

"I'm so sorry, Sarah." Julie broke down. "I should have been there for you. Will you ever forgive me?"

I got up out of my seat and hugged my sister like we were innocent children again and we'd had the simplest of fallouts like over who had the most sweets. She clung to me and we stayed in our embrace as the cathartic tears began to shed. It had been a long time coming, and we hadn't communicated properly for so long, that it felt like the air in the room was so much lighter than it had been over the last year or more.

"I should have found a way to talk to you about my feelings," I apologised. "I bottled everything up and became resentful and it caused the divide in our relationship to grow. You tried to invite me to a baby group but I was stubborn in my response because it didn't involve Lena. I should have explained why I felt she was being excluded – you aren't a mind reader!"

"When I replied that mum could have Lena it was only because I thought it wasn't the right place to take her," Julie confessed. "I didn't really think about it properly or how you would feel about that."

"You tried to get us back on track, but I couldn't find the words to explain why I felt so upset. I should have been more mature about it all. I know that I've excluded you from my life since, and that's not fair either."

"Looks like you've been carrying a lot of weight on your shoulders, Sarah." Mum joined us. "I think we all recognise that we should have understood a bit better. I'm sorry that I told you not to bring her to any more family events. That was wrong of me and I was acting on emotion."

"I guess she does work on her own agenda," Nick spoke. His admission was small in front of everyone, but I sensed by his body language that he felt he had let Lena down. I tried not to push it any further; I had the feeling that we still had some conversations between us that needed finishing.

After a little more explaining on my part about the added profile of Pathological Demand Avoidance (and how the features of this extra layer differ), we decided to call it a night and that maybe we could all find a way to research it better, or even attend a course online or something.

"This is going to be a learning curve for all of us," I finished. "We might not always get it right, but our mistakes are where we learn best."

As I hit the sack that night I felt proud of myself. I was no longer shrinking as a mother but becoming the parent that my children needed me to be. It felt like the truth was out and I had been freed from the accumulated blame that had been building for so long. Not only that, the news was bringing my family back together and starting to repair the void that had developed between us all.

The diagnosis was an answer. I knew from this judgement day that I would be able to protect our family unit. I remembered the CAMHS session with Theresa and her phone call a week ago where she'd reminded me that Lena's mental health was the most important thing. I had taken her advice and was leading the rest of the family along too. That day marked the rebirth of understanding Lena's autistic identity. It would be the start of better support and guidance to follow. As a fierce mama, I would make sure of it.

***

It was finally Thursday and I was looking forward to the first video call with my friends since our fallout. I was nervous, I knew I had some stuff to admit to and the embarrassment was consuming me. Would we be able to move on from this and just go back to normal? We'd had disputes when we were younger, but this was the first time in our history that we hadn't properly spoken. We may have texted each other, but it was more difficult to face them properly. I took a deep breath and poured myself a mocktail from a can in the fridge. I was ready to go online.

We began the conversation fluffing around the surface of topics, which was pleasant enough, but I could sense we were still avoiding the elephant in the room. I put my big girl pants on and decided to go in.

"I know I text to say I was sorry," I slowly started, "but I didn't really explain why."

"You don't need to apologise," Shelley answered.

"We get it!" Vic joined. "Besides, all friendships have their ups and downs."

"I got scared," I confessed, "and it hit me all at once... knowing that Nick would be free to start over again put fear into me. Panic took over and I lost control of myself, hurting you both and myself in the process. I even had a small lump on my head to prove it!"

"How did you do that?" Vic asked in a caring tone.

"I hit myself with a notebook out of frustration that I was sabotaging everything in my life," I confessed. "It certainly wasn't the best coping strategy."

"Have you thought about going to the doctor for some help?" Shelley asked. "Counselling might be something to think about?"

"That's a great idea," Vic agreed. "Remember you've been holding so much together by yourself. I mean, a marriage breakup is tough enough, but fighting for an education for your child, and coping with a school who tried to exclude her and blame you in the process, is huge. That's without wider family struggles. Getting help for it all is not a sign of weakness, it's actually an indication of strength."

"I guess you're both right," I admitted. "Maybe I'll make an appointment and go from there."

"You've already put things in place," Shelley commented. "Choosing to be sober was a step in the right direction."

I raised my non-alcoholic beverage and smiled at the screen.

"Cheers." I smiled. "It doesn't have quite the same potency but I definitely feel better when I wake up every morning!"

"I need to take a leaf out of your book." Shelled laughed. "Although I won't ever be running, that's for sure. Oh, that reminds me, whatever happened to that run with the beast? Have you seen him again?"

"I've been putting him off for a while now," I said sadly. "I didn't have the headspace to even contemplate seeing him."

"Maybe it's time you made that step?" Vic suggested. "Remember the feel-good feeling you had after seeing him? Sarah, that night at yours after you'd ran with him? Your whole aura was glowing! I don't think we've ever seen you like that for years."

"That's right," Shelley joined. "It's why we were so disappointed when you were wobbling about returning to Nick; we were worried you were about to make a decision you'd end up regretting."

"It's not that we don't like Nick," Vic spoke softly. "So if you do repair things, then of course we will support you all of the way. But you were wilted for so long whilst you were married – years before you ever reached breaking point. These last few months the real Sarah has started to bloom and we're relieved to see it!"

"There was also the issue that we saw he controlled who you were," Shelley admitted, "it was something we didn't like to witness."

"That's right," Vic agreed. "It was a red flag of being a victim of domestic abuse. You see, we did some homework and there were plenty of other signs too."

"So we are sorry too," Shelley confessed, "we had concerns and we were too frightened to tell you in case it meant we lost our friendship."

I thought deeply about their words and I knew they were true.

"I had a reality bolt that my marriage was abusive the moment I confessed to you guys in Benidorm," I opened up, "it's surreal that when you are living it you get sucked in to being submissive, to survive without even realising it's happening. It's only afterwards that it dawns on you how much control you're living under."

"Exactly!" Vic agreed.

"That's why I went a bit cold on you after Nick made his move again," Shelley admitted. "I just didn't know what I should say. I told you I'd seen him with another woman, but I wasn't entirely truthful about the whole of my concerns."

We continued analysing my past relationship and I heard from Shelley and Vic about all of the times that they had witnessed moments they were unhappy with. It felt a lot to take in and it was no doubt something I needed therapy to help free my mind of in order to make future choices that were healthier.

I then went on to tell them all about Lena's recent diagnosis. They listened and asked the right questions. I knew I had their full support.

"Now, I don't know what to do about Tim, he won't wait around forever. Should I still text him or is this just simply not the right time?" I asked my friends nervously.

"That's a fab idea!" Vic said with excitement. "You can take things slowly whilst you make sense of learning from the past!"

"One last thing," Shelley began, "we think this belongs to you!"

Shelley held a sparkling rose-gold necklace up to the screen, trying not to wobble the camera so that it could focus on the tiny rainbow charm in the middle.

"No way!" I could feel the tears of joy surfacing. "Did you buy it for me?"

"We both did," Shelley said.

"I absolutely love it." I beamed gratefully. "It's perfect."

"We thought it would be a celebration for completing your rainbow!" Vic informed me.

"But wait!" I interrupted. "You know I still have to work on indigo, right?"

"You already had indigo and you didn't realise it!" Vic answered cryptically.

"I don't understand?"

"You have an indigo child..." Shelley started to explain. "Her recent diagnosis confirmed that too!"

"What's an indigo child?" I asked, intrigued. I had never heard of the term before.

"Indigo children are believed to possess special, unusual – or sometimes supernatural – traits or abilities," Vic explained. "You have one of them already in Lena. And now you understand who she is, both of your indigo hues will shine even stronger."

"We've come to the conclusion that she inherited her wonderful and colourful persona from you," Shelley suggested.

"Consider yourself one mighty indigo mama!" Vic declared.

I tried to process what my best friends were telling me, but I couldn't shake the feeling of being incomplete no matter how much they wanted me to be celebrating. What if they felt disappointed after all the help they had given?

"I'm so grateful but... I just thought once the rainbow was complete, it would solve everything."

"We're always on a journey of discovery," Shelley began, "the layers may just be your starting foundations."

"What would I do without you?" I sighed. "I promise to not take things out on you both again!"

"Here's to being friends even when our teeth are in a drawer and our tits are on the floor!" Shelley proclaimed devilishly.

"Hah!" squealed Vic. "I love that one!"

We raised our glasses again for a virtual cheers. We had managed to overcome a difficult situation with love and compassion, just as we had done through all the milestones that we had experienced with one another.

They were the kind of friends I knew I'd grow old with. They were the ones who would hold my hand through any situation – from holding my hair back when I was a drunken, sick teenager down an alleyway, to being my sounding board through relationships and to challenging my limits in life. They were always there and would be with me every step of the way. Our conversations would always be deep, whether over a coffee or a gin, always sprinkled with a touch of laughter. They were an intrinsic part of my rainbow that held all of the layers together. I realised that my rainbow was never really black to start with because they had been there with me all the time. I sent one late night text before I went to bed.

> Thank you, girls, for the necklace and for being the magical gold dust that has held my rainbow together! xxx

The next day I thought a lot about what the girls had said and I decided to put their advice into action. First, I made an appointment with my GP to ask for a referral to a counselling service. My best friends were right; I had been bottling so much up that it was a healthier release to find a way to talk to someone so I could deal with the bigger emotions that I had been suppressing for too long. It might have only been the one occasion that I had become so mentally distressed that I had harmed myself physically, but I had been harming myself by relying on alcohol for so long before that. Accepting my mental health was also a priority so that I could keep my rainbow shining brightly and looking after my children was important. After all, if I were on an aircraft with them and we hit an emergency, how could I save them without putting my own oxygen mask on first?

Two days had passed since I had dropped the bombshell on Nick and my family. We hadn't spoken since and I was wondering how they felt now that the news had had a chance to settle in. Most of all, I thought about Nick and felt compassion about the grief he was probably feeling. Instead of my past-state of being bitter, I started to feel genuine care. He had deeper issues relating to his need to be in control – heck who knew whether he was built just like Lena too and hadn't realised for his whole life? I was on the pathway to understanding and if he didn't change his ways, he would never be happy deep inside. I knew it was the time to offer another olive branch, but this time from a place of support. I called him as I dropped Lena at school for her session with Tariq. I started the call pleasantly and gave him the reason for why I had unexpectedly rung:

"I know it's come as a shock and I'm sorry that it's not what you expected to hear..."

I hesitated and made the decision to talk through Nick's silence.

"It's also difficult finding a way forward now that we've separated," I consoled, "but some things will stay the same and one of those is that you are Lena's father, nothing is ever going to change that."

"I just don't understand... why... I just wish that..." Nick trailed off as he struggled to find the words. "I wish this happened to somebody else. It wasn't supposed to be our family."

"Life is never the way we plan it," I comforted. "Instead we have to adapt to the direction it heads in."

"She's my baby! She's my Spitfire!" Nick broke down. I had heard him cry more in the last few weeks than I had through our entire marriage. It reminded me that during all of the arguments we'd had whilst together, he was hurting just as much but showed it in different ways.

"She still is your Spitfire – she hasn't changed," I reassured him. "We just have to enable the funny, creative, sassy-pants that she is destined to be."

There was a small bubble of laughter through the fuelled emotion of the call.

"The report also suggests that Lena could have an exceptionally high IQ but they were unable to continue with their assessments. They didn't want to put her under any unnecessary distress," I informed him. "We should be incredibly proud of what she has to give already and who knows what that will lead to in the future."

"I've always thought she was a genius!" Nick's voice peaked suddenly with a hope of positivity.

"Exactly! Look, if we do this right," I led, "and if we do this singing from the same hymn sheet, then who knows how her strengths will develop. There's no reason why we can't both be there for Lena if we respect one another."

"I wasn't ready for our marriage to break," Nick confessed suddenly.

"I don't think either of us were," I replied genuinely.

"I kick myself extra for not understanding better," Nick admitted, "that's why I made the move the other day. I think it was a last-minute opportunity to glue things back together."

"We haven't resolved any of our issues to pick up where we left off," I confessed. "I don't think it would help either of us. You know that, deep down, just as much as I do."

"I guess you're right," Nick accepted, "it's going to take me a while to adjust to this."

"I will be a supportive space for you," I reassured, knowing in my heart that I would never wish any harm Nick's way. Sometimes couples could come out stronger, even after a breakup. I could but hope that we could stay amicable for the children's sake and that we could grow into new roles.

I thought again about the fact that he had been spotted with another woman. The more I considered it, the more I was able to feel comfortable with the knowledge that if not now, but one day in the future, Nick would be with somebody else. He would make a partnership with someone and we would be acquaintances with only the children cementing the need for us to be in contact. It felt strange, but I was starting to feel that I could accept and adapt to that, one day at a time. The image of Nick with another woman was no longer enough to make me want to give things another try; it was no longer holding the emotional force that it first had which had made me doubt myself and weaken. Was it a sign that I was becoming detached and healing?

We ended the call with the feeling that some of our underlying issues were now out in the open and, unlike the last time I'd offered that olive branch, this time it had been met with open arms. At the very least – we had finally found a way to communicate better with one another. It left me with some hope that we would be able to make this work.

I rushed back to collect Lena from school and buzzed to go through the gate, taking my usual walk along the pathway to the reception whilst scanning the play area in order to locate where she was with Tariq. I felt a little uneasy as her noise always carried through the air and I normally wouldn't have to question where she was. I leaned around the edge of the building to see if they were on the giant tyres or hanging upside-down on the climbing frame, but it was eerily quiet in the school grounds and they were nowhere to be seen.

That's strange, I thought. *Where have they gone? What if she's ran away again?*

I hurried into the reception to find out. As always, the glass shutter remained frozen and I was met by a rigid stare from the other side. *This school really needs to get a more welcoming admin,* I thought. *Or maybe she is friendly to others and it's just me that rubs her up the wrong way?*

"Where is Lena?" I demanded. There was a hint of blame in my voice but I was too worried to act more like a professional parent.

"She's in her classroom," the receptionist answered. "I'll go fetch her."

Her classroom? I was stunned.

She walked away and returned after a few minutes with Tariq. No Lena. Tariq signed out of the visitor's book and beamed a huge smile at me.

"Sarah, you won't believe this – Lena ASKED to go to her classroom today!"

"That's incredible!"

"By building trust and allowing her to feel in control, it has allowed Lena to be able to do this," Tariq confirmed. I glanced around to see the receptionist eavesdropping through the glass. She quickly looked away. It must have been shocking for staff to hear that a child was allowed to be in control and that things were being done differently. I smiled. *Change happens slowly and trickles down to everyone eventually, even if they're reluctant to it.*

"It sounds like we're making a breakthrough!" I said excitedly.

"We sure are," Tariq replied. "Look, I have to leave now, but Lena was busy in the class and wanted to stay. I've asked the teacher to call you if anything changes. I hope that's alright by you?"

"Of course!" I exclaimed. "I would never want to pull her out when she wants to stay. The bridging work you have done is fantastic and I can't thank you enough."

I looked around. The school was silent but I knew that those walls had ears. We were veering away from the set times the school had agreed to have Lena and we were no longer working on their terms. I tried not to worry about the comeback knowing that this had been Tariq's decision.

"This only happens when we work together." Tariq paused and then said, "If you're leaving too, shall we walk down?"

We carried on our conversation along the path and out of earshot once we buzzed through the gate. He must have sensed our privacy was being invaded just as much as I had.

"I'll send an email and copy everyone in to inform them of today's progress," Tariq told me. "That way it will be on record that we need to be flexible and have Lena in school longer on the days she can manage."

"Oh my," I expressed with a grin, "Mrs Ramsbottom will just love that!"

"She will have to get used to it," Tariq retorted. "That headteacher has been playing a funding card for too long to cover her illegal negligence to provide supportive education to a child with SEND. It's been exposed in a big meeting, so now she can't say no to having Lena in because of staffing issues. That's a *her* problem and not a *Lena* problem."

"I have an update to tell you too," I squealed. "I've downloaded the EHC assessment form and started to fill it in. Tomorrow, I will also be calling the GP to request a referral for an ADHD assessment."

"That's fantastic news," Tariq responded. "She's going to need a long-term plan to make sure she gets that high level of support delivered. Understanding her full profile is going to be paramount to getting those needs identified in a plan."

"Hopefully it'll be sent off and I can give an update at the next TAC meeting."

"Whatever happens," Tariq began cautiously, "if the outcome is not in Lena's favour, there are ways to appeal, okay?"

"Uh huh." I nodded apprehensively.

"As you've seen already, this journey is often arduous and complex." He lowered his voice. "One where you have to advocate continuously as Lena's voice because the system is not fit for purpose."

"It's scary that after all we've been through, I seem to always be at the start of another journey," I confessed.

"But you're acquiring knowledge and skills at speed and will be a warrior parent to lead others by example. I have every faith in that," Tariq complimented.

I threw my arms around him and hugged him before I let go quickly, realising his professional status.

"Thank you, Tariq," I said emotionally. "You'll never realise how much you've helped our family."

"The pleasure has been all mine," he confirmed. I could see his eyes welling up as he took a deep cough to conceal it.

I walked away feeling content and secure by the support network that I had managed to find around me. It dawned on me that they were like my rainbow arc and the foundations that were needed to propel my curved trajectory; this was a journey that looked like it wouldn't have a definitive end point. It had been naive of me to think that everything would be neatly tied up; life never worked that way.

We are always learning. We are always facing new milestones and adventures. Lena was also only an infant and we had many phases ahead that would no doubt be met with new challenges. And then there was Charlie. What would he be bringing to the mix as he grew older and developed his own personality? What if he was autistic too? I hadn't even thought about that before.

The arc in my brain was continuing to circulate new thoughts as I began to contemplate the next chapter ahead of us. Lena was beginning to access school again which meant that I would hopefully be able to return to work in January as planned and get back on track. I knew my mum would be able to cope with Charlie alone and I would bring in a wage to keep our family independently. I could feel the biggest, proudest smile explode onto my face. Things were turning around and I was learning how to pull everything together so that I could be the maternal leader my children needed me to be.

22

A Myriad of Colours

"I can't procrastinate anymore!" I declared to Shelley who had popped over for a quick cuppa the next morning whilst Lena was in her session at school. "I want to text Tim but I don't know what to say."

"Just be yourself," Shelley urged me, "he will understand. Besides, you've given a hint that things have been tough and he said to take your time. Sounds to me like he has no expectations."

"Well I guess I could ask if he's free this weekend as it's Nick's turn to have the children?"

"Do it now before you miss your chance!" Shelley instructed playfully.

I picked up my phone and fired off a quick text message to Tim asking him if he was free at the weekend. I typed that I had some time and would love to meet up. A pang of fear fluttered through my stomach like butterflies as I anticipated reading the negative response that might follow. I tried to tell myself that I had nothing to lose.

"What if he doesn't reply?" I asked Shelley in angst.

"Well, if he doesn't, he's not worthy of being involved in your life," Shelley declared. "Remember how much you have to give and how lucky that person will be to know you or your family because you are a catch any man could wish for."

"I'm not sure about that," I replied modestly, "but I appreciate the sentiment."

Suddenly my phone beeped as if this conversation was being radiated to the intended subject to give them a virtual nudge to respond.

"Is it the Beast?" Shelley looked over my shoulder excitedly. "You do realise I'll tell him his nickname when I get to meet your new romance, don't you?"

I laughed nervously as Shelley was jumping ahead of herself. I mean, we'd only been for a run and a coffee together, how did I know if he even liked me like that? I read the message in my head speedily before repeating it aloud.

"He said he's pleased to hear from me and he has no plans so he'd love to meet up." I clasped my hands around my cheeks in relief. The text was friendly and it didn't seem like I had ruined my chances. Then another message beeped through. "Would you like to go for a meal?"

"Yessss!!!" screamed Shelley eagerly. "Quickly, reply yes!"

Tim and I texted each other back and forth to secure the arrangements. By the end of our exchange we had made plans to go to an Italian restaurant in the marina by the canal on Saturday evening. My lips crept upwards with a feeling of nervous excitement that was impossible to conceal.

"See what happens when you take that risk?" Shelley smiled. "Life has a way of creating opportunities when we open our arms out to them."

"Are you proud of me, Shel?" I laughed. "I may be forty but I'm finally finding my feet."

"It's never too late to start anew." Shelley hugged me as she started to get herself ready to leave. "Talking of which, here's your necklace."

I touched the beautiful rose gold and stroked along the patterned chain until I reached the embellished charm – the rainbow colours had been painted with pastel hues. I flipped it over – there was a message engraved with the words: 'friendships are rainbows'.

"You guys got this personally engraved for me?" I asked, shocked by the thought that they had forked out on such a detailed gift.

"We wanted you to know we love you deeply." Shelley was choked up.

I unclasped the connector and fixed the necklace around my neck. The sensation of the cold metal against my skin reinforced the notion of newness and change that was slowly transforming over my body and into my whole life. I instantly felt as if this proud emblem would be loud and clear for everyone to see.

"Rainbows are just relationships we make by connecting to others." I squeezed my best friend with love. "When I make a bridge with you or the kids or with my family, then we form a rainbow together. That goes for any connections we have with people, if our minds meet, then we make that rainbow together."

"That's a good way to think about it," Shelley agreed.

"We spend our whole lives thinking we have to find a partner to fulfil that goal," I continued, revelling in my own wisdom. "But rainbows are often found in places when you're not looking for them. I forgot to focus on what I did have instead of worrying about what I didn't. All of the relationships in my life were rainbows, I just didn't have enough rain to see they were already there. My failing marriage was also preventing me from seeing that."

"See, you did have your colourful rainbow already. Now go get that sunshine out this weekend and make it fabulous, darling! Even if it is bloody freezing!"

"I'll try!" I winked as Shelley put her warm fur coat on to make an exit into the cold, December air.

"I'll be sure to text in the group chat to update you both after Saturday!"

"We will look forward to it," Shelley responded genuinely. "Bye for now."

I wrapped Charlie up snugly and set off to school to pick Lena up, this time without any urgency. My mind was no longer fretting about school or Nick or my family for that matter. Instead, my thoughts were replaced with something that was happening which I was looking forward to and was for me. What should I wear? How would it go? If he brought me home, was it acceptable to ask him in? Would he make a move? I talked my mind through each of the scenarios to internalise the possible options and to enjoy the moment of anticipation. It felt good to know that my role of being 'Sarah' was just as important as being a good mum or a good friend or even a good partner. My identity was shining brightly and my smile had returned. I felt alive again.

As soon as Lena saw me her eyes were drawn to my new necklace. She always noticed the tiniest change of detail and was transfixed by it until she was able to process it.

"What's that?" She pointed as she brushed my skin to lift the necklace away for a close inspection.

"It's a necklace," I responded, "it's a present from Vic and Shelley."

"Why?" Lena demanded, confused. "It's not your birthday!"

I laughed warmly inside at her literal thinking – the giggles weren't something I could externalise or she would have been upset with me.

"Sometimes people might buy you a gift when it's not your birthday," I began, "but sometimes when they want to surprise you or even make you feel better."

"Are you sad?" Lena quizzed, looking up at me. "You don't look sad now!"

"I was feeling a little sad a while ago," I confessed, trying to make the conversation as honest and as child-friendly as possible, "because that happens sometimes, even when you're a grown up, and we might need a little help from our friends or our family to feel better again."

"I was sad at school," Lena contributed, "but I'm not anymore. I get to play again."

"Exactly!" I stroked her beautiful strawberry-blonde hair. "The teachers needed to help make you not feel sad anymore."

"They didn't buy ME a present for it. That's not fair!"

"Maybe their present is playing *Paw Patrol* with you?" I suggested, trying to avoid the path towards an emotional overload from Lena. "Sometimes gifts are the actions people do because they care and want to make us feel better."

"You give me presents all of the time because you play with me, Mummy." Lena slipped her hand in mine. "You're my best friend."

I couldn't contain my emotions. A small tear rolled down my cheek. I felt the happiness and joy of the small rainbow bridge from my daughter's words.

"Why are you crying?" Lena asked, alarmed. "You said you weren't sad anymore!"

"I'm not," I reassured. "I'm crying because I'm happy."

"You're weird!" Lena laughed.

"I'm lucky to have three best friends in my life."

"Four!" Lena shouted.

"Huh?" I looked confused.

"You forgot Charlie!" Lena reminded me loudly. "He has to be your best friend too!"

"Of course!" I laughed. "How could I forget Charlie!"

We stopped walking the buggy and both crept down to Charlie unexpectedly. He beamed his one-tooth, muddled smile back up at us. Lena used her tiny finger to gently tickle under her sibling's chin with deep love and affection, simply mirroring my interactions with her. I felt pleased that the scaffolding I was using was working.

There were some things that I had tried to change in Lena

because I hadn't understood her, but the one thing that I could teach her was how to love someone unconditionally. That skill in itself would help her through life because I knew she could reciprocate what she had already experienced. *Love is the strongest element to any rainbow.*

We continued our journey as Lena jumped from one conversational topic to another, eventually holding her concentration on Christmas.

"How many days until Santa comes?"

"Nineteen," I responded, having just catapulted my brain into mental arithmetic in preparation.

"I want Santa to bring me some friends like yours," Lena stated. "They're kind to you. I don't have real friends at school. I'm just acting when I'm there."

It was such a profound thing to say and an acknowledgement that Lena was unable to take her mask off at school in order to be the authentic child she needed to be. It was further confirmation that she needed extra support to be herself and to socially navigate at school. I felt a tinge of sadness that she wanted friends but found it impossible to make them. It would be the next thing on my agenda to ensure school could support her in this area too. These were the gaps that were being identified and I felt confident that I could voice those needs to others from now on in.

"Friendships can take a lot of time and patience," I replied. "Santa won't be able to bring you friends, sweetie. But Mummy can ask the teachers to find a way to help you make those friends at school so that you're able to be yourself." I paused before concluding, "You're the best friend anyone could wish for."

"Why is there a rainbow on the necklace?" Lena abruptly asked as she changed the topic. I sensed that the subject of having no friends was too triggering and she had artfully bypassed her emotional response with a tactical conversation change as usual.

"Because I found the colours in my rainbow," I answered softly.

"You've found colours in your rainbow?" Lena asked. "What do you mean?"

"Remember that day when you said you felt like a black rainbow?" I reminded her.

"Uh huh," Lena responded, still trying to make sense of what I was saying. I could see her mind searching through her memories for clarity.

"The day we went to see the lady in the clinic and you spotted a picture of a rainbow with sunshine and rain?" I built a picture to help Lena's memory.

"Oh then!"

"Well, you made me think about it more and I realised that I felt like a black rainbow too," I explained. "So I wanted to find a way to make my rainbow colourful again."

"Did it work?" Lena asked.

"It sure did." I could feel the colours radiating from inside me. "You see, I discovered red for finding some new friends."

"But you already have friends?"

"Sometimes we need friends for different reasons," I replied quietly, thinking of Flick. "So meeting new ones can be good for us too."

"Only if they will play *Paw Patrol*!" Lena answered bluntly.

"Good point!" I smiled before I continued with my detailed rainbow analysis. "And then I got the colour orange for just learning to be myself. Next there was yellow..."

"What was yellow for?" I could see Lena's eyes were full of intrigue.

"That was learning to have fun again!" I smiled and cringed thinking back about that dreaded banana skin.

"Yay! I think I like yellow the best. Being an adult is boring. All you have to do is work all day and you don't get to play. What fun is that?"

"Exactly!" I beamed. "Yellow is important. We NEED to have

fun!"

"What was green for?" Lena was jumping ahead as she looked diagonally aside to her temporal lobe to recall the order of the rainbow.

"I reached green because I tried to get a bit fitter. Being healthy is good, it helps me feel stronger."

"Is that because of your jelly belly?" Lena questioned innocently. "I like bouncing on it. Don't get rid of it, that's my trampoline!"

"Don't panic!" I laughed. "It doesn't look to be going anywhere fast. But green is just about making some healthier choices."

"Blue!" Lena's hyperactivity levels were rising with increased focus. "Did you get blue, Mummy? You know that's next, don't you?"

"Blue..." I thought about the incident with Nick. "Yes, that was for making changes that are needed and so people want to be around me more."

"Is that why Vic and Shelley don't get bored and make a new best friend?" Lena asked seriously, frowning.

"I guess you could say that." I felt like I needed to move past this one before we entered a deeper subject matter. "Then I got the next layer."

"What for?" Lena moved on.

"For not being the timid girl trying to fit in anymore," I declared. "I learnt to not be a shrinking violet!"

"You haven't said the last one?" Lena was impatiently waiting for the conclusion. She hadn't shown much interest in violet, although I feared it had gone over her head.

"Indigo is for learning about being autistic," I explained. "This colour is for helping us all understand the world better through new eyes."

There was a brief pause for a moment whilst Lena took in my analogy.

"Wow! That is so amazing!" Lena wrapped her arms around me.

"Can you help me find colours in my rainbow?"

"Of course! Lena, your rainbow will be the brightest one there ever could be!"

"Will you buy me a necklace too?" Lena asked hopefully.

"I sure will!" I undid the clasp. "How about you have a turn of wearing my one in the meantime?"

"Yes please, Mummy!" Lena replied, delighted.

Our walk home felt fresh and clear. Our relationship was consolidated further. We had gone full circle since that initial assessment with Theresa at CAMHS. So much had changed; we were growing into a new way of life and adapting along the way.

When I got home, I had an impulsive idea and I followed it up straight away. As Christmas was looming, I'd been thinking about how this year we could do it differently. I decided that I would have to take the reins for a family meet-up. It would have to be adapted to what my little family needed – rather than trying to conform to what others expected of us. A wave of strength washed over me as I set up a *WhatsApp* group entitled – ***Paw Patrol* Does Christmas!** I added all of my family members as well as Vic and Shelley. Next, I added my new friend Flick, and after a slight apprehensive pause, I typed Nick's name to add him to the group too.

I will be hosting a Paw Patrol themed gathering on Christmas Eve at 2pm and everyone is welcome to join. We will have a buffet and there will be some entertainment (which Lena will be in charge of choosing). If we are lucky, we may get to listen to the odd Christmas song (although this won't be a traditional event and will adapt on the day to what Lena can manage). I can't promise we won't be dancing to the Paw Patrol theme tune in the living room or that you might be enticed to dress up as a character here or there! Please do let me know if you can make it ahead of time, Love Sarah x

My phone beeped instantly with messages in the group from Shelley and Vic saying they would love to come and thanked me for the invite. Shortly afterwards my sister replied that she would make it with Mike and Andrew. She also said that she would find a costume for Andrew to wear and join in with Lena's fun. I had goosebumps. I couldn't believe that things were turning around so well and that my sister was embracing the new way I had decided to do things. I felt so excited, things were finally improving between us, maybe our relationship would be reaffirmed.

After a few hours my mum text into the group and confirmed her attendance. She said to include Dad in the numbers but that he was too much of a dinosaur to get *WhatsApp* on his phone and be able to text back himself. I laughed loudly at the message and sent back an emoji of a dinosaur and a laughing face with tears.

This was then followed by Flick who said that it would be a pleasure to join in with the festivities and how she missed the excitement of her son being young at this time of year. I responded that she may live to regret that once coming over and being at the mercy of Lena's games! My family must have wondered who Flick was – it was a name they had never heard of before. Well, we would just explain the connection on the day. I felt relieved that I was being joined by another parent who had shaped her family to suit the way she needed it to be. She would be my moral strength on the day – although I doubted that I needed it anymore as I had learnt to finally navigate this by myself.

The last person to reply was Nick. He said that he would try and join the gathering but he had plans so it would only be a short visit. I wasn't fussed, just grateful that he would briefly show his face. If

I was honest with myself, that was probably enough in terms of the participation we needed from him in order to put the children first. I wanted him to be included so that things were amicable and that the kids grew up with having their dad in photos as part of their memories.

I had images in my mind about how I would decorate the living room with a mix of Christmas decorations interspersed with some *Paw Patrol* party supplies. I knew that Lena and Charlie would be in their element at something so fun and at a family do that was being centred around their interests and needs. I could get Lena to help me make a themed cake and lay some masks around so that the adults could join the children in the games. I felt so happy in the realisation that my family would be coming back together and this time I felt in control of what would be happening and, for once, we would be able to make it a positive memorable occasion. My rainbow of colours radiated and pulsated with pride.

The next two days were spent packing a bag for the children for their weekend with Nick and getting myself prepared for meeting Tim for dinner. My mum had arrived to ferry the children to Nick's (although Nick and I were starting to communicate better, it felt easier to keep the space between us whilst we figured out this whole new situation), and as usual, I was running late. Some things were just never going to change, but rather than beat myself up about it, I tried to tell myself that perhaps it was just something that I couldn't help. I was learning to reframe my internalised judgement maker; allowing me the capacity to let a lot of negativities disperse.

"I'm sorry I didn't have the kids ready on time," I apologised to my mum as I ran back down the stairs with Poxy Rabbit, Blanket and Charlie's onesie all balancing in my arms. I was shocked at the scene in front of my eyes. Instead of my mum's usual impatience and disapproval of the way that I did things, she was sitting on the living room floor playing *Paw Patrol* with Lena and Charlie together. She was no longer acting in judgement or towering above them with an expectation that they should be conforming because she deserved the respect as the adult. She was lying on the carpet and entering into their world. My eyes filled with happy tears at the positive change that was happening in my family and our ability to reconnect after the earlier struggles we'd faced.

"It wasn't a problem," Mum reassured me. "It actually worked out in my favour because I got to play with the kids, and I learnt all about Lena's favourite pups ahead of the Christmas *Paw Patrol* party!"

I was left momentarily dumbfounded. My mum had taken a complete U-turn on her approach, it felt like I was dealing with a different person. Had the diagnosis changed her thought pattern that much? Or maybe she felt guilty that she had made some pretty awful statements when actually her granddaughter was autistic – an invisible disability that she didn't understand. I wasn't complaining, I was just in shock that she was suddenly acting like the mum I needed her to be. Maybe she was starting to understand her own self too, how much she was trying to conform to what people expected of her.

Mum soon left with the kids to be passed over into Nick's care and I was left with the solitude of the house to fill my thoughts. My mood felt lighter and it was something my sensitive offspring had acknowledged earlier that day. Lena's words seemed to ring back into my ears, the poignancy of what she had said in the morning was permeating my mind as I was getting ready for my date.

"Mummy," Lena had begun as she curled up onto my lap with Rex sandwiched next to her from the other side. "I think your rainbow could be working because you have your smile back!"

"I think you're right," I'd answered, "I didn't like it when it went."

"Neither did I, Mummy. It made you look different, and you know that I don't like things changing," Lena had said as she tugged on the chain. "You can have your necklace back now. It belongs to you."

As I came to from the earlier flashback, I realised I was still touching the necklace and smiling at myself in the mirror. It felt a bit abnormal to actually start liking my appearance and to feel good about the person I was becoming – the feeling of being repressed had felt so ingrained in me that it was good to be freed. I pictured the inner child inside of me and the innocence I once had. The young person who was born so autonomous and who was trying to find her place in the world. The girl who liked climbing trees and roller skating freely around the estate. The child who stood up for the underdog in any situation. The young lady who had a strong mind and would follow the rules that she felt needed to be adhered to. She would have smiled back, after all these years, at her ability to relearn how to be herself all over again.

You can do this. The last-minute flutters of nervous anticipation swept over me before I stole one last chance to check over my outfit, before leaving to walk the journey down to the marina. My black shimmering jumpsuit, woven with a fine layer of glitter, felt like a fitting choice – it had the ability to be casual but dressy at the very same time. I swung a colourful scarf around my shoulders to add a final rainbow statement of personality to my attire. Would I find Tim attractive? Was I ready to get involved with someone new? So many questions were swirling around my consciousness in waves of trepidation, but I wasn't about to let my anxiety get the better of me.

I walked through the same alleyway that I had ventured through the time I had spontaneously ended up having coffee with Tim in his cottage. Then I saw the brambles and grinned at Shelley's references to me meeting 'the Beast'. The picturesque view, as I walked the remainder of the route, kept me entertained until I could see the water open up into an orderly marina with ornate barges lined along the bays.

My eyes scanned around the boats and the water until I spotted the nestled restaurant – covered with ivy that trailed along the walls – it was camouflaged as a hidden gem in the vicinity. The outside seating area was out of use, as the tables and chairs were stacked away for the winter dip, but the condensation against the glass walls indicated the invitation of warmth inside. At the nearest table to the door, with his face looking out of the window, was Tim. As I approached, he left his seat and met me, opening the door on my arrival. The aroma of Italian herbs wafted through the door and hit me with a pang of yearning.

"It's so good to see you again," Tim said with a twinkle in his eyes that made my heart stop. His eyes studied me. "You look amazing, Sarah."

I didn't know what to reply as I nervously giggled away the compliment.

"I'm sorry I'm late," I confessed, "there's not even a valid reason for it. I've resigned myself to the fact that I just have poor time-management skills."

"It's fashionable to be late anyway." Tim gestured for me to come into the restaurant, and as I followed his lead, I could feel his palm gently resting behind me. I didn't flinch, because for once, it was starting to feel natural.

"I would have ordered you a drink to have waiting, but I wasn't sure what you would like." Tim passed me a copy of the drinks menu. "I thought I'd go with what you choose tonight."

I noticed that he seemed eager to please and that the control was being passed over to me. It felt strange but in a good way.

"Well, I've been cutting down on drinking alcohol," I admitted. "I took a leaf out of your book on that one, I think."

"Good for you," Tim said supportively. "I tend to save alcohol for special occasions so that it's just not a regular habit. I'm happy to have a soft drink tonight, if you would prefer? I'm happy either way."

"It would be nice to have a glass of wine," I suggested, "but I think

I'll start as I mean to go on. I've masked for too long under the illusion that alcohol brings."

"Sounds like you've been on quite a journey in a very short space of time," Tim acknowledged.

We had a brief catch up of the events of the last few weeks. Tim filled me in with some details about the men's support group he was running and how Oscar was doing in his alternative secondary provision. The waiter came over to take our orders, but we were too busy making conversation to have concentrated on the task at hand. Eventually we had some extra time to peruse the menu and then decided on some sharers to start and opted for individual pasta dishes for our mains. The waiter arrived with two fizzy colas in glass bottles; they looked appealing as the bubbles popped whilst being poured into the accompanying glasses onto the rocks of ice and lemon.

"Cheers!" Tim clinked his glass into mine as we smiled across the table and leant in closer as if we were being pulled by two magnets.

"Cheers indeed!" I replied, taking a sip of my drink whilst thinking about the next topic to chat about. I had to fill the gap as I could sense the chemistry that was growing between us, and for some reason it fuelled me with verbal energy to ensure my feelings were not so obvious. I fidgeted with my new piece of jewellery to keep my fingers busy – my emotions needed to be channelled.

"That's a very unusual necklace." Tim had a puzzled expression. "It looks like it's been personalised."

"You're very observant!"

"Uh huh." Tim nodded. "I become fixated on the smallest of details and notice the tiniest of changes."

We both laughed as Tim shook his head with the indication that it was a challenge just as much as it was a strength.

"Sounds just like Lena!" I said affectionately.

"So, what's the message say on the back and who got it for you?" Tim asked curiously as he pointed to the engraved writing on the rainbow. "It's okay if you'd rather not tell me."

"My two best friends got it," I answered. "And the message reads *friendships are rainbows* on the back."

"That's cute," Tim replied warmly. "I can't imagine my friends doing that for me!"

We both laughed at the incongruity of a group of men exchanging such sentimental gifts. I took a moment to compose my thoughts. How could I tell him about the deeper context of the story without making it sound crazy?

"Well there's a bit of backstory behind it..." I began.

Tim sat engaged, listening to me relaying the details of the rainbow and what it had signified. He asked questions and showed a deep interest in the metaphor of the black rainbow.

"It's phenomenal that your young daughter had the ability to look deeply at her life," Tim began, "in a way that's so much older than her years."

"I know," I agreed, "her analogy also applied to me, but I didn't have the internal awareness or insight to see it."

"Perhaps you have been forced to comply for far too long," Tim suggested. "Have you thought about your own neurodivergence?"

"I have and it feels like a bit of a mystery still," I admitted. "There are questions rising to the surface that may still need answering."

"It's a bit like your rainbow. It will never just be linear. I'd think of it more like a colour wheel where the layers are more intermittent than seven separated colours."

"How do you mean?" I asked inquisitively.

"Think of it more like a myriad of colours!" Tim explained. "Where the individual spectral colours have overlapped and mixed. A rainbow is not a pure spectrum."

"Shit this is deep!" I said with a grin. "My brain cells are trying to recover some strength!"

"I'm sorry." Tim smiled back. "I do tend to get overexcited when I'm in mid-flow with something that I find interesting."

"Don't apologise. I'm enjoying it. In fact, I hate doing small talk."

"Me too!" In our moment of agreement we were finding some similarities between us.

"So much of this makes sense," I said as I dug a fork into my plate of linguini and swirled the fresh blades of pasta around the prongs. "I think it explains why I felt unsatisfied when I had tried too hard to focus on seven simple steps for the rainbow to be complete."

Tim had stopped eating as he remained absorbed in what I was saying. He shuffled his body weight on his chair. I'm sure I wasn't imagining it but it felt like he was getting closer with something pressing to ask. Sensing the shift of dynamic, I carried on talking through my shyness.

"I can't stop now," I began, "I need to keep bringing all of the other colours into my life now that I'm going in the right direction. Who knows, maybe that means finding out if I am autistic or ADHD or something else in the mix too?!"

The energy between us was blazing, I could taste the electricity in the air. I was no longer relying on alcohol to cope with a new or difficult situation and I was managing just fine.

Eventually, Tim reached across the table and gently stroked my hand. It felt like dynamite and the tiny hairs on my entire body shot up in an excited wake-up call. Something was changing and I didn't need the words to be spoken because, for once, I was able to read the social situation just fine and respond with confidence.

"Will there be room to date someone amongst all of your new colours?" The corners of Tim's mouth raised as he looked deeply into my eyes.

My cheeks blushed in anticipation, knowing that we were finally talking about where this arrangement could be leading to.

"There is definitely room." My smile was insatiable and I couldn't hold it back.

Tim unexpectedly leant across the tablecloth and, with one delicate hand reaching onto the side of my face, gently held me still as he scooped his lips against mine with a passionate kiss. I reciprocated the desire as we stayed like that for a few seconds, unsure of who would be the first to break away or what would happen from that moment.

"My friends did tell me that there is always room for glitter to decorate the rainbow!" I declared as we pulled apart and continued with the date.

"I'm very pleased to hear it." Tim smiled and his shoulders seemed to lose some weight. I realised right then that it was just as difficult for both of us to move out of the green zone. Shelley may have been right about that. "I might have panicked then if you said you were waiting it out for a pot of gold!"

"I was hoping the glitter may turn to gold!" I joked.

We continued talking animatedly until it was time to pay the bill and make our exit from the restaurant.

"Would you like me to walk you home?" Tim offered politely.

"That would be very kind," I happily accepted. I donned my leather coat, wrapped my scarf around my neck, and placed my hand in Tim's open, awaiting palm. We set off on our journey along the narrow towpath, our hands clasped together against the pain of the wintry wind, our bodies riding on excitement as we absorbed the energy of the moon which was shining a fine, white beam on the black, limitless body of water.

Made in the USA
Middletown, DE
19 September 2024